CATALINA

THE SIREN POINT SERIES: BOOK 1

BRYAN SANDERS
& CHARMAINE ZABAT

woodside
publishing LLC

CATALINA

Copyright © 2024, 2025 by Bryan Sanders & Charmaine Zabat

No artificial intelligence was used in the creation or development of this novel or cover art.

Front Cover Design: Bryan Sanders & Charmaine Zabat
Stock Photo: RJMS (istockphoto)
Manananggal Art: Bryan Sanders

ISBN: 979-8-9996406-0-4 (ebook), 979-8-9996406-1-1 (paperback), 979-8-9996406-2-8 (hardback)

Woodside Publishing LLC
www.woodsidepublishing.com
First Edition: August 2025
10 9 8 7 6 5 4 3 2 1

CONTENTS

BROOKLYN BELIEVER STAFF

JERRY SAMBROOK - Founder and Publisher

Jerry Sambrook started *The Brooklyn Believer* in 2005 from his couch in Williamsburg, Brooklyn. His upstart supernatural blog grew into a sensation that's been thrilling New Yorkers for two decades now with NYC's "Spooky Beat" and a variety of offbeat features for the discriminating reader. Jerry lives with his wife Elisa, their dog Renfield, and their three children in Park Slope, Brooklyn.

TIFFANI MILLER, PMP - Managing Editor

Tiffani Miller is an award-winning journalist, filmmaker, and activist. Her work has appeared in *The New York Times*, *The Atlantic*, and *Deadline*, and her reporting has been featured on CNN, NBC News, and countless other outlets. Tiffany lives in Yorkville with her loving husband, celebrated novelist C. Baldwin Miller, and their three corgis Finnic, Rhodes, and Bradford.

KORINNE GO - Advertising Sales Manager

Originally from California, Korrine studied business at UCLA before relocating to NYC, where she manages *The Believer*'s sales team. Korinne is an entrepreneur, an influencer and lifestyle coach, owns her own fitness brand, and is passionate about sharing the stories of other incredible women. She resides in the Upper West Side.

BECKY MANCINI-SLATER - Office Manager | Ad Sales Rep | Tip Line

Born and raised in Queens, Becky graduated from Grover Cleveland High School, where she excelled at volleyball. After two decades working in a department store, Becky changed careers to join Jerry in 2009 and became the heart of *The Brooklyn Believer*. She lives in Jackson Heights with her sister Alice and her cat Mistress Bucket.

BRAD GARCIA - Digital & Social Editor | Video Editor | Reporter

Brad graduated from the School of Visual Arts in 2011 with a BFA in Film. A multi-disciplinary talent, Brad built a highly successful freelance career before joining *The Believer* in 2018 as a multimedia journalist. Brad loves exploring subcultures, particularly at the intersection of technology and sustainability. He lives in Crown Heights, Brooklyn.

TANNER VOS - Investigative Reporter | Chief Photographer

Tanner Vos is an award-winning visual journalist and writer, based in NYC. Tanner is a master of many trades. He's a photographer, a musician, an adventurer, a chef, a designer, and a poet, but–most of all–Tanner is a collector of stories. Tanner and his work have been featured by *Buzzfeed, Gizmodo, and Mashable.* When he's not traveling the world's most dangerous roads, Tanner lives in Greenpoint, Brooklyn.

DAISY SCOTT - Investigative Reporter

Daisy Scott has a B.A. in journalism from NYU. She lives in Long Island City and plays the drums in her spare time.

LIAM RUDDOCK - Calendar Editor

Liam handles all the scheduling duties for the paper while juggling undergraduate business studies at NYU. He intends to focus on arts administration and hopes to eventually complete his MBA. Liam is a skilled bassoonist, enjoys comic books, and lives in the East Village.

PROLOGUE

* * *

A coming roar announced itself from the city to the west and barreled closer. The noise crescendoed into thunder, which rattled the building like a small earthquake as the air screeched and howled.

To fifteen-year-old Miguel, the sound was exactly what he'd been waiting for. It was his signal to move. The floor-rattling scream of the 7-train passing by on the elevated tracks outside the window was a regular nuisance to anyone living or working nearby, with subways running several times per hour in both directions. But tonight, the noise would provide cover, as Miguel escaped from his family's single-room unit in Flushing Creek Houses, a family shelter in the Corona neighborhood of Queens, in New York City.

As the building shook, he pulled back his blanket and, fully clothed, scooted to the front end of his mattress and began to climb down from the top bunk of his bed.

Miguel moved carefully, trying not to wake his six-year-old brother Gabriel on the bottom bunk, who had finally fallen asleep about an hour earlier. He was unconcerned about waking his mom, who was passed out drunk in a cot at the foot of their bunk bed.

1

Miguel silently slipped on his jacket and unzipped his backpack to retrieve a vape pen. He opened the door, just enough for his torso to squeeze through. In the total darkness of their room, even the flickering old bulbs from the hallway were substantial enough to cast a blinding wedge of light through the cracked door which opened up like a chasm, bleaching everything it touched inside the room like the midday sun.

"Where are you going?"

DAMN. Gabriel had woken up despite all of his precautions. If his mom woke too, Miguel's night would be ruined.

"Shhhh," he cautioned his little brother. "I'll be right back. It's nothing. Don't wake Mom. Go back to sleep."

Miguel immediately slipped out into the hall and closed the door behind him, not giving his brother a chance to ask follow-up questions. He hoped that by keeping the incident brief, Gabe might fall back asleep before waking up enough to get curious. His brother had been up late that night anyway, thanks to their mom, so he figured Gabe must be exhausted.

The teenager tiptoed past a few other private family rooms, toward the open stairwell at the end of the hall, and then descended to the first-floor entry way. At the bottom of the stairs, he turned left and exited through a set of double doors into the mid-October New York City night.

* * *

Gabriel listened in the dark for any sounds of his brother returning but he couldn't hear anything over his mom's snoring. His mom was always asleep. She wasn't fun like his big brother.

Where did Miguel go?

The little boy figured his brother was probably doing something exciting–BIG KID FUN–that he wasn't supposed to be a part of.

If Miguel gets to stay up late then I do too, he decided, and rose to his feet.

Careful not to wake his mom, he slowly turned the doorknob. The door made a loud squeak as he pulled it halfway open, and he was sure he would get caught, but she didn't even stir on her cot.

He peeked into the dimly lit hallway, hoping his older brother was still out there, but was disappointed to find it empty. Fully awake now, Gabriel put on his shoes and coat, to match Miguel's attire, and then stepped into the dark hallway, closing the door on his sleeping mom behind him.

The building was scary at night, and he had never walked through it alone before. Each door he passed seemed to be restraining something terrible inside it, based on the weird and threatening noises escaping into the hallway. The leftover scent of a cleaning product tugged sharply at his sinuses like he was at a swimming pool but there was another smell mixed in which unpleasantly burned in his nose. He knew that smell from streets and public bathrooms–urine. He covered his nose with his shirt as he continued.

At the bottom of the stairs, he was faced with an unexpected choice: To his LEFT was the front door of the building, but to his RIGHT was another door, which he'd never used before, that was cracked open like someone had just been through it.

Which way did Miguel go? he wondered.

As if to settle the decision for him, an orange tabby cat peeked its head into the room through the right door and looked around the room, as if sizing up the place. Apparently, it wasn't to the cat's liking because it immediately disappeared back outside.

KITTY!

Gabriel had learned about animals in school already and he loved cats. He ran toward the cracked door and felt cold air spilling in from the streets outside. He peered through the crevice, desperately hoping the cat hadn't gotten away. He couldn't see much but sensed excitement calling from the other side.

I'm not supposed to go outside at night… he warned himself, knowing it was the last chance to turn back before likely getting in serious trouble. *What would Miguel do?*

Quickly arriving at his answer, Gabriel bounded through the cracked door, escaping on a nighttime adventure.

BRRRRR!!

It was colder than he'd expected. And gosh, it STANK. He emerged into a small, enclosed alley. He'd never been on that side of the building before. He searched for the source of the bad odor and discovered it all around him.

This place is used for storing garbage, he realized. The building in front of him was a grocery store and the piles around him smelled like they contained rotting food.

He looked to his left and, under the subway tracks, a large metal gate blocked entry from the street. To his right, the small alley terminated in a dead end which was filled with garbage bins, tied plastic trash bags, and stacked plastic crates.

"Kitty? Little kitty?" he called out into the alley.

Answering his call, a pile of trash stirred to his right. His eyes darted toward the movement, and he watched intently until it moved again. He noticed a huge, overstuffed black garbage bag seemed to be the center of activity, so he crouched down next to it, finding a long tear in the bulging side with some garbage hanging out. The movement seemed to be coming from behind the hole in the bag.

He nervously reached out his index finger and poked at the sides of the hole, pushing into the bulk of the bag repeatedly to encourage the cat to come back out and play. There was a lurch from inside and then a large, dark shape came flying out of the opening, startling Gabriel as it scurried past him.

YUCK! A RAT!!

Thankfully, the rat immediately disappeared under a dumpster and made no further appearance.

Gabriel searched all around the piles of garbage for the orange cat and was about to give up and go back inside when he heard it meow from somewhere deeper toward the dead-end back wall of the alley. He followed the sound until he discovered the cat lounging on a discarded chair. He knew that not all animals were friendly, even cats and dogs, so he approached it slowly. The cat didn't seem very interested in him, busily licking its left paw clean.

Can I pet it?

Gabriel very slowly reached out his hand and touched the fur on the cat's back. It didn't seem to object so he began slowly petting it with two fingers. It was so soft.

A gust of wind ripped through the small alley and sent paper and trash flying through the air like a wind tunnel. The cat got spooked and bolted past the boy, escaping behind him toward the gated street on the other end of the alley, and Gabriel was plunged into darkness. Something had entered the alley and was blocking the light from the street.

SOMETHING BIG.

Frightened now, Gabriel slowly turned to find out what had scared the cat and cast a shadow over the entire corridor.

OH WOW! This is even better than a cat, he thought.

It was no wonder Miguel came outside every night. He hadn't realized what he'd been missing. It was practically a zoo out there. Yet *another* animal, a *flying* one, had landed next to him. He walked closer for a better look. Gabe recognized this animal too, because of the wings.

A Bat!

But, then again, were they supposed to be this big? And actually, as he got nearer to the animal, he realized this one seemed kind of frightening, like a mean bat that would hurt people in a scary movie.

Its enormous wings were unfolded, translucent black velvet crisscrossed with veins, filling the entire width of the alley with their wingspan. The flaps of the wings were partially transparent and shined softly before him, as if from an inner glow, thanks to the city lights behind them. Then, the huge beast pulled the wings inward. They collapsed like an umbrella into two smaller folds on its back, allowing more light to pour into the alley, creating a backlit halo around the bat's torso.

Without the wings spread out, the shape that the animal cut through the backlight almost looked like a person to Gabriel. It started inching closer to him, revealing itself in more detail, and the frightened boy began to cry. With shaky legs, he tried backing away from the animal, but it began to follow, matching his pace.

His mom had warned him that the city could be dangerous at night. But he hadn't expected anything like this. Now he was sorry he had followed the cat.

"Go away!" he screamed at the animal, which continued inching closer. "I said GO AWAY!"

He picked up a crushed soda can off the ground and threw it at the bat, but his aim was poor and it landed low. The giant beast didn't seem to even notice, still creeping closer. It wasn't walking; it seemed to be *dragging* itself on the ground, which made it even scarier.

The creature was now blocking the door to the building and the big gate prevented him from reaching the street, so Gabriel had no means of escape. His only choice was to retreat even further, back into the dumpsters behind him, and try to hide or call for help.

NOW!!! RUN LIKE THE CAT! he instructed himself.

Gabriel bolted for the back corner of the dead end but only managed a couple steps before another gust of wind filled the alley and something heavy collided with him from behind, knocking him to his stomach.

He landed hard, first hitting the concrete with his arms, then banging his right knee on the asphalt as the rest of his weight came down.

Gabriel yelped in pain. His body screamed all over. He realized he'd never been injured this badly before. He attempted to lift himself back up, but the bat was ON TOP of him now, sitting on his back, and its weight was much too heavy.

IT WANTS TO EAT ME! he worried in terror.

"HELP ME!" the sobbing child cried out into the alley, trying to grab for anything to pull himself away from the animal or gain leverage to lift himself up. "HELP ME! MIGUEL!! HELP ME!"

* * *

Miguel heard his little brother screaming and threw down his vape pen. He knew the difference between Gabe's real screaming and performative screaming. This was real. His brother was in trouble and the sound had come from outside.

SHIT. He probably followed me out here, he worried.

His pulse began to throb in his throat. Was Gabe being taken by someone? Was he being hurt?

This is all my fault.

He steadied himself and tried to locate the source of his brother's calls.

Maybe one of Mom's boyfriends showed up on drugs? Maybe someone came into our room after I left?

STOP IT. FOCUS.

He cleared his head and listened. *Which way is the sound?*

He walked out into the empty street under the subway tracks and yelled. "Gabe! Where are you?!" He looked to the east and noticed a Manhattan-bound subway approaching in the distance. He wouldn't be able to hear anything once it got closer.

LISTEN, MIGUEL! He commanded himself. *LISTEN!*

"Help Me!"

Miguel took off running toward the sound, to his right, and zeroed in on his brother's screaming. On the other side of the shelter was a small alley for deliveries which was blocked to the street by a huge metal gate, taller than Miguel's head. He looked through the bars–

SOMEONE'S HURTING GABE!!!

He tried to open the gate, but it was padlocked. It looked like Gabe's attacker was wearing a Halloween costume with a long black wig and huge bat wings.

WHAT THE FUCK? He wondered if the guy was a YouTube prankster or if it was a social media stunt that had gone too far.

"HEY! STOP!" Miguel called out to the man attacking his brother. But the man didn't turn around or even give a reaction.

Gabriel heard him though: "MIGUEL!! OVER HERE! HELP ME! PLEASE–"

Gabe's pleas were cut short by the roar of the subway finally passing overhead.

"I'm coming, Gabe! I'm here!" he tried yelling through the racketing noise, but he could barely hear his own voice through the rumbling.

With no other options, Miguel summoned a burst of adrenaline-juiced energy that surprised even himself and launched upward, almost to the top of the gate and grabbed a pole with each hand. He found temporary footing with his sneakers, which squeaked and slid on the slick bars, but he managed to shimmy his way up until he could grab the top rail and pull himself up the remainder of the distance and heave his leg up onto the gate.

Miguel jumped. He launched himself out and downward, a bit too aggressively given how high up he was, and overshot a bit, colliding with the costumed thug with a glancing blow. He knocked the guy off his little brother but was unable to control his landing and crashed hard, taking most of the impact with his left shoulder.

"AHHH!!! FUCK!" he screamed.

His entire left arm howled with pain. The gravel had scraped off a chunk of skin from his forearm when he slid to a stop, and he worried his left shoulder was dislocated because his arm didn't respond correctly when he tried to move it.

He repositioned himself on his knees, fire burning throughout his left side, and wondered if a rib had been cracked too.

This fucking guy is gonna pay bad now.

Miguel moaned in agony as he prepared to rise up and finish the fight, intent to make sure the other guy's injuries were worse than his. He put all his weight into his right hand, pressed into the ground, secured his feet, and pushed upward toward a full stand.

But the attacker was no longer on the ground and the reprisal was already inbound. The costumed thug rammed into Miguel, strikingly fast, sending him back to the concrete, flat on his back this time.

FUCK! His shoulder and ribcage burned worse than ever now. *It wasn't supposed to go like this.* He risked a quick look to his brother to make sure he wasn't injured.

"Run, Gabe! Run!" he commanded. His brother rose to his feet but refused to move, paralyzed with fear. Miguel realized Gabe was terrified of the attacker but even more scared of leaving without him.

Miguel began to yell at Gabriel more intently, but the costumed man struck again. The injured teenager saw it coming this time but was helpless on his back and could only feebly try to push the guy away. The assailant landed on top of him and pinned his arms to the ground.

HOW IS HE SO STRONG?

"Gabe! Just go! Run! *GET HELP!!*"

That finally got a reaction. His brother bolted to the back door, squeezed through, and took off into the building screaming for help at the top of his lungs.

THANK GOD, Miguel thought.

He turned his attention back to the thug hovering over him. As Miguel's eyes adjusted to the light, he realized the mop of long black hair obscuring the face wasn't a wig but seemed to be real. The ears, however, were clearly fake, coming to long pointed tips, like when people dressed up as elves.

The man opened his mouth to snarl at Miguel and, through the strands of hanging hair, he saw elongated fangs where the upper canines should be. They didn't look like cheap plastic fangs from a Halloween store, more like the expensive ones creepy people got installed by dentists.

Miguel's left arm had become useless, so he put all his remaining strength into freeing his right arm and took a swing at the guy's face. His knuckles connected with the cheekbone, sending a jolt of pain through his hand, but the man's head didn't even budge from the force. Suddenly, Miguel felt a sharp pressure in his outstretched hand–

HE FUCKING BIT ME!

The situation now seemed very different. This wasn't a prank video or a stunt, Miguel realized with panic. This guy was truly out of control and might kill him.

"HELP!" he screamed, "PLEASE HELP ME! SOMEONE GET HELP!!"

He ripped his hand away from the man's clenched jaws, tearing the punctures wider as he pulled free. The attacker's open mouth was now red with blood.

MY BLOOD, he shuddered. And then, Miguel finally noticed the eyes...

Miguel, are you sure this is a costume?

The eyes were impossible. They clearly weren't contacts, but there were no irises, just dark maroon voids, almost black throughout, except for the pupils, which somehow emitted a red glow. These two little points of bright red light transfixed him with their iridescence, shining like pinprick lanterns in dark hollows. The lights had a hypnotizing quality.

They're not pure red, he thought to himself, *there's just a little bit of orange in there.*

The assailant's eyes were more feminine than he had previously realized, almost beautiful, in fact. The person's mouth then opened wider, unleashing a rotten odor, and what Miguel saw inside made him lose interest in the eyes.

A *SNAKE* slithered out of the mouth, long and sleek, unwinding and stretching its way down onto his abdomen.

No, that's not right. It's not a snake. It was too thin to be a snake and there was no head, instead coming to a sharp point at the end. And yet, the thing moved with a mind of its own, a single fiber of living muscle.

IT'S A TONGUE, he realized, not knowing if that was better or worse for him than a snake. The filament on his stomach gathered itself into a coiled bunch, and then the sharp pointed end began to drift upward, tracing over Miguel's shirt as if it was searching for something. *Smelling? Tasting?*

He grabbed the tongue with his right hand and tried to pull it away, but he couldn't move it at all. His hand was slick with blood, still running from the bite marks, and the tongue was unnaturally strong, like a heavy-gauge metal wire. The needle-tipped muscle continued its climb upward until it reached his collar bone, where it paused for a moment, and then retreated back down to the bottom of his rib cage.

There, the living fiber paused for a moment, just hovering, as it lightly probed the shirt over Miguel's belly. Then, without a sound and with no warning, the dagger PLUNGED into his stomach. It was like getting a flu shot through an icepick. A fiber of hot blazing pain shot deep through his chest.

"AHHH!!!!!" he cried out. "STOP!!! PLEASE!! STOP! STOP!! I'M JUST A KID!"

MY GOD, he realized, *THIS IS FOR REAL. THIS PERSON MIGHT ACTUALLY KILL ME!!*

The pain grew unbearable as the muscle wriggled its way deeper inside his body.

"SOMEONE HELP ME, PLEASE!" he tried to scream again into the empty alley, but his voice began to falter. No matter how hard he pushed air from his lungs, now only a sad little rasp could escape, "hEEelllppp…" He wondered if his brother had found an adult yet.

HE'LL BE BACK ANY MINUTE, he convinced himself, *HELP IS COMING!*

His energy was fading, and he noticed drowsiness setting in. He couldn't fall asleep before help arrived! He had to keep fighting until then.

Miguel gathered all his remaining courage and, again, pulled at the tongue. Fighting for his life itself this time, he even managed to will his left arm into action, and yanked at the appendage with all the combined strength he had left. He wrestled with it left and right, attempting to remove the intrusion from his body, but he struggled to gain purchase on the moist fiber with his bloody hands.

Instead, the tongue pushed even harder, like an arm-wrestler that had been humoring him but was now ready to show his real strength and finish the match. It plunged even deeper, disappearing through his tattered shirt into his helpless body underneath.

The burning sensation was gone, replaced by a coldness instead. A huge icicle had been inserted into his chest. Miguel felt like a big snowman, helpless, melting on the ground.

Pinned to the asphalt, with his strength gone, Miguel could only stare helplessly forward, with morbid amazement, as his chest rippled and danced before his eyes.

Oh no. IT'S EATING ME!!!!

He realized the creature was feeding on his insides, *piercing, scraping, and slurping.* The pain was gone entirely now, and the experience felt dreamlike. Miguel couldn't even believe the body opening up in front of his eyes was his own. It couldn't be. He began to have trouble holding his eyes open and worried Gabe might not make it back with help in time.

IS THIS HOW I DIE? he wondered sadly to himself.

Knowing he could only stay conscious for another moment, Miguel turned his attention back to the person's face. He wanted to see it in full and in detail–the face of his *KILLER.*

He'd never gotten anything he'd asked for in his short life. His dying wish was only to know who was responsible. But as he gazed up into the light, expecting to see the face of his destroyer, he realized it was already too late.

He was instead greeted by a vision from the afterlife, the face of an enchantingly beautiful woman, a siren calling him to the other side.

* * *

Sometime later, a crowd gathered outside Flushing Creek Houses to see why ambulances and police had gathered in the middle of the night. It seems a teenage boy who'd been staying at the shelter had been stabbed in the alley.

As it turned out, the kid was a known troublemaker. A delinquent. So, it was lightly suggested by a few onlookers that the child may have been to blame somehow. Perhaps the crime scene was the result of a failed gang initiation?

"A couple bags went missing in the building," an older woman whispered into the night for anyone near her that wanted the gossip, "and I heard maybe it was him that did it."

Eventually, the cold night air made everyone lose interest and return to their warm beds.

* * *

A very safe distance away, the orange tabby cat sat alone, leisurely licking its paw, trying to get it perfectly clean, completely oblivious that anything had happened in the alley.

PART ONE

"The viscera suckers are fabular beings who are reported by the folk to have an attractive appearance during the day..."

"But at night detach the lower portion of their body," "fly out in a monstrous shape, and suck out the entrails, sputum, and foetus of their human victims through their long, tubular tongue."

DR. MAXIMO D. RAMOS
The Creatures of Philippine Lower Mythology
Phoenix Publishing House, 1990

CHAPTER 1

Tears of a Clown

* * *

Daisy Scott considered her options. She'd entered the self-storage facility that afternoon with a mission: to reverse the dramatic rate increase recently imposed on her small, climate-controlled storage room. She'd initially liked her chances. There was a new guy working the front desk who looked like a pushover. She'd buttered him up with a little small talk and then gone in for the kill.

To Daisy's surprise, the employee had forcefully pushed back. He'd started arguing with her and now she needed to wrap it up to leave for an upcoming work appointment.

"Come on, dude..." she said. "A forty dollar increase for my tiny little storage room? You were already bleeding me dry at $115 a month. You know, it was only $80 when I signed up a few years ago. It's almost doubled now."

"I don't set the rates, ma'am. Corporate does. They said it's because of inflation."

"Forty dollars, though? For what? The only expense they have here is you, and I know they're not giving you any of that extra money. It's probably all going to rich guy shareholders somewhere. This is ridiculous. I oughta just take my drums home and store them there instead. It's free."

"Okay, then do it," he dared.

That caught Daisy off guard.

What the fuck? she wondered.

Was he actually calling her bluff? Was he allowed to do that? He'd be losing a customer. This guy was off the rails. Maybe she'd underestimated him. Maybe the new guy was a wild card.

"Well, I can't do that," she parried. "There's no room. And I can't play drums in my apartment building. I have to keep them here until I find a good space for them. Come on, can't you cut me a break on the rate? For a long-time customer?"

"I really can't. I'm sorry."

As a black woman, Daisy couldn't help but wonder if another customer asking for the same thing would have better luck.

"Is this what everyone pays now?" she asked.

"Yeah, it's automated. I don't decide the rates. Corporate does. Sorry."

"Well, then at least get rid of these bogus fees," Daisy said.

She pointed out an extra charge on her bill. "Like this one."

"That's your insurance, ma'am."

"Oh," she said.

"That covers your drums in case anything happens to them."

"In case anything happens to them?!" Daisy asked. "But isn't that kind of like your whole deal? I pay money to store my drums here, and you make sure nothing happens to them? Isn't it already your responsibility to keep them safe? Why else would I be here?"

"I don't make the rules," he said.

"I know," Daisy agreed. "Corporate does. Okay, fine. But one more rate increase and I'm done with you people. I mean it."

Daisy grabbed a magazine off a display rack near the clerk's desk. It had a picture of an open box on the cover and was called "*Self-Storage Now!*"

"And I'm taking this magazine. I know it's only supposed to be for first time customers, but I don't care. I like the look of it."

Daisy flipped through the free "magazine," which was filled with moving tips and coupons for special storage offers.

"Will that be all?" the employee asked.

"Yeah, that's it I guess."

Never late to an appointment, Daisy arrived for her assignment in the Woodside neighborhood of Queens several minutes early and decided to kill time by walking around the block to inspect the local Halloween decorations, or lack thereof.

Daisy was a reporter, and it would be a late night for her. She'd bought a large coffee after she stepped off the subway–hot, with two Splendas and a dash of milk. She pulled her coat a little tighter. It was a vintage, 1970s tan leather jacket with center buttons and broad lapels which she'd found in a thrift store a couple years earlier.

Slipping the leather jacket on for the first time had felt like reuniting with a long-lost piece of herself she hadn't known was missing. The previous owner must have been Daisy's clone because the world's best tailor could not have improved on the way it clung to her body in the mirror. The leather jacket had immediately become her signature garment, and she wore it every day of the year that the temperature would allow, which was most of Spring and Fall. It was usually paired with jeans and a rotation of classic rock band t-shirts, today a black Soundgarden shirt.

Daisy had always been a Halloween fanatic. The twenty-nine-year-old mustered some perfunctory enthusiasm for Christmas each year and managed to tolerate other holidays and birthdays as long as drinking was involved, but Halloween was special to her; it was *her* holiday.

As Daisy walked, she thought about the fortune she was paying to store her drum set, a candy apple red 1990 Pearl Export Series 5-piece. If you added up the years of monthly payments, she easily could have bought a new drum set with the money. But those were *her* drums. They had history together.

The reason Daisy held onto the drums was the same reason she never left home without a pair of drumsticks in her bag; it was her identity. Even if her band had broken up long ago, even if she wasn't currently drumming, she still felt naked without the drumsticks near her.

She finished her reconnaissance around the block and arrived back at her destination, the home of her interviewee, Gertrude Walcott, still one minute early, so Daisy watched her phone screen until it read 7:00 PM and then hit the buzzer for apartment 4B.

About thirty seconds went by without a response at the front door, so Daisy felt a quick moment of concern that she'd buzzed the wrong door and double checked her email for the apartment number.

Nope, apartment 4B. I'm right, she confirmed.

She hit the buzzer again, holding the button a little longer this time. Finally, a woman answered:

"Who is it?!"

"It's Daisy. From the paper. Is this Gertrude Walcott?"

"You're early!" the woman screamed through the small speaker.

"No Ma'am," Daisy corrected, "It's 7:00 on the dot."

"Ugh!" the woman scoffed, although Daisy wasn't sure why. "Well at least give me a minute to clean up!"

Daisy took a deep breath and prepared herself for the next couple hours. Her official title was "investigative reporter," although it was ceremonial at best, and she never called herself that. She worked for a trash rag called *The Brooklyn Believer*, a glorified blog specializing in local NYC "supernatural" stories.

The website started as just a hobby by the owner in the early 00s but somehow flourished into an unlikely small business success story, with predictable ad revenue, steady readership over the years, and a compact, but sustainable, skeleton crew of full-time employees and a revolving roster of freelancers.

The Believer, one of the absolute worst newspapers in the USA, had withstood every anti-journalism trend of the 21st century so far and was still standing, all because they still had "investigative reporters" on the ground, gathering original stories. They may print garbage, but it was *brand new garbage* and, in an over-consolidated landscape where every other newspaper and website had been strip-mined for profits and lost its ability to perform any original newsgathering, the meek could thrive, and so they had.

But the unstoppable success of *The Believer* had lately become its own worry for Daisy. Since the website turned a small, reliable profit, she knew it reeked like "an investment" to all the worst people in the world. She had learned through office gossip that Jerry, the website's creator and her boss, had already turned down at least one offer to buy the company. He'd been steadily winding down his involvement the last few years and it was only a matter of time until he felt the pull of retirement and relative riches calling and sold them off in an acquisition. The new owners would then decide to outsource the site's content-gathering to cut expenses, "lean into video," "embrace AI," and the newly unemployed Daisy would be dropped into a nonexistent job market and end up bagging groceries.

The door finally buzzed, and Daisy entered the building, a pre-war five-floor walkup that had seen better days. She made her way to the fourth floor and knocked on the door of apartment 4B.

"Who is it?!" the woman called from inside.

"Daisy!" she responded, as before, "From the paper!"

"Well, you can never be too careful," the woman explained through the door, followed by a series of clicks and sliding chains. The door opened just a crack, and she peered through to inspect Daisy before allowing her further.

The woman seemed surprised by something. After interviewing hundreds of people the last few years, Daisy had become an expert at reading faces and had come to expect little micro-expressions like that occasionally from people who had seen her name on the website or spoken to her on the phone but had pictured someone different in their mind's eye. She didn't sense any hostility in this case. The woman opened the door wide, and Daisy made her way into her home.

The apartment was stuffy and smelled like the combined remnants of the last several meals which had been cooked inside. She noticed the unit was a duplex, with an old wooden staircase to the left of the front door leading to a second floor.

Daisy tried to get straight to business. "So, Gertrude–

"Please, hun," she corrected, "call me TRUDY. Everyone does." The woman was short and squat with long gray hair and small glasses that made her look a bit like Ben Franklin in mom jeans.

"*Trudy,*" Daisy repeated, "Sure thing, got it. Hey, do you mind if I start recording our conversation for the record?"

Daisy pulled a digital voice recorder from her bag. The device was about the size of a Roku remote, with a bright OLED screen at the top and large manual control buttons at the bottom. The recorder had a great microphone, could record for days nonstop on a charge, and had a built-in USB plug that popped out the bottom to easily transfer files afterward. The tool allowed Daisy to record hours of audio at a time while freeing up her phone for other tasks, which would be necessary tonight. The woman had submitted a claim to *The Believer* that a 16-inch porcelain doll in her possession, a *hobo clown doll*, had been *weeping*. And she was there to interview Trudy and try to record footage of the phenomenon.

Daisy started recording a new audio file and asked Trudy to say and spell her name into the device for the record. Afterward, Trudy continued to stare at the $99 piece of Sony hardware with awe.

"I still can't believe *The Brooklyn Believer* is here to interview me," she said to herself.

Trudy's wonderment relaxed into a mask of worry, as she looked toward the top of the staircase. "Daisy, I always had a feeling that something like this would happen to me. You know, I'm attuned to this stuff. I've been reading *The Believer* for years."

"Is that so?" Daisy muttered.

"Oh yeah," Trudy continued, "I've read 'em all. I even remember some of yours. DAISY SCOTT." She made eye contact with Daisy again for added emphasis, "You had the one about the lady in Staten Island that was experiencing TIME SLIPS. Remember that?"

"Oh yeah, of course," Daisy said. They'd actually run *two* such articles, detailing the plight of local NYC women claiming they experienced time skipping, and the stories were some of the most embarrassing drivel she'd ever seen printed by their team.

"I mean, wow! Can you imagine?" Trudy seemed to recall the details of the article in her mind, reliving the Staten Island woman's peril. Her eyes widened with private amazement, then suddenly narrowed into an accusatory squint. "Hey, whatever happened to the guy that used to write the really *good* stories? Jerry?"

"He's still around," Daisy explained. "He still runs the place. He's the publisher."

"Oh? she replied. "I guess after all these years he doesn't show up personally for every little story that comes in?"

The oldest fans of the website sometimes seemed to idolize Jerry. In their minds he had become the arbiter of supernatural phenomena in New York City, and they wanted his approval for their own experiences, like a competitor on a TV singing competition demanding the *most famous person possible* be present to hear their horrible crooning.

"He doesn't do any reporting these days, Ma'am, but he sent you his best," she assured the woman, biting her tongue to prevent herself from saying that Jerry would never waste his time taking the train out there to see her stupid clown dolls, even if he was still reporting and desperate for a story. Their office had an informal ranking system for prospective articles using letter grades. Daisy was pegging Trudy's "haunted clown doll" claim as a *C-grade* at best, and that was only if the doll was spooky looking. She hadn't even seen it yet.

Trudy stared at the top of the stairs with an evil eye, and shook her head slowly, as if mentally revisiting the scene of a crime. "I moved all the dolls upstairs into storage. I used to keep them down here in our bedroom but NOT ANYMORE!" she explained with exasperation.

"You'll see why," Trudy said, as she began up the steps.

The upstairs duplex room looked like a finished attic with slightly inward-slanted walls and three small windows on the right. Both sides of the room were lined with tall shelving which formed a path toward the back wall, which had a small closet and bathroom on the left side and more shelving on the right. Daisy's vision was reduced to a palette of blacks and grays so she couldn't tell what was on any of the shelves around her.

"Oh! I almost forgot!" Trudy said, stopping in her tracks. "Don't worry about Toby. He doesn't bite."

Daisy wasn't sure what Trudy meant until she followed her pointed finger down to the ground and noticed a geriatric Cocker Spaniel sound asleep on a dog bed by the stairs. It was black with a white beard and was morbidly obese, maybe the fattest dog Daisy had ever seen.

"He's 14 years old and blind as a bat," Trudy said. "He's got it all now, unfortunately: dental disease, an enlarged heart, skin rashes. My poor baby. He just eats and sleeps. He only gets a temper when we do his diabetes shots. Isn't that right, Toby?"

At the mention of his name, the old dog's eyes opened halfway to briefly reveal a white-glazed, cockeyed stare underneath, before declaring a false alarm and letting gravity pull his eyelids back to their natural state. He began panting, as if he'd been winded by the exertion.

"I wish he wouldn't sleep up here with the dolls, but he loves that spot for some reason, and he's always been stubborn as hell! So, we keep his bed up here by the stairs. I think maybe he senses something is wrong with the doll and is standing guard for us."

Standing guard? Daisy scoffed to herself. She doubted the dog could stand at all anymore. There were a couple drenched pee pads spread out nearby which she was careful not to step on as she followed Trudy toward the back of the room.

It was probably her imagination, but the temperature seemed to fall a few degrees as she got closer to the back wall. She felt a brief moment of hope—

Is this one real?

It never failed. She'd spent four years investigating the daily supernatural claims generated by a city of over eight million people, and the process had inadvertently crushed any belief she previously reserved for such phenomena.

Ultimately, paranormal explanations for events had the same trade off as religious dogma, Daisy reasoned. You were given immediate answers, but must accept them on faith rather than any available evidence. And yet, her job was to collect *empirical* evidence where it did not exist, from people who did not require it, and she was growing weary of the thankless task. Still, the horror movie-obsessed kid inside of her couldn't help but wonder about each new call—

Could THIS ONE be real?

As Daisy's vision adjusted, she began to make out details around her, noting the shelves upstairs mostly featured collections of dolls, toys, collectibles, and snow globes. Stacks of dusty old bankers boxes were taking up any leftover space along the walls.

"I wish I'd never seen this damn thing," Trudy said, as she reached the shelf against the back wall, which was tall but had just two shelves. The top shelf held an elaborate Catholic altar display with framed images of Jesus and Mother Mary, at least a dozen candles, statues of various saints, palm leaves, and trinkets. Several crucifixes of various sizes—one gigantic—were mounted on the wall above. Daisy thought she noticed the smell of garlic still fresh in the air but didn't see any around her.

The bottom shelf was reserved for the "Hobo Junction" clown dolls, just five in total. Two of the 16-inch porcelain dolls were still in boxes and the other three were loose and freestanding.

Daisy had done a little research on the topic earlier that day. The old trend of "Hobo Clowns" was in essence a combination of circus clowns and vaudeville-esque "Tramps," or Depression-era drifters and con men. The characters were usually pictured with both beards and clown makeup, which made for a disturbing combination. She wasn't sure if anyone actually found them cute, or just pretended ironically.

Daisy grabbed her audio recorder and held it between her and Trudy to get started. "So, who have we got on the shelf here, Trudy?"

Trudy was busy lighting candles on the top shelf altar but, at the sight of the recorder, put down the lighter and took a step back. She seemed to gather her thoughts first, and then performed a solemn roll call of the clown dolls from left to right:

"BOX CAR BILLY, CAMP FIRE CHARLEY, FAST-FINGERED JAKE, POKER-FACED PETE, and SMILIN' FREDDY."

Daisy noticed each of the dolls was unique, in a custom patchwork outfit with individual flourishes like an oversized derby hat or a scarf fashioned from a potato sack. Most of the figures had red noses and five o'clock shadows. Cigars dangled uniformly from all five of their creepy grins.

"May I?" Daisy asked, as she reached for one of the boxed dolls to examine it.

Trudy nodded her approval so Daisy carefully extricated the box, which was clear plastic on the front side, from the lower shelf and turned it around to study it. Text on the back of the box read:

COLLECTIBLE PORCELAIN DOLL

YOUR NEW, SPECIAL EDITION HOBO DOLL
COMMEMORATES THE FREE-SPIRITED
ADVENTURERS WHO RODE AMERICA'S RAILS
FROM WHISTLE-STOP TO WHISTLE-STOP.

EACH ADORABLE ROGUE IS CRAFTED IN
GENUINE HAND PAINTED PORCELAIN BISQUE…

"Let's see how good you are," Trudy challenged. "Which one is the troublemaker?"

Oh, just great, Daisy thought, as she returned the box to the shelf. She had nothing to go on. Her guess would be just as wild and random as a person off the street.

Okay, who cares if you get it wrong. Get it over with. Just take a guess.

She knew it had to be an unboxed doll or the "tears" might have gone unnoticed. The outer dolls seemed to be spaced further away from the one in the center, which was directly under the altar display and the largest crucifix.

Was it that simple? The middle one?

She contemplated whether or not Trudy might try to trick her by arranging them like that on purpose.

Nah, it IS that simple, she decided.

"The middle one. Fast-Fingered Jake," she declared.

"Bingo!" Trudy affirmed. "You're good!! Yep, he was trouble from day one, Daisy! Day one!"

"Okay, let's start from the beginning," Daisy suggested, trying to hide the relief in her voice that she hadn't identified the wrong doll. She held out the recorder again to get things back on track. "How long have you been collecting these dolls?"

"Oh! Way back," she recalled. "Well, I picked up the first one over twenty years ago–Smilin' Freddy. But I wasn't collecting them back then. It was just another doll I found somewhere. It wasn't until a few years ago I started tracking down the others, and I had a hard time finding Jake."

The middle doll, Fast-Fingered Jake, was unboxed and Daisy noticed it was unremarkable compared to the others. It had similar features, with ratty long hair under a wool beanie, red plaid pants and a shabby jacket with sewn-on patches.

"I finally found him three months ago," Trudy continued, "at a flea market upstate, with my best friend Tina. I remember things were feeling weird that day already, because of the weather… but when we got to the flea market, we both felt compelled toward the back of the building, where this strange old man had a stall set up. And guess what he had for sale?"

"Fast-Fingered Jake," Daisy added rhetorically.

"Practically giving him away too!" Trudy confirmed, "At a price that seems *suspicious* in hindsight. You should have seen that old guy running that stall, Daisy. He had a look in his eye like he wasn't playing by *our rules* anymore, if you know what I mean."

Daisy wasn't sure what she meant but nodded in agreement.

"I remember he was selling a framed 8x10 photo of a shark," Trudy continued. "Me and Tina kept asking him about it. "What's with the shark?!" And he told us his wife had been killed by a Great White. So, we listened to this long-assed story about her—she was Australian. And then at the end, Tina asked the guy, point blank, "Is this a photo of THE shark that killed your wife?" And can you believe what he said? "NO!" It was just a photo of *A SHARK.* Can you believe the nerve of that guy? He probably made up that entire story."

Daisy tried to move things along, "Okay, but then you bought the doll, uh, Jake, and brought him back here?"

"Yeah, so, the dolls used to be downstairs in the bedroom. I didn't show you that room. We think *it's* safe now. But he started causing trouble on night one. At first we'd notice little things, like he had just moved a little, or fell off the shelf. None of the other dolls ever did that. That's how it started. But then things got really scary."

Trudy took a deep breath and looked soulfully into her eyes, "Daisy, do you believe in ghosts?"

"Well, I…" Daisy struggled to come up with a quick explanation that would satisfy Trudy without wasting time or getting into Daisy's actual skepticism about supernatural phenomena, which would be unhelpful. Thankfully, the woman didn't wait for a response.

"–Now me? I was raised Catholic, but what we're dealing with here isn't the work of any God or Devil I ever learned about in school." She leaned in closer to whisper the next part, "I wonder if it could be… *pagan*."

This conclusion seemed to bring a wave of dread over the middle-aged woman, whose left eye began to water and produced a droplet which turned into a streak down her face as she continued with a quivering voice. "My husband Ronny and me… You know, we went back to that flea market after this all started. Ronny was gonna have some words with that old man, but he was GONE. We tried asking around, and it was like he'd never even been there."

Trudy somewhat composed herself and wiped her tears away with an angry determination as she continued, shaking her head at the dolls. "It's an *infection* is what it is. I'm worried about some of the other dolls now too." She turned her back on the dolls, as if they had betrayed her. "I'm getting worried we've got a full house here, Daisy."

"We'll get to the bottom of it," Daisy assured her as she set the recorder down on a box and began removing items from her bag. "Let's get to work and show the world what you've got going on here."

This refocused Trudy, who seemed impressed by the equipment being pulled out. "Is this like your ghost hunting stuff?" she asked, poking at the pile forming on the floor.

"Well, sort of," Daisy tried to explain. Her "equipment" consisted mostly of a small tripod for her phone, a ring light, and a few cables. "We're going to roll footage on the doll for a while, including while we're out of the room, to see if we can get the behavior on video. I also have a frequency scanner that can pick up paranormal audio signals."

The Ghost Box scanner was her only piece of special equipment, and it hadn't proven useful in the field a single time.

"Oh wow, that's smart," Trudy declared with reassurance. "See, I figured you guys would know what to do."

Daisy scoured the room for electrical outlets for her gear but every plug on the far side of the room was buried behind shelving. The only free outlet was over by the stairs, next to Toby the dog, which was too far from the dolls, and she didn't want to move them from their natural position.

"Do you have an extra extension cord up here by any chance?" Daisy hoped.

This seemed to catch Trudy off guard. "Well, not up here…" she said, "but I know Ronny has some downstairs. I'll go check! Can I get you a drink?"

"No thanks," Daisy said, pointing to her giant coffee cup.

"I'll be right back!" Trudy said, running off toward the stairs. "Stay!" she commanded Toby as she passed by his bed and hurried down the creaky steps. The sleeping dog didn't seem to notice.

Daisy was thankful for a moment without the woman's presence and took a deep breath. She assembled her tripod, set the appropriate video settings on her phone camera, and then situated the assembly with the camera shot focused on Fast-Fingered Jake's face to set her focus.

She studied the doll and its bleak smirk in closeup on her phone screen. Even without the ring light plugged in yet, her phone picked up a lot of detail thanks to the legions of candles flickering on the top shelf and the brighter light streaming through the little windows to her side. The moonlight created hard shadows on the clown's face which made it appear sinister on her screen.

At least it looks creepy. That's good.

The doll's painted eyes were rendered in more detail than the other features on the face. They were angled, reaching higher toward the nose, which gave the face a dumb, ugly expression, and yet pale blue circles around the dotted pupils made the doll's stare look sadly expressive. The eyes seemed to have witnessed horrors and been unmoved by them. It gave Daisy another chill.

She noticed Jake's eyeline faced upward and to the side, so Daisy repositioned the tripod to the left and raised it up slightly until the clown's eyes were staring directly into the camera lens, peering into her soul, and she began rolling some test footage.

Her audio recorder was still running, so she set it on the lower shelf, out of frame of the camera shot. She zipped up her bag and placed it against the side wall so it would be out of the way during the shoot and then dropped to her knees and began assembling her ring light.

Daisy was startled by the feeling of something warm and wet making contact with her right hand, and she recoiled.

She looked down to find that Toby the dog had silently wandered over and deposited a slobbery greeting on the palm of her outstretched hand. He sat silently, peering into the void with milky white useless eyes, as if waiting for something. Daisy gave Toby scratches on the head and then moved to the side of his neck which produced some involuntary leg spasms.

That seemed to be all the acknowledgement he required because he then lumbered onward and, nose hunting furiously through the air like a bloodhound on a hunt, proceeded over to the bottom shelf, where he greeted Fast-Fingered Jake eagerly with the broad, slimy tip of his tongue and applied a thick streak of drool onto the doll's face.

His nightly routine complete, Toby waddled slowly back over to his dog bed, where he collapsed and promptly returned to snoring.

Daisy checked her phone screen again to find a weeping clown doll staring back at her in 4K. She rose to her feet, grabbed her coffee, and took two huge gulps. It was going to be a long night.

CHAPTER 2

Ghost Notes

* * *

Daisy slept in and woke naturally without the use of an alarm clock the following morning, a privilege reserved for Tuesdays and Thursdays, when she worked from home instead of reporting to *The Believer*'s office. The flexible hours allowed by the paper were a considerable perk, given that she was essentially allowed to make her own schedule when working remotely.

Despite her incredible punctuality and sense of timing, Daisy wasn't a morning person. She threw on a playlist of rock songs to provide some background music for her morning routine. Daisy never ate breakfast, and the thought of food usually turned her stomach in the morning; caffeine was the chief commodity in her daily ignition sequence. She reminded herself to buy filters later as she pulled the last one from the box and set her small coffee-maker to work.

Daisy's apartment in Long Island City, Queens wasn't much to look at, but it was in good condition and affordable on her budget, despite being a stone's throw from the Court Square subway station, standing firm at the outskirts of an expanding wave of construction and modern prosperity that would eventually engulf it in the coming years. The rapid evolution of the neighborhood resulted in an unusual mixture of old and new, huge and tiny, often within the same block, which Daisy found oddly charming.

Daisy had lived in her LIC apartment building for over three years. Her pay raises at *The Believer* had failed to keep up with her annual rent increases, but she was still comfortable for the time being. Eventually the building, and the neighborhood, would price her out, but she was holding strong until then. Her building was old and problematic enough that the landlord couldn't justify a *drastic* uptick in lease rates. And yet it wasn't *quite* old enough to be on the neighborhood chopping block for demolition; it needed to wear out its welcome a bit longer first.

Daisy's apartment had a small "living room," which was really a glorified hallway extending from the front door past her kitchen and bathroom. It wasn't wide enough for a full-sized couch. Thankfully the bedroom had much more floor space, enough for a full-sized bed, her desk, a clothes dresser with a TV on top, a large over-filled bookshelf, and a small blue loveseat positioned against the wall behind her work desk.

Daisy was proud of her little one-bedroom apartment. The job at the paper had allowed her to forgo roommates for the first time in her life and she'd grown accustomed to the privacy, as well as the ownership she felt over her manicured little abode. She might have joined the "adulting" party a bit later than some of her friends, but it felt like she was finally there. Of course, her walls were still largely decorated with posters of horror movies and rock bands, but they were framed now, dammit.

After browsing the morning news and putting a couple cups of coffee in her system, Daisy got ready for work. She showered, picked her t-shirt for the day, and got dressed.

When she retrieved her phone from its charger, she noticed she'd received a text message while in the shower from her friend Greggory, an assistant medical examiner for Queens County.

She'd met Dr. Greggory Matthews years earlier from a dating app. They'd had a fun little fling but quickly realized they weren't right for each other. Daisy and Greggory had parted amicably, and then maintained a loose friendship afterwards. Relationships didn't usually end like that for Daisy, but Greggory was one of the most laid-back men she'd ever met. She had decided that if he honestly wanted to remain friends with her and didn't feel uncomfortable, then she could be mature enough to do the same.

Greggory's text read:

> yo Daisy!
> I have a case you might be interested in 😜

The text was peculiar, not just because Greggory rarely reached out to her these days, but because he never volunteered information about autopsies. It was unheard of! Medical Examiners operated under strict guidelines regarding the release of information, especially to reporters. Even when they'd been dating, he'd refused to budge on the matter. It had been frustrating for Daisy; she had a close contact with the city who was first to know about interesting deaths in the borough, but all the details that would make an article compelling were the very things he was forbidden from disclosing. It was only the tease of access, without anything actionable.

As a reporter, Daisy was expected to publish at least one self-generated story per week in addition to the shared work of following up on submissions to the website's tip line. The paper made a point of avoiding political content and rarely engaged with celebrity stories but anything else was fair game. She had to submit her story ideas for approval before she could commit additional time and resources, but after years on the job she knew what kind of content got clicks and had free reign to use any sources and leads at her disposal in New York City.

She'd found the process exciting in her early days on the job, but the novelty had long worn off. She'd come to realize that everyone was desperate for attention and their stories were usually unsubstantiated and painfully derivative. After her first month on the job, she'd heard almost nothing new. Most of *The Believer*'s fodder fell under a few broad categories:

BIZARRE HUMAN INTEREST
CONSPIRACY THEORIES
GHOSTS, HAUNTINGS, & DEMONS
CRYPTID & MONSTER SIGHTINGS
OCCULT HAPPENSTANCE
SPOOKY NYC HISTORY

Whatever Greggory had up his sleeve would be unique at least. But it was a hassle to get out to the Queens Medical Examiner's facility, which was about an hour commute one-way from Daisy's apartment in Long Island City and required a transfer to a bus. She was allowed to expense cab or ride share services for certain situations but generally had to make use of mass transit for her work errands around the city. It would eat up half her day to see what Greggory had for her, and she still needed to type up her article from the previous night's investigation and interview, but Daisy knew her stories had been lacking lately and she couldn't pass up the unusual opportunity.

She replied:

Dude you're a lifesaver
Absolutely. Heading your way
I'll text when I get there

Daisy quickly brushed her teeth, threw on her leather jacket, and headed out her front door. She made her way down two flights of steps before remembering she'd left her drumsticks in her bedroom.

Take two.

She ran back up the stairs, added the sticks to her bag, and then left her apartment to begin her day a second time.

Daisy took the E-train to Kew Gardens and then transferred to a Q46 bus to finish the job. Many New Yorkers have an aversion to using buses but Daisy didn't mind them. Compared to the subway, they were often cleaner and in better condition. The heat and air conditioning usually worked and, except for the busiest routes and times, she could usually get a seat. Of course, when trips on the bus went wrong, they had a tendency to go *spectacularly* wrong, so there were pros and cons.

Daisy took a shortcut through a medical plaza and approached the glass and steel facade of the Queens Office of the Chief Medical Examiner—OCME. It was tucked behind a hospital and looked modern compared to its surroundings. She waited outside the west employee entrance and texted Greggory to let him know she was there.

Within a couple minutes, the door opened and Greggory Matthews appeared with a beaming smile. He was average height and solidly built with dark skin and shoulder length dreadlocks. He was wearing camo cargo pants with sneakers, a dress shirt buttoned to the top, and suspenders.

Greggory looked and acted like several people had accidentally been combined into one guy—a doctor, a hippie, a mad scientist, and an artist. It might explain why he seemed to be bursting at the seams with enthusiasm all the time; it was too much for one person to contain. Greggory could be a little scatter-brained and was such a perfectionist that he sometimes kept technicians at work until the wee hours of the morning, waiting on him to complete his overly thorough autopsy so they could clean up and go home. But Dr. Matthews was a rising star at the OCME and any eccentricities about him were easily tolerated in light of his effectiveness and amiable personality. He had a zest for medicine and forensics, as well as science in general, that Daisy, like everyone else, found infectious. He would have made a great teacher.

She gave Greggory a big hug.

"Long time no see, kid," he admonished. "I used to hear from you all the time. What's up with you lately? Are you still a reporter, or what?"

"Technically," she scoffed, as they made their way inside the facility.

"I mean, I know you're burned out and all but I'm gonna need that old Daisy Scott spice on this one. You gotta wake up that tiger inside."

Daisy laughed. "Why? What is it? Something good? I can't believe you're reaching out to me about a case."

"SHHH! Not just yet." He seemed concerned about people overhearing them. "Let's just say," he hinted, "that for the first time ever, I'm stumped."

"You?!" she asked. "Okay, you've got my attention."

They walked down a hallway with a large floor scale and two walk-in freezers to the left and the main autopsy room on the right. Daisy wasn't allowed into most areas during the day but Greggory had given her the full tour one night when they'd been dating.

She was always disturbed to see the tools on display. On TV, autopsy rooms were filled with futuristic, high-tech gadgets and flat screens. In real life, the OCME's tools were unsettlingly banal. It was the same assortment you'd see in a storage shed: scissors, pliers, giant garden shears. She'd expected cutting edge technology, and certainly there was, but the work of medical examiners required dismembering cadavers, a chore as old as mankind itself and uniquely unsusceptible to "disruption." According to Greggory, the most important and revolutionary tech development in the history of medical forensics was still the bone saw.

Despite her love of horror movies, Daisy only enjoyed fictional carnage and didn't have the stomach that Greggory did for viewing human anatomy and crime scenes. It was obviously a prerequisite for his job. He routinely saw murders, bodies mangled in accidents, every form of disease, burn victims, and worse. He'd told her about a case where a woman had caught her husband cheating and stabbed him 134 times with a butter knife and then raked the corpse with a pizza slicer, since nothing sharper had been available.

One time she'd asked Greggory if anything on the job ever got to him. Without pausing a second to reflect, he'd told her that the only thing that ever disturbed him was simply the old people they found who had died alone and had no living contacts who cared. No spouse, no friends, no family, no pets. There were no red flags, missed appointments, unanswered calls, or wellness checks, just a life snuffed out and no one to even notice, at least until the smell set in.

Greggory said it haunted him, knowing such people were out there now, all around us, living out their sad, final days all alone before they'd find themselves on his table. His job was to write their final chapter, meaning he might be the last soul on Earth to ever care about those forgotten people. That was what kept him up at night.

At the end of the hall, they turned left and Greggory scanned his badge to let them into a smaller autopsy room with only two tables, used for special procedures, which was not currently in use. This room had a one-way mirror along the back wall leading to a small seating area where authorized visitors could view an autopsy in progress without scrubbing up. A built-in desk spanned the side wall along the left half of the room, loaded with equipment and two computer terminals. Greggory logged on at one of the stations and pulled up a file from the case management system.

"There's no active investigation on this… yet," he said. "Once that changes, I'll have a press blackout and you'll be on your own until the death investigation is complete, which could take a long time."

"What is this, Greggory? What have you got?" Daisy begged, eager for any clue about what he was building up toward. She noticed he was less enthusiastic than usual. Whatever he had in store for her, it wasn't something light-hearted.

"We've had three cases in the last month," he explained, "two undocumented women and a teenage boy. They all died the same way, but the manner of death is undetermined."

"Undetermined?" she asked.

"Daisy, I can't tell you how these three people died. But it looks like a pattern to me."

Daisy's heart started beating faster. This was a reporter's dream. Mysterious deaths? A pattern? This case sounded like the sort of opportunity journalistic careers were built on—*real* careers.

"Is there a killer? Do you think it's homicide?" she asked.

"Not so fast," he said, shaking his head. "I told you. This one is weird."

"Can you show me?" she asked.

"The photos aren't pretty. Are you sure?"

"I need to see what we're dealing with," she said. "Why is there no police investigation?"

Greggory began pulling up crime scene photos from the system. "I just told you," he said. "Two undocumented immigrants and a homeless kid."

"Jesus, no one cares?" she asked.

"It's not that no one cares. It's a matter of priorities. In Queens alone, we see dozens of deaths a day. For the whole city? You're talking about 150-plus New Yorkers dying every single day, thousands a month. The police can't investigate every death in the city, and there's no reason to. Most deaths are natural and easily explainable. These, on the other hand..."

An image popped onto the screen of a dead woman lying in a patch of reeds by a waterfront. Daisy instinctively flinched from the screen but steadied herself and looked again. It was clearly a pregnant woman, and it looked like she'd been in the water for a while based on the bloating.

"This was the first decedent," he explained. "Female, estimated age mid-twenties, no match in any U.S. record database."

"Mid-twenties…" Daisy repeated sadly.

Greggory clicked through to a new photo, this time closer. The woman looked pale and ghastly, with her wet shirt pulled up to reveal a wound in the middle of her stomach.

"Unnatural death?" she asked.

"Oh yeah," he laughed. "That much I can tell you. But beyond that?"

"What am I looking at here?"

The smile left Greggory's face, and he sighed. "The fetus was missing. My first hypothesis was a failed unlicensed abortion. The wound is very small, consistent with vacuuming. Then we got the second body, same M.O., also pregnant and undocumented. Now I'm thinking, maybe we've got a backroom clinic somewhere? Where are these women coming from? But then I get the third body and I'm thrown back to square one."

Greggory rubbed his eyes. "It was a teenage boy. Definitely no baby or abortion, but similar injuries. In his case though, the liver was missing. Do you want to see the other case photos?"

"No, that's okay," Daisy said. She already had the gist of it. "Was it surgical removal?"

"Through a hole the size of a magic marker?" he scoffed. "No, that's the thing. None of these removed parts were viable. In fact, I'd say they'd been hacked up before being removed."

"Why?" she wondered. "What do you make of it?"

"I wish I knew!" he said, with accumulated frustration obvious in his tone.

"Do you suspect foul play?"

"That was my second hypothesis. The extractions were very clean. The kid's body was found at the site of his death and there was very little blood on the scene despite the internal trauma involved. But I can't say this looks surgical. This isn't a demonstration of skill or talent. This isn't like Jack the Ripper showing off, saying "Look what I can do. Can you catch me?" Other than some basic knowledge of anatomy, the only thing impressive about this is that they got the tissue through a small opening without making a mess."

"It sounds like you went through more than two guesses here."

"You have no idea," he agreed. "Because I haven't even got to the weird part yet."

"What?"

He switched to another tab in the software and then paused.

"This next part is off the record until I say otherwise," he said. "I need your word on that."

"Of course," she said.

"On the boy's body, I noticed some inflammation around the opening of the wound. It looked like an allergic reaction, so I had toxicology run some samples. Well, they tried. Long story short, they come back stumped. Now they're getting into the mystery of it too, right? We're busting our heads on this, so we say, "fuck it." This one won't beat us. It's time for asymmetrical warfare. We send some tissue to a university for protein analysis, okay? Well, the report just came in. And it only raises more questions."

He pulled up a lab document on the screen and zoomed in on a list of terms Daisy didn't recognize:

> Neutrophil stimulating factor 1 (NeSt1)
> LTRIN
> Anticlotting serpin-like protein (AT)
> Adenosine deaminase (AD)
> Putative 34 kDa family secreted salivary protein
> Putative secreted protein (VA)
> Serine protease CLIPA3
> miRNA-100
> miRNA-125
> Bacteria-responsive protein 1 (AgBR1)
> N-acetyl-5-methoxytryptamine

"What am I looking at here?" she asked.

"The kitchen sink, Daisy!" Greggory's natural excitement was beginning to reemerge as he got into the details. "We've got a little bit of everything and none of it should be here," he said. "First of all, these samples lit up their system with unknown matches. This is only what they could identify. The protein profile is a mixture of bioactive components known to modulate vertebrate hemostasis, immunity, and inflammation, plus multiple anticoagulants. It's like the wound was flushed with chemicals to temporarily inhibit the body's natural responses and blood clotting."

"What? Have you ever heard of anything like that before?"

"Never."

"Why would somebody do that?"

"You got me!" Greggory declared. "There's no *good* reason. I guess, if you were trying to extract organs while the body was still alive, then these agents might be useful but, like I said, these organs and fetuses were not harvested. They were hacked up and sucked through a hole. It's reckless. If there's a killer, he's a "*Sloppy* Jack the Ripper" and just wanted to get the organs out as fast as possible and didn't care about keeping them intact or viable. But then why go for the fetus and liver in particular?"

"You said "*killer*,"" Daisy noticed. "And then why the chemicals?"

"I said *IF* there's a killer," he corrected, "and yes, that's it exactly. Why the chemicals? A killer wouldn't use the chemicals. See? We're in a loop. It's got me stumped. That's why I figured you might be interested."

"Have you ever seen a collection of compounds like this before?" she asked.

"No, not from a crime scene."

"But somewhere?" she asked. "Tell me."

"No, it's nothing," Greggory laughed. "Just a coincidence. It won't help us. I just spent so much time thinking about this now, I remembered something from medical school. This mixture of proteins is similar to the cocktail found in mosquito saliva."

"Are you serious?" Daisy asked. "You're not suggesting a giant mosquito killed these people?"

"No!" he laughed. "Of course not. But it sort of looks like someone tried to make it look that way. Right? It's weird. Look, whatever this is, it's a new one. I'm concerned. And I'm ringing alarm bells until somebody outside the Queens OCME takes notice. I'm worried somebody's playing a sick game out there."

Greggory closed the files on the screen before continuing. "And they're picking off the least fortunate people in the city."

"And there's no investigation?" she tried again. "What about the other boroughs?"

"I don't know about the other counties yet. I'll check that out for you while I still can. Eventually the city will take notice. Like I said, the one thing I can say with certainty is this looks like a pattern."

"Does anyone besides you and toxicology know about this yet?"

"Yeah, of course," he said. "Every case that goes through Queens OCME has our full eyes but we're busy here night and day, and will be until the day people stop dying. There's a bad shortage of medical examiners. So, we have to pick our battles. We don't even have ID on these women yet."

Greggory looked at Daisy sadly. Before they'd dated, she'd assumed medical examiners were part of the police department. That's how it always looked on TV shows: the detective and the forensic medical examiner, best buddies, working tirelessly side by side to solve crimes.

But she had learned that NYC'S OCME, like all medical examination units, was vehemently independent. Autopsy reports are completely separate from police death investigations and are usually completed far in advance. Medical Examiners only care about cold, hard facts. Daisy admired Greggory for his choice of profession. A medical doctor had many desirable paths to choose from. They could pursue a specialty or go into advanced research. They could build a large practice and make a lot of money, or they could hide away in a suburb, administering flu shots and patching sprained ankles in comfort and obscurity, earning a sizable income without ever exercising themselves too much.

Greggory hadn't picked any of those paths. From what Daisy had seen, his job seemed to provide all the hassles of the other options with none of the perks. He would never be super rich. He'd never be famous, unless he was involved in a high-profile case. What's worse, his job was extremely difficult. Each case presented a unique set of problems. He could never "phone it in" for the day. Plus, he was exposed to every horror a set of human eyes could behold. And he did it all simply because someone had to do it. And because he was curious.

"These people were just looking for a better life," he said. "But they ended up losing everything."

She noticed Greggory was nervously scratching the nails of his right thumb and index finger together as he spoke. She could picture him doing that for hours, wearing his nails down as he puzzled over one problem after another.

"You know what they say about medical examiners?" he asked.

"What's that?"

"We're speakers for the dead. My job is to find out how people died and tell their story for the record. I'm supposed to bring closure to their loved ones. But how am I supposed to do that when somebody's completely slipped through the cracks like this?

"I keep thinking that these people are sort of like little spare parts, screws and bolts, left over after you put something back together. You know they're supposed to be in there somewhere; they had a purpose at one point, but no one cares as long as the machine's still mostly working. You know? What am I supposed to do when no one cares?"

"That's why you called me, right?" Daisy offered, placing her hand on his shoulder. "Everybody failed these people in life. We've got one last chance to not fail them."

"Thanks, Daisy," he said with a handsome smile that made her remember what she'd seen in him when they started dating.

"Just remember," he said. "They can't keep this quiet long. If you want the scoop, the clock's ticking."

CHAPTER 3

Utopia Parkway

* * *

Daisy left the OCME facility with a list of three victims but knew she only stood a snowball's chance in hell of following up on one of them.

Victim One was a pregnant undocumented woman found along the riverbank at Willow Lake. The body had been discovered along a poorly maintained walking path. The crime scene had long since been cleaned up and exposed to the elements so it would be a waste of time for Daisy to inspect the area. The woman wasn't in the country legally and had no records, so outside agencies had to be involved to begin identifying her and Daisy couldn't wait on that.

Victim Two was also a pregnant undocumented woman. Her body had been found fresher and in better condition in Flushing Meadows Corona Park near the Unisphere, a giant steel globe erected for the 1964 New York World's Fair. The space age monument was a central gathering point in the large park and had become the de facto symbol to represent the borough of Queens. The body had been dumped behind a row of concrete police barricades out of view of any security cameras and no witnesses had come forward. It would be a waste of time to blindly walk around the park asking strangers if they knew anything. Instead, Daisy planned to post on social media asking for information about the first two deaths, hoping someone with real information might come forward.

That only left Victim Three, who had been positively identified. Miguel Mercado, fifteen years old, was found dead in an alley behind Flushing Creek Houses, a family shelter in Corona. The mother, Lucinda Mercado and her surviving son Gabriel had been moved to private housing in a different neighborhood. Greggory had warned Daisy the phone number on file for the mom was disconnected but Daisy confirmed it herself anyway before heading there unannounced.

The new shelter was inconveniently located, off Utopia Parkway, either twenty minutes by bus or a thirty-minute walk from the OCME. Daisy opted for the walk since the weather was nice, and she let her mind wander as she breathed in the fresh fall air and covered ground down a stretch of Union Turnpike and passed Saint John's University.

This case might be the most important of Daisy's career. It would require every ounce of her skill and cleverness. The problem was that Daisy had been on autopilot for a long time and she worried her skills had gotten rusty and might betray her. She felt like a weightlifter who had taken a season off and was now staring down the heavy weights again.

In her earlier days at *The Believer*, she'd looked forward to these situations—tests of her merit, requiring detective skills, improvisation, misdirection, people skills, and boldness to get the job done. The job had been thrilling at first, traveling the city, meeting interesting people, and putting her degree to work writing about it all. And to be investigating *paranormal* stories? One of her passions? It had seemed like a dream come true. Even the late nights and oppressive workload had been tolerable, sometimes stimulating, under the infatuating lens of novelty.

The turning point had come about two years prior. Daisy's ambitions had outgrown the little supernatural blog, and she'd decided to move on. The job was entry level, after all, and she'd always intended the position to be a stepping stone toward bigger things once she'd built a portfolio of professional work to demonstrate her skills.

She had dreamt of writing for a large national outlet or doing serious investigative work—murders, corruption, political scandals, corporate misconduct. She knew she had the talent and, with a couple years of professional work to pull highlights from, had felt ready to conquer the world of *real* journalism. That brief moment had been a high point of Daisy's life. She had felt brave, confident, and hopeful about her life ahead.

It had been her second act. Her mid-twenties had been consumed with a mourning period over the breakup of her band. She'd dropped out of college to pursue music with her friends, putting all her eggs in that basket, and had been completely crushed when those dreams fell apart with no backup plan. The slow process of resuming school, completing her journalism degree, and beginning her real career had culminated in that moment. She had been ready for anything.

Daisy Scott, Investigative Reporter.

Ready to become the 21st century's Ida Tarbell, she'd spent months applying for every job that seemed like an upgrade to her work at *The Believer* but received only form-letter email rejections. Eventually, she began entertaining lateral moves, even lesser jobs, to get her foot in the door at a more respectable publication. Through a mutual friend, she'd managed to get her work submitted to an editor at *National Geographic* and went through the interview process to become a new freelance writer.

After two rounds of interviews, she'd discovered she'd never actually been in consideration. They'd only met with Daisy as a favor to her friend and would only hire people who were already "in the room." Why they had bothered with the *second* interview, just to get her hopes up, she couldn't understand.

The experience had made Daisy realize *The Believer* was a dead end. She had branded herself as a minor-leaguer and didn't have the connections, heritage, or Ivy League degree necessary to jump any rungs on the ladder. She could likely get work with other novelty or entertainment sites, but she had inadvertently closed the door on her dreams of anything more substantial. And she had no one to blame but herself.

Daisy had climbed out onto the tip of a branch, blowing in the wind, with nowhere left to go. She could either hang on to the little branch, or fall to the ground, injuring herself and having to start her climb all over again. Ultimately, she didn't have it in her to begin a third act so soon into her second, and so she had decided to cling to the limb. Not climbing, not falling, just bouncing in the breeze.

Just like the drumsticks in her bag, her job had become a hollow reminder of a former glory. She went through the motions of her work as a reporter, sustained only by custom and momentum.

Did she have the determination to try again? Was it worth getting her hopes up, knowing the inevitable police investigation would bring real reporters out of the woodwork before she could gather any evidence? Daisy felt that hope was a coin with two sides; it drives us to persevere over life's horrors without succumbing to defeat or nihilism, but hope can be crushed as well and, each time it is, it becomes more difficult to muster it in the future.

Daisy arrived at a nondescript multi-family building along a row of two-story buildings spanning as far as the eye could see down Utopia Parkway. She knocked on the front door of the address Greggory had given her and waited for a response. The neighborhood around her looked nice. It was a bit bland, sure, and there was a major thoroughfare running outside the front door, but each building had a patch of grass, if not trees and shrubs, and the area looked pleasantly residential. These weren't homeless shelters at all. Daisy realized the mother and her surviving child had been upgraded to an unusually nice living arrangement in the aftermath of the murder. She wondered how long the charity would last.

Daisy heard the locks clicking and then a woman greeted her at the door. She had weary, darkened eyes, tangled black hair, and was wearing a bathrobe.

"Yeah? What?" she demanded.

Daisy caught the whiff of liquor on her breath at the close distance even though it was still early afternoon.

"Hi, I'm looking for Lucinda Mercado."

"Oh, what now?!" the woman exclaimed. "Just leave us alone, please."

"My name is Daisy," she explained, undeterred. "I'm sorry to bother you. I was wondering if I could ask you a couple questions about your son? Miguel? I just came from the medical examiner's office and–

"We already answered everybody's questions!" she yelled.

Despite her verbal protest, Ms. Mercado opened the door wide to allow Daisy inside. The woman was clearly so used to being herded around and given orders that she didn't feel she had enough agency to refuse. *Poor lady.*

"I'll make it quick," Daisy promised as she entered the home. "I'm not with the city, or the police. I'm a reporter."

"A reporter?!" she demanded. "With who?"

Daisy considered just saying "freelance" to maintain the plausible ere of respectability, but she didn't have the heart to lie to the woman, and "freelance" might sound like "unemployed" to her, which would be worse than the truth.

"*The Brooklyn Believer,*" Daisy said with as much authority as she could gather.

"Oh Lord!" the woman railed. "Are you serious right now? Do you think Bigfoot killed my poor Miguel? What are you doing here? Leave us alone."

Daisy noticed the woman was slurring her words.

"It's not like that," she explained. "I want to find out what happened to your son. For real. And I want to share his story."

"Well, good luck," she laughed, taking a seat on a small loveseat in front of a TV and then adjusting her bathrobe tighter. She daintily took a sip from the straw of a large plastic Taco Bell cup that Daisy knew was filled with booze of some kind.

Daisy guessed the apartment came pre-furnished since there was a full assortment of furniture but few signs of personality or individual daily life. A small boy, Gabriel she presumed, was in the room as well but wasn't watching TV with his mom, instead lying on the floor a distance away and coloring with crayons.

"Did you see anything that night?" Daisy asked Ms. Mercado.

"Hell no," she replied. "I was already asleep. The boys get into all their shit after I go to bed. They know what to do. Miguel started getting into trouble a while back. He started taking after his dad. I saw it and I knew then. I knew I was gonna lose him one way or another. It always happens. They reach a certain age and they just turn on you…

"He'll do it too," she said, looking at her six-year-old on the floor. "He loves me now but you just wait. That gratitude disappears once the hormones kick in and they go feral. Like animals. Every time. One day they love you, the next? Rip out your throat. No gratitude."

"Do you mind if I talk to him?" Daisy asked.

"You can try," she scoffed. "Gabe didn't talk much before. He don't talk *at all* now."

Daisy slowly approached the boy with a warm smile on her face. She kneeled down and admired one of the pages spread out on the floor which depicted the planets of the solar system.

"Wow, this is great," she complimented.

"Thanks," the boy replied, in an impassive tone.

That's good, Daisy thought. *He's not completely unresponsive or anything.*

"What's your favorite planet?" she asked. "Seems like most people like Mars."

"I hate Mars," he said. "It's ugly. And there's too much radiation there."

"Oh, is that so?" she asked, amused at his trivia. Daisy didn't spend much time around children, but it always occurred to her that they had a better understanding of math, science, and civics than your average adult since it was still new and fresh in their minds from school. Once Americans reach the age they are no longer *forced* to learn these things, the facts begin to drift away. These days, people even take pride in their ignorance of basic knowledge.

"I don't like Mars either," she said. "It's overrated. My favorite planet was always Mercury."

"That's the *worst* planet," he said with obvious disappointment that indicated he'd decided Daisy didn't know enough about planets to justify further dialogue.

"Oh," she floundered. "Then what's your favorite?"

After a long pause, he mumbled "Jupiter."

"Of course, the King of the Planets. I should have remembered."

"Are you a policeman?" the boy asked.

Daisy laughed at the thought. "No Sweetie, I'm definitely not a policeman. I'm just a friend. Listen, I know it's scary, but I need you to tell me everything you can remember about the night your brother was… hurt. Can you do that for me?"

The boy shook his head to indicate "no" and turned away from her in what looked like a mixture of natural shyness and fear. It was a moment when the child's mother should have moved in to comfort him, to assist with the exchange, but Ms. Mercado seemed uninterested. The woman just sat in front of the TV and sipped her drink, leaving them to manage on their own.

Daisy tried another approach. She fully sat down on the floor next to Gabriel and flipped through his other drawings. She found one which obviously depicted himself with his mom and deceased older brother.

"Is this your brother Miguel?" she asked.

The boy remained in a huddle, as if trying to physically protect himself from her presence.

"He looks strong and brave," Daisy complimented.

That got a reaction. "Uh huh," he agreed, sadly.

"Gabriel, I want to help other people like you and your brother. What do you remember? What did the man in the alley look like that night?"

"It wasn't a man," he said.

"What do you mean?" Daisy asked.

Gabriel began to cry. She was losing him.

"What do you mean it wasn't a man, Gabriel? Was it a group of people? Please, tell me."

The memory was too much for the boy and he began to sob, which finally activated his mom to action.

"Oh, look what you've done now! That's it!" she declared, rising to a stand. "No more questions! All we do is answer questions and listen to empty promises and what good has it done us. Go away and leave us alone!"

"I'm sorry," Daisy said, making her way to the door. "It was nice meeting you, Gabriel," she called out to the crying boy, but he didn't acknowledge her. Ms. Mercado gave Daisy a nasty look as she retreated into the hallway and closed the apartment door.

Daisy walked back to the subway with a nervous excitement brewing inside her, a restless anxiety stirring in her stomach that she hadn't felt in a long time. It was the same little tinge of fear that had accompanied her early reporting when the job had been fun. Unfortunately, the sands of this hourglass were falling quickly. She felt a sense of urgency and yet had nothing useful to act on.

Daisy took a seat on the train and began carefully composing a message for social media asking for information about the first two victims. She had to be careful with her wording. She didn't want to give too much away. She wasn't very active on social media and her public request for tips would be noteworthy. She might draw the attention of her bosses or co-workers before she was ready. Still, she had no choice if she wanted to break this story.

The nervous feeling in Daisy's stomach was still there, but she found she didn't mind it. In fact, she realized she had missed it. It meant she was onto something big.

CHAPTER 4

Pappas

* * *

In Astoria, Queens, some binoculars trained their gaze on the windows of a luxury apartment building and began hunting through the grid of darkened rectangles for evening entertainment.

The building is unusually quiet tonight, Danny Pappas thought to himself, reviewing the mostly empty homes from his kitchen across the street.

He kicked a pile of trash out of the way to make room for his feet up against the wall, revealing three small cockroaches. At first, they seemed too paralyzed by the change in the status quo to even move, but then sprinted apart in different directions at top speed. Pappas attempted to squash one of the roaches with his slipper, but his reflexes were no match for the insect, which disappeared to safety under the refrigerator, living to fight another day.

There were swarms of the things everywhere in the building. Pappas had made good-faith attempts to get rid of them. Every pest guy in Queens had taken his shot, but ultimately the bugs always came back so Pappas and the roaches had reached an uneasy truce.

They're disgusting, but harmless, really, he rationalized. *And they clean up our spills, don't they?*

His wife even called them "LITTLE HELPERS," so they'd mostly grown accustomed to sharing their home with the legions of bugs. That said, he'd occasionally see squashed roaches under his wife when she rolled over in bed, which gave him pause, realizing the roaches must crawl all over them while they sleep. *Crawling over my face...*

He aimed his binoculars through a gap in the old blinds where a couple slats were missing and continued his search. Only about a quarter of the apartments showed signs of life and all were a disappointment. He mostly just saw big glowing TVs in the windows–some watching the news, others a movie or reality TV. One guy on the 3rd floor appeared to be watching softcore porn, although the plot seemed to involve aliens. The people watching these screens were invisible to him, buried behind couches and cushions and sheets. *BORING.*

"Danny, I need a Diet Coke!" a woman screamed from the adjacent bedroom. His wife's voice had a deep, low pitch and was gravely, like an engine trying to start, thanks to decades of chain smoking. She sounded like an over-the-top CGI villain in a superhero movie.

His wife "hated water" and would only drink Diet Coke from sunrise to sunset, the sole exception being one cup of coffee in the morning. Of course, she was supposed to be on a low sodium diet, but she always lied to their doctor and claimed she drank one soda a day. Pappas had long ago given up trying to change her ways and didn't care anymore. He had attempted to switch her to a generic brand to at least save a little money, but she'd claimed it "didn't taste the same," so never-ending cases of Diet Coke were a regular weekly grocery expense. He decided she could wait a few minutes for her next can and continued peering through the binoculars.

Elsewhere in the building across the street, he saw a tall Chinese man cooking dinner in his kitchen, a dog sitting alone by the window, and a red-haired woman working at a desk in her bedroom. *BORING!* He saw a man trying on various ties with a suit in the mirror, and a couple sitting by their window and just talking. *BORING!!!* Most nights were like this. Nothing exciting. Sometimes he questioned why he still did it. He'd taken up this habit of "people watching" completely by accident while the building across the street was being constructed years earlier, during the pandemic.

The lot across the street had previously been occupied by a decrepit pre-war walk-up, much like his own building, but the crumbling eyesore had been demolished to make way for a new modern "luxury" apartment building. After an argument with some construction workers, Pappas had purchased the binoculars to peer down at the work crew across the street, in hopes of observing violations he could report to the city as revenge.

He'd fantasized about the construction guys packing up their tools and retreating from his street in shame, millions of dollars lost because of their failure. And who would be there, watching on the sidewalk? *Danny Pappas* would be there, with a beer in his hand, perhaps even slipping the guys a knowing little wink, to make sure they knew *he* was the one who got them.

But before he could collect such evidence, the big empty pit in the ground across the street had become a shiny, modern edifice looking down on him.

He hated the new building for what it represented. For a city as old as NYC, the two years of construction had been just a blink of the eye and now his block was forever changed. It was a wrinkle that appeared overnight. The demolished apartment building, along with all the stories of the lives it had contained, had been replaced in a heartbeat. The new structure in its place shouted promises of a fresh new start for those inside, with their eyes on the future, while ghosts of the past could only whisper their triumphs and tragedies to the few like him that would still listen, those with their eyes on the past.

The new building was seven stories tall, not much higher than the old one, but that was where the similarities ended. The luxury apartments were filled mostly with well-to-do young people. He imagined they all had made-up email jobs or worked on "an app" and made more money in a year than he saw in a decade.

The reason he'd kept up his voyeuristic hobby so long, and moved the base of his operations from the bedroom, where his bedridden wife was stationed day and night, to the kitchen window, was mostly due to his interest in one window across the street in particular–*her* window.

Her name was *Peppermint Sage*. She was tall; he guessed much taller than him. And was a real *hardbody*, probably into some kind of athletics in her free time. She had long blonde hair, curves in all the right places, and features that appeared through his binocular glass to be of solid breeding, good German or Scandinavian stock.

"Peppermint Sage" was just the name he imagined for her, of course. He didn't know her real name. But to Pappas, she'd always looked like a "Peppermint Sage." Refreshing and sweet, with an earthy twist.

Peppermint was as gorgeous as any actress or model he'd ever seen on TV, and her life was like a private movie screening just for him, right across the street. She was only home on weekday nights, seemingly occupied with work, responsibilities, or her social life almost every waking minute. Her apartment seemed to be mostly a "crash pad" in between exciting activities.

Like most NYC apartment dwellers, she had no curtains for the large living room windows. The bedroom had one smaller window, with a roller shade, but she thankfully only employed it about half the time. Most of her activities were boring as well, but she routinely paraded around half-dressed and on three occasions he had seen much more.

Pappas had spent so many hours watching Peppermint now, he imagined an entire fictional life for her. She was a Republican and always single. She was too old-fashioned for the young men around her, and was looking for an older Greek man to teach her the ways. Sometimes she would stand at her living room window, just looking outside, and her glance would pass by his direction. His heart would beat quicker. *Does she know I'm here? Does she know I'm watching?* His mind could stretch even further: *Would she even care? Does she like being watched?*

"I CAN'T TAKE MY PILLS WITHOUT THAT FUCKING DIET COKE!" his wife screamed from the bedroom, making Pappas jump.

"I'm bringing it! Give me a fucking minute!" he responded, "Christ!"

His wife had been through half a case of Diet Cokes already that day, Pappas remembered, so he was doing her blood pressure a favor by stalling. He found Peppermint's apartment with his binoculars. *Lights still out. Where are you?* he wondered.

He hunted through the other apartments again and his attention was drawn to a window lighting up. A young woman on the 5th floor seemed to be coming home from work. He hadn't seen her before. She removed her coat and shoes, dropped her keys into a bowl by the door, and proceeded straight to her bedroom, where she flung off her top to reveal a red bra underneath.

HERE WE GO, Pappas thought to himself. *This woman is no Peppermint*, he admitted, but she was a beauty nonetheless, a brunette. She had olive skin with no tan lines. He wondered if she was maybe Middle Eastern or Latino. He preferred blondes and, in general, white women, but beggars can't be choosers, he reminded himself.

Show me your goodies, he commanded the woman with his mind. Then, as if she had heard him and was eager to obey, she quickly removed her skirt and added it to a pile on the floor, revealing matching red panties underneath. It wasn't a thong, exactly, but very skimpy. He decided he would call this woman *Cinnamon Spice*.

"That's it, Sweetie. Show me your *goodies*," he whispered aloud now, forgetting himself in a trance as he stared, unblinking, at the shapely half-naked form.

"Show me your goodies..."

He felt a sneeze building from leaning against the dusty blinds. He started to reach for the paper towel roll on the counter, but it was too far away, and buried behind piles of dirty dishes. He quickly improvised, and lifted the neck of his t-shirt up over his nose just in time to trap the wet blast.

Pappas felt a moment of guilt, knowing his late mother would not have approved of the disgusting behavior, and he felt gross with the warm splatter mixed into his chest hair, but he soaked the mess up with his shirt and decided the transgression was forgivable since the shirt wasn't clean anyway.

With this understanding–that the shirt was already filthy beyond the point of justifying any further maintenance–he went ahead and covered each nostril in turn with a finger and gave a big blow, to fully clear his sinuses into the dirty cotton fabric. He found his right nostril to have been unusually loaded because a hardened little wad of heavy buildup unexpectedly shot out like a rocket, disappearing somewhere into the dark reaches under his neckline.

He pulled in a deep, clear breath through his emptied nostrils to admire his handiwork and then drew his shirt into a bunch and lifted it to his nose to give it a quick dab for final cleanup. He noticed some moisture from the ordeal had penetrated onto his hand. He'd learned from his father that *A MAN ALWAYS RESPECTS HIS TOOLS*, so he wiped his fingers on a clean-looking area of his pants before picking up the binoculars again to resume peeping.

Pappas quickly resituated himself against the blinds, knowing he potentially had mere seconds left before Cinnamon disappeared from view or put on new clothes. But in his upper periphery, he noticed some movement at the very top of the building, something large enough to detect with his unaided eyes.

That's weird, he thought. The building had a large outdoor rooftop area above the penthouse, and it wasn't uncommon to see the heads of people bobbing around up there, but this person was on the level above that, a smaller structure that would likely contain electrical and mechanical equipment for the building. A resident shouldn't be up there.

Young punks, probably, he figured, as he tried to get a bird's eye view of the person with his binoculars. It was easier said than done. The magnified view through the lenses offered none of the reference points he needed to zone in on his target and the rooftop was very dark. Finally, he aligned his view with the top ridge of the upper roof of the building and searched for movement, but saw only shades of black in the night sky. He scanned left and right.

Did I miss them? Was it the lower balcony after all? Was it my imagination?

He was about to give up and resume leering at the brunette when the rooftop shape moved once again.

GOT YOU, he thought, as he centered his enhanced view on the moving form. *But what is it?* Something large and fluttering, like big flags, or a dark fabric.

NO, he realized with a shudder...

WINGS. He was looking at two absolutely gigantic wings, not feathered, but sectioned into flaps. *BAT WINGS*. They were stretched out into the moonlit sky, blending into the inky depths without a trace, except during movements, when the glints of soft reflections would subtly shift and reveal themselves to him.

Pappas immediately ruled out the possibility of the wings being part of a simple Halloween costume. They were too complicated and lifelike for that. He considered it could be part of an expensive mechanical decoration. *But why install it now? With just one week left in October?* It couldn't be intended for an upcoming roof party; it was on the wrong roof.

YOU IDIOT! He chided himself, realizing he should have been getting the incident on video. He dropped his binoculars to the floor and looked for his phone. *Where is it?* He searched frantically around himself for the device—it was nowhere! *Shit! Did I leave it in the bedroom? I'm gonna miss this!* he worried.

Then, a miracle—

YES! He felt a pressure against his backside as he shifted in his seat, and discovered he'd been sitting on his phone the entire time.

"Bless the Lord above!" he thanked out loud, not caring if his wife heard him, and then brushed food crumbs and debris out of the large crack down the center of his phone screen so he could unlock the device.

He opened up his camera app and aimed it through the crack in the blinds. It didn't look anything like his view through the binoculars. *Too dark!* He tapped to adjust the brightness until he could see details in the picture, started recording, and then aimed upward toward the roof.

YES! It's still there! he rejoiced to himself, pinching the screen to zoom in tighter on the phenomenon. The wings seemed to be stretching themselves, rippling slowly, almost airing themselves out in the breeze, and then they suddenly collapsed inward on themselves, like a bat folding in its wings. *MY GOD*, Pappas realized. *This is an animal. ALIVE.* And it was no bat, but something MUCH larger.

"DANNY!!" his wife screamed from the other room. "Do I have to disobey my *doctor's* orders and come get that fucking soda myself?!"

He ignored her and kept rolling footage of the rooftop. *You'll soon have all the Diet Coke you can fucking guzzle,* he smiled to himself. Because their lives were about to change forever, and they'd be living on Easy Street from now on. *Hell,* he figured. *Maybe they'd even move across the street.*

Pappas knew that once people saw his video, his life would never be the same again.

CHAPTER 5

The Brooklyn Believer

* * *

The next morning, Daisy stepped off the elevator and swiped her fob key to enter the office of *The Brooklyn Believer* two minutes early for her shift. It was a Friday, so she walked into a mostly empty office.

The Brooklyn Believer's physical office space was, ironically, located in Queens these days, overlooking Queensboro Plaza, and had been planted there since long before Daisy started at the paper. Sure, once upon a time, Jerry had famously started his blog and newsletter from his shithole apartment in Williamsburg, succeeded by a series of commercial leases across Brooklyn, relocating every few years as the paper's fortunes rose and fell and rose again, but the current base of operations was a half-floor commercial sublet in Long Island City, making Daisy's commute a trivial ten minute walk from her apartment near Court Square.

The office was essentially a glorified co-working space. The other half of the floor was divided into two smaller sublets, each leased by a different company, and they all shared a set of bathrooms by the elevator, a small conference room, booked ahead of time by schedule, and a partial kitchen.

The Believer's office space came largely pre-decorated which meant, on the one hand, they had not been able to put much of a personal stamp on the appearance of the place. The long wall across from the windows, for instance, featured a wall-sized mural print of a beach scene, complete with sand, sky, and palm trees, which could not be less relevant thematically for the work they were doing. On the other hand, Daisy came to work everyday in a clean, modern, and stylish–if perhaps a little cookie cutter–office that they could never have managed otherwise.

The space was mostly one large open room, with three glass-enclosed offices along the back wall. Two of the private offices were generally empty since once belonged to Jerry, who worked limited hours these days, and the other belonged to Korinne, the Ad Sales Manager, who was important enough in the hierarchy to claim one of the only three offices, despite never actually being there to use it, since "networking" meant being outside the building. Daisy's direct boss Tiffani, the Managing Editor, essentially lived at work and was *always* in the third office.

The large open space was filled with "the bullpen," two long wooden tables, constructed from co-working-requisite reclaimed wood, each containing three iMac workstations for the reporters. There was also a seating area for guests by the front door, as well as a small private desk for Becky, the office manager.

Only four of the reporter computers were currently assigned. The other two iMacs rarely got used, but *The Believer* employed several part-time freelance writers in addition to its full-time staff, so it was nice to have the extra machines for the busy times when freelancers needed to work on site.

Daisy gave a nod to Becky as she walked into the bullpen. The 50-something Italian American usually had a stack of paperback romance novels on her desk to fill her downtime. She'd been married once a few years prior, in a whirlwind romance resulting in hyphenated last names, but had ultimately discovered that her Prince Charming had another castle, and another queen, in Poughkeepsie, and the experiment had ended in divorce. Becky had never gotten around to reverting back to her maiden, unhyphenated surname.

Daisy plopped down at her seat, at the far end of the first long reporter table, removed her headphones, and slipped them into her bag. She peeked at the back office to see if Tiffani had noticed her entrance yet. It didn't seem that way, so Daisy opened a paper bag to pull out a large pumpkin donut and kicked back in her designated Steelcase chair.

She admired the plump donut for a second, still warm in her hand, and then took a large bite. The soft fried cake melted into a warm, pumpkin-spiced goo in her mouth. She sipped her piping hot coffee—rich and chocolatey, just slightly bitter—letting it pool under her tongue, sizzling. She let the combined flavors bite at the sides of her tongue for a moment, savoring it, before swallowing. This was a flavor profile she only got to enjoy a few weeks of the year, so she indulged herself with the slow, purposeful admiration of a ramen enthusiast in Japan.

"DAISY!" a voice screamed from across the room.

SHIT, Daisy thought. Tiffani had noticed her. Tiffani was technically Daisy's direct boss, and she didn't like the woman, who she believed had fallen upward due to an aggressive personality. Tiffany was uncommonly self-assured and assertive in a manner that seemed to blindside people into submission, no matter how dumb her ideas were. It was like the presence of an assertive person resets people to their default factory settings—following orders—because, in the end, most of us are just thankful that anyone is brave enough to guide the sheep, even if they don't actually know where the hell they're going. The humble rarely lead the way. It's people with *bold ignorance* who inspire those with *meek ignorance*.

"We've got a shit show again, today, girl!" Tiffani said, storming over to Daisy in her high heels. "Look, I know it's Friday, but I need you to squeeze in an interview today if you can. We got a video submission last night that Jerry's already had eyes on, and he wants to run it ASAP, for the weekend."

"What? Where?" This was the last thing Daisy wanted to hear. She had enough work to finish up before the weekend already.

"In Queens. Close by, don't worry. You can knock it out real quick this afternoon and then come back here to type it up and finish your other assignments. The footage speaks for itself, trust me, we just need you to get a statement and take a couple photos."

"Can't Tanner cover it?"

"No, Daisy," Tiffani admonished, "You know Tanner can't do it today. Come on."

"Fine," Daisy relented. "What's the video?"

Tiffani's ruby-red lipsticked grin stretched into an excited, narrow smile. "Wait until you see THIS one."

"This is the fakest shit I've ever seen, Tiffani," Daisy said, looking at a frozen still frame of the shaky cellphone video they had just watched together in Tiffani's small, partitioned office.

"Well…" Tiffani began, with an exaggeratedly sarcastic tone, "He may not have *your* level of expertise, but BRAD says it's real, and he's the *video guy*, so…"

"Brad said this is a REAL GIANT BAT caught on video, Tiffani?" Daisy didn't believe her. "Bullshit."

"He *said*," Tiffani glared at her for emphasis, "that the video hasn't been manipulated. He said…" She reset her reading glasses and glanced down to her handwritten notes for exact wording, "The footage is genuine, unaltered smartphone video. It's not computer-generated or AI. No signs of editing or composite alterations."

"Oh, how does he know?" Daisy retorted. "And why doesn't he go do the interview himself, if he's so bullish about it?" Brad had the cushiest job of them all. He mostly worked from home and his assignments always took *weeks* to complete, not days. He was probably getting paid to watch Netflix while on the clock. "Isn't he supposed to be a "reporter" as well?"

"This is his field, Daisy," Tiffany countered, "He has software at home he can use to check these things. And NO, he can't interview the guy. Brad is still behind on the "Spooky Beat" videos, and he's also tied up with Tanner's project, which is top priority. Jerry only had Brad check this one out for us to make sure it was worth your time before I assigned it. And it IS. Besides…"

She leaned back in her chair before continuing, "You said you were sick of running all around the city and wanted to focus on Queens stories, remember? Well, this story is your beat. *The Queens Beat.* Besides, have you got something better to work on?"

Daisy was relieved Tiffani hadn't seen her post online about Greggory's victims and she wasn't ready to mention the lead to Tiffani until she had something more concrete. She just remained silent and stared at a framed photo on Tiffani's wall which depicted a younger, tired-looking Tiffani with her husband, a stern-looking bald man, both wearing brand new, expensive "outdoor gear" in front of a religious site somewhere in a jungle. She guessed the photo had to be at least a decade old.

The couple were still married but it was office gossip 101 that Tiffani's marriage was a slow-boiling disaster. Tiffani hated everyone, but seemed to despise her husband most of all. Daisy had only ever seen the guy a few times at Christmas parties and special events, but it sounded like he was even more pretentious than Tiffani, so she couldn't imagine how insufferable their conversations must be together.

Or maybe they barely spoke at all? Tiffani spent every waking hour at work, likely to avoid the man, a perpetually-underemployed writer with an Ivy League degree, who fancied himself a "political pundit" and "novelist," so perhaps, their meals together at home were filled only with wordless, seething resentment for each other, accented with occasional passive aggressive arrows shot across the table, while their three corgis watched uncomfortably in a protective huddle.

"Where's Jerry?" Daisy asked, hoping she could stall until he rolled into work and then plead her case to him to get this reassigned. This new interview would add hours to her workload that day and she'd been hoping to leave a little early since it was Friday.

"He's out today. On the boat."

Fuck. Jerry had bought a little sailboat in June and had spent most of the summer breaking it in. He would still take a weekday off now and then to enjoy himself out on the water. To Daisy, it seemed a little late in the season for that, but it sure was a gorgeous day outside.

"Okay, even if it's real footage, so what?" Daisy said, attempting another approach. "It's Halloween next week, Tiffani. This was just some kind of Halloween stunt on a roof. Have you seen all the crazy stuff people buy and build in their yards for this holiday? People love Halloween, and this is New York City. It's nothing. Besides, this video is so dark you can barely see anything."

Daisy worried the footage was actually unusable. She would feel embarrassed running it on the site. She hoped Brad was planning on brightening the footage later before they thought about putting it in an article.

"That's why I had Brad brighten it already first thing this morning. This is the *enhanced* video that he sent back."

"This is the *improved* footage?" Daisy questioned. "What the fuck? Come on, Tiffani, at least let me save this for Monday. This is a *D-minus* story and I've got a lot to do."

"Well, Jerry thinks it's a *B*, Brad thinks it's an *A*…" Tiffani stared at her with eyes that were knots of loathing, scrunching the skin of her face, "and I think it's an *A+* so it's settled."

Daisy stood at the wall of floor-to-ceiling windows along the side of the main room and sipped her coffee, which was now lukewarm and had a slight aftertaste after each sip that made her want to stop drinking it. She'd barely made a dent in the giant drink yet though, so the pull of the necessary caffeine outweighed the bad taste, and she kept sipping.

She looked out on the formation of modern office towers, gleaming windows, and rooftops as they popped against the backdrop of the sky. The blue was so vibrant, she noticed, that in photos it would be accused of unrealistic over-saturation, and yet there it was, in its unlikely azure glory. She noticed two small puffy clouds slowly drifting their way over the giant rooftop jetBlue sign visible out their windows. It was an absolutely perfect day outside today. The temperature was ideal as well, just chilly enough to justify her jacket and make her hot coffee extra delicious on the walk to work, but not cold enough to ever feel uncomfortable. It was a day to be OUTSIDE and to be FREE, like Jerry on his boat, but now she would be working until late that night.

Daisy took the moment of downtime to check on her social media post about Greggory's two victims. She had several responses already but, as expected, all were clearly spam or off-topic. She reminded herself to check the replies again later.

The front door swung open and a rattled twenty-year-old exploded into the office.

"I'm so sorry!" Liam the intern exclaimed to Becky at the front desk, pausing a moment to catch his breath, before finishing the last leg of his race to collapse at his seat, the opposite end of Daisy's table, breathing heavily. "The trains were delayed!"

"That's why you leave early, young man. They're always late," Becky explained with a booming Queens accent that was too motherly and matter-of-fact to be malicious. "You need to make up that time this afternoon."

"Yes, Becky," Liam replied, taking off his jacket.

"Good morning, Daisy!" the intern beamed. "I saw a great movie last night and I thought about you."

Uh oh. She thought. *What's this gonna be?*

Liam considered himself a "film buff" because his customary diet of blockbusters and superhero movies had recently expanded to include a couple Scorsese films and movies with subtitles. Daisy, on the other hand, watched several movies each week and was almost a decade older than the intern.

Her first love had always been horror, particularly vampires, and she'd seen it all from silent films to the latest and greatest offerings. She loved the old *Hammer* horror films above all. She was planning to attend a Halloween party the following night, which would be her first costume party in years, and would make her grand entrance dressed as Dracula, specifically, *Christopher Lee's* Dracula.

With Daisy, the question usually wasn't *if* she'd seen a movie, but *how many times*, so Liam's rudimentary recommendations were never anything new.

"You've got to check this one out," he continued, proudly. "It was called *The Thing*."

"Liam, don't talk to me until I've had my coffee," she said, taking her seat.

"You've seen it before?"

Daisy put her headphones on to dissuade further conversation. She shook her mouse to wake her monitor screen, which was framed in post-it notes around the perimeter. Her station at the desk was sparsely decorated compared to all the other assigned seats. There was a printout, typed as large as possible to still fit on the paper, reminding her which typefaces were currently approved for use. Her computer came with a landline phone next to it, as did every seat at the table, not because they wanted them, but because they came pre-installed with the lease. She had never used her phone and didn't even know her own extension.

Other than a couple cheap Halloween decorations she'd picked up at a dollar store, the only evidence a human being with a personality worked at Daisy's station was the *percussion practice pad* on her desk—a thick, round slab of rubber intended for drumsticks. Her use of the practice pad was largely tolerated by others in the bullpen because it produced virtually no sound in the large room, just the fidgeting of Daisy's arms in the corner of their eyes. Sure, she sometimes ventured off the pad striking things that made noise, and she usually got her feet involved in the beats, but she tried to be respectful.

She logged onto her computer and opened up a small web browser window in the corner of her screen, streaming local NYC news. Daisy hated cable news, believing it only actually took a few minutes to explain the day's events to people, and that the rest of the airtime was stuffed with Talking Heads arguing about why the viewers should be angry and terrified by what they were hearing. She could make up her own mind about politics, as well as the nature of right and wrong, without being preached to by angry teleprompter-readers in blue suits, sandwiched between pharmaceutical ads.

But she loved local news. In fact, she was somewhat addicted to the constant flowing stream of NYC news the way most people were addicted to the never-ending gush of social media. She knew it served a practical purpose; the newscasts often helped with her work, even providing leads. But she'd grown so accustomed to the habit that she felt cut off from the city, UNPLUGGED, if she went too long without checking in. Even on her days off, she spent hours sitting at her desk with the chattering of local news serving as background noise at the edge of her radar, while the rest of her mind was occupied with other things.

She tried to access the third-party publishing system the team used for most of their work duties, but when she entered her password and tapped 'enter' to gain entry, the app refused with an animated flourish.

Damn, Daisy thought, recalling she'd been forced to change her password earlier in the week. She hadn't written it down, so she struggled to remember the replacement. They were required to change passwords regularly and she tended to cycle through percussion related terms. The latest iteration finally popped into her head, and she carefully typed it in:

Paradiddle96!

Successful this time, the kingdom of *The Brooklyn Believer* opened up before her. She checked her email and then began to prepare for her upcoming call with the supplier of the "giant bat" footage, Mr. Danny Pappas.

She found the original, unaltered video submission and watched it a couple times, stretching it out large the second time to inspect for clues. The most glaring omission from Tiffani's presentation of the edited footage was its first few unfortunate seconds, in which a topless woman moves about her apartment on screen, as our hero, the camera operator, adjusts the settings to improve the picture before continuing upward to the top of the building to finally capture the supposed phenomenon.

As for the thing on the roof, Daisy wasn't very impressed. But she also couldn't figure out what she was looking at. She ruled out the possibility it was a large bird; the form was clearly supposed to represent either a comic book character with a bat-like cape, or a person with bat wings attached to their back. The large wings had a range of motion and fluidity that didn't look mechanical and would be impractical for a costume.

It was difficult to perform much detective work on the footage because there was so little to work with. It wasn't just dark; the camera angle was too low compared to the rooftop across the street, meaning most of the figure was blocked by the ridge of the building and only the thing's "head and wings" could be appreciated much at all in the pitch-black scene. Like most videos sent to *The Believer*, the low quality and ambiguity of the footage was a feature, not a bug. If she could see it better, it wouldn't be a mystery. And the truth was probably too mundane to make a good story.

Either Brad or Tiffani had already created a record in the system for the case, titled "Giant Bat Video," but most of the fields were still empty, awaiting Daisy's data entry. The contact info only said "PEEPER" along with the guy's phone number. She was tempted to leave his name unchanged after seeing his unedited submission.

It was standard practice to check contact details against prior records in their archives, so Daisy searched their database for the man's name and it returned one prior result—but then, she searched for variations on "Danny Pappas," "Dan Pappas," and simply "Pappas," to discover *several* older entries in their tip line she suspected might be from the same guy, covering a range of different nonsensical reports, claims, and discovered injustices, none of which ever seemed to have warranted a field call from a reporter. *I guess his ship finally came in*, Daisy thought to herself.

She managed to reach Mr. Pappas on his cellphone. He was a grumpy sounding man with a thick Queens accent who seemed oddly defensive as they made plans to meet at his apartment that evening at 6:00 PM.

In the meantime, she planned to barrel through the rest of her existing work before her meeting with Pappas, so she would at least be caught up for the weekend. Even if Tiffani was correct, and the interview was brief, Daisy knew it would be another late night for her by the time she got back to the office, typed up this new article, and got it published on the site.

Daisy sat between a giant image of a beach on one side, and a beautiful autumn day out the windows on the other, wondering what Jerry was up to that moment? He was out there on the water somewhere, probably marveling at that same blue sky, while sipping a hard seltzer and filling his eager lungs with the crisp sea air.

CHAPTER 6

Astoria

* * *

At 6:00 PM, Daisy stood glaring out the windows of a stalled, above-ground Astoria Ditmars-bound subway car, fuming inside with the knowledge she was officially late for her interview. It was simply unheard of. For anyone else at her paper, the tardiness would be a trivial *non-event*, even the expectation for some of her colleagues. They were always late. But not Daisy Scott. She prided herself on having punctuality you could set a clock by. She thought of it as a core, defining trait.

The subway had screeched to a halt just two stops away from her destination and she'd been standing there, packed in a tin can with the other increasingly frustrated passengers for a full ten minutes. Daisy would gladly have escaped from the train to complete the remaining distance on foot, but the subway had come to a stop between stations and was parked in the middle of nowhere on the above-ground track so there was nowhere for passengers to exit until it resumed its lurch to the next stop.

Despite the cool weather outside, there was no air circulation in the deactivated N-train and the human body-filled contraption was beginning to get uncomfortably muggy. Daisy distracted herself by checking her map again to make sure there would be no mistakes or delays finding the guy's address once she was finally allowed to disembark. She was considering removing her jacket to cool off when the conductor mercifully announced the train would resume its course. A furious hiss announced that the decades-old stretch of stainless steel was resuming its progression, and the passengers began adjusting their coats and fixing their hair. Daisy made her way through the car to position herself at the far door so she could make a mad dash toward Pappas' apartment the moment the doors opened at her stop, and she waited.

"Yeah?" a gruff Queens accent barked from a front door speaker a few minutes later.

Daisy had sprinted to Danny Pappas' building and thankfully he had answered the buzzer quickly. She recognized the man's voice from their call earlier.

"It's Daisy, from the paper!" she replied into the door buzzer, with an uncharacteristic extra-touch of optimism she hoped would distract from her tardiness.

"YOU'RE LATE," he replied, sternly.

DAMN. She was only six minutes late. Now she would be on the defensive.

"Sorry," she explained. "The subway got stalled—

Her explanation was cut off by the door buzzing to allow her inside. She hurried through the door and launched herself up the stairs towards his floor.

"Sorry I'm late, the trains were stalled," Daisy repeated to Mr. Pappas through his cracked door a moment later.

"EXCUSES!" he erupted. "I shouldn't be surprised! Not from *The Brooklyn Believer.*"

73

As she followed the angry man into his apartment and then watched him close the door, Daisy promised herself that this interview would be quick and she would leave ASAP.

She employed a *"Three-Strikes, You're Out"* rule with her interviewees. She left IMMEDIATELY at the first sign people or environments might be unsafe; the job wasn't worth putting herself in danger. But for smaller transgressions, she allowed the accumulation of three violations which could range in nature and severity. Danny Pappas had almost struck out before he had even closed his front door. He was at two strikes:

STRIKE ONE - The guy was clearly an asshole and a homebody, the sort of person who's waited months for the opportunity to be cruel to another human being face to face. He hadn't shown a level of aggression to her yet that made her fear for her safety, but her alarm bells had been activated and she was watching keenly for escalation.

STRIKE TWO - The odor in the apartment was horrific. Pappas hadn't bothered to clean up at all for her visit and she guessed he must be at least a moderate hoarder. Piles of food, trash, Amazon boxes, old papers, and clothing filled the living room, and the couch appeared two-toned thanks to a black layer of grime partially covering the vintage, orange flower-print velour upholstery.

Daisy was fighting the urge to pull her shirt over her nose for the remainder of the interview or just say "fuck it" and bolt back into the hallway to call this one a bust. She smelled rotting garbage, mildew, and the specific reek that comes from dishes that have sat unwashed far too long in a damp sink. As she got closer to Pappas, she picked up a noticeable body odor. It wasn't the fresh musk of a clean person who's just broken a sweat, rather the smell of a body on which perspiration had been allowed to dry and then gone unwashed for days. The sharp odor had a sort of *aftertaste* as well, burning in her nostrils with a heat like horseradish.

Daisy decided to begin with a litmus test before she began her interview questions, to see if Pappas was reliable enough to interview at all.

"Is this your first time contacting the paper?" she asked, knowing full well he had made several prior attempts.

Pappas contemplated her for a moment and then, with a self-congratulatory smirk that revealed crooked brown teeth, shook his head as if to say, "nice try." He leered at her like a raven taunting a house cat through a window. "No," he scoffed. "It's not the first time. Don't you know that?"

He chuckled to himself like a crime boss who had easily detected a double cross. "Sure, I'm a citizen informant. And I reported a couple tips that got lost in the shuffle. But you can only lead a horse to water, you can't make it drink. And *The Believer* isn't much of a paper these days, is it? But my *video* is different. Because here you are, begging at my door…"

"So, *you're* Daisy Scott…" he continued, feeling he had the upper hand now, and inching closer to ogle at her.

"Not bad… You're cute. I like that jacket," Pappas complimented, eying her up and down with a raised eyebrow. "With the big curly hair, it makes you look like a hot 70s chick, like Pam Grier. You ever heard of her? Big rebel attitude… and an even bigger chest."

STRIKE THREE.

"No, don't think so," Daisy countered, to shut down the discourse. She was lying through her teeth. Any self-respecting fan of horror, b-movies, and cult classics was familiar with the work of Pam Grier and, coming from a fellow film buff, she might have taken the comparison as a memorable compliment. But she knew this pervert was no connoisseur of Blaxploitation films and had made the suggestion for all the wrong reasons.

"And I do take offense!" she continued. "I don't need your opinions about me, just your statement about the fucking video. Alright? It's up to my discretion whether this story runs on *The Believer* at all. Me and only me. And I'll leave right now if you don't learn some manners real fucking quick."

It was no idle threat, and Pappas seemed to realize this, standing down. "Okay, okay," he said, offering his hands up in a "stop" motion.

"I'll be good. I was just *saying*, is all…" he muttered. "Just thinking out loud… It's a shame not every beautiful woman can take a compliment these days. But I understand."

"Let's just get on with this," she said, unzipping her bag to remove her audio recorder.

"Don't worry. I can DIG it," he said, unable to restrain the impulse to throw the 70s slang in as a little taunt, despite their truce.

She shrugged it off and began rolling audio, eager to just finish up and leave.

"Please state and spell your full name for the record please," she instructed, holding out the recorder.

"Huh?" he grumbled, "You haven't been recording this? What the fuck? *Amateur Hour!* And why do I have to tell you my name? Did you forget it? I already fucking told them on the phone–

"It's just a formality, sir, to be sure we spell your–

"Oh, for fuck's sake!" he roared. "Daniel Spiridon Pappas, P-A-P-P-A-S, PAPPAS! Two Ps! They used to be able to spell at *The Brooklyn Believer,* back before it turned into socialist trash…"

Daisy tried to interject, "Every reporter does this sir, it's–

"I know the old *Believer* crew broke some good stories back in the day," he interrupted, "It used to be a big deal. But now it's a gossip rag run by a bunch of dumb college kids."

He began pacing the room as his grievances with the website began to flow out of him, "You know, it's one thing to have typos in an article, but I'm seeing typos in fucking HEADLINES on the website these days. I even stopped reporting them on the site because nobody ever fixes them. Nobody even fucking cares anymore, do they? I bet you… I bet. *Yooouuugh*–

His voice choked up, halting his rant with a gargle, and he started coughing in a wild spasm, eventually lurching across the room for an open beer can to rinse his dry throat.

"Are you from the neighborhood?" Daisy asked, trying to use the opportunity to de-escalate.

"Oh yeah," he retched, "born and raised…" He paused to force two quick, hard coughs into his closed right hand and then took another long swig of stale beer, which seemed to finally restore his voice to its initial, less alarming level of raspiness.

"…born and raised here in the neighborhood," he proceeded. "Believe me, I've got some stories. When I was seventeen, I was in a fender bender. The first cop that shows up, he tries to blame it on me! It turns into a whole fucking fiasco. Finally, the other cop shows up. Thankfully, he knows my old man. He says to the other guy, "You dumb fuck! This is Prokopios Pappas' boy!""

Daisy tried to follow along with his story but wasn't sure where he was going.

Pappas realized he was losing her and clarified, "See, he knew it couldn't have been my fault! Because he knew I learned to drive from the same person that taught my older brother Markos to drive, and that taught my Momma to drive–my old man, who had, quite possibly, the most expert understanding of defensive driving in the history of this city. He ran a carwash in Queens for forty years, for fuck's sake! I remember later that night, when my pop finally saw the damage to the car, the first thing he said was, "Now I KNOW this wasn't YOU!""

Daisy became worried that Pappas would be hard to keep on track and decided to skip a couple of her prepared questions to avoid rambling responses that might keep her there longer than absolutely necessary. She was starting to acclimate to the bad smells in the room after being in there for a few minutes, which disturbed her even more than the odors themselves.

"You said you're married, correct? Did your wife see the thing on the roof? Did anyone else?"

"Fuck no. She doesn't see nothin'," he scorned. "My wife's been on bedrest for years. Sponge baths and all that shit. She only rolls out of bed when I change her sheets. I don't even wash 'em anymore. If I go to the trouble and put down fresh clean sheets, she just *immediately* covers them in piss again, so why bother? I just throw them in the dryer at the laundry for 20 minutes and then call it a day. "Here are your sheets!" I mean, why bother? Just fuck it!"

Daisy gagged at the mental image, imagining the unfortunate person at the coin laundry who was next in line for that dryer. She moved onto the next question.

"Would you say you have an interest in conspiracy theories?" Daisy wanted to poke him a little bit, hopefully not enough to unleash a torrent, but enough to get a couple embarrassing quotes for the article she could actually use.

"Define *conspiracy theory*," he retorted in a pompous-sounding mimicry of some right-wing podcaster he'd probably heard, "Sweetie, you don't realize this because *The Believer* is part of the mainstream media now, and you've never known anything different, but most of the news is bullshit. You're just a pawn in someone's game."

"Is that so?" she probed.

"The news media has been co-opted by the deep state since the Clinton era, at least," he said. He wasn't interested in having a conversation, just administering a lecture to a captive audience.

"And they had a pretty good run for a while. Shit, in my old man's day, they almost ran him out of town for speaking the truth. But social media changed everything. It gave the little man a voice for once, and people are waking up. That's why your industry is dead. Some of us figured out the game. People used to say you were crazy if you thought the moon landing was fake or vaccines were dangerous. Now you sound crazy if you believe the opposite. You can't bury the truth on the internet. It's a new world out there. One where *you're* the dinosaur. How's that feel?"

"If I'm obsolete then why did you contact us, and why am I the one here trying to share your story?"

"Well, I guess this one's so good even you guys managed to figure it out. Congratulations. We've got Woodward and Bernstein here."

"It's a slow news day," she countered. "Can you show me where you recorded the video?"

"Hmph. Sure, okay. It's not like it's up there right now or anything. I don't see the point," he grumbled, leading her into the small kitchen. Pappas started struggling with the ratty old blinds over the window trying to pull them up. "It was over here, across the street."

She was thankful to see Pappas open the window after lifting up the blinds, which she hoped would introduce much-needed fresh air. There wasn't much to note in the kitchen; it was overfilled and filthy just like the living room. There was a horde of food stashed in every available crevice, mostly 2-liters of Diet Coke and dollar store junk food brands. She noticed a few dead cockroaches among the other debris on the floor.

"The second I saw it, I knew I had something special," he explained as Daisy joined him by the kitchen window. A pair of binoculars were resting on a chair by the window.

"Doing a little sight-seeing?" she questioned, pointing to the lenses.

"Ha!" he scoffed. "Bird-watching."

Daisy peered out the window. She didn't even see any pigeons. The only birds this guy had seen lately were fried chickens. She studied the building across the street for a moment, including the rooftop. It was already getting dark outside and she couldn't see much with her naked eyes. She leaned her head out the window and gulped in a deep breath of clean air before pulling her head back into the smelly kitchen.

"I've got a great title for your article," Pappas said proudly, *Neighborhood Hero Discovers Species.* No, wait. That wasn't it. Shit. *Neighborhood Hero Discovers SINISTER THREAT.* That was it. Nice, right?"

"You think this is a new species?" Daisy asked, genuinely curious what fantasy explanation he had settled on.

"Well, actually. No," he corrected. "I think it's an *old* species. Hang on."

He retreated back to the living room to dig through a pile of papers and junk on his desk to produce a computer printout of a science article from the internet noting the discovery of a fossilized giant vampire bat from the Pleistocene epoch in the Americas. It looked like his printer had been low on ink and most of the small text was stretched into blurred lines and illegible.

"I've been doing some research," Pappas explained. "And I think one of these ancient beasts has survived into the modern day. It's somehow gone undetected all this time… that is, until I came along."

As a lifelong vampire fanatic, Daisy knew enough about bats that she didn't need the fine print of Pappas' article to doubt his interpretation. Vampire bats, even huge extinct ones, are tiny in comparison to harmless fruit-eating bats still alive today. It's possible that a *flying fox* could be large enough to produce the wingspan seen in the video. But aren't stationary bats always hanging upside down instead of standing upright like in the phone footage? And why would a giant fruit bat even be in New York City? She wondered if the Bronx Zoo had flying foxes.

"People probably disturbed its habitat somewhere," Pappas continued, "installing pointless wind turbines or solar panels. And so it came here. Imagine it! A prehistoric terror, loose in the city, feeding on the blood of innocents. It's like I discovered a living dinosaur or something."

Daisy still believed the same hypothesis as when she'd walked through the front door–that the giant bat was simply an elaborate Halloween prank captured in low enough quality video to make the methodology undetectable.

Pappas asked Daisy several questions about when he could expect the article to go live on the website and how she would refer to him. He suggested some specific verbiage to highlight the dramatic nature of his encounter and then began explaining his intentions to monetize his video once it had enough views, thanks to *The Believer's* upcoming article.

Daisy only half-listened to him and slowly worked her way back toward the front door as he rambled. Her mind was busy with an internal argument, trying to decide if she should bother inspecting the rooftop across the street.

This information wasn't actually necessary for the article. Jerry only cared about clicks. And this particular mystery was probably more compelling if left unsolved. But at this point, Daisy's curiosity about the matter had overflowed its container and she knew she wouldn't feel content calling it a night until she took a quick look for clues at the actual scene of the crime. Perhaps it would be a waste of time, but she was already there, wasn't she? This was always the question for a perfectionist working on nonsense: where should she draw the line, for her own sanity?

There's no cheat sheet for gathering information about a past event and, unfortunately, there's never a guarantee that all the evidence you need still exists. In the end, no matter the talent or training, reporters, detectives, investigators, and archaeologists all rely on the same essential commodity, which is both fickle and dangerously opaque. It's a muse which can open any door, or bite the hand that feeds–CHANCE.

Or, put another way, Daisy was counting on some dumb luck.

* * *

Once the reporter was gone, Pappas took a seat on his couch to finish off his beer and contemplate his coming fortunes. *The Brooklyn Believer* was small change. But he had to start somewhere. They'd run his article over the weekend, and by Monday national news outlets would want in on the action and he would go viral.

There was big money in a video like this, and the associated merchandising, but Pappas had even bigger plans. He'd suffered a lot in recent years, after his "awakening." He had discovered information networks online, capable of unraveling the web of lies constructed by liberal elites and the deep state, and he considered himself privileged to have joined in that work.

But standing up for truth and liberty, and casting a finger at the true villains, had cost Pappas dearly. His own family had abandoned him over petty politics, calling him an extremist for simply telling it like it is. The family his father had built! Gone now. Dissolved.

All because those idiots wouldn't listen to the truth. He'd tried to share the fruit of knowledge, but they'd been too timid and pre-programmed to taste of its blessings. They had been cowards, Pappas felt.

But that was all in the past. God was just clearing a path for Pappas and removing negative energy. Maybe his family didn't listen, but others would. He'd have a chance to set things straight for millions of people. Heads would roll and the puppet masters would be revealed. He might start a revolution.

Pappas felt an electrifying thrill, and not just because his story was getting out there—HE was getting out there—with fame and fortune to follow. There was also a lingering excitement from the presence of the young, female reporter in his home. She'd been much more attractive than he'd anticipated.

There'd been something alluring about her standoffishness with him, and now he couldn't get her out of his mind. Her parents had picked a terrible name with "Daisy," he figured. She's not soft and delicate like a flower, but bold and unwavering like a strong cup of coffee.

Mochaccino.

That's the kind of woman she was, and that's what he'd call her. Mochaccino.

It'd been a long time since he'd been alone with a woman like that. He felt flush with libido from the contact and wanted more. He rose from the couch and stood in front of the mirror to scrutinize his physique.

He'd been quite a stud back in high school, hadn't he?

He closed his fist in a tight grip and mimed a few biceps curls. It's true, what his wife had been telling him, he realized. He'd let himself go a bit the last several years. He pinched and pulled at the rolls of fat around his stomach with his hands. The blubber on his sides felt soft and pliable like dough in his fingers. It didn't feel manly having love handles.

But when he poked at his front beer belly, which jutted out proudly in a solid mound, he sensed strength and muscle underneath the outer layer of cushioning.

Yes, there's still a fighter inside of this old dog, Pappas hoped.

He resolved to cut back on the beer and pastrami, to resume his old habit of banging out a few pushups in the morning, and that—by hook or by crook—he would get back down to his fighting weight of 250lbs. He was about to spend a lot of time on television, after all. It came with the territory, and he needed to look the part.

It won't be that hard, he reassured himself. And besides, what was it his old man always used to say?

"THE BODY IS A TEMPLE."

Yes, his temple needed some repairs, but it would be worth the trouble. Mochaccino might have a lot to learn, but she had reawakened something in him. An animal craving, a lust to exert action on the greater world outside his little dwelling, began to reassert itself.

"Why just watch?" Pappas asked greedily, sizzling in the titillating juices of his upcoming machinations, "when the world is out there for the taking?"

He grabbed a fresh beer from the fridge and took a seat in his chair by the window to crack it open. Hey, the moment called for at least a small celebration, so he could allow himself this one final indulgence. It was just to sip on, as he made his plans for the future.

Mochaccino...

Yes, he would get himself into shape, he schemed, and much more. He was navigating a world run by evil forces, openly hostile to truth-tellers like him. What's more, he was surrounded by sleeping, oblivious *normies,* like his family and the reporter. They too played a role in the grand scheme, as patsies, bag-holders, and collateral. He would try to save them, sure, but would they listen?

Pappas stared out the window, wondering what he had actually discovered on that rooftop. Would it return? Are there more of them somewhere? The creature could be dangerous. Was he safe? And who might try to stop him from informing the world about it? What role would the government eventually play in all this?

The road ahead would be treacherous.

THE BODY IS A TEMPLE… BUT WHAT OF THE HEART? THE SOUL?

He would not simply rebuild his body.

For the fight ahead, he must become glorious.

Pappas would don the Armor of God.

CHAPTER 7

The Impluvium

* * *

"Luxury" apartment buildings in NYC tend to have pretentious names and the one across the street from Pappas was no exception. Daisy stood outside "The Impluvium: Astoria," vaguely remembering the word *impluvium* from somewhere in college. Unable to recall the missing trivia, she resorted to Wikipedia to jog her memory. The term referred to a style of ancient Roman atrium, in which an open ceiling allowed rainwater to pool in an indoor fountain. This seemed like an inauspicious and ill-advised name for a residential building in a city frequently suffering from hurricanes, floods, and large-scale water damage, but it must have sounded fancy to an investor somewhere.

Daisy needed to get to the roof of the building. She entered the lobby and walked confidently past the doorman, a young guy watching a movie on his phone who looked stoned out of his mind. To the right, she found the elevators. She hit the 'R' button for the roof level and then studied her tired reflection in the mirrored glass wall as she made her ascent. The overhead lighting in the elevator was awful, casting deep shadows under her eyes and it made her look a hundred years old.

The elevator opened to a small hallway with double doors at the end leading to the roof deck. The doors were shut, which gave Daisy a moment of concern as she approached, worried they could be locked or that the outdoor area was already closed off for the coming winter. Thankfully, the door opened without hesitation. She stepped outside and tested the door to make sure it opened both ways and she wouldn't be locked outside on the roof.

Daisy wasn't incredibly high up, but the air was much cooler on the roof than it had been on the street. She pulled her jacket tighter. A stone path stretched to her right, toward the tenant roof deck area, which took up about half the square footage of the roof level and provided multiple seating areas for residents along with a few tables. Daisy had seen much larger and fancier roof decks, but this one was notable at least for the lush greenery filling every crevice, including full sized trees, bushes, and ferns. Otherwise, there wasn't much to see on that side.

To her left, a long brick planter filled with small trees formed a barrier, with a small, closed gate and a "restricted access" sign at the other end of the stone path. A low mechanical hum built in intensity as Daisy neared the gate and peered over to inspect the rest of the roof. She saw only the usual–HVAC and electrical equipment and exposed ventilation shafts, but there was a set of metal stairs leading up to the higher level, which was exactly what she needed.

She gazed around the area for cameras, noticing a couple near the tenant area, but it was too dark to perform a rigorous search and ultimately knew she'd have to take the risk that her unauthorized activities would be brief enough that no one would notice. When was the last time she had to worry about security cameras? She hadn't pushed herself this hard in a couple years.

Back in the saddle again, huh?

Daisy hopped the small fence, landing more gracefully than she'd expected on the other side with a satisfying swish of her jacket that made her wish someone had been with her to witness it. She began ascending the side of the sub-building, noting that the narrow metal stairs barely had a guardrail on the side. These stairs were built for climbing, and nothing else. Every plank and screw had been selected on the basis of keeping costs as low as possible while meeting only the basic legal requirements.

About halfway up the rickety stairs, she noticed she was already about eight feet in the air and for a moment felt like a kid getting on a haphazardly-assembled ride at the county fair, putting her life in the hands of a troupe of scruffy nomads evading arrest warrants who she hoped had dutifully tightened every screw necessary to prevent a tragedy.

Daisy continued to the top of the stairs and reached a small overhang with a proper railing. She looked down at the field of humming boxes and guessed she was about fifteen feet above the main roof level. Before her, the path divided into two narrow railed ledges. One side had a door into the roof equipment building and the other side had a red metal ladder attached to the wall leading up to the highest level, where she needed to go.

Daisy started bravely up the rungs at first but then paused after placing her fourth step. She could feel the force of the wind blowing against her, like it was ever slightly trying to pluck her off the cold metal bars she was clinging to.

This would sure be a stupid place to fall and injure myself, she warned herself, and continued carefully to the top.

A pang of disappointment hit Daisy the moment her eyes peaked over the horizon; it looked totally empty. She hoisted herself up the final rungs and emerged to a small square level of finished concrete with a red railing stretching around. A small air shaft popping up through the ground in the middle was the only feature at all.

The rattling of the machinery was quieter at the top and Daisy realized she was thankful for the lapse in the noise to gather her thoughts. She tried inspecting the concrete for clues but there wasn't any lighting up there and it was too dark.

An inspiration hit Daisy—she used to carry a small, high-powered tactical flashlight in her bag at all times. Her father had gifted it as a Christmas present, for use on the job and for general safety in the city.

She opened her bag and began searching with false hopes, already halfway remembering she'd stuffed the device in a drawer trying to eliminate deadweight from her daily bag. After confirming she'd left the flashlight at home, and that her bag needed a deep cleaning later, Daisy proceeded to a backup plan. She improvised and shined the flash of her phone camera to cast a weak beam she could use to inspect the ground for clues.

After a walk around the perimeter, she concentrated on the side of the roof facing Pappas' building. She stood in front of the railing, right on the spot where the bat had been, but didn't see any evidence left behind. One detail seemed important—there were no electrical outlets up there. If the bat figure had been mechanical, the perpetrators would have had to run extension cords down to the lower roof level or one of the apartments for power. However, all of the units had small outdoor balconies attached, so it wouldn't necessarily be a prohibitive amount of work to climb up there and then throw a long extension cord down to a friend on a balcony.

But getting the device up there? After experiencing what the ladder at the final stretch was like, it seemed very unlikely anyone had carried anything large or heavy with them to the top level. That indicated to Daisy that the stunt had likely been a person in a costume after all. As a horror buff, Daisy could recount several films off the top of her head that featured incredible looking human-sized bat wings, practical costume effects that looked realistic even to close detail and in bright light. If filmmakers could manage that decades ago, then a person who was good with their hands these days, with access to modern materials, internet marketplaces, and 3D printing, could easily construct something that would hold up to light scrutiny, at least on a dark, blurry phone video.

Daisy looked across the street and searched for Pappas' window. She was thankful to see the blinds had been closed again. She was a little creeped out about the idea he could be over there right then, peering at women in the building or even watching her on the roof.

Daisy crouched to get her phone light close enough to the pavement to make a difference and waved it over the ground like a magic wand back and forth looking for clues left behind. She wished she could inspect the site during the day under full sun but knew she couldn't delay the story, and it would be harder to get up there unnoticed during business hours.

Daisy scooted over a couple feet on her knees and began waving her light over a new area and immediately detected a clue which made the climb up there feel justified. The cone of light from her phone came across a stain on the concrete, large and dark. She rubbed it with her finger. It was perfectly dry. Old. It reminded Daisy of parking spots with oil stains, accumulated from leaking cars over time. You couldn't wash off those stains. They'd become ingrained in the asphalt, like tattoos. Why would there be a stain like that, the result of repetitive exposure, on the very top of this roof where no one ever came?

A plane flew overhead toward its landing at LaGuardia. A thick fog was starting to set in so the plane dissolved into the distance and faded away into the clouds as it descended. Daisy rose to her feet and shut the phone light off as she walked to the railing facing the Manhattan skyline.

Her perch atop The Impluvium: Astoria wasn't particularly high by NYC standards, but the view was unobstructed and near the waterfront, meaning there was nothing before her but the rolling dark velvet of the East River and the glittering Manhattan skyline, looming in the distance.

People imagine the NYC skyline as a shining ember lighting up the sky, illuminating the darkness with its neon, electric glow. But the NYC skyline didn't look like that to Daisy. Instead, the mostly-unlit buildings were like pillars of black obsidian glass, draped in a few Christmas lights, stretching up through the haze of the sky—which is what actually glows, from the spillage of millions of lights underneath. It looked beautiful to her, not the world's largest or most resplendent skyline, but one that seemed to somehow reflect the nature of the city.

Daisy watched as countless red aircraft safety lights on top of the distant buildings blinked on and off, each with its own pace and pattern, like red fireflies communicating in the night. Her mind began to wander as she took in the lovely sight and she felt a warm pang in her chest as memories of her time with her band, The Pathfinders, came spilling over the defensive wall. It was usually nighttime when these introspective feelings hit Daisy. And it was always when she was alone, able to disappear into her head without distractions.

Was she still even the same person who had played drums in that band? That was the question that scared her. People think of themselves as having fixed, preset personalities, holding true throughout their lives and resistant to change.

But aren't we more like that doorman downstairs? We show up for our shift and there's a changing of the guard. Then we're forced to extinguish all the fires set by the previous person. We clean up their old messes, unable to reconcile that the idiot on the earlier shift was ourselves. Eventually, *this* Daisy Scott would pass the torch to another. But she wasn't living for her future self, was she? Treading water at a dead-end job? She was living the dream of a prior Daisy that no longer existed.

The skyline began to feel threatening instead of inspiring. Those high-rises represented success, the dream everyone is chasing, and there she was flaming out in Queens, as far as she'd ever felt from success.

Daisy retraced her steps back down the ladder and paused at the lower level before continuing back down the staircase. The equipment room on the other ledge was probably locked, and she'd have to slide past a bunch of obstacles on the narrow railing to reach it, but it would be negligent not to check it since she was already up there. The path was tight, and she stepped over a minefield of tool cases and piles of gear while holding onto the railing. At the halfway point, a huge exhaust fan blew hot air in her face, and she had to turn to her side to squeeze past a large duct jutting out of the building. Finally, she reached the end of the ledge and was surprised to find the door unlocked.

It was pitch black inside, so she lit her phone flash again before proceeding through the door. An awful smell was the first thing she noticed. The only thing worse than an ordinary bad smell was an unconventional one and the equipment room reeked with a specificity that had no precedent for Daisy. The closest comparison she could retrieve was the smell of her Grandpa's fishing tackle box when she was a child and went fishing with him on vacations to Georgia. She had never liked fishing, but had loved waking up at the crack of dawn to go out on the river with him in his little old motorboat. It was so pretty and peaceful on the water and the scenery around them had been so quiet and still it had seemed unworldly.

She remembered her Grandpa had an old, rusted metal tackle box for his fishing lures and bait which had always given her a gross laugh due to its disgusting smell, which seemed unique in all of creation. It had smelled both dry and wet at the same time—arid mustiness wrapped in something fresh and biting. The odor was similar to that of fish or the ocean, but somehow a derivative of the source, like the musk that trails behind the coat of a chain-smoker which is not the same smell as a fresh cigarette or an ashtray, but something new, formed only over long periods of exposure.

If her phone flash had been inadequate upstairs, it was now completely useless in the equipment room. The falloff of the light was so abrupt that the device could only assist in revealing what was already right in front of her. She waved the light around to confirm the room seemed to hold elevator equipment. There was a row of breaker boxes to her right and the floor space to the left was crowded with tall metal cabinets and large machines which looked like motors. She was careful not to touch anything as she took some tentative steps deeper into the room. The smell seemed to intensify with each step and her light became less effective the farther she got from the relative brightness of the open door.

This is actually scary, she thought to herself, pulling her shirt over her nose to block the smell and questioning why she had come in there. She had only walked a few steps into the room, but the doorway seemed menacingly distant now. She couldn't tell how much farther the room stretched or where the smell could be coming from.

There might be chemicals stored in here. Or there's probably a leak or mildew problem, she figured. She began to push ahead to the end of the room but stopped herself.

What are you doing, Daisy? You've already got your bonus points on this one.

She'd only be punishing herself by pushing ahead through the stinky room in the dark. It wouldn't solve the mystery or make the story better, only delay her return to the office to write the article and go home for the weekend.

With that settled, she retraced her steps back to the door of the shed, and then down to the lobby, where she stopped to ask the stoned doorman if he was aware of any costumed people or Halloween displays occurring on the building's roof.

"Not that I know of but it's my third week," he replied, unhelpfully.

"What about in the lobby," she tried to clarify, "have you seen anyone in a costume like a giant bat?"

"Like Batman?"

"Yeah, I guess, whatever. Anything that looked like a bat, with big wings."

"I'm not sure," he replied, scratching his goatee. "It's possible that I did."

"It's possible?!" she demanded, "you don't remember if you saw somebody walk through here dressed like a damn bat?"

At this, he finally set down his phone to break away from his movie. "Lady," his glazed tired eyes met hers for an appeal, "It's Halloween."

It was after 11 PM by the time Daisy completed her article and submitted it into their system, and she was the only person left in the building except for the cleaning crew which came after hours. The distant sound of vacuum cleaners had gotten closer and closer until they finally arrived at *The Believer*'s floor and Daisy had made her final revisions under the howling roar of a vacuum inside the office. The noise abruptly stopped, and Daisy noticed the woman packing up the vacuum to move onto her next room.

Of course, it's quiet now that I'm done and heading home. It felt like a mean-spirited twist on top of a bad day, like the noise had only existed to bother her.

Either Jerry or Tiffani would have to approve her story in the queue before it would go live on the site, but she didn't intend to wait. Knowing Tiffani was a workaholic and stayed logged in 24/7 while at home, Daisy assumed the story would be up by the time she got home.

At this point in her tenure at the paper, it was rare for any alterations to be requested before publishing a story like this. Daisy didn't make typos and knew how to construct an article correctly. When changes were suggested, it was usually on more prominent features. Tanner's articles got much more scrutiny for two reasons. He was a lesser writer, living life in the fast lane with no time for proofreading, and he also worked on high profile puff pieces involving city officials and institutions. Even if *The Believer* still maintained a little street cred as a "counterculture outlet," it had only lasted so long due to a certain maintenance of local politics that was careful not to make the wrong people look foolish with their reporting.

For coverage of ordinary New Yorkers, like Danny Pappas, the paper towed a deliberate line between taking claims seriously or lightly mocking the individuals reporting them. Steady readers of *The Brooklyn Believer* seemed to enjoy both flavors in equal measure, willing to ridicule one person for their fantasy account of an alien abduction, only to lose sleep that night over the following article about a haunted brownstone in Brooklyn.

The giant bat story seemed to fall in between. With the edited version of the video embedded in the body of the story, Daisy explained that the phenomenon was an unsolved rooftop mystery and offered some of Pappas' select comments and theories to give it a little spice. She restrained herself from orchestrating a bloodbath. After the way he'd treated her, she had been tempted to frame the guy as an unhinged wacko pervert, but that would only have resulted in the article getting kicked back by Tiffani and she could find other ways to vent later without causing herself to pull an all-nighter.

"*DIYOS KO!!*" a woman's voice cried out from behind Daisy, startling her.

She turned to see the cleaning lady, an older asian woman, making the sign of the cross as she continued, "*Panginoon, ilayo nyo po kami sa mga kampon ng kadiliman!!!*"

Daisy couldn't place the language. The woman was staring at her computer, transfixed by the frozen image of the rooftop bat from her article. She looked petrified.

"I'm sorry?" she asked the woman, "Are you okay?"

The cleaning lady let go of the vacuum and moved a little closer, not taking her eyes off the screen, but then stopped, as if she didn't want to get *too* close. "What is this?" she asked, with an accent unfamiliar to Daisy's ear.

"This?" Daisy questioned, pointing at her screen. "The bat? It's an internet story. That's what we do here. It's like a joke."

"No!" the woman corrected, looking away from the image and meeting Daisy's eyes. The woman looked truly spooked, like she'd seen a ghost.

If she thinks THIS is scary… Daisy thought to herself, *imagine if she saw a good one.* The woman might faint from watching even a middling horror film.

"It's just a bat costume, Ma'am," she tried again to explain.

"No!" the woman challenged more firmly. "That's not a bat. It's a *MANANANGGAL.*"

"What?"

"Manananggal. It's from my country, the Philippines. Very evil. There were stories about them in my village."

"This?" Daisy tried to clarify, pointing again to her screen.

"Yes!" the woman agreed, now refusing to look at the screen again. "Please," she begged. "Tell me, where was this?"

"The video?"

The woman nodded in agreement, pleading to Daisy with her eyes like the information greatly mattered to her somehow.

"It was here. In Queens."

A mask of fear overcame the woman's face as she signed the cross a final time and rolled her vacuum out the doors into the hall without saying another word.

That was interesting, Daisy thought to herself. Typing "*manangal*" into an internet search before it left her mind.

"Did you mean *manan**anggal**?*" the results suggested.

Daisy clicked on the correction and was presented with a large sketch of a winged monster and a list of search results, including a couple YouTube videos at the top. The manananggal was a mythological creature from the Philippines that looked like a woman who'd been cut in half with giant bat wings. Daisy compared the image in the search result to the still frame in her article and realized she had missed something important.

Holy shit.

The cleaning lady had been right. That's why the form on the roof didn't have ears on top like a Batman costume; it wasn't a bat. She realized the incident had likely been a prank or stunt by Filipinos in the area and the clueless peeper across the street had gotten a glimpse of something he didn't understand and had led her on a wild goose chase. The horror fan in Daisy chastised herself for not previously knowing about the manananggal, which seemed like a cool monster that she wanted to read up on, but was it worth pulling her article for a revision?

It didn't change the nature of the story, which was about Pappas and his video. She still had no idea who the perpetrators were or why they had gone to the trouble. It was a stray detail, important perhaps if she was trying to actually solve the mystery, but just a distraction at this point. Only a handful of their readers from the Philippines might even notice the omission.

Daisy shut down her computer and packed up her bag. The last person out the door at night was tasked with closing down the office, so she hit two switches by the door, plunging the office space into pitch blackness, save for a red emergency sign in the back of the room and the soft shine of city lights from the wall of windows.

I missed a trick, Daisy chastised herself about the Filipino connection to the video. Had she missed some clue along the way that might have led to that discovery sooner? If she was going to write an article about the murders to save her career, she'd have to be more careful, and cunning, than that from now on.

CHAPTER 8

Kylie Rhinelander

* * *

Kylie Rhinelander sat by herself on her couch, scrolling through old Facebook photos she had posted back in high school. Sometimes she found herself daydreaming about her old hometown in Iowa. She'd been in such a hurry to leave that crummy little place and get to the big city, but had it actually been that bad? Looking back, it seemed less certain now.

She would never want to move back there. Her husband Brett would never go for it, and she knew the kids would find it depressing compared to what they were accustomed to in NYC. Still, she imagined the challenges of parenthood might be lessened with her whole extended family around to help contribute.

Things were about to change, she worried. It was hard enough with Brett's three kids, especially considering the youngest had disabilities, but adding a fourth? She had barely gotten used to the idea of being a mother, and was still struggling to grow comfortable with Brett's children, when she'd found out she was expecting a child of her own.

They'd moved into a huge luxury high-rise on the Long Island City waterfront with extra bedrooms for when they had custody of the kids– Brett Junior, who had cerebral palsy, and the twins, Loftin and Wilder. Compared to her previous apartment, a shared loft in Brooklyn, the expensive tower home seemed like the culmination of a rags to riches story. She had an apartment up in the clouds in New York City, with the crushingly expensive panorama of Manhattan's skyline filling her view from floor to ceiling. It was like paradise, everything she'd wanted from New York and more.

She had only been twenty-two when she'd met Brett. She had considered herself a city girl already by then, pursuing her dream of becoming a model. She'd finally booked a high-paying job, a photo shoot for a local plastic surgeon named Dr. Rhinelander. It turned out she had been hand selected from a pile of headshots by the doctor himself, to represent the platonic ideal of beauty.

When she'd shown up for the gig and met Dr. Rhinelander, it had been love at first sight. He had a full head of dark hair, a strong jaw, and deep, mesmerizing gray eyes. He had been significantly older, late thirties, and she would later learn in the middle of a bitter divorce. He was also a father of three sons, which she didn't discover until after they'd been dating for a month. She never saw the kids much back then since the mom usually had custody in the early days.

After they'd moved in together, and the kids became a regular part of their lives, Brett had started working later hours and would frequently come home drunk. They'd also been having arguments.

Brett had provided her with an amazing life, but it felt like she'd been saddled with all the responsibility of taking care of his children, and now there was a baby on the way? She wasn't even twenty-five yet. Was she ready for all of this?

"Christ what's that smell?!" Brett called from the entryway, followed by the clank of keys and the slam of the front door. Kylie had been so lost in memories and worries she hadn't heard the front door open.

"The whole fucking hallway reeks of cabbage or some shit," he continued, taking off his coat. "It's those damn Eastern Europeans– Russian? Ukrainian? Romanian? I don't fucking know. At the end of the hall. I told you, it's like every day now they're cooking cabbage. I'd rather smell fish in a fucking microwave. How can they eat that shit? It's disgusting. And it's all they eat. Have you seen the menus at those places? Beets and potatoes and cabbage, fucking boiled roots. Zero spices. But they stink up the entire fucking building because they're raised to love that crap."

"Oh please," she replied. "My day was fine, by the way. And the smell's not even noticeable except in the hallway. You're just a complainer. You were complaining about the food in London, too."

"That's different," he countered. "You're pregnant, and they should have had some decent options by the hotel, so we didn't have to take a car. That's all I was saying."

"You said the Brits pretended like they invented curry because they didn't have any good dishes of their own," she remembered. "And you also complained about *them* not using spices."

"Okay fine," he agreed, "but you're just proving my point. British food sucks so they're smart enough to eat Indian food instead. Why are the people down the hall still boiling cabbage every night? That's my question, Kylie. It's New York City. They could eat anything they fucking want."

"I'd ask you about your day, but I guess I have my answer already based on your mood. Why are you so late? I thought you were doing consults today."

"Yeah… I was. Yeah," he said slowly, walking into the bedroom to change out of his work clothes while continuing his explanation, "But I met a couple of the guys for a drink on the way back. Sorry, it was meant to be a quick thing, so I didn't text. Mark's having woman troubles and needed some advice."

"Again?" she called out, trying to be just loud enough that he could hear her in the bedroom without waking the kids.

"Yeah," he replied, returning to the living room in his boxer shorts before slipping on a pair of sweatpants as he continued, "It's that chick–Monica? or whatever–I mentioned it before. He doesn't know what's going on with her and he needed to bash it out with the guys. It was no big deal. Time just got away from us. Hey, why the interrogation? Am I on a schedule here? It's Friday night? What's the big deal?"

"Nothing. No, it's just…" Kylie tried to choose her words carefully. Brett was drunk and in a bad mood, but he was home so rarely these days she needed to seize the opportunity to discuss some things.

"My projected due date was two days ago," she said with the least accusatory tone she could manage. "You know, it just seems like if you're not at work, you'd want to be here so we can be ready when my water breaks."

"I will be!" he roared. "Where am I right now? I'm here right now, aren't I? Jesus!"

He retreated to the kitchen to grab a glass and a bottle of Johnnie Walker Blue from the wet bar, while shaking his head silently in disagreement as if she was still speaking.

"I wish you'd come straight from work is all I meant," she said.

He poured a double Scotch before proceeding.

"You're complaining about me not being here to my face," he continued, ignoring her last remark, "as if I'm not standing in my own fucking kitchen right now."

He took a quick gulp of his whiskey, followed by a grimace and a hiss. He was hours past the sipping portion of his night. He only took big gulps like that once he was already trashed.

"Besides," he continued, softening his voice, seeming to recognize his temper had been building, and raising his eyebrows to soften his delivery, "I've told you a million times. You're an insider here. The second that baby announces he's ready to come out and get started, I'm gonna activate a network of the best guys I know to swoop in and provide us with the most flawless delivery this borough has ever seen. You're in Dr.

Rhinelander's hands." He finished with a broad grin and then raised his glass to his lips, this time taking a restrained sip.

"Was Hannah there tonight?" she asked.

"Jesus Christ!!" he screamed. "What is your fucking obsession with her?!"

"Honey, please," she hushed. "Don't wake the kids."

"I don't–" he shook his head as if he couldn't process it. "No. I don't care. They won't wake up. This is important. You gotta get her out of your head because there is nothing going on between us and I am not going to fire her. You're just imagining shit. I'm a cosmetic surgeon. I can't have somebody UGLY answering the phones. Can I?! And she's not even really my type. You know that."

He realized he'd left off a crucial part of his argument. "And I'm married, for Christ's sake," he finished as an afterthought.

"So, if I sat on another man's lap that would be no big deal?" Kylie questioned, no longer caring if he got angry.

"I told you, we were just horsing around! The whole office was!! I was sitting on Martin's lap just a second before you walked in. Am I having an affair with Dr. Haan as well? You just walked in at the exact wrong time. Jesus almighty!"

He took another large gulp of his Scotch. "You have to learn to trust me. We can't argue about this every fucking night. Not with the baby on the way."

"You're right," she agreed, concluding she'd make no further progress with him that night but would continue the discussion later when he was sober. She turned away from him and focused on the skyline through the windows.

It's lovely tonight, she thought, admiring how the arrival of a deep fog had transformed the familiar landscape into something both alien and beautiful. She'd only just learned from Brett that fog and clouds were actually the same thing. But it made sense. The clouds outside an airplane window looked just like the fog outside their apartment.

Who was to say where the fog ended and the clouds began? She wondered.

Kylie rose from the couch and walked silently to the windows to get a better look at the Big Apple, blinking through the distant haze outside the windows of her large living room.

A strong hand reached from behind her to softly cradle her swollen belly.

"We're almost there," Brett reassured her, tenderly, from behind. The delayed scent of liquor and bad breath hit her nostrils a couple seconds later, as he delivered a sloppy kiss to her neck, needle pricks on her skin from the stubble on his face.

"Did you think about my suggestion?" she asked, hoping the topic of baby names would be less controversial for him. Her due date was already here, and they hadn't picked a name for their son yet. Brett had been brushing her off anytime she tried to discuss it.

"I told you the name," Brett responded, chuckling to himself. "Coconut." He rubbed her stomach with his hand to demonstrate the resemblance. "It's perfect."

"I'm serious, Brett."

"Yeah, okay," he said. "Coconut is a girl's name anyway. We'll save it for our daughter."

Kylie didn't find his jokes funny anymore. He never took these things seriously. All of her friends and family thought they'd picked a name already and she just wouldn't tell them for some reason. What would they put on the birth certificate? She worried Brett had decided on a name she wouldn't like and hadn't told her because he intended to make it one of his "executive decisions" and surprise her once it was already set in stone.

"What about my suggestion?" she offered hopefully. "Richard?"

Her father, who'd been named Richard, had passed away from an aneurysm shortly after she'd moved to New York. She had continued on with her life, at first coping by partying too much and tearing down barriers in her life. Then, she'd met Brett. He was mature, had seen it all, and had a comforting wisdom she found reassuring. And yet, he was young at heart and energetically dragged her on adventures all over the city and across the world. The whirlwind of excitement provided by Brett, and eventually his kids, had created a welcome distraction from her pain.

Deep down, however, the loss of her father was still very raw for Kylie. She had discovered that the grieving process takes so long because the world was filled with triggers and associations that brought him to mind, and they each had to be individually processed. When a loved one passes, memories aren't reclassified all at once. Instead, each fresh reminder of her dad reignited the mourning with a sharp sting of loss, like an aftershock to a long distant earthquake, because it had to be rebranded in her mind as something lost to the past.

Earlier in the night, she'd been scrolling for a movie to watch and been stopped in her tracks by a listing for an old action movie. She had watched the film with her dad when she was little. Such an innocent little thing, a random movie title, now forever cast in a bittersweet light, another reminder of heartache added to her list.

"It would be a nice tribute, I get it..." Brett began, removing his hand from her stomach and adding some distance between them before finishing off the rest of his glass with a gulp. He followed with a reflexive hissing sound through his teeth as if to demonstrate how much the drink had burned.

"But a name is forever, you know?" he continued, making his way back to the kitchen to refill his glass. "*Richard?* That's a little old fashioned. Isn't it?"

"Not really," she said softly, not looking away from the window.

"And besides. DICK. They're gonna call him 'Dick.' You know kids. Fucking monsters. *Dick Rhinelander? Little Dicky Rhinelander?* No way! What the fuck?! Sorry. It was a good name back then. But no."

"I understand," she said.

"I'm anxious for that baby to get here. We've been rerunning commercials for six months now. Do you realize that? Six months. I know you say you've been hitting the gym, but you'll have to really kick into high gear after you deliver. You know that, right? I'd love to run some

Christmas ads with the whole family, including the new baby, and you'll be in a tight red dress. BAM! Back in action, right?"

When Brett said, "the whole family," he meant them, the twins, and the baby–not Brett Junior. That had been one of the multiple scandals in their short time together. Brett had never been comfortable including the youngest child in their ads. He had claimed it was for Junior's own benefit, and it's true–the video and photo shoots could be long and tedious, and it was hard enough corralling the twins all day. But she knew by now that Brett's real hesitation was due to embarrassment. A disabled child didn't fit the image he wanted to portray to the world about his medical practice, which was fixated on attaining perfection, which was only just slightly out of reach, one procedure away.

Brett had suddenly changed course on the matter, however, at her behest, when Kylie had convinced him to finally include his namesake in a television commercial.

Lean into it! She had advised. They'd produced a series of ads, tying into Cerebral Palsy Awareness Month, featuring the entire family and *finally* revealing Brett Junior to NYC. The results had been unexpectedly disastrous. And several months later, Brett was still working public relations to soothe over the incident.

Firstly, the expected response from the public–goodwill in light of Dr. Rhinelander's perseverance as a father of a son with special needs– was overshadowed by the general shock from the revelation that the well-known plastic surgeon actually had a third, disabled "secret" son he'd kept out of all the previous advertising. This had earned him a spot in the local news cycle.

Secondly, backlash to the ads led to investigations which purported to reveal that none of the proceeds of the campaign had actually benefited anyone with cerebral palsy, other than their own child. Brett had maintained it was a misunderstanding that got re-printed without consent until everyone mistakenly believed it, but the damage had been done. Since then, she'd known better than to make any more suggestions about his business. Her job was to look pretty and smile. And make babies.

Their apartment was like a display case where Brett stored her and the children. They were his little figures to play with when it was convenient, or keep locked away when it wasn't.

"That sounds great," Kylie mumbled, her attention only on the fog outside, which was even thicker now. The entire city out the window was blanketed in clouds like in a dream. Her entire life in NYC was like a dream. If she woke up, would Brett be gone? Would her father be back?

"Honey, is it safe for me to take an Ambien?" she asked sweetly, like a child begging for sweets before dinner. "This late in the pregnancy?"

"I don't give a shit what you take, Kylie," he replied, walking to the bedroom to leave her behind.

"I'm asking if it's *safe*," she clarified, hoping he was sober enough to give her a reliable answer.

"Yeah, sure, why not," he slurred, closing the bedroom door.

Despite their attempts to keep quiet and not wake the children, Brett Junior's familiar wail began to echo from his back bedroom. Always soft at first, his sobbing would quickly build to a manic, inconsolable screeching if she didn't calm him quickly.

I need help with these kids.

Kylie realized the solution to her problems was very simple—a nanny. They certainly had the money. And if Brett wanted her in the gym all day, then he would need to hire some help, she decided, as she hurried toward Brett Junior's room.

All I need is a helping hand.

CHAPTER 9

Manananggal

* * *

Daisy entered her third-floor walk-up apartment carrying Chinese takeout. She'd realized on the walk home that she hadn't eaten since noon and was ravenous. She carefully hung her coat on its hook by the door and retreated immediately to the bedroom to eat at her desk.

She sat down and woke up her laptop, which was connected to an extra-wide external monitor. She opened her sack of takeout to spread the components of her General Tso's combo across the table and cracked open her Diet Coke before opening up YouTube and searching for the Filipino monster she'd learned about from the cleaning lady.

She typed "mananangal" in the search bar.

The top of the page offered the disclaimer, "showing results for *mananan**gg**al.*"

The perfectionist in Daisy couldn't live with the typo staring back at her, so she searched the term again with the correct spelling. The screen refreshed and she reviewed the videos populated down the page. Most seemed to originate from the Philippines.

She clicked on the top search result but, instead of the video, was greeted by an ad featuring Ryan Reynolds trying to sell her something. After five seconds she skipped the remainder of the commercial and the YouTube video began playing.

An older Filipino man began speaking into his phone, vertically, in a soft voice while loud distracting music boomed from somewhere nearby. He was speaking English, but the audio quality was so poor she could barely understand anything he was saying. The man seemed to be outside a nightclub or busy establishment, standing under a streetlight, while crowds of noisy people streamed by.

He lazily sipped on a bottle of beer and occasionally raised his eyebrows to add emphasis to whatever inaudible thing he had just whispered. She checked the video length, seeing that it was eighteen minutes long, and decided to bail, backtracking to select another video from the search page, this one with a colorful hand-drawn thumbnail image depicting a manananggal.

This video was also preempted by an ad, for a disability law firm hotline–Pinchot, Price, & Simon, a trio of middle-aged white guys with transplanted hairlines and bleached white smiles asking if her Social Security disability claim had been denied. They promised to treat her like family.

After five seconds she skipped the rest of the commercial but was presented with a second, unskippable ad. Ryan Reynolds again. This time, he was dressed "smart chic" in a polo shirt and fake, non-prescription glasses, but with the same irreverent "everyman" approach, now pitching a different product. Daisy liked the actor, but now that he was a business mogul and one of the wealthiest men on the planet, it seemed disingenuous and cynical to still play the act of a snarky, self-aware underdog while begging for even more money.

After a few limp gags and a consumer call to action, the commercial mercifully ended and the YouTube video began, with spooky stock music including a theremin and an animated logo for the channel:

MONSTERS & MAGIC ACROSS THE WORLD
WITH CONEY DE LA CRUZ

The host appeared on screen—a petite, excitable Filipina in large round-frame eyeglasses. She was sitting at a desk stacked with books and trinkets, in front of a green screen backdrop image of a giant European library.

Daisy guessed the woman was a couple years younger than herself, maybe twenty-seven or so. She was effortlessly pretty without makeup in an understated, academic wrapper that Daisy figured probably infatuated a certain kind of guy, except she probably never got a date because they were the same guys too afraid to approach her.

As she spoke, a graphic identifier at the bottom of the screen read:

CONEY DE LA CRUZ
Anthropologist, Bookstore Owner, Content Creator, Author, Researcher, & State-Licensed Driving Instructor

"*Ano na*! Welcome back, friends," she began, "I'm your host—Coney de la Cruz!"

She pronounced her name *KONE-EE*, as in Coney Island, with a hard 'O,' which Daisy found unusual.

"And this is the final installment of my special five-part Halloween countdown…"

The video cut to a new full-screen graphic in a hand-drawn style with the title:

"CONEY'S FAVORITE MONSTERS OF ALL TIME!!"

The host returned to the screen and a panel graphic slid on from the side recounting her previous four rankings with an empty spot open for number one. Her list was:

1) ???
2) Kappa
3) Tikbalang
4) Kapre
5) Werewolf

Daisy was disappointed to see vampires weren't on the list, but she could see how they might be a bit pedestrian for an anthropologist well-versed in broader legends. She'd heard of the kappa but didn't recognize a couple of the others.

"Last week we covered the penultimate entry on my ranking, Japan's ancient river monster, the kappa," she said. "Which means it's time for number one! But, before I get to the reveal," she stalled, "don't forget I have several books available for purchase which are *always* linked below.

"If you're in the tri-state area, my bookstore in Queens, CONEY'S OCCULT BOOKS, is a can't-miss attraction. We've been featured in *Atlas Obscura* and are the city's top resource for modern and antiquarian books and resources on the occult, magic, witchcraft, paranormal science, and esoteric traditions from around the world.

"We're also a state-certified driving school, if that's something you need. We are knowledgeable and enthusiastic and will help you in any way–

Daisy plopped down her egg roll, annoyed at the rambling introduction, and skipped ahead about a minute in the video. She overshot the number one monster reveal a little, but decided to just watch from that point on. The side panel graphic now included Coney's top monster: the *MANANANGGAL*.

"...not that it would matter anyway, but yes, I did factor that into the methodology of my ranking," she was now explaining, "and the manananggal is still the clear victor here, so don't even try me."

Coney paused a moment and crinkled her face in preparation, as if she was about to deliver an overly-rehearsed melodramatic performance, but instead of cringy bad acting, Coney began to deliver a relaxed, sing-song narration that balanced a calm and mature, authoritative style of explanation with a frenetic, youthful enthusiasm bubbling under the surface that made the explanation feel fun. She came across to Daisy like a young student teacher who didn't follow the rule book but was unjaded enough to actually be effective.

"Picture this…" she narrated, as crude hand drawn sketches replaced her on screen to present a slideshow. Daisy wondered if Coney had drawn the pictures herself.

"–a beautiful woman by day, but, as the sun sets and darkness takes hold, she transforms into a flying beast that hunts human beings in nighttime raids."

The drawings on screen depicted a metamorphosis into exactly what Pappas had captured on video, a woman with giant bat wings extruding from her back. Daisy found one detail so exotic as to be downright bizarre; the entire lower half of the creature was missing. It looked like a guillotine had sliced the thing in half at the waist and its guts were literally hanging out the bottom of its torso as it flew around.

Daisy laughed as she took a bite of her chicken with some noodles wrapped around it. She thought this monster sounded like more of a danger to itself than others, having a giant open wound and no legs. She almost felt sorry for it. Compared to traditional fare–vampires, werewolves, zombies, ghosts and demons–she liked her chances against something that was actively bleeding out while unable to stand, walk, or squeeze through tight spaces. If you were in the middle of an open field in the Philippines, this monster might seem scary, but it seemed silly in the context of modern or urban life.

"Spooky right?" Coney continued. "That's definitely not your typical midnight snack! Yikes! And it gets even creeper. In today's episode, my dear viewers, you'll learn all about the mother of all *aswang*–the manananggal! You'll hear heart-pounding tales from the barrios of narrow escapes and secret rituals believed to repel the creatures–

"But this thrilling journey through the supernatural don't come free! So hit those like and subscribe buttons! And buckle up, *mga kaibigan*! Stay curious, stay brave, and let's uncover the secrets of the manananggal together!"

Daisy gave the video a like and then squeezed some spicy mustard onto the opening of her egg roll before taking a big bite.

Coney explained that creatures of Philippine lower mythology, A.K.A. cryptids or monsters, are known as "*ASWANG*." The Manananggal is like a sub-species of these beings. It's a self-segmenting shapeshifter and a "viscera sucker," a creature which feeds by sucking out entrails and organs, rather than blood like a vampire.

The video cut to a scene from an old Filipino movie, in which a pregnant woman was lying in bed and a manananggal's tongue, thin and strong, dropped down from the thatched-hut ceiling and inserted itself in the poor woman's belly. She fought the tongue off, leaving a small incision wound on her stomach, a simple puncture mark, running with blood.

"The manananggal sustains itself," Coney explained in voice over, "on fetuses and internal organs of her prey, particularly the heart and liver, by slurping them out with her long, slithering tongue!"

OH MY GOD, Daisy thought.

She paused the video and put down her plastic fork, trying to process what she was seeing and hearing. The similarity between the cause of death in Greggory's cases and the mythology of the manananggal was unavoidable; every detail lined up with the myth except for the toxicology report. Taken in context with Pappas' video of the creature on the roof, it suggested a connection. Daisy identified two possible explanations for the events.

Either the manananggal, a flying severed torso monster from the Philippines, was real, and had flown to the other side of the world, or the plausible, but more frightening option–a series of murders had been conducted under the guise of Southeast Asian legends.

Daisy found she was too ignorant about the Philippines to deduce any possible motivation. She considered the far-out notion that the island nation was ripe with overly-creative serial killers who, instead of aiming for high death tolls like American shooters, turned their depraved actions into psychopathic, living art installations. If the creature was based on rural tales, perhaps there was an unseen symbolism in the connection; the manananggal might represent the vengeance of rural life and traditions against progress and urbanity, or class warfare.

It seemed equally plausible that the opposite was true; perhaps someone was trying to frame or scare off immigrants with a coordinated threat campaign designed to terrorize specific ethnic communities in the city, like Filipinos, with targeted imagery from their culture. She wouldn't put it past anyone these days.

Without more information, there were so many possibilities. Daisy felt like she'd picked up three or four puzzle pieces off the ground and could only blindly guess at what connections they might make, or what final image they might form if the other hundreds of pieces were available. A blue puzzle piece might indicate the entire puzzle represents a scene of the ocean, or it might just be a red herring, a tiny speck of blue in a field of other colors, falsely suggesting greater importance.

Daisy knew the human mind loves to make connections, even when they aren't there. She wondered if the manananggal similarity was a faulty connection, a coincidental distraction that would lead her farther away from the answer instead of closer. She thought about Pappas and the litany of preposterous ideas filling his balding head. If she looked hard enough for clues, she would find them whether they were real or not. Daisy warned herself to take one step at a time and not commit to any explanation until she had some evidence to back it up.

With her appetite gone, Daisy checked her post about the murders again and found a couple dozen messages had piled up. She quickly identified and deleted about half that were spam and then read the rest individually. Unfortunately, no direct witnesses or relations came forward, and the responses were mostly second-hand gossip that would be

pointless to follow up on. There was one exception–a woman named
Carmen who stated she worked in Flushing Meadows Corona Park every
day and claimed it was common knowledge that multiple unsolved
murders had occurred in the park at night.

The park was pretty far out in Queens and Daisy didn't enjoy the
thought of making the trip, especially given the likelihood that the
woman's tip would just be general gossip, but she had nothing else to work
with. Daisy responded to the woman, asking when she could meet her for
a quick chat.

One thing was for certain, she would keep working. Because she
needed this story. And because Daisy Scott loved a good puzzle. Once a
problem lodged itself inside her brain, it itched like a scab until she
scratched it.

* * *

Kylie Rhinelander opened the door to her balcony, letting a whoosh
of cold air into the stuffy living room. She stepped out onto the
generously-sized balcony, which was formed of concrete with sides made
of heavy glass with no gaps, so she didn't worry about the children's safety.

It was nice having the space to step outside and get fresh air, although
she hadn't decorated it yet, not even a chair. They had placed a small
potted plant out there but, despite her twice-daily watering, the leaves had
turned brown, and she'd given up. She never had much of a green thumb.
Once the baby arrived, she intended to give the balcony space the same
"designer's touch" she'd used on the rest of the apartment.

The balcony extended past the living room down to their corner
bedroom, where a second door led inside the other room. She was glad
to see Brett had pulled the curtains shut before passing out, so she had
privacy from him outside.

A black bird caught her attention as it soared past her through the
fog.

Wouldn't that be something? she dreamed. *To fly through these clouds like a bird?*

The bird had been HUGE—not a pigeon, or even a hawk or an eagle.

What were those giant birds called? she tried to remember. *Albatross?*

Again, a bird flew past, this time from the opposite direction.

Was it the same bird? Is it circling?

After further reflection, she realized that it hadn't been a bird at all. It had been a *bat*.

It's a Halloween celebration! she realized, concluding it had probably been a kite or a drone.

You don't get that back in Iowa, that's for sure.

She contemplated what a great city NYC would be to raise their baby. It was so vibrant and full of culture. Her family didn't understand that part. They steadfastly refused to visit NYC, to the present day. They didn't approve of Brett, of course, but had also been convinced by cable news that New York City was an urban hellscape with open warfare in the streets, too dangerous for any sane, God-fearing person to step foot in. She only saw them twice a year when she flew home. She wished she could visit more often but there just wasn't time.

But if I had a nanny? That would change everything. She could get back in shape, and they'd have time to go on dates again, to travel, to rekindle their spark.

That would change everything.

A warm, chemical buzz pulling her body down into the mattress alerted Kylie that her Ambien was finally working. She grabbed a fresh pair of disposable ear plugs from a plastic jar on her nightstand, a prerequisite for sharing a bed with Brett, and squeezed each piece of foam into a point before inserting it into her ear canals. They expanded, slowly, and the high pitches of the room faded away like she had dunked her head underwater and only low rumblings and bellows could still reach her.

Unfortunately, the sound of Brett's drunken snoring beside her was one of the sounds deep enough to penetrate the defenses of the ear plugs. They were rated for -32 decibels, but Brett's deep chest cavity seemed to contain a dragon or a giant to assist with his noise production. And it would last all night. Kylie had learned that after a night of heavy drinking, nothing would disturb Brett's slumber, or his snoring, until morning.

The ear plugs were like taking an aspirin for third degree burns, not entirely pointless, but woefully insufficient. Still, after months of wearing them every night, she had grown quite used to the sound suppression while sleeping. She even put the plugs in to help sleep sometimes when Brett wasn't there. It added an extra touch of comfort, and every little bit helped since she'd been having difficulty sleeping. She knew the arrival of the baby would only intensify her troubles.

She was still emotional about the argument with Brett, and her mind was attempting to ruminate over how to readdress her points the next time they spoke. To help calm her, she'd opened the bedroom's balcony door to allow fresh air into the room during the night. She always slept better when the room was cold.

Brett wouldn't like it; he preferred the windows and balcony to stay closed, even if the air was off. He seemed to actually prefer breathing canned air that had been piped in for him as opposed to a fresh breeze. But Kylie was from a small town. The open door permitted a slight hint of fresh air and the sounds of outdoor activity into the room, transforming the experience from claustrophobic to pleasant.

Kylie cleared her head and instructed herself to drift away with the warm heaviness filling her body. She felt another moment of guilt about taking the Ambien, but believed Brett would have stopped her if it had been dangerous for the baby. She was just bending the rules a little bit to get some sleep tonight. Life would be full of these tradeoffs soon–trading time for energy, trading her strength to the baby, trading her personal care and well-being for that of Brett and the children.

Bizarre, intrusive thoughts, flickering little lightshow fantasies, began to reach for the steering wheel in her mind. She happily recognized the indication that sleep was here. These would be her final conscious thoughts of the day, until her waking mind began its new shift in the morning, fully rested.

* * *

The apex predator was tense with indecision. It knew this prey would mean trouble and yet there it was—accessible, catatonic, and defenseless. The creature could sense both the female and its mate were inebriated, and they had foolishly opened an access point, allowing for an easy ambush that left them both cornered with no way to escape.

It had moved to a closer vantage point, clinging to the concrete edge of the balcony's support structure with its claws, peering over the top through the bottom of the glass paneled walls to watch as the intended victim slept. Its wings were folded back into neat stacks hanging off its huddled form; they weren't necessary except for flight. The manananggal had other gifts as well, including exceptionally strong limbs and clawed fingers that allowed it to climb vertical surfaces or dig into ceilings to hang in waiting like a spider. It had an unusual form of locomotion but was able to navigate land as well as air.

Without a sound, the creature slipped over the wall of the balcony and into the woman's bedroom. With nails so sharp they terminated in pinpoints, the beast began to climb the wall. With acrobatic muscle dexterity, it ascended, replacing each tiny point of contact with a higher one until it had reached the ceiling. There, it continued onward, crawling horizontally upside-down, until it was positioned directly about the sleeping prey.

A series of reactions and hormones throughout its body cried warning that the critical threshold had been passed and full release of feeding behaviors was imminent. Saliva poured into its mouth and muscles activated as its long, sharp tongue—a marvel of lethality and a testament to nature's cruelty—unspooled from its mouth to stretch downward toward the sleeping woman.

With no time to waste, it aligned the sharp-pointed tip of its proboscis with the life signs of the baby inside the bulging belly. Babies always seemed to know somehow. It had grown motionless in fright at the creature's presence, but that would be no protection from the hunter's many other senses.

The hypodermic tongue slipped into the prey with the deliberate precision of a large needle. The woman didn't even stir. The creature began to feed. Carefully at first, but once the taste hit its throat and ran down to the endless hunger in its ravenous belly, it unleashed a feeding frenzy, attempting to consume as much of the fetus as possible.

The woman began to struggle. Her face grimaced with a mask of anguish as she moaned and tussled as if battling a foe in a nightmare, but she did not wake.

Greedy now, the beast moved onto the liver. It had stayed too long already and should leave while it still could, but the meal was so exquisite, and it had been starving.

It gnawed, scraped, and sucked in a wild mania, with a tunnel vision on the flavors of meat and flesh at the tip of its tongue.

And then the prey woke up. And SCREAMED.

CHAPTER 10

The Unisphere

* * *

Saturday morning, Daisy slept in later than usual. She checked her messages to find a response from Carmen, who said she'd be working in the park all day. She was an artist and gave walking directions to the location of a booth where she sells prints.

Daisy replied that she'd stop by in the early afternoon and then attempted to brew some coffee, only to remember she'd run out of filters and forgotten to buy more. She briefly considered the frugal option of carefully dumping the prior day's grounds to wash and reuse the filter since she hadn't thrown it away yet, but she knew from experience she'd likely end up with a squishy mess and grounds in her coffee, so she used the inconvenience as an excuse to buy a cup on her way to Flushing Meadows Corona Park.

She showered, bought her coffee, and then hopped on the Flushing-bound 7-train. She sipped her drink and listened to music while she watched Queens zip by in starts and stops outside the window.

Daisy contemplated her friend Heather's upcoming Halloween party that night and found she was a little tense about it. The reason she was attending this particular party was the same reason she was nervous—she believed her old friend Jordan would be there.

Jordan had been Daisy's best friend since junior high, as well as the bass player in The Pathfinders. The pair had dropped out of college together to go on tour with the band, and the year they'd spent on the road together had brought them even closer.

Daisy was an only child, but she knew exactly how it felt to have a brother. Jordan might be her opposite in many ways, a tall, nerdy, introverted white guy, but they'd spent so much time together, and knew each other so deeply, that she felt a familial kind of protection towards him and could let her guard down in his company.

At least, that's the relationship they used to have.

Then Caleb, the singer of the band, had announced to Daisy and the others that: his girlfriend was pregnant, they were getting married, he was going to work for her father, and that there would be no more band.

After lengthy denial and bargaining phases, their lead guitarist "Six Foot Dave" was the next to rejoin the real world. Dave was actually 6'4" but had acquired the nickname after an early growth spurt and for some reason it had just stuck.

Jordan went back to school next, leaving Daisy as the final member of the band to give up the ghost and return to the beaten path, re-enrolling in college to complete her bachelor's degree.

The chaos of school and careers, doing the work of creating "real" adult lives, had created an inadvertent wedge between Daisy and Jordan. Time and experience change everyone and it didn't matter how similar their wavelengths had been in the past, life had been altering each of them in unpredictable ways, beyond their own control, in the last few years. A slight change in him, a slight change in her, and suddenly the disparity is compounded, producing two strangers trying to remember who the other person is, or who they once were.

If Daisy was uncomfortable about the night's meetup, she knew Jordan must be a nervous wreck. Jordan was shy and neurotic compared to Daisy and would normally avoid a party like this. It was unlikely to be an introvert-approved "small gathering" if their friend Heather's prior parties were any indication. But Daisy didn't need to be a Pulitzer Prize winner to deduct that Jordan would likely at least make a token appearance.

First of all, Heather was a mutual friend since high school and Daisy knew Jordan still interacted with her regularly online. Secondly, the real kicker, Jordan's new apartment was about a five-minute walk from Heather's place in Hell's Kitchen. After his recent move to the city, he'd need a really good excuse to completely avoid the trouble of a pop-in he could complete door-to-door in half an hour.

And if Jordan *had* to make an appearance at a costume party, she figured her friend was going to wear a costume and stay *just* long enough to justify the trouble. As much as Jordan hated strangers, mingling, and loud groups of people, he was a sci-fi superfan who sometimes attended conventions, and she knew the man had a closet full of wacky costumes that he was dying to take on a stroll.

Daisy got off the train at Mets-Willets Point and took the elevated boardwalk south into Flushing Meadows Corona Park. A picturesque tree-lined boulevard led her toward the Unisphere. Food of every variety was on offer from both licensed and unlicensed vendors. Daisy passed a few guys selling records, jewelry, and knockoff purses spread out on blankets.

Daisy realized she hadn't been to the Unisphere in several years, so she made a pit stop to admire the giant metal globe, the continents of Africa and Asia towering over her head. The park was bustling as crowds of people enjoyed their outdoor activities in the nice weather.

Carmen's note said to head east toward the Fountain of the Planets and that her stall would be set up near a large statue called "Rocket Thrower." Daisy soon found the sculpture; a muscular man with enviable glutes was depicted hurling a space capsule to the stars with his strong arms, through sheer force of will and strength.

Under the shade of trees nearby, a row of folding tables was set up along a broad walking path and vendors had their arts and crafts for sale. Standing in between a young black man selling t-shirts and an elderly Chinese woman offering custom ceramic items, was a thirty-something Latina manning a booth full of art prints. Daisy assumed this was Carmen.

She was selling prints of her paintings in various sizes. The technique and subject matter varied from piece to piece but shared a common theme—the juxtaposition of billionaire prosperity with poverty and suffering for the masses, mostly using NYC iconography in ironic contexts and situations.

CEOs were frequent targets of her satire. One painting depicted a particular unscrupulous mega-billionaire lounging with his plastic-faced, giant-lipped trophy wife in a luxury environment on the moon, both sporting shit-eating grins. A spectacle of light hung in the sky, visible through the glass ceiling of their domed compound. It was a fiery gemstone, a dazzling centerpiece for their delight among the bleakness of the airless void: the doomed planet Earth burning beautifully in the distance.

But a different painting caught Daisy's eye, sending a shiver down her spine. It depicted the Unisphere at night, with the unmistakable outline of *bat wings* on top. The same shape from the rooftop. The manananggal.

Daisy felt a rush of adrenaline as she approached, and her mind surged with questions.

Is the rooftop video connected?

How long has this been going on? And why?

Is someone trying to scare immigrants?

Are these Filipino symbols connected to the murders?

"Excuse me, I'm looking for Carmen," she announced to the artist.

"Yes. That's me," the woman replied. "Are you Daisy Scott?"

The guy selling shirts at the table next to Carmen overheard the exchange and interjected, "What?! Daisy Scott? From *The Brooklyn Believer*? No shit?!"

"Guilty as charged," Daisy said.

"Damn, now that's a coincidence," the man said. "I was just reading one of your stories on the train the other day. What was it... Oh! The food truck that found an image of the Virgin Mary grilled into a beef patty. Wasn't that you?"

"Yeah, that was mine," she told him with a glare, before turning her full attention back to Carmen. Daisy pulled her audio recorder from her bag.

"Carmen, do you mind if I get this on tape?" she asked.

"Sure, that's okay, I guess."

Daisy started recording a new audio file.

"*Aliens abducted my French bulldog*! I read that one too!" the man shouted, unable to mind his own business. "That was you..."

His inflection on the last three words sounded like an accusation, and Daisy almost felt guilty, like she'd done something wrong.

"Yes," she acknowledged. "Now, if you'll excuse me, sir..."

"That one, I didn't believe for one second," he said, not taking the hint. "Aliens crossed the whole galaxy just to snatch that old lady's dog? Nah. I don't think so. It's a waste of technology."

Daisy ignored the guy and had Carmen say and spell her name into the recorder.

"What can you tell me about the murders?" Daisy asked her.

"There's been many of them!" she said. "Everybody around here knows that. You said online that there was just one murder here in the park, but it's been way more than that. Lots of people have disappeared. They just haven't found the bodies. Or they don't care."

"Did you lose someone?" Daisy asked.

"No, not me. Not yet. But word gets around. People around here know not to enter the park at night. That's when it gets you."

"It?" Daisy asked. "Do you mean–"

Daisy pointed at the woman's painting of the wings on the Unisphere.

"This?" she asked. "Is that what gets you?"

Carmen nodded in confirmation. "Yeah, that's what they say it looks like. This park is its hunting ground," she explained. "The Beast of Corona."

"The Beast of Corona?" Daisy repeated to herself. "Do you know someone who's seen it firsthand?"

"There was a pregnant woman who used to sell fruit cups out here," Carmen said. "Anna? That was her name, I think. We only spoke a couple times. She said she saw it one night. But she hasn't been around in a few weeks. The Beast probably got her."

"That thing is all about population control," the shirt seller said, coming closer to officially join the conversation uninvited. "In this country, we've got mass shootings. You gotta work four jobs to make ends meet. We got two broken, corrupt political parties that sold us down the river and won't let us vote for anyone else. Nothing works, everything's a scam and full of poison, and if somehow none of that gets you? That's where The Beast comes in. That's how they keep our numbers down. Picking off the undesirables. Get it? Population control. They'd rather get rid of the problem than deal with it."

"Who's *they*?" Daisy asked, a little hopeful despite herself that he might actually know something.

"Rich guys and politicians, probably," he said. "The victims are always poor people, aren't they? It's purposeful. And I'll ask you this—were any of the victims white?"

Huh. Daisy noted the observation but deemed three victims and some hearsay insufficient proof of any racial motivation. Three victims were barely even a pattern.

"I believe The Beast is *La Lechuza*," Carmen said. "Because everyone sees wings."

"La Lechuza?" Daisy asked.

"She's a witch who is very evil and transforms into a giant owl," Carmen explained.

"Enough nonsense! It's a Harpy Eagle!" a woman's voice bellowed from the other direction. It was the old Chinese lady on the other side of Carmen, listening in.

"Probably escaped from the zoo!" she explained. "I've seen pictures. They're huge and have horns on their heads. That's all it is. It just escaped, and they're too stupid to catch it. Everybody wants to make up conspiracies these days."

The old woman looked at Daisy's recorder. "Hey, am I going to be in the paper?"

"It's just *The Brooklyn Believer,* Ms. Liu!" the man called out.

"Oh, no wonder," the woman said, losing interest and returning to her seat behind her ceramics. "I don't read that stuff. Rots your brain. You're a bad influence on kids!"

"Is there anything else you can tell me?" Daisy asked, directing her question toward the entire group this time. "Do the victims have anything in common? Is "The Beast" seen before or after a person disappears? What does the lower half of it look like? Does it make a sound? Is there a smell? Has anyone taken photos or video?"

"Daisy, all the people with those answers are dead," Carmen said. "I hope that I never have those answers."

After an awkward silence, Daisy thanked the group for their time and returned her audio recorder to her bag.

As she walked away, the t-shirt seller yelled out to her one last time. "Whatever it is, I'm not scared of it."

Daisy turned back to face the man. "Why not?" she asked.

"Cause it's a bottom feeder," he said. "It's scared of a real fight. It only picks on women and children."

That night, Daisy assembled her Halloween costume while listening to the background noise of local news. The streaming channel had mostly been looping the same packaged stories, including a report about an elderly man falling down the elevator shaft of his building. Outrage was growing after it had been revealed that the slumlord owner of the structure had a long history of building violations and had long neglected basic maintenance.

Daisy walked around her apartment in witch-themed socks, saving the final touch of her costume for last. She had acquired giant 6-inch platform boots on the internet to complete her transformation into the statuesque Christoper Lee version of Dracula. She would still fall several inches shy of that lofty goal, but the extra boost would be enough to lift her eye-line above most of the masses for maximum effect.

She wore a black suit and a long black cape with red inner lining. She pulled her hair back into a bun, but decided to forgo wearing contact lenses to replicate Lee's bloodshot eyes. She slipped her vampire fangs into her pocket so she wouldn't forget them later.

Daisy was painting a false widow's peak under her hairline when a breaking news alert caught her attention. The anchor announced that the wife of a plastic surgeon, a minor local celebrity, had been murdered the previous night. Authorities had responded to their Long Island City home, only about a fifteen-minute walk from Daisy's apartment, to find the woman bleeding out from injuries. The paramedics had attempted resuscitation, but she'd been pronounced dead at the scene. No information was available yet about the investigation or possible suspects.

Daisy had seen Dr. Rhinelander's ads over the years. He mostly stood out for the nepotism and manufactured enthusiasm on display in his grandiose commercials, as well as his tacky, ubiquitous subway ads. Daisy had spent many hours of her life holding onto a pole, forced to stare at one of his print ads, featuring his face and catchphrase: "Magnify Yourself." He'd been in business long enough that newer posters sometimes ripped and tore away to reveal his ancient sales pitches of perfect beauty hibernating underneath. The surgeon was a familiar source of tabloid controversy, considering he had a colorful past, had obscured the existence of a disabled son for years, and had even swapped his old wife for a younger model in between commercials not too long ago like no one would notice. He was the sort of public figure that thrived somewhat on an undercurrent of notoriety, simply by maintaining his status quo as a guy some people loved to hate.

Daisy made a mental note to follow up on the story later and finished changing into her Dracula costume. After brushing her teeth and double checking that her drumsticks were in her bag, she set off for Heather's Halloween party.

Daisy took the train to Columbus Circle, noticing many other people in costumes along the way. As she exited the station, a large group of teens hopped the turnstiles to avoid paying the fare. The violations went unnoticed by four uniformed police officers stationed nearby for that very purpose. They were too busy chatting and scrolling on their phones. Everything else in the city had been defunded to maximize the number of cops in the subways, but the only concrete result so far had been astronomical overtime pay for the police.

From the subway, it was about a ten-minute walk to Heather's building near the Hudson River. Daisy arrived at a sprawling new condo tower in Midtown West. This building eschewed a pretentious title like "The Impluvium" for over-simplicity instead–56 WEST APARTMENTS. She slipped in her vampire fangs and headed through the revolving door.

Inside, there were two security guards stationed at the front desk, which had a wall-sized water feature streaming behind them. One of the guards looked up to see Daisy entering and gave a smile in recognition of her costume. Daisy paused at the desk.

"Heather Montash?" she asked, with her best attempt at a Dracula accent.

"18th floor, Dracula. On the left, I believe. You'll probably hear it from the elevator," he laughed.

Daisy thanked him with a fang-filled smile and headed toward the elevators.

CHAPTER 11

Jordan Farmer

* * *

Jordan Farmer leaned his back against the wall of his friend Heather's cramped living room, wincing at the volume level of a top-40 song the thirty year-old electrical technician didn't recognize. The apartment was a one-bedroom unit with the bedroom closed off for storing coats. The combined living room and dining space was really large by Manhattan standards, but the turnout for the party still managed to overwhelm the space, and the room felt like a chaotic sea of sweaty bodies and noise to Jordan.

Almost every attendee had made at least a perfunctory attempt at assembling a costume. His friend Heather was dressed as a princess and her husband was a football player. Most of the costumes were off-the-shelf standards but a few notable exceptions stood out. One guy appeared to be dressed as William Howard Taft in a bathtub, based on the fake mustache and large styrofoam basin strapped around him. Another heavy-set gentleman was dressed as a giant baby, wearing only an oversized diaper and a bald cap. His giant, hairy gut hung down in a flap over the diaper as he guzzled beer.

Jordan had considered a few different costume options for the event. The party hadn't been important enough to justify building or buying a new costume, so he'd dusted off one of his old favorites, from the British sci-fi show *Doctor Who*.

He realized he'd been standing alone without speaking to anyone for a noticeable stretch of time and worried he should probably intermingle again. He looked around the packed apartment, only seeing the same unfamiliar faces he'd awkwardly shuffled past during his previous rounds through the room. He'd made his obligatory greeting with Heather when he'd walked in but, as the host, she was understandably too busy bouncing around and entertaining her guests to chat much with him.

The kitchen island and wet bar were packed with snacks and hors d'oeuvres, as well as a generously stocked selection of beer, wine, liquor, and a few flavors of soda and non-alcoholic drinks. The casual abundance on display, likely an afterthought to Heather and her husband, a VP at Goldman Sachs, forced the comparison with Jordan's own standard of living, but it was nice to get a taste of such creature comforts. It was one welcome thing about attending functions at the homes of rich friends, he reflected.

Valuable floor space in the room had been sacrificed to erect a folding table near the front door for the DJ, in a Satan costume. Jordan assumed he was one of Heather's co-workers as opposed to a professional DJ, given that he seemed to just be playing a Spotify playlist off his laptop. There were also two large free-standing speakers connected to his computer, taking up additional space.

Jordan didn't regret coming to the party, necessarily, but realized his timing had been terrible. The invitation had read "8:00 PM-??" which he felt had left too much room for interpretation. Without a ballpark estimate of when Heather expected the event to end, how had he been to decide when to arrive? Especially if the visit would be brief? What time would the party hit its peak? Eventually, some parties with open bars could descend into bedlam, until only the drunkest and most dedicated partiers remained to fight for the cause. Certainly, he wouldn't want to stick around for that. There were so many variables. It was too much wiggle room for Jordan.

He would have left the party already, except he knew his best friend Daisy would be showing up eventually. They'd fallen out of touch a little the last couple years and he wasn't expecting an emotional reunion, but he wanted to catch up with her. Their friendship had suffered some slight slings and arrows due to busy schedules and misunderstandings. It was neither person's fault, but their relationship had definitely changed.

They still texted almost every week, usually about an upcoming movie or something music related, but Daisy was no longer a person he might contact anytime he had the impulse. His once effortless friend now required some effort, and a slight anxiety flavored his interactions with her now.

Jordan checked the time on his phone and ran through the mental gymnastics of assumptions he'd used earlier to estimate what time Daisy might arrive. She was always on time—it was Daisy Scott, that was a given. She was freaky when it came to that stuff. But the real question wasn't when Daisy would show up; it was when Daisy thought HE would show up, and he'd screwed the pooch on that one.

He'd finished his beer a few minutes earlier and was still holding the bottle because he felt more comfortable having some busy work available for his hands. He'd been keeping an eye on the wet bar hoping a gaggle of finance guys would clear out so he could properly consider the options for his second drink in peace. There would be no third drink. Jordan couldn't stand the crowd much longer. If Daisy didn't show up by then, it was not meant to be, and they would catch up another time.

An opening suddenly appeared in the kitchen as the groups of people resituated, like an alligator had lurched out of a watering howl and scattered all the drinking animals. Jordan seized the moment to cut through the crowd of people, trying not to get elbowed or have a drink spilled on him. A hair over six feet tall, Jordan couldn't exactly get buried in the mass of people, but his lanky build and lack of assertiveness made navigating any thick crowd a dodgy affair. Most people ignored his polite taps on their back or shoulder to indicate his need to pass. Even as they parted to let him slip through, they did so without fully acknowledging his presence; he was just a hiccup in their conversation as they allowed him to wade through.

At the bar, he debated his beverage options, trying to choose between another beer or something more exotic. A young woman dressed as Katniss from *The Hunger Games* series approached the bar and stationed herself next to Jordan to refresh her mixed drink.

Say something to her. Jordan told himself.

Anyone else would talk to her right now. Do it. Just say "Hi."

He wasn't even particularly attracted to the woman, or interested in her. He just knew the situation compelled him to speak up since their paths had converged simultaneously at the bar. He would look awkward and foolish if he didn't say anything. He needed a quick, throwaway remark. But what should he say?

"I like your costume," he complimented. "Katniss?"

"Who?" she asked, with a perplexed look, sizing him up. "No. I'm *Hunger Games*. It's a movie."

"Yeah, *Hunger Games*," he agreed. "You're Katniss. The main character."

"No…" she corrected, irritably, "I'm just *Hunger Games*."

"Oh," Jordan muttered in confusion. "Okay, that's cool."

He waited, but she didn't reciprocate with a question about his costume. Jordan's gut told him to just say "goodnight" and walk away to protect against upcoming embarrassment, but his heart was just too proud of his costume to listen–

"I'm 'The Doctor,'" he announced with a faux British accent and a smile full of pretend confidence.

"That's nice," Hunger Games said, hastily adding a couple ice cubes to finish the assembly of her mixed drink.

"You're supposed to say, "Doctor Who?"" he said, despite sensing from her body language that she was about to walk away.

"Excuse me," she said.

She immediately penetrated the crowd behind her and vanished without a trace. For some reason the polite dismissal stung Jordan worse than a rude rejection might have. When a person tries to soften a blow, you get to see how much effort they're willing to put into it, how much effort they're willing to put into *you*. In the mind of Hunger Games, Jordan had only been worth two words: "excuse me."

You're supposed to say, "Doctor Who?"

I sounded pathetic.

God, why did I say that?

Jordan felt like his insides had fallen through the floor and only a shell remained. No one was looking at him, and yet it seemed like every person in the room was judging him somehow. He barely knew anyone there, all those bankers and yuppies. What in the world was he supposed to talk to them about? It was one thing to catch up with Heather in smaller groups, but he needed help navigating uncomfortable social situations like a giant Halloween party filled with rich strangers. He was out of his league.

You're supposed to say, "Doctor Who."

He imagined how ridiculous he had probably sounded to the woman, who had clearly never heard of the show. Embarrassed and dejected, Jordan grabbed another beer and slowly inched his way back toward his hiding spot in the rear of the room.

* * *

True to the doorman's prediction, the auditory mayhem of booming bass and a packed crowd projecting through the closed door of Heather's apartment was sufficient to guide Daisy toward the appropriate apartment. A stranger dressed as a cheerleader opened the door and gave her a disappointed look, clearly waiting for someone other than Daisy to show up. She politely nudged past the woman and searched the crowd for familiar faces, finding a surprise advantage thanks to the higher vantage point provided by her heeled boots.

Heather was nowhere in sight–in another room, on the balcony, or buried in the sea of costumed partiers. Daisy saw Heather's husband speaking to a small group near the kitchen, but decided she could wait to check in with him since the two were barely acquainted.

Then her eyes hit the back of the room.

There you are.

Unmistakable. Her best friend. Jordan was wearing a retro cricket sweater, off-white with red trim, and a matching hat and coat. The jacket was accented with what appeared to be a piece of celery pinned to his lapel.

What the fuck, Jordan? she laughed to herself.

Daisy was pretty sure his costume wasn't from *Star Trek*. That left Jordan's other nerd obsession, *Doctor Who*, as the likely culprit. Daisy had humored him enough over the years to sit through a few episodes of the decades-old show, which featured rotating protagonists, but she didn't recall any of the heroes wearing root vegetables as fashion accessories.

She noticed Jordan looked sad and uncomfortable, like a traumatized puppy trying to hide from the world behind an oversized, red-banded Panama hat.

Poor Jordan.

All the unease and bitterness that had formed between them seemed to wash away for Daisy, as her protective loyalty to her old friend resurfaced to eclipse everything else.

An idea for a dramatic entrance occurred to her, so she approached the guy at the DJ booth to take her shot. The DJ was dressed as the Devil, in red spandex that was a little too tight to be flattering against the soft ripples of his torso, and bumping along to the terrible song he was playing.

"Hey!" Daisy screamed, waving her arms to get his attention. "Could you do me a favor?" she asked.

The guy turned to address her, still gyrating his hips to the beat. He looked plastered.

What have we got here?

Daisy tried to assess the guy to find an angle. The man's appearance was slightly schlubby and disheveled and the Satan costume was new, but it looked bargain bin, probably from a big box store or Amazon. She didn't peg him as a finance guy, or else he would have overcompensated for the lack of effort by overspending. No, the DJ wasn't one of Heather's husband's rich friends.

The man danced with a confidence unearthed by drink. Daisy could give him that.

Or could she?

No, as she watched further, he clearly danced with a *false* confidence. This wasn't his raw, true self emerging, only a performance afforded to him by the booze. He was a bird puffing up its feathers to appear larger and less vulnerable. The proud masquerade of the insecure.

"What's up?" the DJ asked, shuffling insincerely to the music.

"I wanna surprise someone here with a song," Daisy said with a big smile. "Can you squeeze *Rosanna* by Toto up next in the mix? Thanks!"

The Pathfinders had never covered *Rosanna*, but the song's half-time shuffle drumbeat performed by Jeff Porcaro was infamous among drummers for both its utility and unassuming difficulty. Non-drummers tend to believe fast and loud percussion is difficult and impressive, even when it's not actually the case. *Rosanna*'s half-time shuffle was an opposite case study—a drum part with a complexity lost on most people but which stood out to drummers. Daisy had practiced the tricky pattern incessantly during downtime over the years, often to the chagrin of the bass player parked idly by her side—Jordan Farmer.

"I'll add it to the queue," the DJ replied dryly. "I've got LOTS of requests tonight."

Damn, Daisy thought to herself. She'd wanted to walk over to Jordan with the song playing as a callback to their days on the road. But she could tell the DJ wasn't bluffing. She recognized the tone in his voice. It was the robotic delivery of a person who's received the same request all night long, with each person approaching him thinking they're the first to think of it.

Daisy decided to try another approach since she had nothing left to lose.

"Hey DJ, what's your name?"

The man seemed surprised that she had asked. "I'm Buck," he said.

His languishing dance moves became revitalized thanks to her attention. He even added some tiny swings of his arms.

"No, what's your *NAME*?" she demanded. "Your *DJ NAME*?"

"Oh."

He looked surprised, like no one had ever asked him that before and he hadn't been prepared for it. After a moment, he formed a sheepish smirk and leaned in closer to her like the information was a closely guarded secret. With a quieter voice, he divulged, ""DJ Hotcakes," is the name I've been toying with."

Ugh. Gross. What the fuck?

"Yeah! There it is, your *real* name. DJ Hotcakes. I love it," she lied. "Hey, do you know what I like about you, DJ Hotcakes?"

He shook his head in confusion.

"You're a working man," she said.

Luckily, the DJ concurred because he nodded proudly in agreement with Daisy's estimation of him.

"You know who else was a working man?" she asked, before producing a weathered five-dollar bill from the pocket of her black dress slacks and pointing at it.

"Abraham Lincoln," she said. "He worked on the rails. Did you know that?"

The DJ gave her a perplexed "maybe" look.

Daisy studied the crumpled face of America's sixteenth president in her hand. "Now, *this* was a working man. And he made it all the way to the top, didn't he?"

"Sure," DJ Hotcakes said. But then he furrowed his brow as if troubled by something. Daisy worried he was considering Lincoln's fate all the way to its conclusion.

"And we working people gotta stick together," she said. "Isn't that right, DJ Hotcakes?"

Daisy worried that she'd blown it at the end but she followed through anyway. She placed the five-dollar bill on the table next to the DJ's laptop, gave him a smile and a wink, and then spun around, turning her back to him, not waiting for a response or a rejection. She pushed her way to the front of the crowd, flared the cape of her Dracula costume theatrically, and waited, hoping…

* * *

The music abruptly shut off and was replaced by a familiar, long-forgotten rhythm booming through Heather's apartment. The beat was a call to alertness for Jordan, a personally relevant song playing in a public environment. Jordan knew the song very well. But more important than the melody or the lyrics was its beat. He'd heard the pattern played hundreds of times on drums, knees, floors, and tables. It was almost a calling card.

Then, he locked eyes with Count Dracula, her head elevated above the crowd, dancing toward him with a proud, fanged grin.

Thank God.

It was his friend Daisy, here to save him.

"All I want to do when I wake up in the morning is see your eyes…"

She was waving the ends of her cape with her hands in tune with the music as she indiscriminately bumped people out of her way to clear a path toward him in the back. He already felt his mood improving as he watched her. She was always so carefree. It seemed to unlock his ability to be that way as well.

"I figured it was you the second I heard the intro," he told her.

"Come here!" she yelled, drawing him in for a hug. "How are you?"

"Good. I'm good," he said, as they pulled away. "I've been working too much lately, but I'm trying to get back out into the world."

"Dude, same here," Daisy said. Thanks to her platform shoes, Jordan was seeing almost eye to eye with her.

"Those boots are crazy. You're almost as tall as me," he admitted. "It's weird."

Daisy laughed. "Christopher Lee. You can't skimp on the details. What about you? What is this?" she asked, referencing his costume.

"The Fifth Doctor," he said. He didn't expect her to get the reference. No one had understood it since he'd left home that night. This wasn't a proper crowd for any of his good costumes.

"Ah of course," she joked. "Who could forget the Fifth Doctor? What's the celery for, in case you get hungry? Did you take it from the snack table over there? Honey, those are for eating, not wearing. Bless your little heart."

"It was the 80s," he explained with a laugh. "I'll show you some episodes. You'll get a kick."

"Raincheck," she said.

"Didn't you already do a Dracula costume back in the day?" Jordan asked. "Freshman year of college?"

"Yeah, but that was more of a *generic* Dracula," she said. "This costume is specifically the Hammer Films version of Dracula. I'm also planning a Gary Oldman Dracula one of these days, but I need money first. Gotta do the hair right. Where's the bar?" she demanded. "I'm parched."

Jordan followed Daisy as she picked a flavor of hard seltzer from the bar. The pair exhausted the necessary catchup small talk about work, their inactive dating lives, parents, and how Jordan liked his new apartment in Manhattan, which he'd moved to a couple months earlier after spending most of his life in Queens.

Afterward, Daisy made a pitstop to greet Heather and her husband. Jordan found himself effortlessly joining in the conversation. With Daisy beside him as an anchor, he talked more than he had during his own entrance and greeting earlier in the night.

Jordan realized the small things about people seemed to be what slipped his mind first. He hadn't seen Daisy much lately, and was now reminded about her confidence with other people. He'd taken it for granted before but, with fresh eyes, he realized how comforting it was to have her with him in a crowd.

Daisy's personality, and approach to persuasion, was friendly, but resolute. She was kind, funny, and caring but also had pride, willpower, and an ability to stick up for herself that looked like a superpower to Jordan. If a fast-food worker forgot to give him a straw, he would probably stand there feeling like an idiot for five minutes, if that's what it took, waiting for a perfect moment of eye contact to alert someone, hopefully without causing them any extra hassle, that they had forgotten his straw. Daisy, meanwhile? "Excuse me! Straw please? Thank you!" In and out. Done. All without being rude. She lived her life knowing she had a right to be here and she didn't need to apologize for anything. Jordan wished he had Daisy's ability to stand up for herself and handle social situations with ease, but it felt forced and unnatural when he tried it. It just wasn't him.

CATALINA

* * *

Daisy parted ways with Heather and then made her way out to the balcony with Jordan for some fresh air. It was a small area with only two chairs and several people outside, mostly smoking or vaping. Jordan seemed hesitant about the crowd on the balcony, but Daisy dragged him through to the other side where they found comfortable standing room and could look out over the railing.

An assault of high-pitched barks was erupting from below. Daisy looked down to see the luxury building had a built-in astroturfed dog park on the ground floor which wrapped around the side of the building underneath the balcony. Two small dogs, a Pomeranian and some kind of Poodle mix, were in a serious tussle. Their playful rousing had apparently escalated into all-out conflict and their owners were struggling to untwine their leashes and pull the tiny combatants apart, all while shouting apologies at each other and chastising their embattled little dogs.

"Listen to them," Daisy said, in a Romanian accent. "The children of the night. What music they make!"

Luckily Jordan got the *Dracula* reference and laughed. He seemed more at ease now outside on the balcony. Daisy noticed his slender frame looked a little sturdier than normal. Jordan would never be the type to lift weights but she knew his job as an electric technician involved some heavy lifting so it might come with the territory. He looked healthy but he also looked a little bit older, and she wondered if he saw the same thing when he looked at her.

The night sky was clear, and Daisy wondered if the "Beast of Corona" was out there hunting that very night. Was she on the trail of a serial killer? Or was she just in over her head?

"Is something on your mind?" Jordan asked.

Daisy realized Jordan's perspective might be helpful for her case. She was stuck and needed a push, but she intended to choose her words carefully. She didn't want to put all her cards on the table just yet, and also worried she might sound foolish to Jordan if she explained too much about the supposed "manananggal."

"If you were trying to solve a puzzle," she asked, "and you had several pieces of circumstantial evidence which pointed to a conclusion you knew with absolute certainty was false, how would you proceed?"

"Is this about your job? Last time we spoke you were still burned out. I thought you'd closed the book on this stuff. Did something change?"

"I don't know," she replied. "It's not that. Just think of it as a hypothetical."

The wind on the balcony kept catching the brim of Jordan's hat and threatening to cast it away into the sky, so he removed it and held it in his hand. His curly blonde hair was trimmed short around the sides and back but allowed to form a small mop on the top of his head.

"What's the false conclusion?" he asked.

"You can't laugh," she warned. "I know it's silly. That's the problem."

"Just tell me."

"What if it looked like a... bat monster was killing people in the city?"

"Huh." Jordan grinned. "I thought you were gonna say a ghost or something. At least this is different than your usual crap. No offense."

"None taken."

"You said several pieces of evidence?" he asked.

"Let's say there had been sightings of a "creature" and unexplained homicides that seemed to be connected. Why would someone make murders look like a monster did it?"

"Real murders?" Jordan asked. "Is this for real?"

"Shhh. Hypothetical, remember? But keep your voice down."

"Hmmm." Jordan took the question seriously and rubbed the stubble on his chin. "Specifically, a bat? My first thought would be vampires."

"No, forget vampires," Daisy said.

"Okay then. Well, Batman dresses like a bat to scare people. He uses fear as a tactic since he doesn't have superpowers. He's just a rich guy."

"No, wrong," Daisy said, at risk of getting side-tracked. "Batman has *lots* of superpowers. He's the world's greatest athlete, detective, fighter, logistician, leader, martial artist, and problem-solver, while never taking a day off, or sleeping, or eating a French fry."

"Oh yeah," Jordan agreed. "Okay. That sounds less realistic than Superman, when you put it like that. At least Superman has French fries to look forward to later."

"So, scaring people?" she asked. "You think that's it? What if the people targeted were immigrants? The symbolism of this monster is very specific to an Asian culture."

"Sure," he said. "Why not? Think about the imagery used by the KKK–white robes, burning crosses. That's much scarier than a racist guy just showing his dumb face and overalls. It could be intimidation tactics, making it personal. What immigrants are targeted by a bat?"

"Filipinos, I think? Except none of the victims are from the Philippines," Daisy sighed.

"Oh," Jordan said, clearly confused.

"It's also possible I'm just imagining all of this. I could be headed further and further down a dead end and not know it yet."

"Hypothetically," Jordan reminded her, as the pair of old friends looked out over the rooftops of Manhattan.

CHAPTER 12

Coney De La Cruz

* * *

The next morning Daisy woke with a slight hangover. She'd eventually had a few drinks while catching up with Jordan at the party. She'd left the prior night feeling really good about reconnecting with him and they'd made plans to meet up again soon, possibly even the following week. She guzzled a couple glasses of water hoping her headache would dissipate as she fully woke up.

Daisy realized she'd forgotten to buy coffee filters again, so she threw on her shoes and jacket to head downstairs and buy a cup of takeout coffee. As she headed back to her apartment sipping her drink, she was stopped by an impulsive thought. She grabbed her phone and pulled up the address for Coney's Occult Books, the bookstore owned by the manananggal expert on YouTube. Sundays were usually lazy days for Daisy, reserved for laundry and chores. She was at an impasse on her case and it might be worth a trip to that woman's store to see if she could learn anything helpful. Of course, she had no clue if Coney could even help her, and she might not even be working at her store that day.

Oh, what the hell, Daisy thought. She'd never been to an occult bookstore, and it seemed like an omission given her ostensible line of work. Her only plan for the day was a hair appointment that afternoon. Until then, she'd just be watching *Halloween Wars* and folding socks. She had time to spare. She reversed course to head for the subway entrance.

Daisy took the 7-train to Jackson Heights-Roosevelt Avenue and then walked toward the address on the map. Coney's bookshop was located on a busy stretch of storefronts in a slightly seedy area near a major transit junction. As she walked down the street, the smell of barbecue from a street vendor wafted through the air and produced a gurgle in Daisy's stomach, even though she was usually never hungry in the morning.

The neighborhood seemed like a microcosm of the *real* New York City. The daily grind of the outer boroughs was all around her. It was a mixture of the old and the new. As Daisy neared the dot on her map, she heard a variety of languages, some she recognized and others she didn't. Daisy loved Queens because it felt like each block transported her to a new corner of the Earth, like a lived-in Epcot Center. One minute she's in South America, the next? Asia. The next? She's at the steps of a Banana Republic outlet store. It was like someone had grabbed a neighborhood from every country in the world and just stuck them together to see what would happen. Then, to the god-like prankster's surprise, all the denizens had just resumed going about their day like nothing had happened, intermixing and intermingling, sharing food, culture, and ideas.

Coney's bookstore was situated in the middle of the block, between a Mexican restaurant and a nail salon. A white hatchback was parked out front with "Student Driver" and "Coney's Driving School" emblazoned on the sides. The large sign over the shop's front doors read:

CONEY'S OCCULT BOOKS AND DRIVING SCHOOL

A second, smaller sign underneath it and to the right read:

& NOTARY PUBLIC

But this smaller sign had been spray painted with a giant red "X" crossing it out. As Daisy entered the bookstore, she wondered what the story was behind the little sign. Why hadn't Coney just taken it down if she no longer offered the service? Why leave it up there, along with a permanent record of her odd venting? As Daisy walked through the doors, she got her answer. Coney de la Cruz was a strange person.

The jangle of sleigh bells on the door announced Daisy's entrance to the bookshop but it was drowned out by Devo's "Baby Doll" blasting at inadvisable volume over busted speakers.

The store was narrow and cramped like an undersized bodega and the shelves on either side stretched up fully to the ceiling. Daisy noticed a bizarre collection of items for sale.

Closest to the door, there were grocery items she didn't recognize, mostly chips and bakery goods, which she assumed were Filipino imports. Beyond the first few steps, there were books as far as the eye could see, but it wasn't arranged like a normal, modern bookstore. There were no splashy "book club tables" with pastel and neon rows of the latest derivative young adult romance novels penned by Instagram stars and billionaires' kids. It looked more like a library or a bookstore in an old movie. It smelled that way too. Daisy knew and loved the odor of freshly-printed books, but Coney's store projected a different kind of pleasant, nostalgic scent—*old* books.

As Daisy proceeded down the path of shelves and neared the clerk's table at the end, she noticed trinkets, art, collectibles, and occult items for sale near the checkout area. Some decorations that caught her eye were downright bizarre.

A taxidermied animal was on display in a tall glass case, mounted in a predatory pose on top of a fake rock. It looked like a ferret or a possum with too much fur, blaring its sharp little teeth.

Is that a fucking wolverine? Daisy wondered.

There was a price tag on the case—$3999. It was for sale. Everything there was for sale. Coney was a hustler! Daisy might wonder who could be dumb enough to drop $4K on a dead wolverine behind some glass. But Coney only needed to make that sale one time for it to work, didn't she? And until then, it was certainly a centerpiece.

She was pleased to even see a few Halloween decorations added to the mix. She would have forgiven an occult store for skipping that step since the entire room was essentially Halloween-themed. Behind the sales desk, Daisy noticed a retro Ninja Turtles Halloween poster which read "Cowabunga! It's Halloween, Dudes!" in yellow block letters. The poster revealed its great age through dozens of thumbtack holes around its ragged perimeter. Those Turtles had probably been in Halloween service since before Coney was born.

A pair of red Chuck Taylors were propped up on the desk next to a can of Diet Dr. Pepper and tapped along to the beat. The face of their owner was buried behind a book, something about European werewolf lore.

"Girl of my dreams, she don't love me."

"Excuse me," Daisy announced, trying to raise her voice over the Devo song.

The person behind the desk didn't seem to hear her and kept bopping to the music.

"Always the way it seems to be."

"Excuse me!" Daisy tried again.

This time, without moving the book, the woman flung her hand up toward Daisy, forming an urgent "stop sign" gesture. As she did this, the instruments in the music dropped away to leave only the digital bass doing a funny little climb until a loud snare hit brought the full band back in. The stop sign hand was replaced by a synchronized snap of the woman's index finger toward Daisy when the drum hit.

Only afterward, as the vocals began a repetitive call of "My Baby Doll," did the reader finally lower her book to peer at Daisy through round-frame glasses. It was Coney, the owner of the store, and exactly who Daisy wanted to see.

"Hey! Can I help you?" Coney asked.

With the book put aside, Daisy saw she was wearing a belted coverall jumpsuit. It was the sort of unisex style worn by laborers, mechanics, or exterminators except the pastel green color was too vivid and conspicuous for pure utility. Coney was dressed like the resident engineer at a colorful goo factory in a children's movie.

"Well, not exactly," Daisy replied. "Maybe. I saw your YouTube video. The one about the manananggal?"

"That was you?" Coney asked. "I saw my view count went up by one. Thanks."

Daisy wasn't sure if she was joking or not. "I love your store," she replied.

"Yeah, it's great," Coney said. "Well, no. It's awful. A money pit. But I inherited it from my Grandpa, and I'm hanging in there. He loved this store so much and, no matter what, I can't let him down."

Daisy followed Coney's eyes over to a framed photo of an elderly man, she assumed was Coney's grandfather, on the wall of the store. The man looked very kind, and Daisy wondered how many years it had been since he had passed away. She felt a little sorry for Coney, who seemed to have some sadness troubling her underneath it all. Daisy decided she would buy something before she left.

"They mentioned my store on the Travel Channel once," Coney continued, with a smile. "It was pretty cool."

"Oh yeah?" Daisy asked. "That's awesome."

"Yeah, they didn't say the NAME though."

"Oh."

"Yeah, it was a guy from a ghost hunting show. A BIG one. If I told you who, you would know him immediately, but I'm not a name-dropper so I'm not gonna do it, okay?"

"Okay," Daisy agreed. "Sure, I respect that."

"But this guy came into the store, bought a couple things. Said he loved the place, and he'd do a shoutout on the show and tell people to visit. Well, on TV he only said it was a bookstore in Queens and then he didn't give the name. So, that didn't help with business or anything. Nobody's gonna make travel plans based off of that, are they?"

"I suppose not," Daisy said.

"He was gonna send me a signed headshot too and never did."

At this, Coney sat up straight in her chair, getting more agitated. "I didn't even want it! I don't watch his show! But he offered it when he was here, so I said sure. What was I supposed to say, no? But then it turned out he was out of headshots or whatever. So, he said he'd mail one instead. That was like a year ago. And nothing! Like I said, I don't even want it. It's just the principle of the thing. I don't care about him. I don't even believe in ghosts."

"You don't believe in ghosts?" Daisy asked, surprised to hear this from the owner of a paranormal bookstore.

Coney took a sip of her Diet Dr. Pepper through a straw as Devo's synthesizers wailed. "Oh, of course not," she replied, matter-of-factly. "Do you know that most Americans who believe in the existence of ghosts are Christian, even though the notion of a deceased soul being cursed to rattle around in an attic for eternity directly contradicts *The Bible*'s explicit explanation of the afterlife?

"You have to be ignorant of both science *and* religion to believe in ghosts and I'm neither. If scientists and theologians can both agree there are no ghosts wandering the Earth, then why would I listen to less-informed people? But the world is strange like that. People will base their whole life on a book and never get around to reading it. Still, I love ghost stories though."

Daisy was amused by Coney's rationale, and it raised her hopes that underneath the bizarre exterior hid a true expert who was immune to flights of fancy or an over-willingness to believe. The only thing better than a paranormal enthusiast who believes everything, was a paranormal enthusiast who wants to believe but is deeply skeptical and needs real evidence.

"Can I ask you a question?" Daisy said. "Have you ever heard of a manananggal showing up someplace–

"Mananan**GGAL**!" Coney corrected, accenting the end of the word more heavily than Daisy had been prepared to mimic in casual conversation.

"ManananGGAL," Daisy repeated. "Have you ever heard of one showing up somewhere other than the Philippines? Like, say, Europe? Or... America?"

Coney paused a few seconds to admire a section of the Devo song and then returned her attention to Daisy.

"A manananggal? No, never," she said. "These are rural folk tales from the provinces about creatures that perch on the roofs of bamboo shacks and hide their detached legs in groves of banana trees. It's meant to scare village kids and stop them from running off into the woods at night to get into trouble. They're local legends. They don't translate. It's like looking for the Loch Ness Monster in space. OOH! *Loch Ness Monster in space*. Actually, that's good. I would watch that. Maybe it's like the Loch Ness Monster has been captured in the future and is contained on a giant spaceship or something? Then it goes wrong? It writes itself. But they don't have the balls to do it."

Daisy pulled out her phone and quickly retrieved her last article from work to show Coney the image Pappas captured on the rooftop. She zoomed in on the photo and held it out for Coney to see.

"What about this?" she asked. The very action of showing the photo to Coney seemed like a minor victory. It felt like she was finally making up for her original sin of missing the Filipino connection to her story and was now connecting real pieces of her puzzle for the first time.

"Didn't you read the article?" Coney asked. "It was a hoax. That guy was bonkers."

"I wrote this article. I'm Daisy Scott."

"Then why am I explaining this to you?" Coney asked. She pushed up her glasses. "But if you're looking to learn about Filipino folklore, you did come to the right place. I'll put together a few of the essentials!"

Coney began dancing along with the music as she ran around gathering books.

"Why did you do it, Babydoll?"

"This one has a funny story about a viscera-sucking mother-in-law. You'll crack up!"

As two books became three, and three became a stack, Daisy started worrying about the eventual cost.

"Full disclosure, I'm throwing one of my books in here too," she said. "A girl's gotta eat. Don't worry. I'm legit."

"Let me ask you this," Daisy said, "Are there many serial killers in the Philippines? And would they ever use the symbolism of a manananggal for some reason?" Daisy corrected herself before Coney could have the chance: "Manan an**GGAL**," she added.

"Serial killers are mostly a U.S. thing," Coney said, returning to the sales desk with a pile of books. "There are sensational cases everywhere–there's crime in Antarctica–but is it common? The numbers show the U.S. is actually a *major* outlier per capita."

Oh. She's probably right.

Daisy felt a little foolish. It was easy to forget that daily mass shootings among civilians were a strictly American phenomenon.

Coney held up a trashy-looking paperback romance novel.

"Maybe a little something for those lonely nights?" she asked. "I won't judge."

"No thanks," Daisy said. "So you don't think there's any truth to this stuff? It's all just spooky bedtime stories?"

"I'll put it this way, uh, Daisy. There are things in the Philippines that make me glad I'm on the other side of the world."

"So, you do believe?" Daisy asked.

"I didn't say that. By the way, are you interested in driving lessons? I'm running a special."

"No thanks."

"But I can absolutely guarantee you there are no manananggals posing on rooftops here in New York City," Coney said.

She closed her eyes as Devo's bluesy solo wailed arpeggios. Daisy sensed it had been a great struggle for Coney to keep her attention from the song while speaking with her and those muscles were at their failing point. It was time to go.

"Will that be cash or credit?" Coney asked.

Later that afternoon, Daisy bought groceries, finally replacing her coffee filters, and then went to her regular hair appointment. Her friend owned a small salon and gave her a great rate on maintenance of her twist-out. She flipped through one of her new purchases, a book on mythology of the Philippines, as she waited on her friend to finish with another customer. She skipped to the chapter on "viscera suckers" to read about the manananggal and found most of the content seemed to be exactly what Coney had described–rural folktales. It felt discouraging.

Daisy tried to recall her initial impression of the monster. What was that first feeling when she'd learned about the manananggal? Ridicule. It looked like it was more of a danger to itself than anyone else. The idea of such a thing might be scary in an open field, but in a major city? She had started to take the idea seriously but now, with a primary source in her hands to remind her of the myth's true nature, Daisy worried she'd made a faulty connection somewhere.

When it was Daisy's turn, they changed the TV channel from the Spanish language program it'd been on since she arrived to a local news channel since she was a regular and they knew her preference.

She tried to hold her head still as she sat and watched news coverage about a subway incident. An elderly woman had been pushed onto the tracks and killed. A few soundbites from an activist calling for modernization of the subway system and the installation of protective barriers along the tracks was followed by a response from the city. They weren't doing any of *that* but intended to increase the police presence in the afflicted station.

Daisy's restless mind finally settled as the background noise of the hair salon and the television lulled her into a sleepy trance. Her eyes grew heavy, and she worried she might fall asleep in the chair.

Until the breaking news alert came on TV.

Oh no.

She watched in horror as the looped news package was interrupted by live reporters coming on camera to describe breaking new details emerging about the death of Dr. Brett Rhinelander's wife Kylie.

The woman had been killed in the same manner as Greggory's victims.

And they had a suspect–Dr. Rhinelander.

After rushing her friend to finish her hair, Daisy hurried home. A soft rain began to fall just as she neared her front steps. By the time she'd made it upstairs and thrown off her jacket, a rumble of distant thunder had erupted, and the smell of fresh rain began to fill her apartment through the cracked windows. She watched out her bedroom window as the sky opened up and flushed Long Island City with water. Daisy counted her blessings that the rain had waited until she made it home. That would have been icing on the cake of a bad day to get her hair drenched walking home from a styling appointment.

She camped out in front of her computer monitor and watched the news in a haze, absorbing all the details. Dr. Rhinelander had been arrested Friday night and released later, on bond. His wife Kylie, nine months pregnant, was found bleeding out in their locked 15th floor apartment. Her baby had been removed through a violent wound. A press conference was scheduled for the following afternoon but few other details were available yet. There was no mention of the other murders. *Yet.* But everything else lined up. It seemed Daisy had her answer.

Seeking some confirmation, Daisy decided to risk a text to Greggory to test the waters and see how much the situation had changed. She sent a short message asking if he was involved in the Rhinelander autopsy. Surprisingly, he responded quickly, but his text confirmed her suspicions.

Press blackout
Rules are the rules.
Sorry Daisy

It was over. "Her" case was solved already, and it would be reported on by anyone and everyone but her. There was no monster in New York City or even a Filipino connection to the killings. Pappas' video had been a red herring. Maybe the old lady in the park had been correct. A bird or bat escaped from the zoo and the sightings were unrelated.

New York being a melting pot, each person Daisy had involved had offered a unique interpretation of the mystery, filtered through the lens of their unique beliefs and cultures—manananggals, La Lechuza, extinct giant bats, escaped birds. She'd been soaking in a brine of lies, conspiracies, and misinformation. What happened to the skeptic inside her that knew better? Hadn't she learned these lessons years ago? Daisy had run all over the city on a wild goose chase, huffing the lore of

Southeastern legends like a fool, while real investigators had been out there getting the job done.

All along, the actual solution to the murders had been the very first thing she and Greggory had ruled out: a "Sloppy Jack the Ripper." That very minute, half the city was probably busy connecting Dr. Rhinelander with the trail of dead migrants.

Worst of all, she'd gotten her hopes up and had nothing to show for it. Where does hope go when you've built it up, but the intended outlet disappears? Hope can't just disappear overnight because it takes too long to form in the first place. It's sluggish and has momentum. Her work on the story had brought Daisy a little bit of much-needed self-pride and she still felt the afterglow of that mental shift, even as the cause for it had evaporated.

But what now? Back to the status quo again? She knew she would resent working at *The Believer* even more after this experience. What now? There would be no article. Her golden ticket had vanished, and she was right back where she'd started.

PART TWO

"Viscera suckers fear knives, light, salt, spices, ashes, large crustaceans, and the sting ray's tail. It is said that the most effective way to kill a viscera sucker is to thrust the sharpened top end of a bamboo [spear] into its back."

DR. MAXIMO D. RAMOS
The Aswang Complex in Philippine Folklore
Phoenix Publishing House, 1990

CHAPTER 13

A Formula for Violence

* * *

Daisy did not sleep well and woke up two hours before her alarm Monday morning. She spent the extra hours searching the internet for any new developments about Rhinelander. Mostly, she found old scandals resurfaced and past transgressions relitigated through the new context of a shocking tabloid homicide:

> "I always knew he was a psycho!"
> "Didn't he settle a sexual harassment claim?"
> "His commercials are so creepy"

A meme from months earlier resurfaced in which a zoomed-in clip taken from a commercial showed the surgeon's young second wife looking uncomfortable on camera with a dead stare. An added caption read "blink if you need help."

Daisy read all the comments on a controversial post suggesting the strange murder of the unborn baby was linked to the Freemasons and rituals in pursuit of everlasting life. Anonymous detectives questioned if the doctor belonged to a cult of devil worshipers. But there was still no talk of a connection between Rhinelander and the other murders in Queens.

Daisy considered the possibility that she was the only person yet connecting the Rhinelander slaying with the other unreported deaths. Her hope returned, burning at her insides. It was uncomfortable, like a physical urge, compelling her to take some kind of action before the opportunity slipped away. But at this point, what else could she possibly do?

Daisy reported to work earlier than usual and walked into a frenzy of activity. Almost every employee of the paper was in the office at the same time. Daisy did a quick roll call as she walked to her seat. Tiffani and Becky were there, of course, and Liam was accounted for. Brad was MIA as usual, but Tanner was perched on the side of his desk, flirting with Korrine, the beautiful sales manager, who was sitting in his seat. Korinne only showed up a few times a month, but Daisy had detected her presence back in the elevator thanks to her trail of perfume. Daisy eyed Jerry's door in the back of the room, which was open.

Good. Jerry's here.

She had some backup today. Daisy had a special relationship with Jerry. Maybe she wasn't his heir apparent at the paper, and maybe she had grown jaded about the job, but Jerry had always recognized her talent and been willing to fight for her. He probably saw a young version of himself in her, however mistakenly. Most of the crew faked an interest in the paranormal out of convenience and would just as easily jump ship to cover entertainment or sports. But Daisy shared Jerry's genuine passion for the content and, with a few drinks in him, he would readily admit that Daisy was the only writer who lived up to his old glory days.

"Didn't you wear that same Soundgarden shirt last week?" someone asked.

It was Liam, not minding his damn business.

"No, Liam," she said, taking her seat. "You're mistaken."

"I dunno…" he said.

Technically, he was wrong. But he was also sort of right. It was a different shirt, but the same design. Daisy loved her faded "Badmotorfinger" shirt so much that she'd bought a new replacement online. She'd intended to reserve the old one, now a faded gray, as a sleep shirt but had accidentally worn it to work since her mind had been distracted with murders and monsters.

"Oh, hi Daisy!" Korinne said, noticing Daisy had taken her seat.

"Daisy's an old soul, Liam," Tanner added, pulling his concentration away from Korinne to acknowledge Daisy's presence. "She likes that classic rock."

Everything that came out of Tanner's mouth, however innocent, landed like the taunt of a jealous younger brother. Tanner Vos had pastel cyan eyes set behind thick curtains of upper and lower eyelashes that put most women to shame. He was perpetually "unshaven" in a meticulous manner that required more daily maintenance than either shaving it clean or just growing a beard.

He wore his hair in a pompadour that curled over to leave waxy strands forever dangling over his eyes. He was constantly brushing the hairs away but would also sometimes leave them there intentionally, to look cool. Daisy couldn't stand it and would start brushing her own forehead trying to spur him into mimicry to get the hair out of his face.

Even Tanner's desk area was annoying. He had a printout stuck to a bulletin board that read "PRESSURE IS A PRIVILEGE" in Gotham Ultra.

"I like anything with a good beat," Daisy clarified.

"As long as it's old," he repeated. "But it goes with the territory. Daisy's the *senior* reporter here, going on thirty."

"Alright now," Daisy cautioned.

"You know what they say?" Tanner continued. "Thirty is the age you're no longer a young adult. Just an ADULT adult."

Korinne came to her defense, "Brad is older than Daisy, isn't he?"

"Who knows," Tanner said, "I swear. That guy is outsourcing his projects to somebody else. He's paying somebody in India $4 an hour to do his work for him. That's why he never comes in here anymore."

"Do you *think*?" Korinne asked, entering into gossip mode.

"I think he's double-dipping clients," Tanner said. "Maybe triple-dipping. He's got Tiffani scammed. And Jerry? He's too…"

Tanner looked back toward Jerry's office and lowered his voice before proceeding. "Jerry's too checked out to notice."

Daisy suppressed the inclination to stick up for the absent Brad. He'd been at the paper

even longer than her but she'd never liked the guy. He was rude, cocky, overly defensive about his work, and had heinous bad breath. Daisy didn't think Tanner was correct about Brad outsourcing his work, but his writing and video work had always been so lazy and uninspired that the change might go unnoticed.

"Daisy?" Korinne asked. "Have you been reading Tanner's *Ghosts of the Second Avenue Subway* series?"

"I haven't had a chance yet," Daisy lied.

"Oh, it's incredible!" Korinne gushed. "And upscale features like that really help me sell ads."

"We know haunted cheeseburgers aren't selling ads. Isn't that right, Daisy?" Tanner said, with a mischievous grin. "I have a connection at the Mayor's office," he bragged. "I lined up an interview with the New York City Public Advocate for my final installment. That's like the Vice Mayor. It's gonna be dope."

"It was the Virgin Mary," Daisy reminded him. "Not a haunted cheeseburger."

"Oh, that's right," Tanner said. It was a "sacred manifestation" at a burger stand near LaGuardia. Great work on that one."

Tanner was technically Daisy's direct competition at the paper, the other "investigative reporter." *The Believer* had always handed out fancy titles like candy, almost as a perk for employees at the bottom of the ladder. Not even Liam was an exception. A disagreement with Tiffani about his schedule had resulted in the bestowment of an official title for him–"Calendar Editor." The kid was 20 years old and about 5 weeks into the job, running errands mostly. Part of his busy-work involved managing the office's scheduling calendar, hence the inflated job title.

Daisy felt pretentious calling herself an "investigative reporter" when the lesser, but much more accurate "staff writer" would suffice at any similar publication.

Tanner felt differently. He proudly brandished and flaunted the moniker, in what seemed to Daisy like stolen valor, along with a second, equally preposterous title, for a position which technically didn't even exist–"Chief Photographer."

This latter distinction was a point of controversy among many in the office, not just Daisy, since Tanner only took photos for his own articles, and they were never particularly *good* pictures. However, he had lobbied for the extra title, pleading his case that it added additional prestige to the staff roster, and Jerry had relented. Of course, Tanner had immediately printed new business cards with the dual title looming large under his name.

Daisy could just imagine him, prowling the bars in Greenpoint with his sleazy blue eyes, thinking he's some kind of all-star, looking for a woman drunk enough to be impressed by his bullshit, and rolling out with the unstoppable line he'd practiced dozens of times in the mirror:

"I'm Tanner Vos, Investigative Reporter & Chief Photographer for a newspaper. What do you do?"

She shuddered at the thought of it. *It would fucking work too.*

Maybe Daisy couldn't stand him, but other women clearly disagreed. He always strolled into work with the quiet cockiness of a guy who just got laid that morning. There seemed to be a heavy momentum to the love lives of overconfident, semi-handsome assholes that allowed them to coast in perpetuity on mere fumes, so long as they never paused their womanizing long enough to let their confidence falter.

Chief Photographer?

He didn't even have a real camera. He used his iPhone. Modern smartphone cameras automatically set the focus, exposure, and lighting of your shot. They suggest improved framing and employ software tricks to counteract your jittery hands and poor impulses. You don't even have to push the button at the right moment anymore. Some people mistook these digital training wheels for previously unnoticed photography talent on their part. Their incredible, natural skills behind a camera suddenly announced themselves, and every shot they popped off was a work of art. Tanner was one of these people, an "artist" pointing his iPhone at the world and deciding the default image staring back must look nice because of his own trivial efforts.

Tanner clearly wanted Daisy to engage in a formal, professional rivalry with their reporting efforts, but Daisy just didn't care enough about him, or the work at this point, to bother.

"It's that time, people!" a man called from the back of the room, with the joyous, breezy command of a carnival barker or a movie pirate.

It was Jerry to the rescue.

Jerry Sambrook was in his late-forties, with graying blonde hair, but still had the excitable temperament of a child. These days he mostly wore Hawaiian shirts with khakis and boat shoes, no matter the occasion. He'd emerged from his office with a huge, manic smile to round everyone up for the weekly staff meeting. Although the group could easily pull up a couple extra chairs to fit at the bullpen, Jerry liked to make regular use of the conference room on the floor, which was available with the lease as an amenity. So, the entire *Brooklyn Believer* staff filed out the door and down the hall to regroup at the larger table.

After a rundown of current projects and an update on how far behind they were with the tip line, Korinne gave an update on sales numbers and then was allowed to leave. The rest of the meeting would be about publishing content and she wasn't necessary.

The remaining group moved onto planning the week's assignments and discussing how well current features were performing on the site.

"Your "clown doll" story was dead on arrival, Daisy. We need you to do better than that," Tiffani chastised, before pivoting from admonishment to delight as she ranted and raved about how many views Tanner's stories had been getting in contrast.

"Our boy's on a damn hot streak!" she gushed.

"Aw shucks," he said in jest, assuming a pose of sarcastic modesty before breaking character to brush the hair out of his eyes and finish with a perfectly-timed clench of his prominent jaw muscles for dramatic pretty-boy effect.

Daisy sat quietly and stared at the box of donuts someone had placed on the table which was totally untouched. They were all strawberry. What kind of madman buys an entire box of donuts and only gets strawberry?

Jerry was also zoned out, smacking on a wad of nicotine gum, a staple for the former chain-smoker since before Daisy had joined the paper. He'd had no trouble switching from cigarettes to gum but could never kick the gum habit. There was always an oversized lump of the stuff in his mouth. Daisy would watch and try not to laugh as he moved the wad around to different pockets in his cheeks like a hamster as he talked.

Daisy noticed Jerry looked a little sunburnt.

Good, she thought. *That's what he gets for being out there on the boat while the rest of us have been here working on his paper.*

Then, Daisy questioned herself. What was Jerry doing that was so wrong?

The man was self-made. No one ever gave him anything. No one at *The Believer* was highly paid given their indie status, but Daisy knew Jerry was paying everyone as much as he could, and that his own compensation, while multiple brackets above Daisy, was relatively meager compared to his peers. Jerry wasn't an out-of-control capitalist trying to conquer the world; he was a successful small business owner treating his people fairly, maintaining a careful balance, and enjoying the fruits of his work. Wouldn't she do exactly the same in his position?

It's nice to preach about collectivism but does the dishwasher really want to earn as much as a brain surgeon? What would they have to look forward to? Humans are built to want nice things and, if someone works twice as hard or as smart, it feels natural they should earn twice as much. Daisy sure wanted to earn more and would be willing to work her ass off given the chance.

But money is power, and power creates an unfair advantage. How does the "humble billionaire" pass on their humility to a child that can never know the value of money or experience the slightest sting of real suffering as they had? The legacy of wisdom can be unraveled by its own success in just one generation.

Good for Jerry, Daisy allowed. *But I've got my eye on you.*

It felt right to monitor his success as he grew richer. In a fair world, the harder the climb, the harder his legs would be working, but to Daisy it looked like the opposite.

"What's on the docket today, Tiffany?" Jerry asked.

"We're still playing catchup from last week, guys," Tiffani said. "Liam is still clearing out the inbox but we're gonna have our hands full. Somebody will need to go to Jersey City this week. We've kept that woman waiting too long already. We need to photograph the area of her home where she says she experienced the "Time Sli–

"No more time slips, Tiffani!" Daisy yelled, unable to contain herself. "These people just copy each other. None of us want to go to New Jersey for that! Even if it was real, it would be boring."

"She's right," Tanner agreed from the other end of the table. "That one's a dud, Tiffani. A couple pictures won't help it."

"My whole life is a time slip!" Becky said. "Next slip it'll be over!"

Becky reached for the box of forgotten donuts, the first to finally make a selection from the formation.

"Liam, did you buy these?" she asked. "Why did you buy all strawberry, honey?"

"I like strawberry," he said.

"But you didn't eat one," she observed.

"I don't eat donuts," he said.

"Well, if you had read the synopsis about the Jersey City time slips," Tiffani interjected, "that lady's story was kind of unique actually, but fine."

With the consensus turned against her, she moved on.

"We got a GREAT lead on the tip line," she teased. "A woman called in claiming her ex-boyfriend, who's a postdoc scientist at a university, has been turning animals INVISIBLE. Becky talked to her this morning."

"OOH!!" Daisy blurted out. "I'll take that one!"

"Be careful," Becky said. "That lady was crazier than a shithouse rat! And drunk on a Monday morning! Must have been on a bender all night long, I'd say."

Daisy was undeterred. "Who cares. I'll take it, Tiffani," she repeated.

The thought of a Fall stroll through a college campus to have a quick chat with an academic about his psycho ex-girlfriend, and whatever boring thing he's actually working on, sounded like a pleasant respite from her recent workload. Even more, this was the best kind of story–a completely *new* one.

The idea of "invisibility experiments" was so silly and specific that it guaranteed big traffic for the article, just based on the title alone. This assignment was the rarest of all breeds, an *actual A+* story.

"Tanner agreed to take that one," Tiffani said, with a satisfied glance in Daisy's direction. "We have something even better for you. It's a good spooky one. Your kind of thing. There's a mystery smell on a Q32 bus that no one can figure out. They say it smells like the same *Drakkar Noir* cologne a bus operator wore before dying tragically in the early 80s."

"Oh, come on!" Daisy yelled, "Jerry, let me have the invisibility one. I got stuck interviewing the pervert last week, for God's sake. Enough short straws."

"I know, I know…" Jerry apologized, smacking on his wad of nicotine gum. "We owe you one, kid, but this science thing is more up Tanner's alley, right?"

"Do you even know what quantum physics is, Daisy?" Tanner asked. "What are you gonna ask a scientist about? His favorite drummers?"

Despite Tiffani's spot at the helm, the paper still operated like a boy's club sometimes. Daisy wasn't allowed in all the good doors. But she saw the chance to make her move.

"Okay, then I want to go cover the Rhinelander press conference at the courthouse instead," she said.

"The plastic surgeon?" Jerry asked. "Why? Everybody's gonna be covering that nonstop. They already are. Why do we care?"

"Daisy, let's leave homicides to the real reporters," Tiffani added.

Daisy didn't even bother trying to defend herself as a "real reporter." But she wanted to attend the press conference and free up some time to finish what she'd started with Greggory. She needed to give the group something to convince them, but nothing more.

"I heard from my friend, the medical examiner," Daisy teased. "He doesn't reach out often. I can't say much."

"Oh?" Jerry asked, perking up. "About the Rhinelander stabbing? Did he give you something exclusive?"

"Look," she dodged, hoping that the tidbit she'd already divulged would be enough to seal the deal, "It's too early to say. But there may be an angle on this that isn't out there yet. Just let me look into it."

Daisy stood up and started pacing as she made her case. "Yeah, everybody's on the Rhinelander stabbing already, but it's sensational. It's gruesome. There may be more to this than meets the eye, and this is my beat, right?" she asked, looking directly at Tiffani. "The Queens Beat."

"Careful, Tanner," Jerry said with a smirk. "If Daisy Scott starts trying again, you'll be in trouble around here."

Daisy wasn't sure whether to take the comment as a compliment or insult.

"Try to get something useful," Jerry said.

YES! THANK YOU, JERRY, Daisy thought, as she sat back down, her heart racing from the impromptu adrenaline rush.

"Motive," he said. "That's what I haven't heard from the press yet. Was this guy always a psycho? Were there warning signs? Or did something turn him?"

"I'm sure there were signs," Tanner said. "There always are. There's a formula for violence."

That got Tiffani's attention. "Ooh, Tanner, that's good! *A Formula for Violence*. I love it! Daisy, that's the title of your article."

"Oh, come on. Seriously?" Daisy asked.

It wasn't a terrible slug, but it was pretentious for the topic, and she couldn't stand these little forced encroachments on her territory. Her articles weren't supposed to be team efforts, and she didn't appreciate the unsolicited help.

"What do you think, Jerry?" Tiffani asked.

Jerry was always the tie breaker. He stared quietly out the windows like he was thinking very seriously about the decision.

"Jerry?" Tiffani asked again.

"Sorry, what?" he asked.

"Daisy's article," Tiffani reminded him. She seemed a little frustrated he wasn't listening, but it had become par for the course with him lately. Even when he was in the office, his attention seemed to only come in little spurts.

"About Dr. Rhinelander," Tiffani said. "We're asking about the title. How's "A Formula for Violence" as the slug?"

"Yeah, great title, Daisy," Jerry said. "A little highbrow for the guy from the subway ads, isn't it? But it sounds good. Nice work. Run it."

"It's settled!" Tiffani agreed.

Instead of speaking up to reclaim his credit, Tanner just made eye contact with Daisy. His smug, satisfied grin seemed to say "I tossed you a scrap. Ha. Eat up."

The press conference was scheduled for 11:30 AM in front of the Long Island City Courthouse, walking distance from *The Believer*'s office.

Half an hour before the start time, Daisy gathered her belongings to leave. She dug through a cabinet drawer under her desk to locate an old "PRESS" lanyard with her name and picture on it and added the ID around her neck.

Worried about her audio recorder's ability to pick up voices in a crowd, Daisy went to *The Believer*'s storage closet and pulled out an old box of microphones. She found wireless mics and an attachment for a camera, but everything used XLR plugs and wouldn't connect to her audio recorder. Finding an adapter for her to use was one thing Brad, the tech guy, might have been useful for if he'd shown up that day. Instead, she decided to just take her chances with her usual audio recorder at a distance.

As Daisy was repacking the microphones in the box, she discovered something else she knew might be of use. It was an old long-range parabolic microphone. It looked kind of like a black laser gun with a big suction cup on the end and headphones attached. It was too large to fit in her bag without hanging out of it, and wouldn't record audio–she could only listen. She would also look ridiculous using it. But it was effective at great distances and Daisy was desperate enough for a break that it gave her some extra comfort to bring the device along just in case. It was nice to have extra cards up her sleeve even if she didn't have to play them.

As Daisy left the office with the weight of her equipment in her bag awkwardly pulling her to the left side, she heard Tanner's voice calling out from behind her.

"Hey, Daisy!"

She looked back to see him preening in front of the bullpen like a bargain bin James Dean.

"See you on the front page," he taunted, with a wink.

CHAPTER 14

Long Island City Courthouse

* * *

Daisy's walk down Jackson Avenue took less than ten minutes, but it felt like an hour thanks to the lopsided weight of the listening device. The strap of her bag sliced into her shoulder thanks to the extra weight, so she had to stop frequently to move the bag from one shoulder to another. The day was unseasonably warm, and she began to sweat due to her leather jacket.

She arrived at Long Island City Courthouse and found pandemonium in the small park at the steps of the picturesque landmark. Daisy passed by the historic courthouse almost daily and never gave it much thought beyond the fact that it offered some park benches and a fountain if she wanted a nearby place to sit outside. The area was usually quiet and sparsely attended except for people walking their dogs or stopping to sit under the trees.

Today was different. A large crowd was gathered in the park with heavy NYPD presence on all sides, even blocking off street traffic. Holding a press conference outdoors at the courthouse was a little unusual. Daisy guessed the department wanted the symbolism of the landmark behind them on camera. She'd assumed on the walk over that the outdoor, public location would grant easy access, but she started to doubt her plan as she reached the courthouse.

A blockade of cops was positioned between the curious crowd on the street and the inner sanctum of reporters and VIPs allowed where the action would happen. Daisy imagined the embarrassment of returning to the office ten minutes later, after being rejected from entering the conference. *Wouldn't that be something?* Tanner would mock her until the end of time.

No, if they turned her away, she would just idle around for an hour, maybe try out the parabolic listening device, and then lie to Tanner and say she'd gotten in.

Daisy held out her press badge as she approached the officers, hoping for the best. Did they know about *The Brooklyn Believer?* And if they did, would that help her? Or hurt her?

A cop leaning on a barricade looked down at her bag and saw the old-school audio equipment hanging out. That seemed to do the trick, because he gestured toward the gaggle of reporters behind him with a bored point of his thumb, granting her access.

THANK GOD.

Daisy worked her way through the mass of people to get closer to the foot of the building where a podium was set up. An NYPD seal on the front of the lectern was flanked by three microphones on each side, each branded with the logo of a news agency.

A couple dozen reporters and camera operators were lingering on standby, all staring down at their phones. The big-name operations were situated up front, with "lesser" writers like Daisy left to fend for themselves at the outskirts. There were too many people in her way to capture good footage, but she only planned on rolling audio anyway.

The assembly began a few minutes late, as a group of officials made their way to the podium in a procession. Most of the men and women were wearing well-tailored black or blue suits with NYPD pins on their lapels. The rest arrived in matching navy-blue coats with their names embroidered on the fronts. The jackets looked a little too warm under the bright midday sun.

"Good afternoon, everybody. Members of the media…" the NYPD Chief of Department began. "First of all, my heart goes out to the family of the victim…"

Around Daisy, anyone who didn't have a microphone or video camera pulled out their phone camera apps. Daisy began rolling a new audio file on her recorder.

The NYPD Chief introduced the bloated lineup of dignitaries encircling him, which included, but was not limited to: the Commanding Officer of the 108th police precinct, the Queens Investigation Chief, two case detectives from the 108th Detective Squad, a lieutenant from Queens North Homicide, and the Executive Officer of the Queens North Detective Bureau.

The Chief explained the mayor would have attended too but he was busy touring a robotics factory and couldn't reschedule last minute.

Daisy felt out of her league in that company. Seeing all the pomp and circumstance rolled out for the Rhinelander investigation brought a new sense of hopelessness over her.

She was an amateur poking around the big leagues, an imposter waiting to get caught and thrown out. She even felt a little ashamed of her presence there. Her self-confidence faltered to such a degree her knees got a little shaky and her hands became sweaty. What angle could she possibly find on the story that no one else in that crowd might see? Why was she there?

With the introductions finished, the Chief began reading from a script. "The information I'm about to provide, about a homicide that occurred here in Long Island City, Queens last Friday night, is preliminary and subject to change, as this investigation is still ongoing."

Three speakers took turns recapping events and explaining the operational picture from their area of expertise. Officers and paramedics had responded to a 911 call Friday night at 11:42 PM at the home of Dr. Brett Rhinelander, and found his wife unresponsive, with traumatic wounds, and she was pronounced DOA at the scene by EMS. The plastic surgeon had been frantic, intoxicated, rambling nonsense, and covered in his wife's blood, providing probable cause to make an arrest.

Other than specific details about the known sequence of events that night, the most important new detail for Daisy was the verbal classification of Kylie Rhinelander's death as a "stabbing homicide," a phrase repeated throughout the speakers' scripts.

Eventually, the NYPD listed the exact charges Dr. Rhinelander was facing—murder in the second degree, criminal tampering in the first degree, and criminal possession of a weapon in the fourth degree, an unrelated extra charge stemming from a pair of brass knuckles detectives found in the doctor's dresser drawer while rummaging the place.

"Cameras can't take the place of police officers!" the speaker exclaimed, making the case for increased NYPD funding. The appeal was met with strong applause from the other NYPD officials. After the clapping faded out, he concluded, "This investigation is ongoing and will be handled by the 108th Detective Squad with the help of Queens North Homicide. If anyone has additional information about this incident, please call Crime Stoppers at 1-800–

A motorcycle stalled in traffic somewhere nearby revved its engines and the angry sound ricocheted through the Courthouse Square. The Chief of Detectives paused his delivery in frustration and the crowd had a little laugh until the motor's purr became a war cry, indicating the distant light had turned green and the eager motorcyclist peeled away.

The speaker made a second attempt at delivering the Crime Stoppers phone number and seemed pleased after his success. "All calls will be kept strictly confidential," he finished.

The Chief of Department reclaimed the platform. "With that, we'll take some *on*-topic questions about this individual and about this case."

Daisy was stunned. There had been no mention of the other murders. "Stabbing homicide?" They'd mentioned medical examiner findings but nothing about toxicology or the biological agents Greggory had discovered in the teenage boy's corpse. Did they even know about his findings? Or care? Was Greggory still on these cases? Was Daisy the only person in New York City connecting the Queens murders with the Rhinelander case?

Her nervousness faded away and her determination returned, providing a floor for her deliberations to remain productive without sinking into self-doubt. Yes, she had to know her standing for sure. But now she was scared to ask leading questions in front of the gathering. She was in a crowd of hungry competition. She was a minnow in the sea with sharks, about to ask if they knew she'd found a feast somewhere. She needed confirmation without fumbling her damn scoop.

"You there–Jeff, up front," the Chief said, taking the first question.

"Is it true Dr. Rhinelander has been released on bail?" a reporter asked.

"Yeah, so Dr. Rhinelander has instructions not to travel..." he started. "Oh. Yes, he's out on bond," he clarified, realizing he'd buried the lede. "He posted bond. He was released early Sunday morning. He's in the city. We're in constant communication, but I can't give more information about that right now."

"Is that safe for the public," the reporter asked in follow-up.

Two questions. Daisy realized it paid to be one of the reporters up front.

"Perfectly safe. All indications are this was an isolated crime of passion. Dr. Rhinelander is not a danger to the public."

Isolated? This is unbelievable, Daisy thought.

She decided that if she got a turn for a question, she would ask about the other murders as vaguely as possible to gauge their reaction without giving too much away.

The Chief took hands for another question. Daisy raised hers enthusiastically, but another reporter up front was chosen instead.

"Is it true Dr. Rhinelander claimed there was an intruder on the night of his arrest?" she asked.

"So, for that one… I'm gonna turn things back over to our Chief of Detectives."

The suits shuffled positions, and the new official continued, "This is early in the investigation, a little over 60 hours since the incident. This is what I can tell you at this phase of the investigation...

"Despite Dr. Rhinelander's claims, there was no evidence of an intruder. The building is filled with cameras. Everywhere. The lobby, the elevators, the hallways. No extra fingerprints were found. Dr. Rhinelander was heavily intoxicated and in a state of emotional distress when officers reported to the scene, and he made some incriminating statements during his arrest. Officers were able to take Rhinelander into custody without incident."

Daisy found this new disclosure interesting. Rhinelander claimed there had been an intruder? Had he been bluffing to protect himself? Or could his claim have been true? What if the plastic surgeon wasn't the killer at all, only implicated in a slew of circumstantial evidence?

"Have you found a murder weapon?" a reporter near Daisy asked. They were beginning to take questions from the outer tiers.

The Chief of Detectives handled this question too. "The murder weapon is still unidentified at this time. We believe Dr. Rhinelander somehow removed or destroyed the murder weapon before officers arrived on the scene. We think there's a gap–between when the incident took place and when Rhinelander placed the 911 call, that's maybe twenty minutes. During that time, we believe he disposed of the weapon and our investigation is focused on that avenue right now. The weapon might be unusual," he added.

That last disclosure was the first recognition Daisy had noticed from the NYPD, on any level, that there had been anything less than textbook about the Kylie Rhinelander stabbing.

The Chief repeated the Crime Stoppers hotline number and urged anyone with knowledge of the case or the missing weapon to come forward, and then took hands for more questions. Daisy jumped in place to draw attention to herself, but they called on someone else instead.

"What about reporting that neighbors heard the couple have an argument that night, and rumors that Mrs. Rhinelander was intending to leave the doctor?"

"I can't discuss that. We have to balance the public's desire for information with the need to maintain the integrity of the investigation and due process. Next question."

Daisy tried jumping again. No luck. Somebody else.

"Is it true Dr. Rhinelander was having an affair with his secretary?" a reporter asked.

"Folks, we need to stay on topic about this investigation. Who else have we got?" he asked.

Daisy jumped and waved her arm furiously.

"You there—leather jacket."

YES!

Daisy cleared her throat. "Do you believe Kylie Rhinelander's death is related to the other similar deaths in Queens?"

"Similar deaths?" he asked. "Sorry, who are you with again?"

OH NO.

They hadn't asked anybody else what outlet they worked for. She had to announce it to the entire group? It was like a nightmare where she's naked in front of everybody.

"*The Brooklyn Believer*," she said.

There were audible chuckles from some of the reporters around her and the Police Chief had a good laugh at her expense too. "I told you *everybody* was here today," he joked to a detective standing near him, before leaving Daisy hanging and moving onto a new reporter's question.

"Next one, over here. White shirt, let's go."

With her shot taken and blown, Daisy listened to a couple more answers and then retreated to the rear of the group. She didn't sense the police were lying. It was possible they really didn't know about the migrant deaths. Or, at least, they hadn't made the connection yet.

Had everyone else missed what was happening right under their noses simply because they didn't have enough empathy for the victims to pay attention? It could still be her story to break, if she acted fast enough.

Daisy felt an electric thrill of anxiety. As a teenager, she would sometimes find an amazing thrift store t-shirt in her size but lacked the money to buy it on the spot. Instead, she'd have to wait for her next allowance, knowing the precious, one-of-a-kind shirt was out there in the world. Only she knew or cared about it, and yet she had no claim to it until purchased. So, anyone else could swoop in if she waited too long.

What had Dr. Brett Rhinelander seen that night? She needed to talk to him directly, but how? He was the most wanted man in New York City at the moment. It would actually be in his interest to speak with her; Daisy was probably the only person in town who might believe his story. But she'd never get close to him or his handlers under all this scrutiny, especially not with her laughable credentials.

As Daisy studied the sea of cops, officials, patrol cars, and flashing lights, she worked up the courage to do what she knew she must. She had to use the giant, ancient listening device she'd dragged along to get some actionable information, hopefully without attracting too much attention in a gathering of the entire Queens police force.

Daisy exited the park through the police perimeter and then crossed a side street where she rested her bag next to a subway entrance and some bike stands. A wave of second thoughts hit her as she began unpacking and assembling the device. She worried the general shape might look too much like a gun at a distance. This wasn't the environment to take such chances. She hoped the parabolic dish on the end and giant headphones attached to it would make it clear it wasn't a weapon if officers took notice of her.

Daisy turned on the device and aimed the large cone at the crowd across the street as she played with the settings. It was very powerful, but not designed for pulling individual conversations from a group like that. She tried homing in on the group of NYPD officials but there were too many people in the way, and she only heard indistinct chatter.

A pair of uniformed officers on the outskirts of the park seemed to be in an animated conversation. They were far enough from the podium she hoped she might be able to hear them clearly. One of the cops seemed to be ranting about something. He had a bulbous bald head, which looked too large for his frame, as if someone had squeezed his body like a balloon and squished extra contents into the top. He was jacked, with huge arms and veins throbbing in his neck. Daisy pointed her microphone at his tirade and listened in.

"Okay, expert," Bald Head was saying, "then let me ask you THIS. If Big Bird bangs his best pal Snuffleupagus, is *that* bestiality?"

"No," his friend said, "because they're both animals."

"Yeah, but Snuffleupagus is a mammoth," Bald Head retorted. "They're extinct."

"What's your point?"

"I'm just saying, I think if you bang an extinct animal it's gotta be bestiality. At least on a technicality."

"Maybe," his friend conceded, "but I don't understand why you're thinking about this kind of stuff, Roger."

Daisy moved on in search of more helpful conversation. She listened in on some other cops discussing what they'd had for lunch. Now and then, a passerby would get close to her on the side street, and she would try to hide the giant suction cup in her hand out of embarrassment. She looked like someone you'd see at the gates outside Roswell, New Mexico. The device was intended for someone's grandpa to listen to birds in the woods and she realized how silly she looked with the contraption in a busy area.

She caught a break when the Chief of Detectives was leaving. Daisy noticed him heading in her direction as he parted with the group, and then he paused to chat with some officials at the edge of the park, within earshot of Daisy's device. They were close enough she worried about being seen, so she crouched behind a parked car and rested the cone of the device on the hood to train it precisely on the small group of cops. She turned the volume up uncomfortably loud to make sure she heard everything.

"...for now, but the guy seems paranoid," an officer was telling the Chief of Detectives. "He's insisting on moving to a new hotel each night and registering under aliases."

Were they talking about Dr. Rhinelander? Daisy wondered.

"The guy's a jackass. I'm tired of him already. You're keeping tabs, right?" the Chief asked.

"Of course. He's moving to the Lexington Continental this afternoon."

"I don't feel good having him out there."

"You and me both. But he's not getting on a plane, and we've got eyes on him."

"Magnify yourself," the guy chuckled.

BINGO! They were talking about Rhinelander, and he'd be staying at the Lexington Continental Hotel in midtown Manhattan that night. But without a room number, that information was next to useless. It was a gigantic upscale hotel. She'd never get the information out of employees, certainly couldn't afford to bribe them, and couldn't exactly go floor to floor checking every room. Knowing Rhinelander's hotel without the room number meant she could go stand in the lobby of the building and know he was above here somewhere, so close, with all the answers. But she'd be unable to do anything about it. She needed more information.

Daisy moved her device around, trying to get the best signal in her earphones.

"His wife was pretty cute," the Chief said. "Did you see the commercials?"

"Yeah," the other guy said, "too bad she picked a snake. Plus, there's a pack of kids left behind. They're staying with the ex-wife for now."

"Can't stay with him," the Chief agreed. "That's for sure."

"Nope. One of the kids saw the mom's body that night."

"Oh, I hadn't heard that. Jesus," the Chief said.

"I also read on the internet he's in some sort of Devil worshiping cult. *Eyes Wide Shut* parties and shit like that. With other rich people. Imagine if you were one of his patients right now..."

"No, you can't believe all that shit you read," the Chief said. "The media's going crazy right now. He's like an infomercial guy so it's easy to believe anything."

"Well, he killed his wife, didn't he?"

"That's true," the Chief said. "Who knows? Maybe he'll get away with it. He hired a top law firm. Sounds like he's going all in on his defense."

"Who's representing him?" the other cop asked.

"Kristoff and Peters."

That piece of information seemed useful at first glance, but Daisy realized it was a distraction. Rhinelander's attorneys would repel a reporter faster than a New Yorker squashing a red lantern bug on the sidewalk. She needed to get to him directly and couldn't just camp out in front of his lawyer's office hoping he showed up. She still needed his room number.

"They're good, but it's a tough case."

"Yeah," agreed the Chief. "Plus, he kept changing his story. Animal attack, intruder... He's been quiet since he got out. Must be listening to his lawyers and finally clammed up."

Animal attack? Rhinelander's initial statement to police had been that an animal killed his wife? That's the sort of minor missing detail that could justify an article even if she failed to locate the doctor, but she couldn't print something as fact if she'd acquired it off-the-record through eavesdropping.

"How are those new jackets?" the Chief asked.

"Real nice," the cop said, "a little warm."

"What are you doing?" someone demanded.

Shit. Am I busted? Daisy wondered.

A woman carrying a Trader Joe's sack was gawking at her unusual audio gear. Daisy realized how preposterous she looked with the listening device and headphones, like a bumbling enemy spy in a comedy movie that just got spotted by the hero.

"I'm sampling the air quality," Daisy said, hoping that would bore the woman enough to leave her alone. "Don't worry about it."

"Is it bad?" the woman asked, looking worried.

"It's not fit for living creatures out here," Daisy said.

This thankfully scared the woman off. Daisy didn't care whether she'd believed the lie or just decided she was a psycho, so long as the woman was gone. But, unfortunately, hordes of people were beginning to stream out of the park, making it harder to use the device incognito. Daisy waited for a break in the exodus and tried to reposition her device on the car hood, but the Chief of Detectives had left already, and she couldn't spot anyone else left in the park who might know anything useful.

DAMN. Without Rhinelander's room number, Daisy could make it right to the finish line but not cross it. She had everything except the one piece of info she actually needed.

She packed up the audio device in her bag and made her return voyage to the office while juggling what she'd learned at the press conference in her head. Was there a way to use the intel she already had to acquire what she still needed? After a series of false starts, Daisy latched onto a kernel of a plan which she developed through to a series of concrete steps, leading to a *theoretical* triumph.

Daisy returned the equipment to the office and was pleased to find everyone except the stalwarts had left already.

Thank God for showboating slackers, Daisy thought, glad the less-tolerable crew had cleared out.

Daisy's plan required multiple bold swings and too many destinations—too many failure points—for her liking. Plus, it was almost 1:00 PM and she had to accomplish most of it before the close of business hours that day. But with no alternatives and a ticking clock, she had no choice. She was headed to the Upper East Side.

But first, she'd have to prepare. And that meant taking one for the team.

How far was she willing to go for this story? For Daisy's plan to have any chance of success, she'd have to do something unthinkable and soul-crushing.

What came next, she dreaded with every fiber of her being. But she was a reporter. And there was no other way to get the story. That's what reporters do, right? Anything it takes.

Daisy Scott was getting an emergency makeover.

CHAPTER 15

Upper East Side

* * *

Daisy's first stop after leaving the office was heading home to change clothes. She swapped her jeans and Soundgarden shirt for some unworn gray and black suit separates she'd been saving for a special occasion. Today was that day. Knowing her dingy Adidas sneakers would ruin her upcoming disguise, she considered trying out the two pairs of high heels from old weddings, gathering dust in her closet before nixing the idea and lacing up a newish pair of Nikes instead. She rarely wore high heels and her inability to walk in them would offset any style benefits they provided.

Daisy admired her reflection in the mirror, as she pulled the remaining tags off her new clothes. She had planned to leave her leather jacket at home, but tried it on over the outfit and it somehow elevated itself to match the dress clothes. It restored a slight sense of danger to her elegance that actually increased the appeal. Honestly, thanks to her hair appointment the previous day, she looked better than she usually did when she dressed up for special occasions.

But it wasn't enough. Daisy wasn't trying to look "good." Her con required that she look like a woman from a different walk of life, and it was the remaining final touch to her transformation which she dreaded–she needed makeup.

Daisy took the subway to Manhattan and got off at 59th street. She'd be running up and down the Upper East Side for the rest of the afternoon and had texted a friend asking for advice on an affordable place to get her makeup done in the area, which is an expensive neighborhood to be in the market for such things. Her friend recommended she try a MAC Cosmetics store, where she could buy some products and get help with the application.

Daisy entered the store, which looked like a black room filled with mirrors and bright color swatches. The girl working at the desk was young, maybe 18 or 19, and looked bored. Daisy explained that she never wore makeup but was headed to a special occasion.

"What products would give me the best bang for my buck, and how do I use them?" she asked. "Would you mind showing me?"

"I'd love to show you!" the girl exclaimed.

The employee said her name was Emilia and proceeded to explain to Daisy that it was her first week on the job and there'd been zero action so far. She'd barely even had customers. She had a lifetime of skills she was ready to demonstrate but they'd been languishing unrecognized. Daisy Scott would be her first proper test subject.

After multiple reminders to Emilia that she was in a hurry and only needed the basics, the cosmetics guru launched into a 12-point inspection of Daisy's face and gathered a pile of products selected for her skin tone. But instead of limiting her scope to the basics, Emilia seemed to rush through an entire primer on makeup products and techniques, all while applying the products to Daisy's face in demonstration–blush, concealer, lipstick, eye liner, eyeshadow. She even gave her fake eyelashes. It happened so fast she couldn't decline it.

Daisy felt like a race car driver on a pit stop with a team of pros doing major fix-ups and replacements in the blink of an eye to get the car back out in the race. Daisy wasn't even clear what some of the products were for, since Emilia went through it all so fast.

When Daisy's makeover was complete, the woman staring back at her in the mirror was unrecognizable. The stranger looked beautiful and like someone important, but it wasn't Daisy. She imagined how some family members might gush at seeing her dressed like "a grownup woman" for once, with makeup and all.

She had a dark thought. How many jobs might she have landed if she'd dressed like that? Her reflection looked like the sort of woman who would get hired instead of her. Hell, Daisy would probably hire her beauty queen copy given the chance. But it was only a costume, and she could never feel comfortable dolled up like that. She felt like a lumberjack in a necktie.

The person in the mirror looked like Daisy's evil twin. In a parallel universe, was another version of her romping around comfortably in lipstick and dresses every day?

Wait, I'm the one that's the slacker. Am I the evil twin?

The cognitive dissonance of seeing someone else's face in the mirror combined with the various perfumes and scents in the store began to give Daisy a slight headache and she was glad the makeover was finished already. But it gave her an idea.

"Do you know anything about perfume?" she asked.

Emilia's eyes lit up like she'd won the lottery.

Daisy left with multiple perfume samples lingering on her arms and neck, which combined into a powerful, noxious bouquet. She fretted over the scent trail she'd be leaving behind her but it would help with her disguise. With Daisy's metamorphosis into a cover girl complete, it was time to begin her operation, which would proceed in three phases. Phase

One required a trip to Rhinelander's attorney's office, which was walking distance from the makeup store, a few blocks uptown.

Kristoff & Peters law firm was located in a large office building. Daisy checked a directory on the wall in the lobby to locate the suite number and then joined a small group of people on an elevator headed up and hit the button for the 8th floor.

Her goal was to leave with a piece of paper or stationery with the law firm's logo at the top, which she would use as a prop to bluff her way through Phase Two. As a reporter, they would turn her away at first sight, so she couldn't just be honest about her intentions. Her logistics required some deception.

The surest way to leave the law offices with her prop stationery would be to book a consultation with one of their attorneys and pitch them a fake lawsuit. She would waste fifteen minutes of their time, but would leave with onboarding documents from the firm. It'd be too risky though; she'd need to prepare a made-up story, and it would create a paper trail for her activities. Also, a lawyer's office might be able to squeeze in a quick consult from a walk-in, but it would be at the very end of the day, best case scenario, and she didn't have time for that.

Instead, she would come at the problem from a different angle, one that would be deeply humiliating, but just might work. She was going to channel her inner Valley Girl and do her best impression of her co-worker Korinne Go: a modern, bobble-headed career woman, stinking of too much perfume, looking for a job.

Daisy exited on the 8th floor and followed signs toward the proper suite.

She wondered: had a guy been checking her out in the elevator? She was pretty sure. He'd been really obvious about it. Guys weren't usually so obvious. Was it the clothes and makeup?

There's no reasonable excuse to ogle a woman who just rolled out of bed, but maybe the act of dressing nicely created some pretense of solicitation in people's brains. "If you're trying, you must care what I think." Did guys assume that if a woman wears makeup and nice clothes it must be to impress them? Or that it was a signal she was open to advances?

Daisy felt a little new respect for Korinne. If she'd been ogled within thirty minutes of her makeover, then what did Korinne experience dressing like that every day? It was like she had forfeited some of her right to privacy simply by making an effort in her appearance. She couldn't disappear into the crowd or be a fly on the wall dressed like that. She'd worn t-shirts and jeans for so long she'd forgotten how many assumptions people made based on your clothes and appearance. It was a disheartening realization. But, as she entered the law offices of Kristoff & Peters, it reassured her about what she had to do next.

Inside the suite, the law firm's reception area was spacious and high-end. To Daisy, it looked more like a hotel lobby than a lawyer's office. A woman around her age was seated at the reception desk, under a large "Kristoff & Peters" logo, eating a salad. Daisy's plan was to dazzle the receptionist with a charm offensive and hopefully leave with some stationery that would serve her purposes.

How would Korinne make an entrance?

"How's it going, girlfriend?!" Daisy asked with a huge smile. "Mmm. That salad looks good. Where'd you get that?"

"Can I help you?" the receptionist asked.

Damn. This bitch is gonna play hardball.

Daisy felt flustered. She'd planned on chatting with the woman a little to butter her up. Now she had to jump right to it.

"I want to fill out a job application," Daisy said.

"Job application?" The receptionist put down her fork. "This isn't McDonalds. We don't have applications. What are you trying to apply for?"

"Uh, paralegal," Daisy said. "I want to submit my resume. That's what I meant."

"Okay, I'll take your resume. But we're not hiring right now."

This wasn't going according to the plan.

"I don't have it with me right now, darling," Daisy said. She wasn't great at doing characters and her attempt to sound like Korrine had accidentally veered into "southern belle" territory. She needed to pull it back together.

"Do you have some kind of handout with contact information? Like a pamphlet for interested candidates?"

"No," the receptionist said. "And, like I said, we're not hiring. But you can send your resume to this email address, and we'll keep it on file."

The receptionist handed Daisy a business card from a stack on her desk. The name said "Veronica." They were her cards.

Fuck.

The card wouldn't be good enough. She needed something larger. Over the top rim of the reception desk, she saw a stack of file folders sitting next to Veronica. They were wrapped in cellophane, freshly torn along the top. It was what they gave their clients. Daisy noticed the law firm's name was monogrammed in clear, proud letters on each folder. A folder would work perfectly, but Daisy would have to get the receptionist away from the desk long enough for her to take one.

"Who responds to the email on this card?" Daisy asked.

"I do," Veronica replied.

"You do?!" Daisy scoffed. "No offense, sweetie, but I didn't get to where I am by taking backdoors. Can you go get me a card for one of the partners? I need to do this right."

She hoped the secretary would pop into one of the attorney's offices to grab a business card off their desk. She'd have to be quick to not get caught, but she'd only need a few seconds to pull one of the folders from the stack.

"Fine, whatever," Veronica said. She reached into her desk drawer.

FUCK!

Of course she has other cards at the front desk. What now?

She'd already made her play and couldn't have a second run at it or try anything else. She was stuck and needed to improvise. Was there still a way to get the woman away from the desk?

She took the card from Veronica, which had one of the partner's contact information on it–MARTIN KRISTOFF, CRIMINAL DEFENSE. The receptionist gave Daisy a look which suggested their transaction was complete and she expected her to leave. Out of time, and nothing left to lose, Daisy tried the path of least resistance.

"Say, darling, could I have one of those folders over there to put these in?"

Veronica was so happy to get rid of Daisy she gave her two.

Daisy's next stop was Rhinelander's cosmetic surgery practice uptown, which was still open and seeing patients thanks to the other plastic surgeons on staff who weren't facing homicide charges. Phase Two was the riskiest step in Daisy's plan. If her tactics failed in the wrong way, she could land herself in hot water or blow her investigation.

She took a city bus about a dozen blocks north and then found Rhinelander Cosmetic Surgery on the ground floor of Park Avenue with a green canopy over the locked front door. She hit the buzzer for the receptionist inside to unlock the door for her. She waited a minute and then pulled on the door in case she hadn't heard the click over street traffic. Still locked.

She tried the buzzer again. She'd called Rhinelander's office before she left home to confirm they were open for business. Otherwise, all her errands and the junk on her face would be in vain. Daisy peered through the glass of the front door looking for any little clues she could see inside. The lights were definitely on. Why weren't they opening the door? She buzzed a third time.

Then, the door unlocked with a powerful clack that Daisy could feel through her face pressed against the glass, and she was startled enough from the surprise to yelp out loud. She glanced around to make sure no one had seen the ordeal and then hurried inside.

Rhinelander's office wasn't what she had expected. The guy's commercials were so shameless and tacky, she'd anticipated grandiosity and gimmicks. Instead, the interior design was very boring and unremarkable compared to any other upscale medical clinic. There was a seating area for patients with a nice rug over the hardwood floors and a Scandinavian sliding door she guessed led to the other rooms.

The receptionist looked exasperated. She was blonde, maybe mid-twenties, and talking on the phone.

"I'd be glad to reschedule you with another doctor, sir" she pleaded. "But December is our earliest date. I'm sure you can understand this is an unusual situation. I'm sorry, can I put you on hold one minute?"

The receptionist switched lines on the phone and was so distracted she didn't seem to notice Daisy, even as she got within feet of the desk. It explained her wait at the front door.

"Rhinelander Cosmetic Surgery, how can I help you?" she asked the next caller.

Daisy waved her hand a little and the woman finally saw her, giving an embarrassed shake of the head and raise of the eyebrows to suggest, "Sorry, one second…"

"No comment," she told the caller. "I said no comment! I'm sorry!"

The receptionist switched lines, resumed her business with the first caller, and then hung up the phone, finally looking at Daisy.

"Can I help you?" she asked.

Here goes nothing, Daisy thought.

"Sorry to bother you, I'm with Kristoff and Peters," Daisy said.

"Oh," the receptionist said. There was visible relief in her face. "What can I do for you?"

So far, so good.

"I have some forms–

Daisy was interrupted by the phone ringing again. She could tell the receptionist was itching to answer it.

"Go ahead," Daisy said.

"Rhinelander Cosmetic Surgery, how can I help you?" she asked. Her lips scrunched into a snarl as she listened to whatever was on the other line. "No comment!!"

"God, I hate reporters," she said, hanging up the phone. "They're like leeches. The phone is ringing non-stop. How am I supposed to work?"

"Life in the fast lane, right?" Daisy said. "I'll be quick. Martin gave me some more forms for Brett to sign," Daisy said, brandishing one of the folders she took from the law firm. "It's super urgent. He said to go directly to Brett's room at the Continental, but things have been so crazy, I forgot the room number."

Daisy went in for the kill. She leaned in close enough to ensure her perfume drifted into the poor woman's nostrils.

"Girl, can you help me out?" Daisy complained with a sad frown. "I'm new at the firm and I'll look so stupid having to ask Martin the room number a second time. I already made a couple little mistakes and now they're being extra hard on me."

"Oh, I know the feeling... It's 312, isn't it?" the receptionist asked.

"Of course!" Daisy bluffed. "312 sounds right. I really appreciate it. So how are you doing?"

"Ready to quit," she said. "I didn't sign up for this. It's insane. We shouldn't even be open right now. Every call is someone canceling an appointment or trying to get information."

The phone rang again.

"Don't worry," Daisy said. "People have short attention spans. This will blow over pretty soon and that phone will stop ringing. Thanks again. I'll get out of your hair."

"What did you say your name was?" the receptionist asked.

Daisy handed her Veronica's business card with a huge smile and made a beeline for the door. Given the quick timeline of events, it was unlikely Rhinelander's receptionist had ever met Veronica, but she didn't want to stick around to find out.

As Daisy exited the building to Park Avenue and walked south, she repressed the urge to run away like she'd just robbed a bank. She almost expected to hear screams of "STOP HER!" coming from behind until she'd put a couple blocks distance between herself and the scene of the crime.

Daisy repeated the room number in her head as she walked so she wouldn't forget it, eventually stopping to save the digits as a note on her phone. She had a good memory and would never forget just three digits, but this was one of the most important numbers she would encounter in her entire life, so she was taking every precaution possible.

Daisy hopped on the subway towards the final destination in her plan, Rhinelander's hotel, the Lexington Continental in midtown. Phase Three. It was time to land the plane. Daisy was less anxious about the final stage of her operation. She had been most nervous about the fake persona and improvisation required to get her to that point. All her efforts had been to achieve access she wasn't supposed to have. Now, she could fall back on a tool unavailable to her in the first two trials–the truth.

As Daisy approached the ritzy hotel from Lexington Avenue, she began to subconsciously anticipate the cold looks she normally got from entering a place like that in t-shirts and jeans. Instead, the doorman gave her a huge flirty smile and swung the door open wide, not just allowing her access, but almost suggesting an entitlement on Daisy's part with the decisiveness of the action. The doorman didn't question for a second that she belonged in that hotel. She was still grappling with the ramifications of her makeover. It had the power to both giveth and taketh away.

Daisy ignored the front desk and headed straight for the elevator bays. She hit the button and jumped in the first elevator that reached the lobby, only to find that a room key was needed to access any of the higher floors.

Damn. What now?

She exited the elevator and scrolled on her phone so she wouldn't look suspicious while she thought of a way to get upstairs. She couldn't just pretend she was a guest to get a key from the front desk. Security and protocols were too tight. She could always buy herself a room for the night, but it'd be a big blow to her pocketbook.

A group of young business people approached the elevators carrying boxes of equipment along with suitcases. They paused in front of the elevators to rest their loads while they waited on a ride up.

"Need some help with that?" Daisy asked, as an elevator reached the lobby.

"Oh, no! That's okay. You're so nice," a woman in the group said. They began piling their things through the open doors. "Everyone here is so nice. They said New Yorkers would be rude!"

"Did they?!" Daisy asked. "I'm going up too. I don't mind. Let me grab one of these."

Daisy grabbed the biggest box still left on the ground, heavier than it looked, and immediately regretted her choice. She swapped the box for another that was thankfully lighter, and then joined the group forming on the elevator, cradling the box in her arms.

"Do you mind hitting the button for the third floor?" she asked.

"Hey!" a cheery guy in the group said, "that's our floor too!"

"Wow, imagine that," Daisy said, hoping it was a fast elevator.

"This hotel is really something. I can't wait to see the room!"

Daisy and the team of executives reached the third floor and began filing out into the hallway.

"Which way are you going?" they asked. "We're 309 & 310."

Shit. That sounds close to Rhinelander.

She checked the sign on the wall to see which direction she needed to go, hoping the room numbers split wings in just the right place. No luck. They were staying a couple rooms away from where she was headed.

"I'm going the other direction," she lied. "Let me drop this off for you."

Daisy deposited the box at 309 and said her goodbyes, declining an invitation for a night on the town bar-hopping tourist traps with the group. She turned down the hall and headed in the wrong direction until she was well out of sight and then hid, leaning on the wall, listening until she heard the business people make plans to regroup in the lobby in an hour and they finally entered their rooms. She waited an extra moment for safety and then resumed her plan.

Daisy knew once she had Rhinelander alone, she could convince him to talk to her. But even there at the finish line, standing at the surgeon's front door, she still had to be cunning. This was a man on high alert for threats, deceit, and ulterior motives. Every action he was taking to stay under the radar was to prevent a reporter like Daisy showing up at his door asking more questions. She needed a way to ease into her true intentions.

Daisy noticed an unpleasant smell in the hallway. It was a familiar odor, something common and cheap, not what she would expect in a fancy hotel.

What IS that smell?

She looked around her and found the culprit. Ketchup. It was late afternoon and used room service carts waiting for collection in the hall were beginning to turn ripe. It gave Daisy a terrible idea.

She gathered three of the carts together and began an obscene game of preparing one cart to look unused. She poured water from multiple glasses into one and wiped the lip smudges from around the brim. She cleared all debris from the cart and wiped the surface clean before returning a big metal lid to one of the large food trays and refolding some napkins to place at its side. She found some unused butter packets and gave them a prominent location in the tableau.

Daisy reflected on her handy work. It looked fucking awful. She was pretty sure she had mixed two different kinds of juice, and the result looked too brown to be appetizing. Her fake food cart would never fool anyone for even a minute. But half a minute? That might be all she needed.

Daisy rolled the cart to door 312 and took a deep breath. She wasn't dressed like room service. In a movie, she would find a convenient closet nearby with extra wardrobe on hand. Or maybe mug someone to steal their clothes. It would depend on the type of movie. In real life, her options were more limited, and she'd have to make do with what she was already wearing. She removed her leather jacket and stuffed it inside the bottom of the cart. She wasn't dressed like a housekeeper but, without the jacket, she could easily pass as a high-level administrator at the hotel, perhaps the sort of person they'd send to check on a VIP under special circumstances.

It was time for one final act of boldness. She knocked loudly on the door. "Room service!" she called through the door.

Unlike her experience at Rhinelander's office, she didn't have to wait long for a response this time.

"Who is it?!" he demanded. "I didn't order room service!"

"I know," she said. "I'm with the hotel. The food is complementary. I know you don't want to be disturbed so I brought it personally in case you're hungry."

There was no response. What was he doing? Probably analyzing her through the keyhole, trying to decide if she was trustworthy. Daisy batted her eyelashes at the door, trying to look pretty and harmless.

"I am a little hungry," he said, before opening the door.

I'M IN. THIS IS IT.

Daisy rolled the cart into the room, which was generously sized for Manhattan, with a King bed and a seating area against the back windows. Dr. Rhinelander immediately began poking at the contents on the tray, so Daisy tried to position herself between him and the food until she could get the door closed behind her.

Dr. Rhinelander was middle-aged but had jet black hair. *Dyed?* His physique implied a man who hit the gym regularly but something about his coloration and the drape of his skin suggested a bit of hard-living and hedonism at play as well.

"I'm starving now that I think about it," he said. "I can't even fucking go outside without the paparazzi burrowing up my asshole. I need to get a disguise."

"Now there's an idea," Daisy agreed.

Rhinelander grabbed the glass of mystery juice backwater and took a sip.

"What is this crap?" he asked. "Normally they ask your order instead of just guessing. What did you bring me?"

He pulled the lid of the food tray to reveal a disgusting pile of half-eaten leftovers.

"What the fuck is this?!" he roared. "Who are you?!"

"I know you didn't kill your wife!" Daisy blurted out.

She'd hoped to ease into her reveal, but he was too agitated for that. If Rhinelander called for security, she might have bigger problems than her plan falling apart–she could get herself arrested.

"There have been other murders, and I know you didn't do it. I want to prove it."

"Who are you?" he spat out.

"I'm a reporter."

"Jesus Christ," he said.

"Off the record, if you want," she pleaded. "I swear it. I just want to know what really happened."

"You just want fucking clicks and attention, just like everybody else."

"You told the cops there was an intruder," Daisy said. "What if I believe you?"

"Reporters will say anything to get a scoop. Who are you with?" he asked.

Daisy avoided answering.

"I'm friends with a medical examiner," she said, "who's tracking *other* murders just like this one. Unless you're a serial killer, I know you didn't do this."

"I didn't kill anybody!" he screamed. "I didn't kill my fucking wife!"

Rhinelander sat down on the bed. The anger seemed to wash away and what remained of him seemed defeated.

"I would never hurt Kylie," he said, in a calm tone. "Or our baby. Why would I do that? I was deep in the process of trying to rebuild my life with her. After everything I'd built before had turned to shit. Do you know what that's like?"

"I do," Daisy said. She wasn't lying.

"Kylie and the baby were my new beginning. And now my entire life is over. Everything, gone. In one night."

"Let me help you, Brett," Daisy said.

"Who are you with?" he asked again.

She had to tell him.

"*The Brooklyn Believer*. But listen to me—

"Oh, for Christ's sake!" he yelled, rising from the bed again. "Leave me alone. I was taking you seriously there for a second."

It was now or nothing. The events Daisy had been tracking in Queens suggested a connection between Greggory's murders, the death of Kylie Rhinelander, and the sightings of "manananggals" in New York City. Daisy had the image from her Pappas article queued up on her phone. She could unlock it and show the photo to Rhinelander. If the phenomena were actually related, say a serial killer dressed as a manananggal was responsible for the slayings, then the image on her phone would immediately convince the doctor she could help.

But if she was wrong, and had been conflating the murders with totally unrelated hoaxes, then showing Rhinelander a picture of a fake monster would only confirm his suspicions about her, that she was a tabloid hack looking to make his story even more sensational with a make-believe supernatural twist. She'd be thrown out immediately.

Her instincts told her to show him the image.

Daisy unlocked the screen on her phone and showed Rhinelander Pappas' image of the manananggal.

What was that look in his eye? She tried to read the man's face.

Analyze carefully. You only get one chance.

What is he feeling right now? It's not surprise. ANGER?

He's seen it before. Holy shit.

"I can't talk now," he said. "I took matters into my own hands. I've got something cooking. I'm fighting back. We can meet tomorrow; I'll know more then."

YES!

She had access. Daisy allowed herself just one second to marvel at her accomplishment. Her plan had worked. Every step of it. Maybe with a few wobbles along the way, but Daisy was a reporter talking to the most wanted man in the city and making plans to meet again. One way or another, she would gain exclusive information on this case now and have a story. It was no time for celebration yet, though. So many things could still go wrong.

"Where will we meet?" she asked. "Can I have your cell number?"

"No," he replied. "I'm using a burner. Just give me your number. I'll contact you when I'm ready. When I have something."

DAMN.

That development wasn't ideal. Daisy hated to leave the next step in his hands. What if he never contacted her? It had taken a full day's work to track him down, and he kept switching hotels. Could she even do it again? None of her tricks would work a second time. She hadn't saved anything for the swim back. She had no choice but to trust the guy. She tried reassuring him again for safety.

"Okay, but do contact me," she said, writing down her phone number. "I really want to tell your side of the story."

"Yeah, right. You reporters are something else."

"Hey, every reporter in town is tearing you down," Daisy said. "If I want to stand out, I need something different, right? Well…"

She waited for his eyes to meet hers before finishing. "I wanna stand out."

"I'll text you," he said. "Now get out of my fucking room. Your perfume reeks."

That night, as Daisy was preparing to microwave some dinner, she noticed a powerful hunger pulling at her from inside. Daisy had an unpredictable appetite. She rarely ate breakfast, and her level of hunger always seemed proportional to how active she was, a trait she considered a blessing. During sluggish winter months, when other people packed on the pounds, Daisy's metabolism seemed to slow, and she ate smaller quantities of food. During warmer months, when she was running all over town, she would make up for lost time with the frequency and proportions of her meals.

The frozen dinner seemed an inadequate reward for all her hard efforts that day. Daisy called in an order to Court Square Diner and threw on her jacket a few minutes later to go retrieve her takeout order.

She returned home and spread her bounty out before her on her desk: a baked meatloaf entree with side salad, baked potato, and steamed vegetables with bread and butter. Daisy put on a YouTube video as background noise and began demolishing the food. She applied a generous dollop of warm butter to each bite of bread with her knife before it reached her mouth. The meatloaf was moist and drenched in savory gravy. She'd planned on only eating half the food and saving the rest for later, but with two thirds of the meatloaf slices and most of the baked potato already gone, she decided to clean her plate instead. There were no leftovers. Even the broccoli vanished, leaving only the empty potato skin and a few pieces of drenched lettuce on the table.

Why was she so hungry? Her body had needed those calories. It had *demanded* them. But it didn't feel like she was simply replacing lost energy from her day's exertions. That meal hadn't been about refueling. It had been preparation. She was nourishing herself for what was still to come.

CHAPTER 16

Museum of the Moving Image

* * *

The next day was Tuesday, so Daisy didn't have to report to the office and was free to focus on her story. The second she woke up she grabbed her phone and checked to see if Dr. Rhinelander had messaged, but there was nothing waiting for her but a text from her mom and email notifications.

She made coffee and scrolled social media to kill time. A local outlet was touting an expose interview with Rhinelander's ex-wife, promising further scandal and intrigue. The video promo suggested the surgeon was a menace to the public who should be behind bars and that anyone in his presence was potentially in danger.

If that's true, Daisy thought to herself, *I did a really stupid thing yesterday*.

Around 11:30 AM Daisy still hadn't heard from Rhinelander. She cursed herself for not insisting on getting his phone number as well. Maybe she'd never hear from him. He'd probably changed his mind about speaking with her after she left. Or maybe he mentioned Daisy to his lawyers, and they told him to stay away. Or even worse, maybe one of the receptionists she'd spoken with had mentioned a suspicious visit. Her plan could have fallen through a dozen different ways without her even knowing about it. All she could do was wait, and hope.

Daisy tried watching TV to keep her mind off the clock. She found AMC was running a marathon of the *Nightmare on Elm Street* series in honor of Halloween. She watched about half an hour of *Dream Warriors* but compulsively checked her phone screen every few minutes.

She decided to step away from her phone and instead lie down on her bed to read another book from Coney's store. After an hour of learning about shape-shifting pigs, Filipino witchcraft, and a dwarf creature called a *Dwende*, her eyes began to feel heavy, and she almost fell asleep. Then, her phone finally chimed.

She retrieved her phone from her desk and read the message with blurry eyes, initially feeling a pang of disappointment since the notification appeared to be spam. She started to delete the message before realizing what she was looking at:

MUSEUM OF THE MOVING IMAGE 2PM

The text was meetup instructions from Dr. Rhinelander.

What the fuck? she wondered.

Museum of the Moving Image? Why does he want to meet at a museum?

The location seemed like an odd choice. If he was trying to lie low, why meet at a public place instead of his hotel? Was he still changing hotels every night? That seemed troublesome and expensive. He couldn't keep it up for long. Did he not want Daisy to know his next hotel? Or maybe he hadn't checked in yet because it was too early. The only consistency in Rhinelander's choices was that he seemed to be sticking with indoor locations.

But why that particular museum? Wouldn't a plastic surgeon choose an art museum? The Museum of the Moving Image wasn't necessarily the first stop on any tourist's visit compared to the MET or the Natural

History Museum but it housed some interesting exhibits on the history of film and television, including old cameras, stop-motion sets, and some retired muppets. Daisy had been to the museum twice before—first, on a school field trip as a kid, and again with some friends a few years prior. The museum was well-trafficked, so it seemed like an unlikely place for an incognito meetup with a reporter.

As Daisy prepared to leave for her meeting and slipped her drumsticks into her bag, she thought again about what Rhinelander's wife had said in the interview promo, that her ex-husband was a "menace to the public." What if she was right? Was it possible Daisy was misreading the situation? Was she ensnaring herself in the web of a very dangerous man under the illusion she was on the cusp of a big story?

Daisy arrived at the museum, a white three-story building that filled an entire block, about ten minutes early and waited in the lobby for Dr. Rhinelander. She'd hoped he would be waiting for her, but he was nowhere to be seen.

2:00 came and went without the doctor showing, so Daisy went ahead and purchased an adult admission to the museum, making sure to get a receipt so *The Believer* could reimburse her later as a work expense.

Daisy proceeded into a large inner lobby area that looked like a post-modern airport lounge, stark futuristic white, filled with tables and seating areas. The back wall of the large white room was all glass, revealing an attractive tree-filled private courtyard on the other side. The museum seemed lightly attended since it was a weekday and the lounge was empty except for a couple of ladies with strollers seated near the entrance and a guy sitting at a table in the back against the windows.

The man made eye contact with Daisy. It was Rhinelander.

"Why the Museum of the Moving Image?" Daisy asked, as she took a seat next to the surgeon.

Rhinelander was unshaven and wearing a baseball cap pulled low over his eyes. There was a manila folder sitting on the table in front of him. For a guy going through one hell of a life crisis and trying to act covert, Daisy couldn't help but notice the doctor had inexplicably taken the step of drenching himself in musky cologne before leaving the hotel that morning.

"I picked it at random off the map. It's perfect," Rhinelander said with a laugh. "It's the last place anybody would ever look for me. I don't give a fuck about this stuff."

He spoke rapidly and seemed very satisfied with himself. He was amped up. Daisy wondered if he was on drugs.

"Ok first off," he said, taking command of their meeting, "show me that picture again. The one from yesterday. Where did you get that? What is that?"

The man's general mood was a strong contrast to the previous day. He was manic, even buoyant, despite occasional paranoid glances out the window to his side to check the tree-filled courtyard for any visual changes.

Daisy didn't have the image ready on her phone like in his hotel room, so she opened her camera roll to find it again. As she scrolled, Rhinelander stared out the window. Daisy noticed something odd. For the most part, his eyeline wasn't checking the ground. He didn't even seem to be looking for suspicious people. He was watching the treetops.

"Is this what you saw that night?" Daisy asked, showing him the photo.

"I don't know what I saw. I was drunk," he explained.

But he took Daisy's phone from her and studied the image carefully, pinching with his fingers to zoom in on details. The man disappeared in thought, seeming to forget she was even there as he analyzed the photo, trying to solve a problem in his head. For a moment, Daisy could imagine a competent surgeon hiding under the layers of cartoonish, treacly branding.

"Tell me what actually happened that night," Daisy said. "What *do* you remember?"

He paused for a moment, staring out the glass, like he didn't want to look away. Daisy bet he would conduct the entire interview looking outside instead of at her if he could. Finally, he turned his head back toward her, but his eyes first spot-checked the manilla envelope on the table before meeting her gaze.

"Wings," he said. "Teeth, claws. That's what I remember. It was an animal attack, okay? At least, when I first woke up, that's what it was. It was like you're in a tent in the woods and you wake up to see a bear fucking mauling your wife. You know, fucking crazy. Nature asserting itself shit. But I remember seeing a face… That's the thing that just kept driving me crazy. I know I saw a fucking face that night. I don't know how they did it, but a person did this. I saw it."

As he spoke, Rhinelander would nervously glance toward the entryway each time a new person entered the lobby or made a quick movement on the other side of the room. Otherwise, if his eyes weren't on Daisy, they compulsively drifted back to the skies outside.

Daisy had him recount his entire story in full, providing every little detail he could remember. She learned his trust in her only went so far, as he would not consent to having the interview recorded. Instead, Daisy had to rely on her memory and hope the details were too important for her brain to forget.

Rhinelander explained the "missing time" prior to his 911 call in which police believed he had disposed of the murder weapon. He had been fully awake and shocked into a semblance of sobriety by that point in the night and remembered his deliberations clearly. He'd been too dumbfounded by the attack to know how to proceed. Whatever had killed his wife, had escaped the way it had arrived, through the open balcony, without leaving the slightest trace evidence of its presence.

After attempting to stop Kylie's bleeding, he'd taken a seat on the floor, catatonic, with the phone in his hand, trying to decide what to say to the 911 operator.

Had an animal entered their apartment?

Or an intruder?

It was the most basic detail of his account, and he hadn't been sure what to say. Rhinelander had realized, even before reporting the crime, that he would be implicated by the circumstantial evidence.

He'd been "fucked. Completely and totally fucked," as he put it.

When the police and paramedics arrived, Rhinelander had told them that an intruder wearing large bat wings had come in through the window and stabbed his wife. The claim hadn't gone over well, coming from a drunken fixture of local tabloid drama.

"One thing I remembered was that the killer held onto the headboard of the bed during the attack. Like for support or something, I don't know. I told the police they should dust the back of the headboard for prints."

"Did they?" Daisy asked.

Rhinelander shook his head with anger.

"They asked me if they should dust for WINGS too. Those jackasses. They got me out of there quick, so I don't know what they did afterwards. I was trying to help them, but they didn't care. They think I'm crazy. The cops…"

He paused, likely remembering his various exchanges with the police.

"Yeah, but that's me!" he said. "Right? Just a crazy guy who killed my wife, right? Right?!"

His voice was rising now, loud enough to draw attention across the room, and Daisy didn't feel frightened per se, but her pulse quickened slightly with the healthy tinge of alarm that presents itself to a reasonable woman, when in the company of an unhinged lunatic who is starting to sound a bit aggressive. Screaming at her wasn't a great way to prove he didn't kill his wife in a fit of rage.

"Yeah, but get THIS…" he continued. "I decided I wouldn't go down without a fight. If we're in fucking "burn it all down" times? Then what have I got to lose? Okay. How's that? So, I hired a private investigator. And not some schmuck either. An expensive guy–this is my fucking life on the line here. I got a top guy. Used to be with the government, high-clearance level shit…"

Rhinelander had calmed down now, his anger replaced by the satisfaction of a coming retribution. He paused a second to see if Daisy was impressed before proceeding.

"Anyway, I had MY GUY dust for prints. Actually, I asked him to do DNA first, cause I figured that'd be even better, but he said there wasn't time, or there might not be a match, or something like that. Whatever. But I had him do PRINTS, right…"

He didn't continue further, instead glaring at her with an unblinking "just scored a home run" victory stare, which somehow dared her eyes to leave his and finally acknowledge the manila folder on the museum table.

Daisy completed the ritual and looked at the folder, which appeared empty to her eyes. Whatever the contents, it couldn't have contained more than a couple pages.

Satisfied with the dramatic pacing of their exchange, Rhinelander grinned and tapped the folder with his finger, but didn't yet open it.

"And he got a fingerprint match," he continued.

Then his smile widened, and seemed to turn a bit sinister as his eyes tightened accordingly. She noticed he had bleached, unnaturally white teeth behind lips that were so thin as to be nonexistent. You couldn't even call the guy "Fish Lips." The comparison would be a compliment compared to the truth.

His smile disturbed her. She understood human faces very well. She often met people during the most subjectively frightening experiences of their lives. Of all the possible configurations of human facial expressions, many were rarely ever seen, because they only presented themselves in the most catastrophic, rare, and unlikely scenarios.

In horror movies, actors are usually tasked with mimicking a particular human emotion—*paroxysm of terror at imminent death*—which the actor has almost certainly never seen in real life. Some emotions are everyday occurrences, but others are "one-percenters."

Rhinelander's expression was very abnormal, a rarity, one she couldn't quite place. It was a giant red flag. It was the sort of look you ignored at the risk of failing to prevent harm somewhere in the near future.

Was I wrong about this guy?

He had the same gleam in his eye as brutal men who've shed all pretense and have prepared to feast on spectacles of pain and violence. Daisy was looking at a man who had lost it all in the blink of an eye–his wife, his career, perhaps his entire life. And whatever he had in that folder, might not undo the wrongs he had experienced, but he clearly believed it would provide the means for an extraordinary vengeance.

"Every *immigrant…*" he said, pronouncing each syllable of the word for emphasis, "that's nationalized here in the U.S. gets *tagged*."

Immigrant? Daisy wondered. *What is this?*

He began slowly picking at the top of the folder with his finger on the table as he glanced out the windows again for a quick inspection.

"PRINTS," he added, more firmly, looking at Daisy again now to make sure she understood. "And I GOT the bitch," he announced triumphantly.

At last, he carefully, with the skill of a surgeon's hands, opened the folder. He treated the contents with reverence, as if they were top secret nuclear codes. He removed a single 8.5x11 sheet of paper and laid it on the table, theatrically spinning it around, before sliding it in front of Daisy. There were only a few lines of text.

Daisy picked up the page and read the contents–a name and an address.

The name, CATALINA CORDERO, meant nothing to her.

But the address…

Daisy felt acid in her throat, the hot burning rush of terror experienced in fleeting doses sometimes, during brief moments of panic. But this feeling didn't dissipate. Instead, it only grew stronger, beginning to turn Daisy's stomach. A wave of nausea produced gushes of saliva in anticipation of an eruption. She swallowed the pools gathering under her tongue in desperate gulps, like tossing pails of sea water from a sinking boat, commanding herself to believe that the sensation would go away, and she would not throw up in a museum lobby.

Daisy realized Rhinelander was still talking across from her and that she'd missed all of it in her daze. She stared down again at the paper and reread the address…

IS THIS ONE REAL?

The little girl inside of her was not *asking* for an answer this time, but *begging*. And, for the first time, the voice was not hopeful. Instead, it wanted reassurance that this story was FAKE, just like all the rest.

She was scared.

Daisy had been to the address on the paper. In fact, she had stared lovingly at the borough of Queens from the high perch of its rooftop. The address Rhinelander's private investigator had found was "The Impluvium," across the street from Danny Pappas.

CHAPTER 17

Gantry Plaza

* * *

After Daisy's meeting with Rhinelander, she was in such a mental fog that, on her walk home afterward, she could barely remember what she had even told the man after he'd given her the printout. She'd instructed him to go to the police with his new evidence–she recalled that much–but she had no idea how the fingerprints had been collected by the P.I. or if they'd be admissible as evidence.

Rhinelander wasn't thinking clearly. Daisy thought again about the dangerous look in his eye. "Burn it all down times," he'd said. She hoped he wasn't planning to confront his suspect on his own. Who knows if his investigator had even found the right person. Daisy wasn't sure whose safety she would fear for if he approached the woman, his or hers? The one thing she was certain of was that no good would come from a coked-up, vengeful Dr. Rhinelander knocking on the door of that lady's apartment in Astoria.

Daisy wondered if she should contact the police herself. If Rhinelander's P.I. was correct, they had identified a serial killer. Or at least a plausible suspect. Daisy's detective work had brought her to the finish line. She had her story. She could stop.

If Catalina Cordero was the killer, and Daisy poked her beehive trying to get confirmation, she might put herself in great danger. And unnecessarily. The police could take it from there, couldn't they?

But what did she have to give them, really? Just a name and address provided unofficially by an alleged murderer. The cops would never believe her. Even if she had more solid proof, they might not listen. She was a young, black female reporter for a hack paper whose name closed doors instead of opening them. If she tried to explain the situation, they'd probably think she was as crazy as Rhinelander.

No, whatever she did next, she'd have to do alone. Or at least in her own way.

Daisy contemplated her new findings and tried out new theories in her head as she walked. This Cordero woman seemed to be tied to both the "wing" displays and the series of bizarre murders. What was her plan? Her purpose?

Daisy wasn't ready to admit anything supernatural was afoot. Sure, she was tempted like never before. But all she really had to operate on was hearsay and imagery. It could all be smoke and mirrors. Deaths, "giant bats," and a woman who may be responsible—those were the facts. Beyond that? Daisy knew that human intuition was powerful, but primed to find patterns, even where they don't really exist.

The very idea of an asian woman being a serial killer seemed both nonsensical and sinister. It defied the usual expectations. Maybe a Filipina killer could hide in plain sight. How carefully did she cover up her activities? Was there evidence inside her home? Was there a way to get confirmation Catalina Cordero was the killer without putting herself in danger?

By the time Daisy reached her apartment, inspiration had struck. She concocted a foolproof way to get herself in and out of the woman's apartment and safely interrogate her in person. All without putting herself in harm's way.

There was just one flaw with her plan, and it was a big one. It required bold assistance from her timid friend Jordan.

Daisy texted Jordan that she had a situation and needed to meet with him ASAP. He was working at a customer's home but said he'd meet her afterwards at Gantry Plaza, a long strip of manicured parks, docks, and recreational spaces along the Long Island City waterfront.

Later that afternoon, Daisy waited under the infamous Pepsi Cola sign, their designated meetup point, for Jordan, who was running late. Daisy took a deep breath, enjoying the smell of the water and the crisp October air. On the walk to Gantry Plaza, Daisy had felt hot and regretted wearing her leather jacket, but the breeze by the East River was a bit chilly, so it had worked out in the end.

The park was crowded but not to the point of annoyance. A steady flow of people streamed by as Daisy admired the scenery. A gust of wind breathed life into the treetops, sending a scatter of orange leaves into the breeze like golden confetti. The leaves in NYC were beginning to display their Fall color spectrum. Only splashes of stubborn green were left, peppered among the yellows and oranges of the landscape.

Take your time. Daisy thought. *Put on a big show.*

Most people thought of Autumn leaves in terms of death; the dying green leaves were putting on a final performance of false vibrant color in a defiant last stand before withering away to forgotten brown crisps on the ground. But Daisy knew enough about leaves to understand that they changed color in Fall because chlorophyll production shut down, removing the organic green tint of energy production. This meant, in a sense, the Autumn leaves were actually revealing their *true* colors to the world at last.

October was a special month for Daisy. It was a time of both reflection and rapid change. At the beginning of the month, the NYC sun sets in the evening but, by the end, it sets in the afternoon. October was a time to celebrate life and to mourn the dead. It was a time to shine a light into the shadows and see what looked back at you.

Jordan came around the corner in an awkward, hurried walk about ten minutes late, apologizing from a distance as he closed in.

"It's okay, dude!" she promised. "Relax."

"I didn't expect to hear from you so soon. Is everything okay? It's not your parents, is it?" he asked.

"No, no. They're okay. I'm okay. It's not an emergency. It's not like that. I just need your help. Let's walk."

The pair strolled along the waterfront, mostly in an awkward silence, as Daisy searched for discussion topics before easing into her request. If they'd broken the ice the other night, it seemed like it had refrozen since then. Daisy felt even more uncomfortable than she had at Heather's party. Then, she'd had the extra confidence that came from a couple drinks and a Dracula costume.

Jordan wasn't any help. He shuffled along next to her, quietly watching the water as they walked. She could tell he wanted to open up but was nervous. Jordan always seemed to be second-guessing himself. She felt it inhibited his full potential. Still, who was she to judge? Jordan had a career, a *real* one, with a foreseeable future. People will still need electricity in twenty years. What will journalism look like then? Will it even be a viable profession? Daisy imagined herself at age 49, bagging groceries. Unlike her, Jordan had been practical with his second act.

Daisy knew the trick to get Jordan talking. He didn't hate conversation; he just didn't need it in great quantities. He had a high threshold and preferred high-quality topics over small talk. When they had been younger and as close as siblings, Jordan had ranted for hours about his favorite topics. He would go on forever. It was like he had unused thoughts bottled up, with so few people who passed his test to hear them, that they exploded out like a volcano once he got started.

"Do you remember that chick from high school…" Daisy asked. "What was her name… the girl who talked with a Mid-Atlantic accent for some reason, like she was trying to be Katharine Hepburn in an old movie?"

Daisy remembered Jordan had a crush on the girl back in high school and had mentioned her a few times over the years when they were drunk.

"Misty?" he asked.

"Yeah! That was her," Daisy said. "Did I ever tell you about the time in college I saw her passed out drunk on the sidewalk at like seven in the morning? On St. Marks?"

"What?! No, tell me," Jordan said. "Misty??"

After recounting her story, they paused under a willow tree to watch traffic on the river. The water was active, with a ferry sitting at port nearby and a large barge working its way closer from the distance. A variety of smaller watercraft were visible in both directions.

The roar of engines and screams grabbed their attention. Daisy and Jordan turned to see a formation of jet skiers approaching. As they passed, Daisy saw all the jet skis had custom banners attached to poles, implying the stunt had been coordinated to deliver a message of some kind, however they were going so fast all the banners were tangled in the swirling wind behind them, so the deeper meaning behind their jet ski joy ride was ultimately illegible to the gawking crowds along the shore, who could only muster a quick moment of surprise before losing interest and returning to their business.

Daisy tried to explain her problem to Jordan without sounding insane.

"Let me ask you something," she began. "All of the dumb, crazy stuff I've printed in my paper. Or any of the silly stories you hear–ghosts, aliens, monsters. Have you ever thought that any of that stuff could be real?"

"My views on these things haven't changed since we were kids," Jordan said. "It's because of stories that people believe those things. Not the other way around. No one ever saw "flying saucers" in the sky until movies put that notion in their heads, and then everyone started "seeing" them."

The old Jordan was starting to come out. He was more comfortable now, focused on the discussion instead of himself.

"If you hear a sound at night and can't explain it…" he continued, "in reality it could be anything. You don't have enough information. But we want answers for everything, explanations, so we fill in the blanks with the only material we have left to work with when the evidence runs out— fiction. "It's a ghost!" But the truth is, sometimes we just don't know. I realize that's too boring to get clicks for *The Brooklyn Believer*. I mean, no offense, your job is more interesting than mine, for sure, and I love that supernatural stuff too. But it's not real."

"I know that," Daisy said. "I'm not talking about demons or boogeymen in the mirror. I don't think Bigfoot is hiding out there in American redwood forests, somehow eluding all detection. You have to be really dedicated to that cause in a world with billions of cameras.

"But could something unimaginable be living deep in the rainforests? At the bottom of the ocean? Remote, inhospitable areas? There are still some undiscovered patches of this planet, and scientists are discovering troves of new species every week, often with huge implications for our understanding of biology. We could still discover a new animal tomorrow that's so bizarre they'd have to throw out all the textbooks and start over. It's highly improbable, but not *impossible*."

"You're starting to sound like a timeshare salesman," Jordan said. "Are you trying to convince me? Or yourself?"

"I'm not trying to convince anyone. My job is to investigate this stupid stuff and so it's nice to have a second opinion on it now and then, from someone on the outside."

"What's going on with you?" he asked. "And why this emergency meeting? I haven't seen you act this stressed since you started your job."

How do I phrase it? she wondered.

"Jordan, I need to ask for your help with something. And it's a big ask. I don't have a right to ask for this, honestly. I haven't been a great friend to you lately. But I don't have a choice. I need help. YOUR help."

"What is it, are you moving? Sure, I'll help. Whatever it is, Daisy, I'll help. You haven't done anything wrong. We've just been busy. That's life. And you're the one who always texts me. You're the one who always reaches out, never the other way around. I know I'm bad about that. It's not because I don't care. I just get busy and forget, I guess. I wish we were still close."

"So do I," Daisy said.

"It's hard to make new friends as you get older. I shouldn't screw around and lose the few good ones I still have. Tell me about your problem, and let's fix it."

"I need you to do me a favor, and it involves your job," Daisy said.

"Oh, Daze. Listen…"

Daze. He was reverting to his old nickname for her to soften the blow.

"I can't do anything about your electric bill," he said. "I'm a technician."

"No, it's not that. My bills are paid, you asshole."

Jordan laughed. "Then what?" he asked.

"I think this woman is a serial killer so I need to tag along with you and pretend to be an electrician so I can poke around in her apartment a little," she blurted out in one breath.

"What the **FUCK**?!" Jordan yelled.

CHAPTER 18

Catalina Cordero

* * *

"Explain just one more time why you can't just call her?" Jordan asked from the driver's seat of his faded white and blue Con Edison van early the following morning.

"I need to get in there, Jordan. I have to. It's my big break. This is like my Watergate."

"Dude," Jordan said, "I saw one of your stories recently, and it was about an old lady who thought a dead rat was her Chihuahua and carried it around in her purse for a year. I love you, but…"

"This is different. I told you. This is a legit story. You've seen the news about Rhinelander. If the killer is actually this Cordero woman, then this article will put me on the map."

Since Jordan had insisted electric technicians don't have the right to enter customers' apartments when they're not home, even in "electrical emergencies," and because they didn't know Catalina's profession or schedule, they'd taken a gamble that she worked 9-5 and timed their visit for early morning. If they missed her, they'd have to try again that evening, and two attempts would look even more suspicious.

Daisy was wearing a pair of Jordan's navy-blue work coveralls, which were so large on her body she had to roll up both the legs and the sleeves. She steadied a bright blue hard hat on her head and admired the extra touch in the passenger seat visor mirror. It was a little big on her head, but it made her look official.

"What do you think?" she asked Jordan.

"You don't need a hard hat. We're going inside an apartment. You'll look ridiculous."

Daisy sadly returned the blue hat to the area behind the seats where she'd found it.

Jordan stared out the side mirror of the van, like he expected to get caught already, before they'd even done anything. Daisy had rarely seen him this nervous. She worried he might have a panic attack.

"Thank you for this, Jordan."

"Sure," he said. "It's no big deal. What's the harm? Worst case, I'll just lose my career and my benefits and my retirement and my entire sad little life."

"No, sweetie," Daisy laughed. "That's not the worst case. We could also get arrested. Or murdered."

"Jesus, Daisy! Don't even say that out loud. Are you sure this is safe?"

"Of course," she said. "I would never put you in danger. Just stay calm. If we do this right, I think it's actually the safest way to get proof without her ever knowing."

"Okay, so what do I say again?" he asked. "We're here to check your gas line?"

"No, I'll do all the talking except for the technical stuff. You stay quiet and make it look real. Only jump in if she asks a question you know I can't bullshit my way through."

"Got it. What's her name again?" Jordan asked.

"Catalina Cordero."

"Are you sure you have the right apartment? That doesn't sound like the name of a dangerous killer. I picture more like a... tango dancer."

"I'm sure. Trust me. But, whoever answers the door, just stick to the plan. We only have one shot at this."

"Okay. Daisy, please, please, let's make this quick."

"We will. But you're a nervous wreck. I need you to settle down and focus. Whatever you used to do to get rid of your nerves before a Pathfinders show, I need you to do that now."

"That was different," he said.

"Yeah, that was even scarier. We used to play in front of hundreds of people."

"*Sometimes*," Jordan corrected.

"Sometimes," Daisy agreed. "But you never freaked out on us. Not once. Your head always straightened out the second you hit your first note. Why?"

"It felt different. You put a bass in my hand, and I'm not just Jordan anymore. I'm the bass player. I've got a job to do. I'm busy."

"Well…" Daisy said, handing Jordan an oversized wrench from the floorboard. "You've got a job to do."

"We're not gonna need a wrench either, Daisy."

Jordan had wanted to make contact with the front desk of the building before proceeding upstairs, but Daisy knew better and had advised against it. This wasn't a real work call. They didn't want to leave a paper trail from their visit.

The duo stood outside their target's apartment and Daisy took the last minute of calm before the storm as an opportunity for a final pep talk.

Jordan was the best bass player Daisy had ever played with. He wasn't the most technically impressive or the most soulful. He wasn't flashy. He wasn't a specialist, or the best generalist. But Jordan was one of the most responsive musicians she'd ever had the pleasure of playing with. As a rhythm section, they'd been the core machinery of The Pathfinders. Once they'd locked in together, Jordan's bass work entered a kind of dance with her drums. They called and answered, syncopated, rose and fell together, anticipating each other's next moves.

That was the magical, loose improvisation she needed from Jordan now.

"Think of it like one of your adventure shows. Like Star Wars," Daisy said, as she knocked confidently on the door.

"Star Wars?" he asked. "I don't like Star Wars. Do you mean Star Trek?"

"Yeah, that one."

"I still don't get it. What does that mean? They're in space."

Daisy wasn't sure what she had meant either. She just thought it would inspire him. She was spared from explanation by the sound of the door unlocking which snapped them both to attention.

"Remember," Daisy said. "I do the talking. Just have my back."

The door opened and they were greeted by a stunningly beautiful Filipina in nursing scrubs. To Daisy, she looked a couple years older than herself and Jordan, maybe early thirties. Then again, maybe not. Maybe she was a little younger and just looked mature for her age. It was hard for Daisy to tell.

"Sorry to bother you, Ma'am," Daisy said. "We're with Con Ed. We need to check your gas lines real quick."

"Oh..." the woman said.

Daisy noticed a spark of irritation in her tone. It looked like they had interrupted her while getting ready for work. *Good.* That was the plan.

"We've got the whole building to check," Daisy said. "We'll be quick, we promise."

"If you must," Catalina said, opening the door for them.

Catalina's apartment was odd. The first thing to catch Daisy's attention was the smell. The room smelled clean–too clean– overpoweringly so. The sting of fresh bleach, or a similar cleaning product, hung in the air, like Catalina had just bathed the place in disinfectant from floor to ceiling right before they'd knocked on her door.

The living space was bright and airy, thanks to open curtains on a large balcony, and the room was filled with plants. Bright colors caught Daisy's eye from every direction. Catalina seemed well-traveled, based on the variety of globe-trotting souvenirs on display.

All of those details tracked with Daisy's ideal of a young woman's home. But the overall vibe of the place was wrong. It felt more like one of her Grandma's friend's living rooms, maybe just more upscale. If she didn't know better, Daisy would assume she was in the home of a wealthy old woman. Nothing in particular made her feel that way, just the sum of the parts. It was the dated vanity, the filled China cabinet. There were hand-carved collectibles and unusual trinkets like glass figurines. There were floral patterns, plus dated reds and greens where there should be blues and whites. It was all just… wrong.

Perhaps Catalina lived with an older relative. It would explain the assortment of antiques around the room—clocks, rugs, paintings, and super old furniture.

"Okay, let's get this over with," Daisy said to Jordan.

"Sorry, may I use your restroom?" Jordan asked Catalina. He looked down at the floor, avoiding Daisy's eyes.

"Sure, it's the door on the left," Catalina said.

"Thanks!" Jordan replied, cowering off to the bathroom, leaving Daisy alone to fend for herself with Catalina.

Goddamnit, Jordan!! Daisy thought.

As Daisy's nose acclimated to the bleach, she began to detect the larger range of fragrances in the room. She noticed the odors of rose and baby powder. Catalina even smelled like an old lady.

"So, the gas line is in the kitchen? Correct?" Catalina asked.

"Yeah, that's right," Daisy said. Thankfully, she knew that much.

"Proceed," Catalina said, pointing to the kitchen.

Daisy led the woman into her kitchen, which was small, but everything was brand new. Catalina had a large double sink with a fancy faucet.

"I always wanted one of these nice sinks," Daisy said. "I know they also spray for cleaning dishes. Do you spray with it?"

"Sometimes," Catalina said.

Would I actually cook if I had a nice kitchen and a fancy faucet? Daisy wondered.

Catalina's refrigerator doors were a blank slate except for four city magnets—Chicago, Los Angeles, New York City, and Philadelphia—the type tourists bought at gift shops. This detail helped Daisy realize what had been bugging her about Catalina's home since she'd walked in—there were no personal touches. Daisy had seen no photos anywhere, no evidence of family, friends, travel, or even the woman's triumphs. Where were the photos of friends' weddings or Catalina posing in front of a tourist trap? Where were the old trophies and mementos? Daisy had come for a sense of who the woman was and what made her tick, but Catalina's apartment offered nothing of the sort. It might as well be a vacation rental.

"Here it is," Daisy said, kneeling next to the oven and opening up her tool bag. She wasn't sure what to grab. She started with a tape measure since that seemed like something a technician would use.

"Looks like we've got three..." Daisy estimated, "Three and five eighths. Not bad. We like to see four though."

"I would offer you something to drink, but you said you would be considerate with my time," Catalina said.

"Yes. I'm hurrying. You work in medicine?" Daisy asked.

"Yes, I'm a nurse," Catalina said. "At a hospital."

Something about Catalina herself didn't add up for Daisy as well. Here was a middle-class immigrant, in the nursing profession. Perfectly ordinary. And yet the cadence of her speech, and the certainty behind it was misplaced. There was a boredom Daisy detected, under the surface, that Catalina was attempting to disguise. If Daisy closed her eyes and listened to Catalina's voice, she heard the song of high society, or wealth, or power. Daisy formed a mental image of an undercover princess in a romantic comedy, temporarily slumming it in disguise as a normie, not fully convincing in the effect.

Daisy's guess was that Catalina came from wealth. Or perhaps she had a VIP boyfriend and jetted off to exotic locations every weekend. Despite the scrubs and basic makeup, there was an underlying glamor to the woman that seemed conspicuous. Perfect hair, flawless skin. Her teeth looked like "after" photos on the websites of dentists. She could easily blend into the collage of any millionaire's Instagram reel. Throw Catalina in a designer dress and she could walk the red carpet with celebrities and models.

Catalina wasn't *cute* or *pretty*. She was *stunning*.

But it was a hard, intimidating kind of beauty. Some people manage to look like supermodels while still seeming approachable. Not Catalina. At no fault of her own, there was a coldness to her features that, while otherworldly, meant only the world's most attractive people could possibly feel confident sharing space with her. Daisy recalled quotes she had read from attractive celebrities who were lonely and struggled to get dates. No one thought they were good enough to ask them out. Daisy wondered if Catalina suffered from the same issue.

"Do you like your job?" Catalina asked.

Lost in her thoughts, Daisy almost responded instinctually about her real job as a reporter. That would have been unfortunate.

"Oh sure," Daisy bluffed. "You get to meet lots of interesting people. Like yourself of course."

She tried redirecting back toward Catalina. "Which hospital do you work at?"

"The brand new one," Catalina said. "Cortelyou. We're still in the process of getting the site fully functional but it's been partially open to patients for a couple weeks now. State of the art. I love it."

Daisy thankfully didn't visit hospitals very often but was aware of the new development thanks to her habit of watching local news. The new hospital was privately funded by David Cortelyou, a mega-billionaire.

The site was part of a rapidly expanding "disruptive" medical system of hi-tech medical facilities.

"Actually, this might interest you," Catalina continued. "I was talking with some of the electricians the other day…"

Shit. If this woman knew even the first thing about electricity Daisy was about to be busted on the spot.

"They were discussing how the building had multiple discrete electrical systems," Catalina said, "so the critical branches and emergency systems are totally independent of the other installations. It got me wondering. Is this building's wiring setup the same way? Or not?"

What is Jordan doing in that fucking bathroom?

Daisy tried stalling.

"Well, I only do consumer work, of course. That's not guys like us doing construction in a hospital."

"But do the basic systems work the same?" she asked.

"Well…" Daisy stammered. She was stuck. Did Catalina already know the answer? Would she know if Daisy was wrong?

"It just depends," Daisy said, pretending like she was too busy working behind the oven to fully participate in the conversation.

What was that look in Catalina's eye? A "gotcha?"

"I haven't worked at a hospital before," Daisy added.

The bathroom door opened, and Jordan finally slinked into the kitchen to join them.

"Almost *done* here, bud," she said to Jordan. "Looks like I could have done this one on my own, huh?" Daisy hoped he got the message.

"Sorry about that," Jordan said. "Too much coffee."

Daisy packed up her bag and the group made their way back to the living room. Thanks to Jordan's timidity, the visit had yielded nothing of use. She hadn't even had a chance to take pictures.

"Hope we didn't make you late for work," Daisy said.

She noticed Jordan was frozen in the living room and went to retrieve him.

"What are you doing?" she asked. "Let's go."

"They're so cute!" Jordan said.

Daisy looked down to see a mother mouse in a cage, feeding a litter of babies in a bed of pine chips.

"Wow, they're adorable," Daisy told Catalina. "Are you breeding them? Or was the pregnancy an accident?"

"I'm breeding them. But they're not pets," Catalina laughed. "They're for him."

She opened a pair of curtains next to the table to reveal a display case with an enormous reptile habitat, elaborately decorated with multi-level rock features, plants, and a scenic photo backdrop. At first Daisy was confused, because the giant tank looked empty. What was the point? Then her eyes noticed the change in pattern along the top of the rocks. A huge bearded dragon was sprawled across a rock ledge near the top of the habitat, basking under a lamp which spanned the top of the tank.

"This is *Gimbal*," Catalina said.

Daisy had once encountered a pet snake at a house party but had never seen a pet lizard in real life. She personally found the reptile house to be the most boring part of the zoo and couldn't imagine wanting one as a pet. They were cold, unaffectionate, and barely moved. Why would this lady choose such an unusual pet instead of a dog or cat? It looked very well-fed and large enough to take off a person's finger if it wanted.

"I didn't think exotic pets were legal in New York?" Daisy asked, hoping she sounded more curious than accusatory.

"Yes, but non-venomous reptiles are allowed," Catalina explained. "He's harmless unless you're an insect. I breed his food myself."

She opened a panel underneath the lizard's tank and inside was a plastic tub filled with writhing mealworms. Next to it was a smaller white plastic container filled with a colony of crickets using paper eggshells as a stomping ground.

"The baby mice are just an extra treat, because he's been so good lately," she said with a proud glance at the habitat. "He has to eat them while they're still suckling and the bones are soft, so he can digest them safely. So, he's been feasting."

"Don't you find this... distasteful?" Daisy asked, looking at the infant mice. They were little more than bulging pink sacks with tiny, scrunched faces on one end. How could a city dweller like Catalina find the impulse to go out of her way to arrange such a gruesome treat for her pet?

"I think cramming cows in stalls where they can't move, get pumped full of antibiotics, and are fed chicken shit so your heat-lamp burger patty only costs a dollar is distasteful," Catalina said. "But in America, cows are food, so no one cares. If you did the same to a housecat, it would make the national news."

"I get it," Jordan said. "It's arbitrary really."

"No. You don't get it. It's not arbitrary at all," Catalina countered. "Every living thing needs to eat. And if you're here? You have a *right* to eat. And a right to eat what you're *supposed* to eat. It doesn't matter if you like it or not."

"Sure, but live baby mice?" Daisy asked. "Your point about the cows sounds like you want to minimize suffering. You're a nurse after all. Why engage in this cruelty?"

"You missed my point entirely," Catalina said. "This isn't cruelty. This is the natural order of things. You're disgusted by the lizard's natural diet because you've been trained to see it that way, while you turn your back to countless *unnatural* horrors used to produce your own low-quality food. Perhaps Gimbal and I are the ones who should be judging you?"

Jordan crouched with his hands on his knees and looked at the bearded dragon up close through the glass.

"Does it ever escape?" he asked.

"He doesn't need to," Catalina said. "I let him out to roam all the time."

Daisy took the opportunity to check the rest of the living room for anything important. Most of the artworks in the room were landscapes but one large, old-looking painting on the wall stood out to Daisy because it was a portrait. The image depicted a beautiful young woman, who looked much like Catalina–perhaps it was a relative–with an infant baby.

The woman had a rosary clutched in her hand. A faded label on the frame said "Nuestra Señora del Silencio."

Our Lady of Silence?

"I'd let you hold Gimbal," Catalina continued, "but I'm late for work, as I said. And I'm sure you have many more apartments to check."

Catalina corralled Daisy and Jordan back to the front door.

"Speaking of which," she said, "Have you two checked the gas line of Mrs. Coleman next door yet?"

"Uh, no," Daisy said. "Not yet. She's on our list. Right?"

"Right," Jordan agreed.

"Oh, really?" Catalina asked. "Well then, I'll take you over there right now to introduce you."

"Oh, no," Daisy said, a bit too vehemently. "That's really not necessary, Ms. Cordero."

"I insist," she said. "Mrs. Coleman is an 85-year-old widow and gets very confused and upset when strangers come to the door."

Catalina gave Daisy a big grin.

Was it a knowing grin?

"But she knows me," Catalina finished.

"Well, fantastic," Daisy said, knowing they were stuck.

"Are you okay," Daisy asked Jordan after they'd finished up and returned to his van on the street.

"Yeah, I think so," he said. "I just hope work doesn't find out about that."

"They won't. But why did you make Mrs. Coleman sign something, Jordan? That wasn't part of the plan."

"Well, you weren't any help!" he said. "You were supposed to do all the talking but you weren't saying anything to the old lady."

"We weren't even supposed to be in there," Daisy said.

"Okay, well I was improvising."

"Don't worry about it," Daisy said. "She's probably already forgotten that we were there."

"Did you get what you needed?" Jordan asked. "I didn't see anything weird except for the lizard."

"Maybe. I promise I'll explain the rest of this to you once I figure it out for myself."

"Catalina was really something, huh?" Jordan said, looking up to the top of the building.

"Yeah," Daisy agreed, lost in thought. "She was really something."

* * *

On her way to work, Catalina Cordero stopped in the lobby of her building to say good morning to Jamal, the young man working the front desk.

"It looks like a gorgeous Autumn day out there, Catalina," he said.

"Yes, I agree," she said. "Tell me, Jamal, is Con Ed working on gas lines in the building today?"

"Not that I know of," he said. "Are you having a problem? Want me to put in a maintenance ticket?"

"No, Jamal," she said. "That's alright. I don't have any problems I can't take care of myself."

* * *

That evening, Daisy stopped by the office to use her work computer and accounts to do some research. *Believer* staff wasn't allowed to use Google search. Instead, the paper paid monthly fees for search platforms that were actually reliable and free of ads, bloat, misinformation, or AI. The insistence on accuracy gave Jerry one less thing to fret about being sued over, a never-ending concern in their line of work.

Daisy arrived as the sun was setting and had hoped the office would be empty but saw a light in Tiffani's office was still on. She tried to stay quiet and not draw too much attention to herself since she didn't want to give any updates on her case to Tiffani just yet.

She pulled up the copy of Pappas' footage which had been brightened by Brad to review it one more time. She zoomed in closely on the face, hoping she might be able to clearly tell if it could be the woman she'd just met or not. But the footage was too blurry and pixelated to reveal anything new.

Daisy ran a search for "Nuestra Señora del Silencio," retrieving generic Spanish results about the Catholic faith. Daisy added the term "Philippines" to narrow down her results and discovered that an infamous 19th century convent in the Visayan Islands bore the name. The structure had been burned down in the early 1900s after a mysterious mass-death event which culled every living soul under its roof. To this day, locals refused to go near the site, but it was a fixture "dark tourist" spot for those seeking morbid curiosities.

"What is this, Daisy?" a woman asked.

Shit. It was Tiffani. *How did she sneak up on me like that?*

"Huh, what?" Daisy asked.

"This? The bat story again?" She was looking at the still frame of Pappas' video, still in the corner of her screen.

"Oh," Daisy said. "It's nothing. There were just a few details about that one I missed that have come to light."

"Absolutely not," Tiffany said. "You're supposed to investigate the articles BEFORE you publish them, Daisy. I think you have things backwards. And this video wasn't even good. Drop it. You're supposed to be working on the Rhinelander story."

"I am. There might be a connection."

"A connection?! That's preposterous. What are you doing?" Tiffani asked.

"I can't explain it right now."

"You can't explain it right now? You always say that! You've got to get your head out of the clouds. You never follow instructions. I'll have to talk to Jerry about this."

"You do that, Tiffani!" Daisy yelled.

Tiffani stormed back to her office and slammed the door.

Daisy realized she'd spent a week working on her investigation, at the expense of her other reporting, and that her job could actually be on the line if she didn't produce results. She shut down her computer and put on her jacket, preparing to leave.

On her way out the door, she stopped for a moment to stare out the giant windows at the street down below. All the people down there were blissfully ignorant of what she knew. Daisy watched a pregnant woman standing outside a store.

What would that woman do—or her husband—if they knew about the murders?

Pandemonium. Even if city officials were aware of the other murders, they could never tell everybody, she realized. It would set off a panic. A murderer is one thing, but a killer who preys only on women and children? It would reduce the city to a millions-strong horde of angry villagers with torches and pitchforks, blood-thirsty for victims.

But was Catalina Cordero actually the killer?

Daisy still wasn't sure. And her investigation was done. Over. Where had she gone wrong? She'd just pulled off the best journalism work of her entire life, possibly meeting the real murderer face to face. She'd been inside the woman's home.

But what did she have to print? Still nothing but her Rhinelander interview. It was *something*, but not what she'd wanted.

What did I expect to find in that apartment anyway? Daisy chastised herself. *A signed confession?*

Something else on the street caught Daisy's attention. It was a person, standing under a streetlight. They weren't doing anything unusual, but Daisy couldn't ignore their presence. They weren't even moving. Why had she noticed them?

Ah, she realized. That *was* the reason. They hadn't moved. The person hadn't budged an inch the entire time she'd been staring out the window.

The figure wasn't very tall, and slight in build. Was it a woman?

Daisy had a fantastical thought—was it Catalina?

No, she was being paranoid.

Daisy studied the shape of the person standing under the streetlight. There was a hood over their head so she couldn't see the face, but the angle suggested the eyes were pointed right at her, as if staring back.

What was it her Grandpa had said about the stars? There are aliens up there staring back down at you? And to them, you're the alien living in the stars. Was the stationary figure down below an alien, involved in mutual study with her? She almost gave them a little wave.

Then, the person moved.

It began slowly at first, like waking from a sleep. Then the arms lifted out to the sides, where they began to rise and fall, up and down. Like wings. The person was mimicking the flapping of wings.

Was it a prank? Someone who read her Pappas article having a laugh? They probably saw a light on in the paper's window and were poking fun about the bat story.

The movements were slow and sinister. Daisy grabbed her phone and opened the camera app. She zoomed in on the face under the hood to get a closer look. The camera app detected the face and tried to square in and focus.

It was a woman for sure. Long black hair.

Is it fucking Catalina?

The main overhead lights came on in the room, startling Daisy and blinding her. The entire street scene out the window was replaced with her own startled reflection. It was gone. She couldn't see anything.

"Turn the lights off!" she screamed.

It was the cleaning lady.

DAMN!

She hadn't had time to get a photo before the lights came on.

"What?" the woman asked. "*No* lights?"

Daisy realized how crazy she sounded and that she'd missed her moment for a picture anyway.

"Never mind," she said. Grabbing her things to head home.

That night, Daisy had a series of unsettling, chaotic dreams. Fragments of madness came together to form quick, disturbing vignettes. She was at her Grandpa's funeral, her first personal brush with the death of a person she couldn't bear to lose–his body there in the casket, not a hair out of place. Wearing his favorite suit. It had felt so wrong to see that suit on a lifeless body. Just a husk, an imitation of the man who'd been taken from her.

Then, she was at work. Except it wasn't just work. It was also the Daily Planet from Superman comics. There was no Clark Kent or Superman. But she was Lois Lane, dressed in 1940s attire. Liam was there at her side, in a bow tie, taking pictures.

"Gee golly, Ms. Scott!"

She was leading him into danger. She knew the risks and he didn't. But they were going anyway. She was being selfish.

Now the bow tie was gone, and Liam had become Jordan. They walked together, bravely, down a long dirt road.

"Where are we, Daze?"

Daisy shone her flashlight ahead, lighting the way.

But now Jordan was gone as well. She was alone.

The flashlight disappeared and she found herself walking through a jungle at night. A dense canopy obscured the cloudless night sky overhead. It wasn't familiar like an American forest. The trees were different–palm trees. The air was crisp. She didn't have her jacket.

Something cracked and crunched under her feet. Daisy bent down to find that it was animal bones. The entire path through the jungle was paved with small animal bones! She continued walking, and a rustling sound from the treetops frightened her. She searched the trees for what had produced the disturbance, something large, but saw nothing in the canopy except the leaves of a palm tree settling to rest from a furious shake.

Daisy stepped on a hard object and kicked it aside with her shoe. With horror, she realized what the lump had been.

She wasn't walking on animal bones.

She'd stepped on the skull of a baby. She was walking on the bones of human infants.

Too scared now to continue, Daisy turned to head back the way she had come.

But where had that even been?

She was lost now. The path had disappeared. She stumbled blindly through the thick brush of the jungle until she broke her way through into a clearing.

She was in an open rice field now, which stretched as far as the eye could see in all directions. The sky was pitch black with no stars. A small Filipino boy was with her. He was petrified.

"Help me, please!" he pleaded, watching the skies.

"What's wrong?" she asked, kneeling down to comfort him. Now the Filipino boy had become Gabriel, the survivor she'd interviewed in Queens.

"There's no reason to be afraid," she assured him.

A ticking sound began ricocheting through the field, like a sinister clock. A countdown.

TIK

TIK

The ticks were uncomfortably loud, like gunfire, coming from the sky itself. Daisy covered her ears, trying to shield herself from the sound, which shook the ground like anvil strikes.

TIK

TIK

Then, like a storm which had passed overhead and was now receding into the distance, the ticks grew quieter. Gabriel cowered, holding onto her.

"Protect me, please," he begged.

TIK

TIK

The ticks were barely audible now, just distant echoes. But it brought Daisy no comfort. Because she remembered something she'd read in one of Coney's books about Filipino mythology. It was a trick. The quieter the sound, the *closer* the danger.

Daisy wrapped her arms around Gabriel. The wind began to pick up. At first it was just a slight breeze on her face, but soon it became a hurricane. Small pieces of rice plants got caught up in the maelstrom, achieving enough velocity to nick her skin as they zoomed by.

TIK

TIK

Something large was circling overhead. They were helpless. In the middle of nowhere. There was no shelter. There was nowhere to run or hide.

Then Daisy looked up and saw it.

And screamed herself awake.

It wasn't even 5:00 AM yet but Daisy couldn't get back to sleep. She gave up trying and made coffee instead. Her apartment was chilly, and they hadn't turned on the radiator heat in the building for winter yet. She grabbed a sweater from her closet and planted herself in front of her computer to watch local news and scroll on social media.

The news was showing a busy crime scene somewhere. Something big had happened.

Daisy turned up the volume. The Chief of Detectives for the police department who had spoken at the press conference was on the screen.

"...but not at this time," he was saying, "however we can confirm it was a suicide."

After a few more details that failed to clarify what they were talking about, the program finally cut back to the news anchor who provided a recap.

"For those just tuning in," he said, "Dr. Brett Rhinelander was found dead of apparent suicide late last night. The disgraced cosmetic surgeon, who was facing murder charges, had a long legacy of notoriety in the New York City spotlight…"

Daisy's concerns about her article vanished. She had made a mistake. A big fucking mistake. Rhinelander hadn't committed suicide. She knew the truth. And even worse, she knew who was next. Daisy had just volunteered herself as a victim to a serial killer.

CHAPTER 19

Eagle Valdez

* * *

Once the sun had risen and it seemed like a reasonable hour, Daisy first texted Jordan, telling him to skip work if he could and lay low for a while, and that she would explain and make it up to him later. Then she placed a call to Danny Pappas, worried he may also be on Catalina's radar thanks to her article.

She dialed Pappas' cell number and tried to think of what to say as it rang.

Oops! Sorry, sir. Either a mass murderer or a literal fucking monster is on our asses thanks to me. Sorry about that. My bad.

The line rang several times and then went to voicemail. Daisy ended the call instead of leaving a message, but then thought better of it. She dialed the number a second time, preparing a quick voice mail message in her head to go over the basic points to keep Pappas safe. But this time, the call connected after the third ring.

"Hello?! Who is this?" a man asked on the other end of the phone. It wasn't Pappas. The voice was much deeper and gravelly, very distinctive. To Daisy, the man sounded a little like Ron Perlman with a throat infection.

"I'm trying to reach Danny Pappas," Daisy said.

"Were you with him last night?!" the man demanded.

"No, sir," Daisy said. She was worried something had happened to Pappas. Maybe she was speaking with the police, who had his phone.

"I'm a reporter, Daisy Scott. I spoke with Mr. Pappas the other day. I just need to follow up on a few things, sir."

"This is Danny's wife!!" the voice screamed.

"Oh, I'm so sorry!" Daisy said. "Sorry! Ma'am! I just need to speak with Mr. Pappas please. It's important."

"Well, good luck!" the woman replied. "He's been gone since last weekend."

"Gone?" Daisy asked. Pappas didn't seem like the type that left the house much. "Where?"

"You tell me!" the woman yelled. "You're probably one of his floozies. I know that's where he is. Well honey, you can keep him!"

"Ma'am, I told you. I'm a reporter. I was there last—

Daisy realized Mrs. Pappas had already hung up.

He's been missing for days. Shit. Did I get him killed too?

This is all my fault. I created a disaster.

She hoped Jordan had listened to her advice.

If Catalina came for her, how would it happen? It seemed that the attacks always happened at night. So she had the day to prepare. Would barricading herself inside at night be enough? She didn't have a balcony. If her door and windows were shut and bolted, what could Catalina do? She nabbed people when they got sloppy. Daisy could stay smart.

But for how long? She had no reason to believe this was a woman who would give up. She was expertly covering her tracks, and Daisy was in her way.

No, she would never be safe from Catalina.

Daisy was out of options and needed a Hail Mary. With nowhere else to turn, she grabbed her leather jacket and drumsticks and headed for Coney's Occult Books and Driving School.

There was no music playing in Coney's store this time as Daisy hurried through the narrow aisle toward the Filipina in the back, who seemed to be asleep.

"Excuse me," Daisy said, trying to wake her. It didn't work.

"Excuse me! Coney!" she yelled.

This time, Coney's eyelids fluttered, and she came to. "Can I help you?" she asked.

"It's me, Daisy, from the other day."

"Oh," Coney yawned. "You read all those books already? Damn, girl. You've caught the bug. Well, there's more where that came from."

This seemed to wake Coney up in full. "We haven't even started on magic and witches yet," she said. She rose and began collecting new books.

"Coney, I think the manananggal is real," Daisy said. "At least, someone is making it look that way. And it's here, in the city. There's been a series of murders."

"I know," Coney said. She set down the books and looked at Daisy matter-of-factly.

"You do?" Daisy asked.

"Yeah, I looked into it the other day after you left. Pretty crazy, huh."

"Uh. Well, yeah. That's an understatement. What do we do about it?"

"Nothing," Coney said. "Don't even worry about it."

"What?!"

"It's been taken care of already. Let's just say I have a friend who handles this sort of thing, and I called him in. He'll be in town tonight. It's better if you don't know anything more than that."

"Coney, she's gonna come after me next."

"Why would you say that? You read the books. They feed on fetuses and young children. You'll be fine."

"No," Daisy demanded. "You don't understand." She looked Coney in the eyes, pleading, "I went in her apartment. I interrogated her. She knows I'm onto her."

"You what?" Coney asked, stunned. "Why?"

"Yeah, I know it was stupid. I'm a reporter. I was reporting."

"You don't make anything easy, do you?" Coney asked.

Daisy left the bookshop with handwritten instructions on where to meet Coney and her friend later that evening. Coney had assured her she'd be safe on her own until then.

Daisy finally heard back from Jordan, who had ignored her instructions and reported to work. She admonished him and begged that he head straight home after his shift and not go outside after dark.

Daisy returned to her apartment and watched local news for most of the day. A sharp implement had been found next to Rhinelander, who supposedly stabbed himself in the stomach, like ritual seppuku due to his shame.

Daisy knew better.

As the hour grew late, she put on her jacket and retrieved the instructions Coney had given her. She was to meet the book clerk at a private location in Hunter's Point, an industrial, waterfront area of Long Island City. But instead of a street address, she had a complicated series of directions based on landmarks and something about crawling under a gate.

Was Coney for real about this?

Daisy exited the Hunter's Point subway station as the sun was setting and walked east, leaving behind the throngs of people, bars, and restaurants to enter a less developed section of the neighborhood filled with old manufacturing buildings. As the Long Island Expressway appeared overhead, Daisy realized she'd reached the first step in her instructions. Daisy proceeded until she reached the waterfront of a creek that ran through the numerous warehouses. The instructions said to hop a fence and cut through a giant parking lot.

Hop the fence?

It was obviously private property. The gate was solid metal, with no barbed wire or anything dangerous, and only about four feet high. Daisy didn't see any cameras around. Sure, she could jump the fence. But *should* she? Was it legal?

Daisy went into strangers' homes for a living. She knew better than most, the importance of "Covering Your Ass" in life. She couldn't control crazy people, or disasters, or prejudice. But she could limit her exposure to them, especially when it seemed foolhardy.

Daisy's "spider-sense" about complex situations had served her well as a reporter and had kept her safe. That sense was tingling now, telling her to turn around. She could still go to the police. Rhinelander was dead. Maybe they would listen to her now.

Coney seemed perfectly trustworthy. But who was this *friend?* Who knows what kind of people the Filipina associated with. Daisy's mind reeled with dozens of ways she could be putting herself in further danger.

The sun dipped behind a building in the distance, darkening everything around Daisy even further. It was night. That's when Catalina attacks. She had to pick the lesser of two evils.

She easily climbed over the short, sturdy gate and walked through a large parking lot until she reached a row of trees in the back. In general, this area looked strangely wild and unkempt for Queens. Since it was a relatively industrial and ungentrified area, the scene of lush trees and the creek hidden behind the warehouses didn't even look like NYC to her.

Then, she reached the aforementioned gate, a long barred structure preventing access to a footpath heading downhill through the brush. Why did she have to crawl under it?

Daisy looked for the handle to see if it was locked. She couldn't even find the latch. Vines had overgrown the structure, and you'd need a weed wacker to clear it. The gate was angled against the ground however, providing enough clearance on one side for a person to slip underneath.

Grumbling to herself, Daisy got down on her hands and knees and crawled under the opening in the gate. She intended to have a talk with Coney later. There had to be an easier way to reach this place.

Daisy walked carefully down the incline, trying not to slip, until she reached the waterfront of Newton Creek and found her destination. It looked very nondescript.

"L.I.C. STEELWORKS," read faded print on the side of a rusted old two-story manufacturing building. A dilapidated wooden fence stretched in both directions, preventing access to the water or to any entrance except the front of the building.

L.I.C. Steelworks? Is this the right place? Daisy wondered.

Who the hell was she meeting? Why here? Was the person a criminal? She still had time to turn around.

But curiosity got the better of her. As she pulled at the rusted old outer door of the building, she saw something peculiar—a recently installed steel security door right behind it. It looked really expensive, like the door to a bank vault or a top-secret area.

Why on Earth would someone go to the trouble of installing such an expensive security door on a shabby old building? Why didn't they just demolish the old structure and start fresh?

Before Daisy could even search for a doorbell or ringer, Coney answered the door, smiling.

"Daisy!" she yelled, giving her a big hug. "Come on in! I'll show you around."

Daisy wasn't sure what she'd expected the inside of the building to look like, but it sure wasn't what she found. The interior could only be described as a giant, industrial, multi-million-dollar man-cave. The decrepit old manufacturing building was just a facade, hiding a new construction, state of the art facility inside.

Now I've seen everything....

The huge, two-story room was open in the center, providing high ceilings over an open floor plan. A prefabricated steel mezzanine wrapped around three quarters of the room to provide a slim second level, accessible by staircases on either side. A couple doors on the mezzanine led to smaller back rooms on the upper level.

The fourth wall of the structure, across from the front entrance, was the most impressive. Two rolled up oversized loading bays left the entire wall open to a private, scenic view of the creek, with the Manhattan skyline looming large in the distance through the treetops. A small dock attached to an outdoor area provided direct water access. A motorcycle was parked inside.

How the fuck did he get a motorcycle in here? Dragged it under the gate?

The walls were filled with complex displays of weapons and tools. There was a home gym, as elaborate as any she'd seen on television. There was a computer workstation with multiple monitors, gear she didn't recognize, and racks of equipment connected.

The place wasn't all business though. A deep well in the floor, perhaps originally used for working on machinery from the underside, had been turned into a living room conversation pit rimmed with bookshelves. An enormous flat screen TV hung before expensive looking seating. Daisy noticed a video game was paused on the screen. It looked like a *Legend of Zelda* game. She guessed Coney had been playing it before she arrived. Coney seemed to spend a lot of time there based on the books randomly left about.

Books and weapons. Who the hell are these people? Daisy wondered.

"Can I get you something to drink?" Coney asked.

Daisy began to politely decline, but realized she was actually parched.

"Sure, what do you have?" she asked.

"This way!" Coney announced, with a grin.

The kitchen put Catalina's to shame. There was a dedicated glass-front fridge just for beverages. Daisy selected a bottled water and thanked Coney, who offered her a snack as well.

Coney opened up a hideaway door to reveal a walk-in pantry that was stocked so well it would make an overfunded tech startup from the early 2010s blush. It looked like a 7-Eleven. An entire shelf was dedicated just to SPAM, with enough cans piled up to outlast the apocalypse if need be.

"I'm in charge of keeping the place stocked with snacks for my friend Eagle," she said with pride. "Everything's arranged in order of protein content per serving. He said that extra step was unnecessary, but I know that man. And when he's gearing up for a job, he always wants protein."

Daisy selected a bag of chips from a shelf and thanked Coney as she closed the pantry.

"I also help clean up around here," Coney said. "And I assist him with his work on some freelance cases. That's the only way I'm able to make ends meet. But it's exciting stuff! We get to travel a lot. I also helped decorate the place!"

Now that she mentioned it, Daisy noticed some bizarre touches around the room. Next to the kitchen, for instance, there was a mannequin dressed like a 1950s diner waitress, holding a tray of condiments. This Coney was an odd duck.

Daisy had to admit, whatever this pair was getting into, it was an impressive operation. The location was barely, only technically, accessible by foot. To anyone on the outside, it looked like an abandoned industrial building. Even from the other side of the creek, it would appear innocuous as long as the loading bay doors were down.

This Eagle guy must be loaded, Daisy realized. She thought she understood people, but this was a puzzler. Where does money like this come from? What sort of person could afford a place like that and be useful against a murderer? Was Coney involved in something shady?

Daisy's gut didn't give her that impression. The anxiety she'd felt outside had faded away. She knew Coney wasn't trying to deceive her.

Besides, she realized, as she reexamined the wall of weapons—swords, daggers, and whips, many whips—if this guy knew how to use any of that stuff, she was in the safest place she could be.

Still, she was a broke reporter. She worried this guy's services were pricier than she could afford.

"Don't take this the wrong way," Daisy said, "but how does your friend afford this place? I can't imagine any line of work that's monster-related being taken seriously, much less leading to all of this. Are his parents rich or something?"

"Oh, they're SUPER rich," Coney said. "But, believe it or not, he built all of this himself."

Coney looked around the giant, hi-tech playground with obvious pride.

"Eagle's parents cut him off a long time ago. He really paid for all of this by capturing and killing specimens, although he blows money as fast as he gets it. We have discussions about that. I always tell him, he could allocate just 10% of each fee to an interest-bearing savings account, and we could build a little nest egg of future capital for–"

"Wait a minute," Daisy interrupted, getting more worried now. "Exactly how much does this dude charge?"

"Let's put it this way," Coney said, "if there was only one rat catcher in a world full of rats, they could charge whatever they wanted, couldn't they?" she grinned.

Jeez, Daisy worried. She'd accidentally found a top-shelf monster guy on a wino's budget.

"Coney, I'm just a tabloid reporter, you know…" she said.

"Oh!" Coney seemed to finally realize her concern. "Don't worry, Daisy. This will be *pro bono*. This problem is close to Eagle's heart, I think."

They moved to the conversation pit and Coney tried to change the subject to get Daisy's mind off of Catalina. The living room area was open and stylish, plus so well-appointed that, under other circumstances, Daisy would have gladly plopped down on a couch to enjoy the humongous TV. But fear for your life isn't an emotion that can be put aside at will.

Daisy was startled by the sound of approaching engines.

No, the sound was higher pitched. It wasn't a vehicle.

"He's here!" Coney exclaimed. Jumping up to run over to the open rollaway doors.

Daisy followed her over to the small outdoor patio and dock to see a motorboat approaching. The sun had fully set now and the two figures on the boat appeared only in silhouette as the shape grew larger and the sound of the whining motor grew louder.

A quick, muffled conversation took place between the two men. Daisy couldn't make out any of it over the noise of the onboard motor. Afterwards, one of the figures athletically hopped over the side of the boat and onto the pier, before kicking the side of the boat to instruct the other man to depart. As the boat followed instructions and returned to wherever it had come from, the man approached them and entered the building.

"Kuya!" Coney yelled, running to give him a hug. "Let me take your bag."

Coney picked up a medium-sized black duffle bag the man had brought from the boat.

"Thanks, Coney," he said. He pronounced her name normally–*KAHN-EE*–instead of like the hot dog. Daisy stored that detail away for later.

She immediately sensed there was no romantic connection between Coney and Eagle. Their bond was obviously strong, but it seemed more like the sibling variety, like with her and Jordan.

"How was it?" Coney asked.

"I can't talk about this one," Eagle said, "and unfortunately, it's unfinished."

He briefly cut his eyes at Daisy.

"But I'm exhausted," he said. "And I need food. Did you get Jollibee?"

"It's in the microwave!" Coney said, running to the kitchen, leaving Daisy alone with Eagle.

Eagle approached her and leaned in close. "Listen," he said, "I trust Coney with my life, which is why you're here. But I don't like reporters, and I can count on one hand how many people have seen this building. One of them is dead. Am I clear?"

"Crystal," Daisy said.

"It sounds like you've made a series of bad decisions, Daisy Scott. But you made one good one. Involving me. First, I need to eat."

Coney and Daisy situated themselves on barstools at the kitchen's long breakfast bar while Eagle opened up his sack of fast food at a small dining table close by. Coney handed her a business card. It read:

EAGLE VALDEZ: MONSTER HUNTER

Seriously? Is this guy for real? Or is he some kind of charlatan?

"Is Eagle your real name?" she asked him.

"No!" Coney said. "But I'll never tell!"

Daisy tried to get a read on the man as he ate his meal. Eagle was clean-shaven, above average height, and athletically built, but he didn't have the overly-pumped physique of a gym rat. To Daisy, the way he walked looked more like a fighter, or even a dancer. There was a gracefulness evident in the control he had over his posture and movements. She could equally imagine him snapping a guy's neck in combat or launching into an acrobatic routine. Skilled martial artists tended to move that way, but there was something else in his movements too—a measure of showmanship, even flamboyance, that crept through the cracks of his nonchalant demeanor. Daisy could picture Eagle Valdez, in a tuxedo, swinging a female partner—or male?—with the gracefulness of a movie star.

Daisy doubted she'd learn enough about the man to test her intuitions. He was quiet and seemed focused on the task at hand. She was one of his clients, not privy to his inner world. She wondered if a guy like that ever fully opened up to anyone, even a close friend like Coney.

"Coney!" Eagle complained. Again, he pronounced her name differently than everyone else. "Why are there veggies on my burger?!" he yelled.

"You've been on the road, Kuya!" she explained. From context clues, Daisy guessed that "Kuya" wasn't Eagle's real name, but some kind of Filipino affectation for close companions.

"You need nutrients!" Coney said.

"Nutrients?! This?" Eagle removed a tomato slice from his cheeseburger.

"He hates vegetables," Coney explained to Daisy. "He's like a little kid. He only wants to eat meat, rice, and desserts. I have to force him to eat well."

She turned her condemnation toward the culprit directly. "You can't exercise away a bad diet, Eagle! You're getting older now."

"Whatever…" he said.

"You have to take care of yourself. One piece of lettuce and a slice of tomato won't kill you."

The offending tomato slice sailed through the air like a projectile, directly in between Daisy and Coney's heads, before smacking the refrigerator behind them with expert, forceful precision. It looked like the tomato slice had moved at fast enough velocity to have stung if it had hit her.

"Mmmmm. That's better," Eagle said, through a greasy mouthful of beef and cheese. He offered Daisy some of his fast-food, but she had no appetite and declined.

"Good. More for me," he said.

Daisy chatted with Coney while Eagle polished off his burger, some fried chicken, a small bowl of spaghetti, and most of his fries. As he picked at the undesirable fries left on his plate, he finally got down to business.

"So tell us, Daisy," Eagle said. "Besides your lack of fashion sense, what seems to be your problem?"

Snarky! What's with this dude? Daisy wondered.

"Oh, you know. The usual. Someone's trying to kill me."

"It happens," Eagle said.

"What do you intend to do about Catalina," she asked him directly.

He picked at his fries for another moment, and then pushed the leftovers away.

"Manananggals feed on fetuses and toddlers, mostly," Eagle said to Daisy. "You would have been perfectly safe if you hadn't gone into its den and poked her in the eye. She's on alert now. Probably preparing to skip town after she kills you. You've made my job much, much more difficult."

"Well, excuse me," Daisy said. "But this is my first encounter with a manananggal."

"Mananan**GGAL**," Eagle corrected. Unlike Coney, who barely had an accent, Eagle's Filipino inflection was more prominent.

Daisy ignored him. "And I'm not even sure I believe in this shit yet, just to be real with you. Maybe everybody in the Philippines believes women's torsos are flying around in the trees, but me? Sorry, it's just a hard sell. I believe this lady is a killer. Yes. But I think she's the metaphorical kind of monster. Not the literal kind."

"Not everyone in the Philippines believes manananggals are real," Coney said. "Actually, only the older generations seem to even tell the stories anymore."

"Legends exist to keep us safe," Eagle said. "But people forget."

"So, you actually believe they're real?" Daisy asked. "Have you seen one? Not photos or videos, but actually seen one in person?"

"I've seen several of them," Eagle said.

"But how can that be?" Daisy asked. "It just doesn't seem... biologically possible that something like that could be real."

"I thought the same thing the first time I saw platypus," Coney added. "It shouldn't be real. If you saw a giraffe outside, it would be impressive. If you saw a goat, much less so. It's all dependent on what you're used to."

"So, you've seen a manananggal too?" Daisy asked.

"No," she huffed.

Coney seemed offended by the question.

"He's always promising me I'll get to see something cool," Coney said, looking at Eagle, "but nothing yet."

"That's not true, Coney," he reminded her. "You're fibbing. You saw an aswang."

"It was a pig," Coney told Daisy.

"An evil, shape-shifting pig," Eagle added.

"Yeah, but still. A pig."

"Next time, Coney," he promised.

"No. This time, Eagle."

"Nope, not tonight. I'm sorry. There's already a trail of bodies in this city. It happened on my watch. I'm doing this one alone."

"No way!" Daisy interjected. "I have to go along. This is my life on the line. And my story. I'll stay behind you–stay outside–whatever. But I have to be there too. I have to know."

"Do you understand how dangerous this is?" Eagle asked. "I've been doing this since I was a child. The manananggal may be half the woman she used to be, but she's twice the trouble. Trust me."

"OOOH!" Coney exclaimed. "Kuya! That's a good line! Did you just come up with that?"

"Not just this minute," he said, "but yes. It's one of my better sayings."

"That's a good one," she said again. "Can I use it on my YouTube channel?"

"Ehhh…. You know, Coney. I would just rather that you didn't," he said.

"I'll give you credit. I promise."

"That makes it even worse!"

"Why?" she asked.

"I do a lot of undercover work, Coney. You know I can't get famous. I can't be a celebrity. Sure, I have the symmetrical features for it, but I can't risk notoriety."

Coney was clearly disappointed. "I meant like a quick shoutout. Not your life story, jeez."

Eagle went over his plan of attack. He truly believed Catalina was a manananggal and intended to enter her apartment, which he called her "den," and "destroy her lower half" while she was hunting on a raid.

Daisy insisted that she knew the layout of the apartment, and of the entire building, even the roof, and that under no circumstances would she disobey an order from him if she was allowed to tag along. Plus, everything about him would remain off the record. Thankfully, Eagle realized the extra pair of hands could be useful and finally consented, retiring to his bedroom to change clothes in preparation. They were going that night.

Daisy sat nervously with Coney in the conversation pit as they waited on Eagle. Was she ready for this?

What about Jordan? Knowing a text wasn't good enough last time, Daisy called Jordan to make sure he stayed put while she went with Eagle to deal with Catalina. Jordan answered and asked if she'd gone to the police. Daisy was vague in her response, just stating she'd found someone able to resolve the issue that night, but that Jordan needed to stay home.

"No, I'm coming with you," he said.

"You can't. It's gonna be dangerous, Jordan."

"Then why are you going? What are you trying to prove here, Daisy? A story isn't worth all this."

"It's not about proving anything anymore, Jordan. It was at first, but things got out of hand. I can't explain it right now. Just promise me you'll go straight home after work and that you won't leave the house."

"First you say it's an emergency, and make me drop everything to meet you in the park. And then, once things get interesting, you cut me off. I'm on a "need to know" basis, now, huh? Daze, you can't ask for my help and then tell me you don't want it anymore. That's now how friends work."

"I know," Daisy said. "And I've been a shitty friend to you. Dude, believe me. VERY shitty. You don't even understand how shitty I've been just yet. But I've taken steps to fix it. Please, just stay indoors tonight. Don't ask questions. Just do it. And I'll explain everything to you tomorrow. No more secrets, I swear."

Daisy ended her call and Coney put her hand on her shoulder to comfort her.

"Don't worry, Eagle is the best," she assured her.

"Are you ready?" Eagle's voice boomed from the bedroom door at the top of the stairs.

His black tactical clothes had been replaced by stylish outerwear. He was dressed to the fucking nines, including a fancy short scarf coiled lightly around his neck, with one end draped in front and the other behind his back.

In his hand was not the menacing black duffle bag he'd arrived with, but a monogrammed Louis Vuitton briefcase.

"Let's get this bitch," he said.

* * *

Catalina hummed a forgotten song to herself as she set bowls of oils and herbs on the ground and lit candles. Her mind was somewhere else, lost in a past only she remembered.

She kneeled on the floor, and began to prepare a concoction, which she rubbed all over her body, coating her skin. She applied an extra layer of oil to her abdomen and her humming became a chant—a hymn.

And as she sang and performed her ancient ritual, her beautiful eyes burned red in the darkness.

CHAPTER 20

Manananggal in New York

* * *

Eagle knocked on Catalina's door with trademark confidence, and then they waited for a few seconds, which felt like a lifetime to Daisy, to see if she answered.

"What if she's home?" Daisy whispered, realizing Eagle hadn't covered that eventuality in his preparations. "Like, what if she hasn't transformed yet and just answers the door?"

"I'm here to neutralize her," he said. "The plan wouldn't change."

He retrieved a small case from his coat pocket. "But it looks like I was right, and she's out hunting."

He knelt down, removed a precision tool from the case, and began picking the lock. Daisy noticed he was wearing expensive looking dress shoes. Why had he dressed up for a posh night out on the town to come kill a monster?

A Monster.

Daisy had spent her whole life hoping for this moment.

What if it's real?

She couldn't even bring herself to thrill at the possibility–she was too afraid. She was seconds away from the biggest event of her life. But, now that the moment was here, now that it was real, she just wanted to turn and run. What if Eagle was right, and it really was a manananggal? Either way, she was at a killer's doorstep. A second time. And she knew better. Why had she even come? She already had her story.

"Eagle, I'm not brave like you," she said, "I've never done anything like this before. I don't know if I can go through with it now."

Eagle was quiet for a minute and kept fidgeting with the lock. Daisy wondered if he would even respond to her admission.

"Daisy, I'll tell you a secret." He paused working on the lock and looked at her. "But you have to promise not to tell anyone, even Coney."

"Sure. Of course."

"I do this for a living. I hunt things that give people nightmares. I've killed dozens of creatures, more dangerous than any known animal. And you know what?"

"What?"

"I'm scared every time."

"You are?" she asked.

"Of course. I'd be an idiot not to be. To stare death in the face and to not feel fear–that's not bravery. It's foolishness. Courage isn't a lack of fear; it's doing things even though you're afraid, because there's no one else to do it. Make sense?"

Daisy realized Eagle was much better at pep talks than she had been with Jordan in the same spot.

"Besides," he added, returning to the lock as he kept talking, "fear is useful. It makes you alert. It heightens your senses and speeds your reaction time. A little fear is healthy before tangling with a manananggal. Believe me, I know. And this one feels different than the others."

Daisy wanted to ask what he meant by that last part, but he finished picking the lock and opened the door before she had a chance.

"Are you ready?" he asked, grabbing his briefcase. Without another thought, he walked into Catalina's apartment, leaving her in the hall.

Daisy wondered what she was about to see. All of her questions had been answered except the final one. And, to the little girl inside of her, it was the only one that mattered.

Is it real?

Either way, she'd have the story of a lifetime now. She just had to survive long enough to tell the tale. In just an hour or two, Daisy hoped, all of this could be behind her. She'd write up her article and mend fences with Jordan.

But first…

Deep breath, she thought. *Here we go.*

The lights were off inside the apartment, so Daisy looked for a switch on the wall. Eagle beat her to the punch and turned on a lamp, which was sufficient to make the room visible enough to navigate, though not bright enough for comfort. The room looked exactly the same as when Daisy had been there the previous day, and the balcony doors were closed. The bleach smell was present again, although there was something different about it this time.

"I thought you said her legs would be in here?" Daisy asked Eagle.

"Something's not right," he said, sniffing the air. "Be on alert."

"I'm already on alert! Look at me. Alert! What do you mean "something's not right?" That's not what you want to hear from the monster expert, dude."

"We're okay," he said. "Just be alert. That's all."

"What are you worried about? Tell me."

"This isn't her den," Eagle said. "It's someplace else. I miscalculated."

"What does that mean?"

"I don't know yet."

He began walking around the room, inspecting Catalina's belongings, looking for clues.

Daisy's suspicions about Eagle returned.

No legs, huh?

That had always been her experience with supernatural claims. You always *just* missed it. Or it will happen again *next* time. For sure. It just never happens when you're looking.

Daisy noticed Eagle had stopped in front of the old painting of Catalina's ancestor with a baby. She walked over to join him.

"It looks just like Catalina."

"It *is* Catalina, Daisy," he said softly.

Eagle sounded strange. His mood had shifted suddenly. He seemed less confident than he had throughout the evening. He inspected the writing on the picture frame with the name of the convent.

"*Hindi...hindi ito totoo...*" Eagle whispered.

"What?" Daisy asked. "What is it?"

He didn't answer. He just nodded his head and snickered.

"Eagle Valdez... Monster Hunter," he said to himself.

He seemed to be shutting down. That wasn't good.

"Hey, you're still with me, right?" Daisy asked. "I can't do this alone. What's wrong with you?"

Eagle laughed to himself, first softly, then building into a loud throaty chuckle.

"What's so funny?"

"She's been on a killing spree here in New York City," he said, "just rubbing my nose in it, and I didn't even know about her."

"Don't beat yourself up about it. So what? One slipped through the cracks. You're here now. Let's get her."

He stopped laughing. "You don't understand, Daisy." He pointed at the writing on the painting. "It's her. It's all Catalina."

"The massacre at the convent?" Daisy asked. "I looked it up. That was over a century ago. What does that mean?"

If Eagle found fear useful, it looked like he'd have plenty to rely on tonight. The adventurer looked terrified.

"She's one of the old ones," he said.

Daisy wasn't sure what that meant, but the fact that he was scared terrified her.

Eagle's head jerked up and he listened intently for something.

"What?! What is it?" Daisy asked.

"SHHHH!!!"

The room was totally quiet. Daisy couldn't hear anything. What did he think he'd heard?

"It's time for the whip," he said, bending down to open the latches on his hardshell case.

"I still don't hear anything," Daisy said, although she was beginning to notice a foul odor in the room cutting through the sting of bleach.

Eagle opened the Louis Vuitton briefcase to reveal a monster-hunting kit straight out of a vampire movie. There was even a crucifix.

On closer inspection though, Daisy noticed the assortment of items carefully strapped inside or nestled in form-fitting cushioning was peculiar. A whip took up much of the area and there were many small vials of chemicals or potions. She saw several pieces of jewelry or stones.

"Are you gonna use those necklaces for something?" she asked.

"Those aren't necklaces," Eagle said, sounding offended. "They're amulets."

Daisy hoped she'd have a chance to look through his briefcase later because it looked fascinating but one inclusion in the case demanded an immediate answer.

"What's with the doll?" Daisy asked, pointing to a tiny figurine of a Wonder Woman-type superhero figure.

"Never leave home without Darna," Eagle said, patting the doll on the head.

Out of the corner of Daisy's eye she saw movement. There was a rippling in the shadows behind an old armchair in the corner of the room. The back wall seemed to pulse and shimmer. It looked like the reflections of streetlights, the way they stretch and morph across her ceiling at night, lying in bed. By the time Daisy realized what she was seeing, the creature's wings had completely unfolded. It was there, right in front of her.

JESUS CHRIST!
IT'S REAL.

The thing in front of her was a vision pulled from nightmares. Daisy knew that she should alert Eagle and then run for her life, but she was too paralyzed for her muscles to behave, not out of fear, out of *revelation*. She was amazed, and wanted to study the creature. If a Bengal tiger suddenly hopped into the middle of your living room, your fight or flight response would be tempered by the unexpected, and rare, opportunity to behold such a stunning animal privately and up close. That moment to see the manananggal was a gift.

But the urge to witness it longer–to *know*–no matter the cost, was the same deadly allure that led storm hunters and wildlife photographers to their demise.

Seeing the manananggal also unlocked an emotion inside her she'd forgotten since childhood. When Daisy was a little kid, she'd easily believed that department store Santas were the REAL Santa Claus. Once she got a little older, she downgraded them to merely "helper Santas." Eventually, she realized all the Santas were just haphazardly employed men with fake beards, and the nature of Christmas changed for her forever. She still loved Christmas, but never again had it been *magic*.

Daisy saw magic in front of her for the first time in over twenty years.

Sure, perhaps, the manananggal could eventually be explained away as just a bizarre unknown animal, or a woman with a medical condition, something ultimately *knowable*, but it was still the most bizarre and incredible thing she'd ever witnessed. And Daisy couldn't pull herself away.

Daisy knew she only had seconds to absorb as many details as her eyes would allow. Her focus darted around, picking out details, trying to burn them into her brain like she'd be tested on them later.

The manananggal's ears were pointed but they weren't oversized like Spock ears, where an attachment had been added. The ears were elfish, long and tapered into rounded points at the tips, but they were narrow, petite and delicate-looking, even dainty. Daisy saw elongated canines peeking out from under the creature's upper lip. She would have noticed giant fangs when she met Catalina, so they too had been part of the metamorphosis but, like the ears, they seemed natural and lived-in, as opposed to a recent addition.

The manananggal's wings began to flap, creating strong gusts of wind current in the room. Daisy needed to alert Eagle, but she'd noticed the face…

My God.

Through the monstrous eyes and nostrils which flared out slightly like a bat, Daisy identified the regal features of that hauntingly beautiful face.

It was Catalina.

"Eagle! She's here!!"

Eagle pulled the whip from its housing in the lid of the case and unfurled it across the floor of Catalina's living room. But the beast was already airborne and collided with him, sending them both crashing into a coffee table.

Eagle banged his arm on the side of the table as he fell. "*Aguy!*" he screamed, losing his grip on the handle of his whip. He heaved the manananggal off him, reaching for his weapon. The creature repositioned—quickly, in a fast burst of movement like an insect—using its long claws to pivot itself around to re-engage Eagle.

Lightning fast!

The movement had happened in a blink. Daisy had imagined the manananggal would be helpless on land. It had no legs for Christ's sake. Part of her had even hoped it might be *comically* easy to defeat such a thing, more of a scary story than an actual brush with death.

There would be no such luck.

If anything, the lack of extra mass below the waist made the thing *extra*-maneuverable. Its arms were narrow but clearly incredibly powerful, and the fingers were stretched out like claws, which seemed to have no trouble supporting the animal's full body weight as it prodded its way toward Eagle. It moved weightlessly like a spider.

Eagle was cornered and couldn't get to his whip. Daisy knew she had to do something. She grabbed a wooden armchair and tried to flip it up so the legs were pointed outward like a shield, but the chair was way heavier than it looked, and she could barely lift it.

Eagle screamed across the room. The manananggal had its claw dug into his chest.

With a burst of adrenaline, Daisy tried again. She lifted the chair and then shifted it around to get a better hold from a different angle. She staggered over toward the corner of the room—towards the monster.

"Yo, Catalina!" she called out, trying to get her attention. "You and your fucking lizard should have stayed out of Queens."

At that, Daisy lunged at the beast with the piece of furniture, managing to trap it between the chair legs. The manananggal pushed back against her, forcefully. Daisy dug in her heel to get traction, trying to hold the animal in place long enough for Eagle to escape its grasp.

The creature, pinned against the wall and unable to fly, began to swing its long claws. The chair wasn't even close to long enough for those claws. Daisy's arms started getting scratched.

No, not just scratches.

They were cuts, she realized. And they weren't like paper cuts she wouldn't notice until later. These claw scratches were deep and each one stung immediately. Her arms would be torn to shreds if she kept this up.

Daisy realized Eagle had already moved and she hadn't noticed.

"Any time now, Eagle!" she yelled.

Daisy's arms were getting weak, and she couldn't hold the chair up any longer. With the final strength in her arms, she tried to keep Catalina trapped a little longer, but her hold loosened as gravity pulled the chair lower and the wings began to flap.

Daisy's arms gave out. She dropped the chair and turned to run. Immediately, she felt the manananggal hit her from behind. The room went dark as a black curtain covered everything. Daisy saw Catalina's apartment through a hazy filter of crisscrossing patterns as she fell to her knees. Her vision had gone dark and blurry, and she was enveloped in a horrible stench.

It's a wing, she realized. It was blocking her face.

Daisy's right arm cried out in pain. It was on fire.

Jesus! She's biting me. What the fuck?!

Daisy wondered how many final thoughts were filled not with the dread of death or reflection on life, but with only a dark laugh at how it all ended.

"This is really it, huh? Wow." Because an unexpected death only provided enough time for your first impulse response. And because death rarely came for you by your own rules.

But, if she died in that apartment, Daisy realized, then she *had* chosen her own fate. No one else had pushed her to that point. She'd climbed a mountain to get there. What she'd found at the top was her problem.

A loud crack ignited in the air and the manananggal squealed, releasing its vice grip on Daisy's arm, allowing her to stagger to her feet and see what had freed her.

It was Eagle, and his whip. Daisy noticed something was attached to the end of the weapon—

A stingray's tail.

"Sorry, Granny," he said to the manananggal. "But it's not your night."

He recoiled the whip and lashed at the creature again, striking it with the sharp tip of the tool, leaving a deep wound across its collarbone. It screamed in pain and began flapping its wings again. In the enclosed space, the gusts became like a wind tunnel. It was hard for Daisy to even stand her ground.

Once the manananggal was fully airborne, it turned to face the closed balcony doors, and then accelerated, crashing right through them, busting the door frame and shattering a glass panel. The creature disappeared into the sky.

"It was her!" Daisy said, running to the window. "And she really looks just like a fucking bat. It's real!" Daisy marveled at the empty clouds where Catalina had escaped, her heart still racing.

Eagle joined her at the balcony, recurling his whip. The air blowing in from the broken door was bone-chilling cold.

"How are you doing?" he asked her.

"I'm okay, I think," she said. "What about you? It looked like she had you dead-to-rights there for a minute."

"Don't worry about me," he said. "But you handled yourself well. I'm impressed. I'm even glad you came along."

That seemed like low praise since she had probably saved his life, but she would take it.

"What now?" she asked.

"It's no use staying here. She's probably watching from nearby. She'll be entirely focused on killing us. We won't get another chance tonight, but we still have to find her den. You can sleep on the couch at my place tonight. We'll debrief Coney and then try again tomorrow."

As Daisy followed Eagle back down to the lobby of the building, it occurred to her that she'd made a terrible mistake in Catalina's apartment. It was the kind of critical error she couldn't afford to make ever again. She'd forgotten to take a picture of the fucking monster.

* * *

About half an hour later, as Daisy was returning with Eagle to his hideout in Hunter's Point, a van pulled up outside The Impluvium.

The driver of the van cut the ignition and nervously approached the building. He'd been there before. He knew the way. He took the elevator upstairs and walked to Catalina Cordero's front door. It was ajar. The lights were off inside, and a cold breeze was blowing into the hallway from the apartment.

The man didn't want to go inside. He knew it was dangerous and he wasn't the risk-taking type. But his friend needed help. And that meant doing whatever it took, even if she'd asked him not to.

"Brave heart, Jordan…" he reassured himself, as he pushed the door open and entered Catalina's lair.

"Daisy?" he called out.

No answer.

There were signs of a struggle—broken glass and furniture. The place looked like a tornado had hit it.

"Daisy?!" he tried again.

Jordan noticed the entire balcony door had been shattered. He bent down to check out a puddle on the ground. Was it blood?

It seemed like Daisy had come and gone already and someone had gotten hurt. Jordan grabbed his phone to check in with her. As he pulled up Daisy's contact in his phone, Jordan became distracted by something on the floor.

Movement.

His heart skipped. Something was crawling on the rug near his shoes.

He stepped back in fright. Only afterward, did he realize what was on the floor.

It was Gimbal, Catalina's lizard. He'd gotten free of his habitat during whatever calamity had occurred in the room.

The breeze from the open balcony picked up in intensity and all the small items that had been spilled in the struggle began to blow around in the room.

This will be a mess to clean up, that's for sure.

The light coming from the balcony behind him dipped, making the room too dark to see anything. The wind picked up even further.

Shit. Okay, time to get out of here, Jordan thought. He knew it had been a bad idea anyway. He had no business being at what appeared to be a crime scene, especially without Daisy there.

He tried walking toward the sliver of light coming from the front door across the room, but the torrent of swirling air made it difficult to keep his balance. He struggled toward the door, with the sound of glass and ceramic breaking behind him from the gale.

Then, a small worm appeared, wrapping around the side of his body. He stopped, grabbing at it curiously.

What is this?

The worm reared back and plunged itself into his stomach, sharp as a knife.

Jordan screamed, trying to pull the unknown object out of his body, but it kept wiggling, further and deeper inside. He slumped to the floor, pulling furiously at the winding filament entering his abdomen. His belly was full of searing pain. He moaned in agony. It wasn't just the torn flesh that hurt, it felt like his wound was full of battery acid.

He collapsed on the floor, helpless, as the worm repositioned itself, moving under the skin of his stomach, feeding. His head drifted backward and hit the floor. He was getting sleepy, was it just a dream?

Jordan's eyes grew heavy.

He wasn't in his apartment. Where was he?

The pain was gone now. In fact, the nightmare had become a lovely little dream.

As he closed his eyes for a well-deserved rest, all his friends and family came to meet him, and he witnessed a miracle–a beautiful angel hovering over him.

CHAPTER 21

Hunter's Point

* * *

Coney paced around Eagle's hideout, feeling useless and ruminating. She was worried about Eagle and their new acquaintance Daisy, and wished she'd been allowed to go with them. Eagle was too protective with her, always reluctant to let her see any real action. Despite their history together—she'd known him since childhood—Eagle sometimes treated her like just a glorified travel agent or research assistant. He always kept secrets from her, including the identity of his primary client.

Things had changed a couple years ago. Eagle had always been a small-time hunter. He'd made a decent living; his tastes were too lavish to settle for anything less. But he could never have afforded to build their new facility in Long Island City without the deep pockets of his new buyer, and he refused to tell Coney who it even was. He claimed it was for her own good.

Lechugas!!

Eagle could never have done any of this without her. Most of the good ideas had been hers. He'd wanted to build his hideout inside a high floor of an office building, looking out over New York City. He'd been imagining the view and hadn't been thinking about the difficulty of getting all that gear and furniture—not to mention the weapons!—up and down through a busy elevator. Eagle was a man of many talents, but he sometimes missed things that were right under his nose. *That's why he needed her*, she told herself.

Coney heard the alarm system disengage—THEY WERE BACK!

Already? She knew from experience Eagle could stay out all night on these missions. Sometimes it took more than one night. They'd made quick work of this manananggal, it seemed. She ran to the back door and got ready to greet them. Eagle would never walk the long way they'd sent Daisy the first time. Daisy's route had been a precaution. Coney tried to imagine Eagle crawling under a gate in his posh clothes. Ha! No, he probably trusted Daisy enough to know about the back entrance by now.

Eagle held the door open for Daisy, who entered first. She looked at Coney and shook her head to say "no."

They'd failed! And Daisy was bleeding. Eagle entered the room and reset the alarm system.

"What happened?" Coney asked him.

He didn't answer, instead heading straight for the stairs without even looking at her. He went into his bedroom and shut the door.

"Are you okay?" she asked Daisy.

"I'll never be okay again after that," she said. The reporter looked horrible, like she'd survived an accident. Coney realized that she had.

What happened in that apartment? She wondered. *Maybe they'd been lucky to make it back at all.*

"So much for my jacket," Daisy said, looking at the rips in her sleeves which were caked with dried blood.

Daisy needed medical attention.

"There's a first aid kit in the closet next to the kitchen," Coney told her. "We need to get you patched up. Go grab that kit and take your jacket off, then rest in the living room. I'll be right back to take care of you, okay?"

Daisy nodded that she understood. Coney worried she might be in shock and didn't want to leave her alone, but she needed to check in with Eagle. She ran up the stairs and didn't even bother knocking. Eagle's door was unlocked, and she found him sitting on his bed, head downcast.

Eagle's bedroom was sparsely decorated and immaculate, not an item out of place. Eagle even ironed his bedsheets. The room appeared humble at first glance, the most notable decoration being the small Catholic altar, but Coney knew from experience that inside his dresser drawers were rows of fabulously expensive rolled ties and glittering watches. She knew that behind the unassuming door to his side was a walk-in closet even larger than the bedroom itself. Of course it was, he'd co-designed the layout of the place.

"She got away," he said.

"I know, Kuya."

Eagle stared down at the floor. Coney hadn't seen his confidence rattled like this in a long time. He wasn't usually the contemplative type, more a man of action than someone that lives inside his own head the way she did.

"So what?" she said. "Since when do you care if it takes more than one attempt? You bragged about camping out for a week–

"I wasn't bragging!" he said. "I was just explaining…" Eagle sighed.

She wondered if he felt threatened by an aswang being in New York, setting up shop right next to them without the "world's greatest monster hunter" even noticing. It was an embarrassing oversight, yes, but one that could be rectified and prevented with more vigilance in the future.

"You'll get her next time, Kuya, what's the big deal?"

"The big deal, Coney, is I've seen Catalina before."

"What?" she asked. "When?"

Eagle stood up and started pacing the room. He was searching for words. She'd only seen him this vulnerable twice before, both times during major life crises. He didn't let people see him like this.

"What happened in that apartment?"

"I've told you the story about the first time I saw an aswang," he said, "when I was a young child in Cebu."

It was a criminal understatement. Eagle had told Coney that story dozens of times and would usually get to it like clockwork if he was drinking long enough. At five years old, Eagle had been in a remote area with his parents and had encountered an aswang—in fact, a manananggal, specifically. The incident had traumatized Eagle. Not just because the creature had been frightening, but because he'd seen his father, a rich, powerful man everyone feared, reduced to complete cowardice in the jungle.

Eagle's passion for the unknown and quest to conquer his fears had eventually shaped a hobby into a lifepath and his offbeat choice of "career" was one of a couple intractable issues his parents had with Eagle's lifestyle choices, resulting in estrangement from his immediate family. It was a sore spot in his life. Was he saying Catalina was *the* manananggal from his childhood? It's not like they were super common, but it seemed very unlikely. They didn't travel. Most were lucky to pick off a few villagers without attracting attention. Hopping continents?

"That was her?!" she asked.

"I think so, Coney. I can't be sure."

"That would make her old!" Coney said.

"Hey!" Eagle yelled. "I'm only thirty-three. Watch yourself."

"I meant relatively," she said.

Eagle stopped pacing and the depressive look came over him again. "I think she's even older than that," he said. "*Really* old. What do you know about Nuestra Señora del Silencio? The old convent. Have you ever toured the remains?"

"No. I haven't been there. I know about it, of course. But there's no reason to go. It's like visiting Chernobyl, just ruins. There's nothing to see. People just go to get a picture to brag they were there."

"Yeah, but do you know the full legend?" Eagle asked. "About the nun?"

"Of course!" Coney said. "This stuff is my specialty. Let's see… Rich girl gets into trouble, her parents send her to the convent to become a nun, but she gets knocked up by a priest. The baby dies and she gets revenge by killing everybody. Right?"

"The other nuns kicked her out first," Eagle corrected. "The legend is, she gave birth, and the nuns cast her out into the jungle, where the baby died. *That's* why she got revenge."

"You believe all that?"

"I do," he said. "And I think the nun was Catalina. It's her. It's all her."

"You think the nun became a manananggal? And it's Catalina? That's impossible. That would mean she's been eating people without getting caught for over a century? I don't buy it."

"Coney, she's just as coordinated as we are! She has a system! We're seeing it with our own eyes! She's careful… so careful." Eagle rubbed his chin. "She's smart."

"It's true," Coney admitted. This wasn't the sort of challenge they were accustomed to. "I never imagined a manananggal being so… industrious."

"But we should have," Eagle countered.

"What do you mean?"

"You know how hard it was to immigrate to the United States, Coney. They do everything to stop you. Anybody who's here is someone who's already accomplished the impossible at least once."

"I didn't think about it like that," she said. "Any aswang that makes it here to the states wouldn't be like a low-level thug. They'd be a crime boss."

Coney realized Eagle was right. They'd assumed a lack of sightings outside the Philippines meant the creatures couldn't spread. But, in actuality, any aswang that had managed to emigrate out of the islands might be good enough to cover their tracks. And for that matter, what else might they have been missing all this time?

She felt bad for Eagle. It was like Sherlock Holmes discovering not only that he had a Moriarty who was his equal, but that he'd been badly losing a game—one he hadn't even known he was playing.

* * *

Daisy sat on the couch, stunned from the events in Astoria, listening to the muffled sound of a Tagalog conversation upstairs. Under normal circumstances, she might have been curious if they were talking about her, but these were abnormal circumstances, and she was completely fixated on the searing pain in her arm. She'd retrieved the first aid kit from the closet, a giant hard case. She'd looked inside and had been pleased to find that, like everything else in the building, it was overly-stocked. It looked like they were prepared for war injuries if needed.

She managed to turn on the TV and found the *Elm Street* marathon on AMC again. They'd made it to *Freddy vs. Jason*.

How long are they gonna be upstairs?! Daisy worried. *I'm bleeding to death down here. No rush!*

At least it was a big TV. She sat on the edge of the couch, looking at the wounds on her bare arms. She'd wanted to go to the hospital after leaving Catalina's apartment, but Eagle had insisted it was too dangerous and he had all the necessary training and supplies.

Finally, the upstairs door opened. Coney came running down with Eagle following behind her. He'd taken off his outerwear and rolled up the sleeves of his collared shirt. There was a red spot on his chest where the manananggal's claw had stuck him but otherwise he looked unscathed.

"Let's get you fixed up," he told her, as he sat down on the couch.

Daisy showed him her arms which were full of deep scratches caked with dried blood. Her right arm had two deep puncture marks and the muscles in her bicep hurt when she moved it.

"I'm not gonna turn into one of those things, am I?" she asked. "It bit me."

Eagle inspected the punctures on her arm. She felt embarrassed. It was like showing a doctor some wound you sustained through stupidity. Except she hadn't done anything wrong. Why did she feel embarrassed?

She realized it was because this probably never happens. Eagle doesn't get bitten. She'd messed up. And now she may have become a liability to everyone if she was infected.

"No," he assured her. "Relax. You won't become a manananggal."

"Are you sure?" she asked. "She got me good. Look. And my arm really stings. They don't infect you through the saliva, like a vampire? You're totally sure?"

"Actually, I don't know," he said. "I've never been bitten. We'll keep an eye on it."

"What?!!"

Eagle tilted his head back and roared with laughter.

"I got you!" he laughed. "You should have seen your face, oh my God. I'm kidding with you. The saliva won't hurt you. But it will itch like crazy later. Trust me, I've been bitten by everything."

WHEW. Daisy relaxed a little. Now that he mentioned it, Daisy noticed a series of scars on Eagle's forearms, including a rather large one near his right wrist.

"Is that scar from a manananggal?" she asked.

"That one? No, that's just from rollerblading in the house as a kid. I was showing off for my cousins and cut myself on the sink. Brace yourself, I'm afraid this is going to sting," he said, before applying disinfectant to the first of her wounds.

"FUCK!!!" Daisy screamed. It hurt even worse than Catalina's fangs in the apartment.

Coney came to join them on the couch, bringing her a bottle of water. Daisy took a shaky sip, feeling relief that she wouldn't spontaneously sprout wings and rip her legs off. But it begged an interesting question, one Coney hadn't addressed in her YouTube video.

"Then how *do* you become a manananggal?" Daisy asked.

"Depends on who you ask," Eagle said. "No one has ever put one of these things in a cage to study it and most people who see it die. That's why myths get so fragmented."

"There are a few proposed methods," Coney said. "Tainted food, rituals, and magic. But most legends trace back to the black chick."

"The only explanation I've seen with my own eyes," Eagled agreed, "is the bird."

"The bird?" Daisy asked. With her mind focused on something besides the pain, Eagle's first aid work on her arms became less torturous.

"Some believe that the power of an aswang is transferred by a small black chick," Coney said, "like a tiny parasitic creature living inside them. Eagle has seen one."

"You think Catalina has a bird inside her?" Daisy asked.

"We don't know," Coney said. "But it's his working theory."

"What do we do next?" Daisy asked. "Try again tomorrow?"

"We won't be able to ambush her at home a second time," Eagle noted. "We still need to find her den."

"That could be anywhere," Daisy said. "Where do we start? This lady's always one step ahead. We don't even know how many victims there actually are."

Daisy thought about the last thing she'd talked about with Greggory before the Rhinelander slaying had ruined their plans. He'd been planning on checking the other counties for similar deaths.

"Could any of those fancy computers over there be used for hacking?" Daisy asked.

"That's a Coney question," Eagle said.

"Well, theoretically," she said, thinking. "But it's probably above my pay grade. I'm not a hacker. Sorry."

Coney looked embarrassed, like she was letting Daisy down by not having the skills. It made Daisy regret even asking. It was a silly assumption. Just because someone has expensive computers doesn't mean they're an expert coder.

"Maybe I could call someone though," Coney said. "What did you have in mind?"

"A friend of mine is a Queens medical examiner," she explained "I'd asked him to check the OCME system for deaths in other counties to see how many victims we were really dealing with. But he cut me off. They can't talk to reporters."

"You just want to check the database of autopsy records for the five boroughs?" Coney asked. "Well, I can do that. I was going to anyway! I thought you meant something hard. I'll take care of it tonight."

"Wow, okay." Daisy said. That was actually a huge relief. It felt like they'd found their next steps. They were still moving, still planning. There was still hope.

"But what about Catalina?" she asked.

"She works at the hospital. I'll go ask around there tomorrow," Eagle said, finishing up work on Daisy's arm, now tightly wrapped in gauze. "Good as new!" he decided.

Daisy took a sip of water and dribbled some on her shirt because her hands were still shaking. Eagle noticed.

"Coney," he said, "we need to get Daisy's mind off of Catalina. Mine too. Guess what I have in mind?"

"KARAOKE!!!" Coney screamed.

She jumped up off the couch and flew over to the TV, where she opened a cabinet underneath, revealing a complicated sound system. She pulled out microphones and started setting up a mic stand.

"Oh no! Guys," Daisy said, "I'm a drummer, and there's a reason they don't give us microphones. Plus, I'm really not in the mood right now. I'm injured. Not tonight, I'm sorry."

"That's fine," Eagle said. "You can just watch."

He grabbed a controller and switched inputs on the television. He began scrolling through a database of songs and artists that looked a little too complete to be a consumer product and Daisy realized it was a *professional* karaoke system.

Eagle picked his track, a Filipino song she didn't recognize called "Halik" by a group named Aegis. Daisy appreciated the effort to comfort her with the distraction, but wasn't expecting much from Eagle in terms of vocal performance. He didn't seem the type for fun and games. She expected a half-hearted, ear-splitting attempt, conjuring memories of similar efforts from co-workers at past *Brooklyn Believer* Christmas parties.

INSTEAD…

Eagle launched into an operatic vocal intro–pitch perfect!–followed by a frenetic, emotional performance that had him bouncing around the conversation pit as he hit every word and note like a pro. With a mic in his hand, the man-of-few-words had transformed into a charismatic superstar and was parading around the living room pit like a fucking diva belting out high notes as Coney cheered him on.

This guy could perform at bar mitzvahs and not miss a beat! Daisy thought. There was a showman under that cold facade, hiding just like his building was–in plain sight.

When his Aegis song finished, Eagle passed the microphone to Coney.

This time, Daisy definitely wasn't expecting much. Coney didn't look like a singer, and she anticipated an awkward but humorous, tone-deaf performance, the kind Daisy would give, that might put a smile on her face and lower the bar a little.

INSTEAD…

Coney picked "Vision of Love" and the opening trill sounded like fucking Mariah Carey herself had entered the building. Somehow, out of Coney's tiny little body, came a booming command performance so powerful it sounded like she could bring the light fixtures down on their heads. And not a single note off pitch! It was like Daisy had stumbled into an *American Idol* audition and everyone was good.

What gives? Was every Filipino a great singer? What do they put in the fucking water?

Coney finished and then passed the mic to Daisy.

"Your turn," she said. Coney seemed to realize that Daisy would object because she countered her refusal preemptively, "Come on, please. Just have fun."

Giving into peer pressure, Daisy scrolled through the list of artists looking for something she knew. She'd never been a singer; it wasn't her thing. She loved music but didn't feel its pull in that particular way. She didn't even sing in the shower. Plus, thanks to her dad, she preferred rock classics over the pop hits they would likely recognize. On the spot, and not wanting to take too long, she selected "Black Hole Sun" by Soundgarden and nervously looked at the mic as the guitar intro began.

"I don't know this one," Eagle made sure to point out.

"It's good for you to hear some new things," Coney told him. "Me too."

As her moment came, Daisy pictured the starting pitch in her mind and imagined her voice belting the opening line perfectly before moving the air from her lungs into the microphone.

"In my eyes, indisposed, in disguises no one knows..."

The sound that came out startled her. She had nailed it. What's more, the high-quality microphone and sound system had a rich, sweet, professional sounding tone that was exciting to use, like playing with a fancy new toy. With a little more confidence, she continued singing and, despite a couple little falters and flubbed words, she impressed even herself.

"Wow, Daisy!" Coney exclaimed.

Even Eagle nodded lightly in reluctant approval.

As she continued, she tried to stay focused on her pitch and the lyrics but her mind began to wander. She thought about the singer, Chris Cornell, who had taken his own life at age 52 and how most lead singers of that generation, 90s rockers, had died tragically and before their time.

You could never see an intact performance of Nirvana, Alice in Chains, Blind Melon, Stone Temple Pilots, Jane's Addiction, the Cranberries, or Soundgarden, because of misfortune.

"Times are gone, for honest men..."

She wondered what it said about Gen-X and their place in the world that so many of their idols disappeared before their time. The contrast was particularly stark with 60s rockers, who seemed to have been built to withstand any storm and continued touring and romping around on stage well into their geriatric years. She dreamed about all the songs the 90s singers had left to sing but we never heard, and wondered how the world might be different if we had.

Daisy realized her rendition of "Black Hole Sun" had become an unusually soulful and somber affair. Instead of proudly belting the choruses as intended, she'd been singing them like a sad, pleading lullaby. She'd been channeling all her dread and sorrow and her catharsis over Catalina into the notes and was surprised to find tears running down her eyes. She wiped the moisture away, a little embarrassed, but noticed Coney's eyes were tearing up as well.

When the song finished, she handed the mic back to Eagle.

"You might not be ready for that," she joked, "but your parents are gonna love it."

They each sang an encore. Eagle performed "Uptown Funk," complete with dance moves, and Coney picked an Ed Sheeran song.

For Daisy's encore, she chose "Put Your Records On" by Corinne Bailey Rae, a favorite song from her childhood. It was one of the first songs she remembered identifying as "her music" instead of something she'd listened to because her parents did. She still knew all the words by heart so she could concentrate on her pitch instead of the lyrics.

After karaoke, Eagle retired to his bedroom for the night and Coney set to work on the computer, breaking into the OCME database of NYC autopsy records. Daisy was curious about how it worked and wanted to watch her at the computer, but she was too exhausted from the night's events and excused herself to rest on the couch, where she promptly dozed off.

Daisy woke twice during the night. The first time, she noticed the room's lights had been dimmed and someone had placed a blanket over her on the couch. It smelled like hotel sheets. The building was very quiet, perhaps because it was away from residential areas and near the creek. The only sound in the big room was the clacking of Coney's keyboard. She was still working.

The second time Daisy awoke, she saw Coney was passed out on the other couch in the living room pit across from her, work finished and snoring softly.

In the morning, Daisy woke to the smell of coffee. Coney had already disappeared from the living room area. Daisy felt surprisingly rested. Despite the unfamiliar surroundings and waking up a couple times, she'd gotten a full night's sleep.

She heard Eagle and Coney chattering in Tagalog in the kitchen and came to join them.

"Is that coffee?" she asked.

"Daisy's up!" Coney said, rising to start pouring her a cup. "How did you sleep? It's great here, right?! The couches are better than my bed at home!"

Daisy would find Coney's level of general enthusiasm annoying from any lesser person, but Coney was kind-hearted and brilliant, which made her manic energy endearing. It reminded Daisy of herself when she'd been a little kid, overly-excited about her friends coming over. She remembered staring at the clock, counting the seconds until the fun would start. To Coney, this was like a slumber party.

"I slept great," Daisy said. "But it seems like you barely slept. Did you have any luck with the autopsy records?"

"Ooh!" Coney said. "Be right back!" She darted off for the computer workstation, leaving Daisy and Eagle alone in the kitchen, sipping their coffees.

"After sleeping," Daisy said, "now everything about last night feels unreal. I was so panicked the whole time, it's like a blurry haze in my mind. I just remember its red eyes."

"She was quite real," Eagle said. "Look at your arms for the proof."

Daisy sensed an opportunity from the discussion, and it sent her heart racing.

Why didn't I think to ask him this before?! She scolded herself.

"Hey, Eagle, since you know about all this stuff…" she began coyly, "what about vampires? Are they real too?"

The man's eyes rose up to meet hers for only a second. It was the look teachers had given her when she'd asked one of the dumbest questions they'd ever heard. He didn't even bother with words. Only a quick shake of his head was required to fully shut her suggestion down.

That's a shame, she thought, *but he doesn't necessarily know everything.*

Maybe these guys are specialists, like doctors. You don't go to a proctologist with an ear infection. Maybe if you have a manananggal problem, you see Eagle. If you have a vampire problem, you gotta see somebody else. She reminded herself to ask Coney when they were alone later since she seemed to be the smart one anyway.

Coney returned to the kitchen with a stack of printouts in her hand.

"You'll want to see this one, for starters," she said, placing a map image on the table which had place-markers all around New York City. "Our manananggal has been busy."

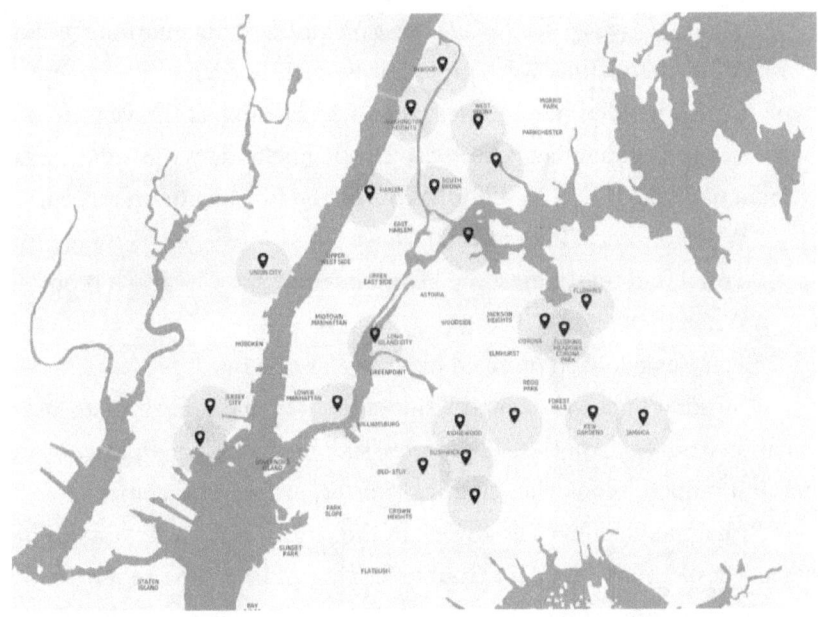

Daisy couldn't figure out what Coney had prepared. What had she done all night? She'd expected a list of victims. This looked more like a search result for restaurants. It couldn't be.

"Coney... you're not saying?"

"Daisy, I don't know what your friend Greggory came up with, but I checked the entire area and found twenty-two unexplained deaths in the last three months where the cause of death was intrathoracic bleeding and organ damage from unknown incised wounds just like the ones you know about. I included New Jersey."

"Holy shit!" Daisy said. "Catalina's a mass murderer. Like for real."

Eagle stayed quiet, sipping his coffee.

"Did any of them have toxicology reports with, uh, protein sampling?" she asked.

"Just the teenage boy's autopsy you told me about. Queens seems to be the only facility that thought of that, but it looks like there are manananggal victims in two states already. And every borough except Staten Island is affected."

Even literal monsters don't want to go to Staten Island, the map suggested.

"All of the victims were pregnant women and children, except for two." Coney handed her another page, which listed all the victims. Two names were highlighted. One was Dr. Rhinelander, the other was a woman named MONICA THOMPSON, the first victim on record.

"Who's Monica Thompson?" Daisy asked.

"You'll find this interesting!" Coney said. "She was also a reporter."

"What?!"

Even Eagle looked up from his coffee at that one.

"But don't get too excited," she said. "The file said she was just on vacation from Los Angeles. There were statements from people who knew her and it doesn't look like anything sinister, just a weird coincidence."

"Imagine Catalina's first week in the city," Eagle said, "establishing herself... she may have had trouble feeding at first. The reporter could have been an opportunistic kill."

"Still," Coney added, "she wasn't pregnant, so it's a notable deviation from her pattern."

"I'd like to follow up on that," Daisy said. Even if it was a coincidence, it was the last thing she needed to hear right then. A good night's sleep had calmed her anxiety enough to function and she had things to do. Worrying that Catalina might also have a sweet tooth for reporters was an extra wrinkle that her brain didn't need at the moment.

But she had to look into it. How could she not?

"I've got the next of kin contact info in her file," Coney suggested.

Good, that's a start, Daisy thought. But what about Catalina? She pulled Coney's map closer on the table to study it again.

Twenty-two victims. And those were only the ones the city knew about so far. Daisy knew Pappas would probably be added to the list very soon. At the Unisphere, Carmen had suggested some bodies weren't even found. Catalina's death toll could be enormous.

"Look," Daisy said, seeing an obvious pattern to the place-markers. "The murders almost form a ring around her building in Astoria."

"Yes," Eagle said. "They prefer their hunting grounds to be away from their home. It's why they go on raids, to put distance between their kills and the den."

"So, her den has to be close to her apartment," Daisy thought out loud. "In the same area, inside the ring."

"It'll be close. I thought it *would* be her apartment," he said. "The lower half is extremely vulnerable during the transformation. She has to keep her legs safe."

And then it hit Daisy in the face like a city bus.

OF COURSE!

She'd been a fool.

"Eagle!!" she yelled, "I know where Catalina's den is!"

How absurd! Why didn't she see it? She'd been there a week earlier. She'd been possibly inches away from all her answers, at the very *beginning* of this ordeal, but had stopped short. Because she'd forgotten her fucking flashlight.

Daisy explained her experience in the neglected equipment shed on the roof of Catalina's building and Eagle agreed it was worth a proper inspection, but they had to wait until nighttime. If that was where Catalina stored her legs during her raids, then they had to catch her in the act to sabotage them. And showing up early would give away their possible advantage.

The group had a lot of work to do and made plans to split up. Eagle suspected the victims were mostly Catalina's patients from the hospital system and wanted confirmation. Unfortunately, Coney wasn't able to access the patient database remotely, so Eagle planned on escorting Coney to the hospital where she could physically copy the files to a USB drive while Eagle asked around about Catalina.

Coney was giddy about her skills being of use and getting to go with Eagle. "I'm doing field work!" she beamed.

Meanwhile, Daisy was running home for a shower and a change of clothes. Afterwards, she was supposed to lie low until they met up again in the late afternoon. Daisy intended to use her time to check up on the reporter from L.A. with the contact info in her autopsy file.

Before leaving, Daisy called in sick to work so they wouldn't expect her at the office and then tried wiping the dried blood off her jacket. She found the rips and holes weren't too bad. At least they were clean tears. It would never look the same again, but it could be mended. She wouldn't abandon her trusty leather jacket just because the 'ole girl had taken a few dings.

Next, Daisy tried calling Jordan to ask him to skip work again. Thankfully, it was Friday, so if they needed the weekend to handle Catalina, she didn't have to ask him to miss more than one day. There was no answer though. It was still early. He probably wasn't awake yet. She sent a text just in case.

Daisy joined Eagle and Coney at a large table where they were examining building plans of the hospital. Eagle was talking about stairwells and escape routes.

"Okay, I'm headed home," Daisy said. "I'll see you back here later."

"Be careful, Daisy!" Coney said.

"What do you call this place, anyway?" Daisy wondered.

"What do you mean?" Eagle asked her.

"You know what I mean. There's gotta be a name for it. I'll meet you at the…. What?"

"Oh," Coney said, "There isn't one really. I say "the river" sometimes. Or "hideout" or "the shop." Eagle used to call it "the building" until we had it fully up and running."

"No good," Daisy decided. "Are you guys even trying? Why not 'The Eagle's Nest?'"

Coney's eyes shot open, and she covered her mouth with her hands like a child learning a new curse word in front of her parent. Her eyes darted to Eagle and then sheepishly looked down at the floor.

"This place doesn't need a name, Daisy," Eagle said. "Does your apartment have a name?"

"My apartment doesn't have pinball machines and a front row view of the Manhattan skyline or–fuck yeah–it would have a name."

Coney walked her to the back door and Daisy felt lucky she'd found these new Pinoy friends. They just might save her life.

"She won't get me when the sun's out?" she asked Coney. "You're sure? I'm safe during the day, right?" she asked.

"During the day," Coney repeated. Her tone seemed to admit she couldn't make the same promise about afterwards.

"Oh!! I almost forgot, guys!" Daisy said, raising her voice so Eagle would hear her across the room as well. "Do you know what day it is?!"

They both stared at her, not understanding.

"Happy Halloween!!"

CHAPTER 22

Cortelyou Hospital

* * *

Cortelyou Queens Regional Hospital's entranceway greeted Coney and Eagle with a large, flattering portrait of the facility's namesake, David Cortelyou. They paused under the glare of his intense blue eyes as Eagle repeated the plan: he would get Coney access to the file system and then she would copy the patient directory while he poked around to learn about Catalina.

"What if we see her?" Coney asked. "She might be working today."

"That would be interesting…" Eagle agreed, considering the possibility. "But I doubt it. We've made New York City too dangerous for her now. I bet she doesn't even come back to work. She will skip town soon. But first, she has some unfinished business…"

Coney knew he was talking about them.

"…and then she'll move on to the next place, I believe. We can't underestimate her again."

"This Cortelyou guy always gives me the creeps," Coney said, noticing the portrait over their heads. The mega-billionaire was devilishly handsome, with graying blonde hair, but there was something off about his steely gaze; it was uncomfortably intense. They just looked like eyes that had seen things they shouldn't have.

"Why?" Eagle asked. "He's using his money to do something good. What's wrong with that?"

"Cortelyou's hospitals cut everyone else out of the loop but him," she said. "He's not some folk hero. He's trying to build a monopoly."

"He can't do that, not with everyone in the world trying to stop him. Besides, it's a private company. He refuses to do an IPO and let investors ruin all this. I admire him."

Coney's opinions sometimes differed from Eagle on these issues. Coney's upbringing had been financially secure, particularly thanks to contributions from her grandfather in the states, but Eagle came from old money and didn't share her aversion to flagrant displays of wealth and power.

"All the easier to avoid scrutiny," Coney said.

Eagle sighed. "God forbid the man opens affordable hospitals. You're always such a cynic! You can't accept that a rich guy might use his power to actually help the world. That's why all the other billionaires hate Cortelyou, because he actually puts his money where his mouth is."

"Sounds like someone's drinking the Kool-Aid," Coney said. "Be careful, Kuya. Gods and gurus deceive by giving us something shiny first as a distraction, so we don't realize what they take."

They reached the top floor, where Eagle considered their logistical options based on both their knowledge of the building schematics and the real-life activity in the building. The records department was huge and full of nurses and staffers so Eagle didn't even consider it as a place for Coney to work her magic. Instead, he eyed the IT department from the other side of a restricted glass door.

"This will do. I'll be right back," he said. "Stay put!"

Immediately, he was gone, leaving her alone—an undercover imposter!—in the hospital corridor. Coney watched the madness of staffers scrambling around her. Everyone seemed angry and frustrated. The new building was in the middle of a soft-opening to the public and it seemed to be going as chaotically as one would expect for such a giant, complicated institution starting from square one. Coney realized the timing could serve them well, since everyone in the building was probably battling private nightmares filled with problems to solve and fires to put out. They might even go unnoticed!

A man in blue scrubs slipped up beside her.

"WHAT ARE YOU DOING HERE?!" he bellowed in English, from the corner of her eye.

Coney's heart stopped.

She'd been caught before she'd even started! So much for field work!

"AH!! I got you!" Eagle roared, reverting back to Tagalog. He'd found scrubs and a doctor's identification lanyard somewhere and was holding a patient's chart on a clipboard. The man sure loved his costume changes. The badge hanging around his neck said, "DR. GALLAGHER." Coney hit him on the arm as payback.

"You should have seen your face, oh my God!" he chuckled. "Whew. That was good. Alright, let's do this."

He'd found a key fob for the department's door somewhere too. She didn't ask. On the other side, they found the IT room and Eagle looked through the small window on the door to peer inside.

"There's only one guy in there. Perfect," he said.

"Let me see too," Coney whispered. The window was too high for her, so she lifted up on her tiptoes to peer inside. There was a middle-aged man's face visible behind a rack of servers. She didn't see anyone else.

"How do we get rid of him?" she asked.

"I see car keys on the table. He drove here," Eagle said.

"So?"

"I know what to do. Stand aside for a minute."

She did as he asked and hid herself behind a cabinet along the wall. She peered around the corner to watch as Eagle knocked on the door. After a few seconds, the man answered.

"Yeah??" he asked. He seemed to be in a bad mood, like everyone else working in the hospital.

"It's almost 10:30," Eagle said, looking at his clipboard. His voice sounded very bored, like he'd said that hundreds of times already. "Last chance. That's when they start towing cars."

"What are you talking about?"

"I'm just making sure you sent your email to HR if you have a vehicle in the lot," Eagle told him.

"What email?"

"About the employee parking lot!" Eagle said. "Today's the day! Anybody who didn't submit their vehicle information is about to get towed."

"Nobody fucking told me," the guy said. "They're doing it when? Right now?! I'm in the middle of something! What the fuck?! I can't right now. Sorry."

"Well, I don't know what to tell you," Eagle replied. "Don't blame the messenger."

"What information do they need?"

Eagle scratched his chin. "Let's see, what all was it… license plates, registration, VIN number, uh, a copy of your driver's license and insurance. You know, all that. You didn't get the email?! Wait, what do you drive?"

"A 2019 Chevy Equinox," he said.

"What color?!" Eagle asked, with horror in his eyes.

"Black."

"A black 2019 Chevy Equinox?! Have you been asleep? They've been calling you over the intercom to move your car. What's wrong with you?"

"What?!"

"Yeah, for like ten minutes. Wow! So, *you're* the guy they're looking for. You really screwed up. You didn't hear the intercom?"

"No! I didn't hear it!" he roared, pulling at his hair like an animal in fury. "I hate this fucking place! I hate it!! Nothing works!"

"You'd better move your car first to be safe," Eagle said. "*If it's still there*… that is."

The IT guy looked petrified.

"And then you should take all your info to HR," Eagle continued. "Don't forget *any* of it."

"You just saved my fucking life!" the man said, running off toward the door to the elevators.

Coney watched it all from behind the cabinet until Eagle curled his finger at her to come join him in the room.

"I bought you some time," he said. "I don't know how much. Use it well."

"Where will you be?" Coney asked, taking a seat at the computer workstation inside.

"Finding out what I can about Catalina. Remember the plan—we won't meet up again. Copy the files to your USB stick and then head straight back to the hideout."

Coney was worried about her escape from the hospital later. What if she got caught? It had been scary enough walking in there with Eagle at her side. On the way out, she'd be alone.

"What if–

"Just keep your head down," he said, knowing her concerns already. "Once you leave this room, it's just a USB drive in your pocket. You're not doing anything wrong. No one will know. You understand? You can do this, Coney."

"Okay, I can do it. Yes."

"Just hurry," he reminded her on his way out the door.

Coney stared at the computer monitors and tried to steady her nerves. Now it was all up to her…

* * *

Eagle slipped a disposable mask over his face and then entered the nearest nurse's station where he sat down at an open, logged-in terminal. He seated himself right next to a nurse, working at the next computer. He didn't care about getting caught. In his youth, Eagle had mentored under a confidence man and walked away with techniques to talk his way out of most situations. In adulthood, he'd faced desperate life and death struggles in the jungle, requiring every ounce of his wit and courage. Compared to his trials in Capiz and Siquijor, a little undercover work in a hospital felt like parlor games to him.

He wasn't even concerned that the men and women around him might know the real Dr. Gallagher and the badge would give him away if anyone looked. They wouldn't look. A well-dressed, confident man could blend in anywhere as long as he acted like he was supposed to be there and didn't overstay his welcome. In fact, this hospital was such a trainwreck, he could probably convince any of these people he was their boss and give them orders if he wanted to.

The situation wasn't without risk but, even in a worst-case scenario, he had memorized the stairwells and exits and could easily escape the building. To Eagle, the little operation seemed like a series of light challenges, each of which he would be overequipped to handle. He was even having fun.

He gave the nurse seated next to him, a blonde in bright orange scrubs, a big flirty smile and she started twirling her hair.

As if, you hag, he thought.

He searched through the employee directory to look for Catalina Cordero. Eagle found her in the registry. She was a prenatal RN and worked with expectant mothers! How devious.

"Which way's OB/GYN?" he asked the nurse next to him.

"Third floor, on the left," she said, turning to face him with a smile. She thought he was flirting with her. "I'm still trying to learn the layout too," she added. "It's a mess, but we signed up for this, didn't we?"

"Thanks again, love," he said, standing to leave. "There are three words you've been waiting your entire life to hear…"

The nurse's eyes squinted in surprise.

He leaned in close, whispering in her ear, "Orange is unforgiving."

Eagle found the department of obstetrics and gynecology and approached a male nurse working in the wing.

"I'm looking for Catalina Cordero," Eagle said. "Do you know her? Is she working today?"

Eagle had told Coney he believed Catalina wouldn't be there. Time to see if he was right!

"Catalina? Of course I know her. I see her everyday…"

The nurse looked at the ID badge on Eagle's lanyard, clearly wondering who he was. The nurse's eyes returned upward.

"But she was a "no-call, no-show" today," he said. "They're still trying to get her on the phone."

Beautiful, Eagle thought. This guy didn't know Dr. Gallagher. And he'd been correct about Catalina.

"A no-show?" he asked the nurse. "Interesting…"

"Yeah, it's not like her. She's always so dependable."

"You haven't had problems with her before?" Eagle asked, turning the pages of his clipboard like the documents pertained to his questioning.

"Catalina? No, never. She's great. Smart. Probably the hardest worker here. A little quiet, but some people are like that."

"How is she with patients?" Eagle asked. "How does she handle the workload? The stress?"

"I've hardly ever seen her stressed. She's like a machine. In fact, she even volunteers for a bunch of work downstairs in addition to all her shifts in OB/GYN."

"Downstairs? What are you talking about?" Eagle asked.

"The free and sliding-scale clinic, downstairs," he said. From the nurse's tone it was clear Eagle had made a small mistake and should have known about the free clinic services. No matter, he could handle it. He just needed to redirect.

"We're already understaffed," Eagle said. "Ms. Cordero should have called to give notice. I'm sure the entire department has been impacted."

"You're damn straight," he agreed. "Donna's working another double thanks to her. It's preposterous. We're already spread too thin."

"Well, I'll see what I can do," Eagle said.

He started walking away from the nurse but then stopped. "Just remember though," he told the man, "we signed up for this didn't we?"

* * *

Coney pushed aside a bag of Flamin' Hot Cheetos and cracked her knuckles before setting to work on the hospital's state-of-the-art computer system. After a little digging, she quickly noticed a huge problem. There were no medical records accessible on the system.

What gives?

She searched every available directory and double checked the surrounding room to make sure she was at the correct terminal.

It had to be. The only other option was an ancient-looking IBM computer set up on a table next to the larger, primary workstation. It looked like a museum display.

Wait, why is that even in here?

The machine was running. It looked like a computer from the 1980s, running some kind of DOS program. Coney clicked through a couple screens and realized with terror why the old device was in the room. Further, as she stared with alarm at the floppy disk drive on the front of the computer's frame, she realized her USB stick would be completely useless.

She wouldn't be copying any files.

The entire plan was jeopardized. She had failed.

It didn't take her super-genius intellect to figure out what had happened. The "disruptive" hi-tech hospital's records system wasn't working properly yet. It looked like they were using the old computer to access existing patient files from the old hospital system they had bought out and assimilated. They probably intended to transfer the database but hadn't figured out how yet.

You've got to be kidding me! What century is this?

Another arrogance-born disaster because a tech bro had been overconfident. Should she have planned a contingency for this situation? How? What could she have done, brought floppy disks? No, she couldn't have known.

Surely Eagle would understand the situation. It wasn't her fault! It was like an act of God! But what would she tell him? How could she explain it without Eagle losing his faith in her?

So much for field work. After this, Eagle would never bring her along again.

* * *

Eagle found the sliding-scale clinic on the ground floor, near the emergency room, and asked around to gather information. It was an extra service offered by all Cortelyou medical systems—not just the hospitals, but the Urgent Care clinics as well—providing low and no cost basic medical care to uninsured and underserved patients.

It all made sense now. Catalina was a fox in the henhouse, using her position of power over expectant mothers to corral them like livestock in the slaughterhouse while she chose which one looked the tastiest. The hospital was her private buffet table. Not only that, her "volunteer" work downstairs provided her with a free list of off-the-radar children along with their last known addresses.

Eagle found it grotesque. He couldn't stand manananggals. It was simply the principle of the thing. To specifically prey on the helpless, to punch down, was both cowardly and contemptible.

Eagle wasn't on some mission to eradicate the world of all monsters. To the contrary: he believed even creatures of the shadows had their place. He sought balance. It was something of a hot take, but he maintained that all beings–yes, even some aswang–were a necessary component of the cosmic dance. They weren't "evil." The only true "evil" Eagle had witnessed had always been wearing a suit and a tie.

Aswang weren't entirely a negative force to be stamped out. They were creatures at odds with us; they were beings placed in an untenable position within the food chain–above people. It led to unavoidable conflict. But some aswang were even benign. It was foolish to generalize. Eagle wasn't a hunter or a poacher. He was a rancher culling the herd.

And yet, many Aswang, particularly the manananggal, were different. How could one compromise with a beast so depraved that it only fed on the helpless despite being strong enough to behave with more honor?

There was nothing else to be learned from sticking around in the hospital. With a thought about Coney, hoping she'd finished copying the files by then, he decided to head back to the hideout.

Eagle walked through the emergency room and paused to take one last look at the frenzy of medical staff and unfortunate patients surging around him. The hospital was a fiasco. Eagle believed in the idea behind the place. It was an incredible facility and the potential benefit for patients and the community once it was fully operational was obvious. But this was a slick new operation trying to build everything from the ground up, all while integrating the existing medical practices from the defunct hospitals it had gobbled up and replaced.

Seeing it with his own eyes, there was a clear arrogance on display. The hospital could barely keep the lights on at this stage. They shouldn't be seeing patients at this capacity yet. All the doctors and staff were running around like chickens with their heads cut off. Poor bastards. He almost felt sorry for them. Not to mention the patients! The kid in the stall next to him had his hand wrapped in a bloody towel and his dad looked furious like they'd been waiting all day. Eagle hated the American medical system. It was so inefficient–even here! What a joke.

He was used to field medicine. No waiting, no paperwork, no deliberation. Just immediate action and results. What was this poor kid even waiting for? He checked the chart.

For simple stitches! The boy had sliced his left index finger open. That was it! What was wrong with these people? This was a five-minute fix, TOPS! Why were this boy and his father still waiting? It was ridiculous.

"Are you the doctor?" the father asked Eagle, hopefully.

Eagle looked at the chart again out of curiosity.

It's just a couple stitches…

He could handle this kid's cut and then disappear before anyone even noticed.

Wouldn't that be kind of funny?

Besides, it looked like no one else was gonna do it and the good deed would almost make up for the fact he was technically committing lots of crimes.

"Let's take a look," Eagle said, slipping on a pair of nitrile gloves.

* * *

It was Coney's worst nightmare. She'd always been the whiz kid, the expert. It was her reason for existing. Eagle expected her to unravel problems, not get stuck on them.

Now what? She couldn't even hack the system later. It wasn't online!

She just *had* to get the records back to the hideout somehow, even if it meant stealing the darn computer itself.

Coney sat down at the old IBM system again and thought through her options. Could she get the CPU out of the room? It was too big and heavy to carry. There was an old dot matrix printer attached to the device, the kind with spools of paper rimmed with small holes on the side. It was sitting on a roller cart. Could she remove the printer and get the computer onto that cart? Then roll it out of the hospital unnoticed?

Probably not. But it looked like that might be her only realistic option left, other than just giving up.

OH NO!!

Coney realized her predicament was even worse than she'd realized; she would need the monitor too! The computer used an old-school port, VGA or something, and she wouldn't be able to connect it to any of the screens at Eagle's hideout without ordering adapters and they didn't have time. It's always something!

Wait…

Coney realized there could be another way to remove the files.

Yes!

But it wouldn't be quick. Not at all! Hopefully the IT guy wouldn't come back anytime soon. And hopefully Eagle hadn't encountered any issues like she had.

* * *

"How are you coming along on that wound vac, Dr. Gallagher?" an annoying female physician working the ER floor asked Eagle. She had been pestering him nonstop!

"I didn't forget! I'm getting to it!" he screamed. "I have to finish dressing these burns first, Rebecca! I don't know how I'm supposed to work under these conditions!"

"Well, what else is new?!" she replied. "We're all in the same boat!"

He'd gotten pulled into the frenzy of activity and they kept giving him more work to do. Now he couldn't get out of the situation without being noticed.

"No, no, no!" Eagle said, running over to supervise the rollout of an intravenous fluid bag on a pole. "That's the wrong patient. Carlisle was moved to stall 18! I told you! Stall 18! Pay attention!"

"Who the hell are you?" the man pushing the IV pole asked.

"I'm Dr. Gallagher!" Eagle screamed. "Who the hell are you?!"

"Dr. Gallagher."

* * *

"CODE GRAY. REPEAT. CODE GRAY ON THE FIRST FLOOR," a nervous voice announced over the loudspeakers. "REPEAT. WE HAVE A CODE GRAY. SECURITY TO THE ER."

OH NO! Coney thought, knowing the alert was probably about Eagle.

Was she out of time?

Coney watched, on the verge of panic, as the dot matrix printer threw ink at the rolling pages, only halfway through printing the entire patient directory from the hospital system onto a growing stack of paper on the floor.

She'd made the only move she'd had to make–PRINT ALL.

The old machine had lumbered back to life and started screeching its ancient song as it spat out pages and she tried to fold them so they wouldn't make a mess.

The pile was already so tall, would she even be able to carry it by the time it finished?

There seemed to be enough paper left to complete the job–she wouldn't have to worry about that. But was there time? If they knew about Eagle, did they know about her?

She was only to the "Ms," and it had taken five minutes to get that far; the machine was so slow!

"Hurry, you old dinosaur! Print! Print!!!"

* * *

Walter Gidley, a thirty-two-year veteran of Empire State Security Services, patrolled the southwest corridor of the building, trying to avoid the bustle of people hurrying in both directions. Unlike them, Walter wasn't in a hurry.

He sighed, as he paused to pull up the waist of his pants. They were annoying him. That pair of pants always fit so nicely after they'd been through the dryer, but only on day one. By day two, they started slipping and falling. He had to stop walking every few yards to hike his pants up again. Maybe his wife Rosie was correct, and he should go back to wearing a belt.

Someone bumped into him on his left side. They didn't even stop to apologize, just kept running. It wasn't like this at the old hospital. He'd spent over half his security career in that old building. It may have been a crumbling, bankrupt mess, but he had liked the predictable, boring routines of the place. Here, they had nothing but fancy new procedures and there was another security team on site that didn't treat him with the respect he was due after his years on the job. He was staring down retirement. The last thing this old dog wanted was to have to learn so many new tricks.

"CODE GRAY," the intercom blared, "CODE GRAY. SECURITY TO THE ER."

What?!

Code Gray? A hostile person? Walter didn't hear that one very often. And certainly not yet at this brand-new building. Cortelyou was barely open to patients. Who would be causing trouble?

Well, whoever it is. They didn't count on running up against Old Walter, did they? He'd put a stop to it.

Walter heard the commotion coming from the emergency room even before he made it to the double doors. He heard the sounds of a struggle and breaking glass. He opened the doors to see two other guards trying to wrestle a man in scrubs to the ground.

What the Dickens is this? Walter wondered.

The man in scrubs broke free of the guards and started running for the exit–towards him! Why were they trying to tackle this guy? What did he do? Walter tried to get a look at the man's face as he approached but only the eyes were visible due to the mask.

"Stop him!" one of the guards yelled from across the room. "He's an imposter!"

The man in scrubs reached Walter and stopped. They studied each other for a second. Then, the man dramatically turned over a large shelf of supplies, sending the contents crashing to the ground, leaped over it, and then disappeared into a nearby stairwell.

"Who does this guy think he is?!"

Walter followed the intruder into the stairwell and looked upward.

WOW!

The man in scrubs was bounding up the flights of stairs like gravity didn't even affect him! He was clearly some kind of athlete. He was supposed to chase after the guy? He wasn't the man for this job! Stuff like this never happened. Walter preferred giving stern warnings. He was already a little out of breath from running the twenty feet to the stairwell. At his age and weight, he might have a heart attack if he ran up all those stairs!

And what would his wife Rosie say about overexerting himself again?

Still, a job is a job. He hadn't patrolled hospital corridors all these decades to let some punk pull a stunt like that.

Walter looked again at the multiple levels of stairs over his head. The man in scrubs was still zipping through them, already near the top.

"Not on my watch," Walter said, as he began huffing and puffing up the steps, stopping every few seconds to pull up his pants.

* * *

Coney exited the IT room holding her huge stack of printouts and two security guards ran past her. They were probably after Eagle. Were they looking for her too? She couldn't walk out of the hospital like that.

She ducked into a small, unoccupied exam room to look for a way to disguise the stack of files so she wouldn't look suspicious on the way out of the building. It was a standard exam room, just a reclining chair with a pillow and a protective sheet of paper over it and cabinets full of useless medical supplies–cotton swabs and hand sanitizer.

Darn!

She needed a case or a bag, but there wouldn't be one just sitting around. She'd have to steal one, and she didn't want to do that.

Unless…

Coney eyed the pillowcase with inspiration.

She pulled the cotton sleeve from the pillow and tried to wedge the stack of paper into it without messing up the pages. The circumference of the case was just large enough to accommodate the files, but she had to deliberately edge it into place, each side a little at a time, until she could scoot the back end of the papers into the case and grab the remaining cloth as a sort of handle.

It wasn't pretty, but it looked less obvious than a stack of patient records.

Then, the door opened.

"What seems to be the trouble miss, err…," a doctor had entered the room and was looking at a chart, "Wallace? What brings you in today?"

Oh no!

What to do?! Should she tell him she's in the wrong room and leave with the bag? It might give them away. Had Eagle even had time to escape yet?

But what else could she do?

"It says here you've been experiencing delayed reflexes?" he asked.

Coney went with what seemed like the lesser of two evils.

"Yeah, a little bit I guess," she said.

"Well," he began, opening a cabinet. "Let's get the 'ole reflex hammer out and see what's going on here."

"*Lechugas!*" Coney said, hiding the bag of files behind her chair.

293

* * *

Dave the window washer made his final safety checks on the suspended scaffolding system on the roof of Cortelyou Hospital before beginning his work. It would be the first proper cleaning the windows of this new building had received, and they definitely needed it already.

Still, it would be an easy job. He wouldn't be free-hanging on ropes and there was zero rigging required for this gig. The building had its own suspended platform system which would lower down the columns of windows. It was pretty nice, even upscale compared to what he was used to. It was an expensive hanging cradle system and the work platform inside the little steel cage was large enough to maneuver around in and still have space for his bucket and tools.

The roof access door flew open and a man in medical scrubs came running out. It was a doctor, not a nurse or staffer, Dave was sure of that much immediately. He could tell from the man's look and attitude. He seemed "official." You knew these things after you spent enough time around people.

The doctor ran up to him and flashed a badge from his wallet.

"Police!" he yelled. "I need to commandeer this vehicle!"

He's a cop. Dave realized. *Of course. Okay, that explains it.*

But "vehicle?" What the fuck? Was he talking about the window washing platform?

"I dunno..." Dave said.

The cop didn't wait for permission. He walked right past Dave and began climbing into the cage.

Fuck it! Who cares? Dave thought. He didn't get paid enough to interfere with a police operation.

"Be careful, I guess!" he told the guy, stepping away to mind his own business.

The police officer stopped his preparations in the cleaning cradle and stared at Dave intensely, eying him up and down. Why was he looking at him like that?

"What size is that jumpsuit?" the cop asked.

* * *

Walter finally reached the top flight of stairs, with his heart pounding so furiously it threatened mutiny if he'd taken even a few more steps. He'd barely made it. In fact, he'd almost given up near the end. He couldn't breathe and a stitch had formed in his side by the second floor which had persisted his entire climb.

But he'd done it! He'd made it to the top. Walter opened the emergency exit leading to the roof level and emerged to find a shocking, bewildering scene:

The intruder was now standing in a big metal basket attached to the exterior of the roof wall. Without the mask on his face, Walter could see the troublemaker was an Asian man. He looked distinguished with hard eyes and a strong jaw, like a model or something. His scrubs had been discarded into a pile on the ground and he was instead wearing a green and black tracksuit.

"You know what? Let's just do the whole outfit. Helmet too," he told another man, who looked confused, and was wearing only a t-shirt and boxer shorts.

"Let's go! Chop chop!" he barked.

The half-naked man acquiesced and handed the imposter his hard hat. It was green and black, like the tracksuit. Walter watched as the Asian guy situated the helmet on his head to his liking.

"How do I look?" he asked the other man.

The intruder then made the sign of the cross and pulled a lever on the suspension controls–immediately plummeting away from view down the wall of the building.

Gone, without a trace.

The man in his underwear turned to look at Walter. He pointed down the side of the building as if to say, "He went that way! Get him!"

"No!!" Walter said.

No way! That's a step too far for Old Walter. He'd done enough already. He would not be following that guy down the side of the building. No, sir. This event was now officially above his pay grade.

Besides, what would Rosie think?

* * *

The window washing platform plummeted at uncontrolled velocity from the top of the West tower of the hospital. Under ideal circumstances, Eagle would have taken the time to familiarize himself with the control mechanism, a simple enough looking mechanical pulley system, but he'd been in a hurry and was pretty sure he'd accidentally loosened a knot that was supposed to stay tight—very tight.

He quickly found an emergency stop lever and yanked it.

The basket snapped to a halt at the end of the dual cables on either side and then bounced wildly from the sudden stop. Eagle went crashing into the side of the swinging cage and then fell, colliding with the big water bucket on the floor of the steel basket which splashed all over him. The cleaning cage continued to swing side to side from the leftover momentum, but Eagle found his balance and rose to his feet.

Through the swaying window in front of him, he saw an old woman lying alone on a hospital bed. She looked at him as well, and their eyes briefly met. Then, she closed the blinds on him.

Eagle heard voices above his head and looked up to see the real window washer and the security guard comparing notes at the edge of the roof as they watched his getaway. Speaking of...

He released the lever again, once more sending the cage falling at full, unrestrained speed.

Not too much!

He yanked himself to a stop again, this time holding onto the side of the basket so he wouldn't get flung around as it bounced at the end of the snagged line. There was another hospital window before him now. This time it looked like an entire family reunion gathered around an old man in the hospital bed. They'd even brought along their dog.

Eagle held onto the frame of the basket as it swung left and right in front of the window, waiting for it to settle so he could descend another stretch.

Uh Oh. He was attracting more attention. Some kids in the room had noticed his basket outside the window. They were alerting the adults. The window opened up.

"Mommy look! An accident!"

"What happened?!"

"My God, look!"

"Stay away from the window, Denise!"

Each time Eagle swung by the family a new face was added to the gawkers. Even the dachshund joined in, barking furiously at Eagle as he rocked like a pendulum in the basket.

"Bad doggie!" he screamed. "Bad doggie!"

"That's why you gotta hire American!" he heard Grandpa say through the window.

Eagle checked the roof again. Not good. Now other security guards had gathered and were on their radios. He needed to get this over with.

He grabbed the lever, preparing for his final descent, and looked down. He was still about twenty feet from the ground. That was unfortunate. There was no tension on the lever so he couldn't ease in and out of his fall. It was all or nothing. If he had stopped lower, it would have been easy to get down. If he was a little higher, he might have had time to brake again before he crashed. But at twenty feet, even his impressive reaction time wouldn't be enough. It was gonna be the express route, straight down.

Eagle took a deep breath.

One of the kids in the window seemed to sense what he was about to do. The kid looked at his hand on the controls and then told him "Don't do it, mister!"

Eagle gave the kid a wink and yanked the lever.

* * *

Darlene puffed on her cigarette outside the ambulance entrance of the hospital. She wasn't supposed to smoke in that area, but the new hospital was such a shitshow she knew no one would have time to complain.

Everything had been a trainwreck since she'd started a couple weeks earlier. At least her first paycheck had cleared. It ought to have. The man who owned all these new hospitals was one of the richest guys on the planet. At least there was that. But they should be paying her even more to deal with all this nonsense.

A commotion caught her attention, coming from somewhere outside. She heard distant shouts, and a squeaky, metallic sound filled the air as well.

What is that?

With shock, Darlene looked upward to find an accident had occurred. It looked like the window washer's cart had broken loose of its restraints and was hovering right over her head.

"SWEET LORD BABY JESUS!!" she yelled, running for cover under the concrete awning of the enclave.

As Darlene would later recount many times, if she'd taken even another second to reach the protection of the doors, that widow washer's giant steel whatchamacallit might have landed right on her, because the entire apparatus came crashing down in a horrible calamity landing only feet from her shoe.

She turned and noticed with astonishment that there was a man in the wreckage.

Should I call for help? she wondered. *That was a huge fall!!*

Well, at least they were already at the hospital. You've gotta count your blessings big and small.

"*Aguy! Aguy! Aguy!*" the window washer swore, as he quickly rubbed his hands back and forth over injured places on his body like he could rub away the pain if his hands moved fast enough.

Darlene watched as the man expertly pulled himself from the wreckage of his horrible accident like some kind of acrobat. She noticed he was tall and handsome and had bulging arm muscles under his shredded work clothes. The way he paused to fix his hair after stumbling to his feet reminded her of a swashbuckling knight in a movie.

He must be Army Reserve, she thought. *That was impressive!*

The man started walking toward her! Was this the meet-cute she'd always dreamt of? She threw her cigarette away just in case.

"It's one of those days, huh?" the man said.

Darlene noticed the window washer had an accent, and she imagined him whispering sweet nothings in her ear.

"Listen, Boss," he said. "I'm taking my lunch break. This side is looking good…"

Boss? He was talking about his work?

He was staring upwards at the windows, so she did too. She wasn't sure what they were looking for.

"I got the West tower looking pretty good, but I still need to do the other faces."

She didn't know what to say. It wasn't her job to talk to window washers. She just opened the door all day. Sometimes she helped with a wheelchair.

"Sure," she said.

At that, the man hobbled away through the parking lot and disappeared from her life forever. Darlene looked up again at the windows the man had fallen from. Now that she took a longer look, she wasn't even sure he'd gotten that side very clean.

Darlene wondered where the handsome window washer had staggered off to. Wasn't that always the way with men in her life? Running away the second she opened her mouth?

Well, Darlene thought, *if that guy's skills in the bedroom look anything like his skills at window washing, maybe I dodged a bullet.*

CHAPTER 23

All Hallow's Eve

* * *

Daisy's morning was thankfully uneventful. After showering and getting dressed—one of her Badmotorfinger shirts again—she'd placed a phone call to the next of kin listed in the L.A. reporter's autopsy report, her brother Jesse Thompson who lived in Bakersfield. There'd been no answer, so she'd left a voicemail explaining she was a reporter in NYC who needed additional details about his sister's passing since there had been many similar deaths since then. If Mr. Thompson didn't respond to her message, Daisy intended to try contacting him just one more time and then let it go. The man's sister had passed away less than three months earlier and she wasn't going to pester him.

Her next order of business was Jordan; he hadn't responded to her yet despite a couple more texts. She tried calling him and it went to voicemail. That meant his phone was still on. Why wouldn't he answer? He ran around town all day for work but had plenty of moments to check his messages and answer a text. She was pretty sure she hadn't annoyed him so badly he could be ignoring her.

Daisy then wasted almost an hour playing phone tag with the electric company, listening to elevator music, and cycling through automated phone systems trying to get a human being on the line who could answer her very basic question: did Jordan Farmer report to work that day?

Finally, she was given a cell phone number for a guy named Rob, who was supposedly Jordan's manager, and he actually answered.

"No, Jordan was a no-show today. It's put us in a bind, but I'm sure he's got a reason. If you get a hold of him, tell him to get his ass to work."

"Yeah, okay. Thanks," Daisy told him before hanging up.

Is Jordan in trouble?

She couldn't even bring herself to consider it. She'd dragged Jordan into this mess. If anything had happened to him, she'd never be able to live with herself.

NO. Now's not the time for that.

It wasn't information that she had; it was the *lack* of information that was stressing her out. Trying to fill in the blanks with imaginary horrors would not only increase her anxiety, but distract her from finding the missing information. She needed to keep moving.

Daisy took the train to the city and stopped by Jordan's apartment building in Hell's Kitchen to make sure he wasn't there. She had to double check a note file in her phone for his apartment number before knocking because he'd moved to Manhattan pretty recently and she hadn't been to his new apartment yet.

After knocking a few times and not getting an answer, Daisy pulled up a small dust mat outside Jordan's door, hoping there might be an extra key, but no luck. Now she was getting really worried. What if Catalina had gotten him? Everyone who had tangled with the Filipina was now dead except for her, Eagle... and Jordan.

Maybe she had screwed up. Maybe she *should* have let Jordan come with them the night before. She had faced Catalina with Eagle at her side and been wounded. Had Catalina come for Jordan when he was alone?

What happened to him? She stopped herself from considering the darkest thought, and instead got back on the subway, since it was already late afternoon and she needed to get back to Eagle's hideout.

"Man, that field work is no joke!" Coney told her later. "My knees are killing me from that doctor's hammer. I really took a beating for this one, Daisy."

She'd been listening to the full debriefing of Coney's adventure for a second time, since she'd heard it all when she first got there but Eagle had just walked in so Coney had started again from the top.

"How about you, Eagle?" Daisy asked, hoping he'd take over from there and tell his hospital story so she wouldn't have to hear about how floppy disk drives worked again.

"Clean getaway," was all Eagle said, as he started up the stairs to his bedroom. Daisy noticed he seemed to be limping.

"Eagle's like a ninja, Daisy," Coney explained. "They probably never even knew he was there."

Eagle had been right about the manananggal bite. Daisy's right arm was starting to itch under the bandages. She reminded herself to ask Eagle how soon she could remove her wound dressing since she'd struggled to keep it dry in the shower. She noticed her arm was swollen too; the entire area around the puncture marks looked inflated under the wrapping and stung if she touched it. She wondered if her body was having an allergic reaction to the saliva and if that was the normal response.

"Hey, let me ask you something," Daisy said to Coney, since Eagle was upstairs, "I get the impression that Eagle has hunted more creatures than just the manananggal. Based on all your work and travels with him, do you think vampires also exist?"

Like Eagle, Coney found the notion so embarrassingly silly that she didn't bother with words. Instead, the "No" gesture she gave her came in the form of another "look" Daisy recognized from her former teachers. It was the grimace of an instructor who really liked you but was a little bit *disappointed* you'd asked such a stupid question.

Daisy realized that many of the legends about vampires were similar to those of viscera-suckers. They have fangs, feed on humans, and are vulnerable to sunlight. Catalina, at least, possessed a kind of longevity and perpetual youth. She even turned into a bat. Daisy realized she'd been feeling disappointed that the world wouldn't confirm the tired tropes of old movies, and yet wasn't she in the middle of a struggle with a *real* unknown creature? Why did she need coffins or Transylvania when she had found the REAL thing? It's always comforting to look backwards but, for once, wasn't the road ahead actually more exciting?

Daisy's phone began ringing and it startled both her and Coney. She checked the caller ID–it was the reporter's brother calling her back!

"I'm sorry, I have to take this!" she told Coney, excusing herself to the other side of the huge open room, near the kitchen.

After quick pleasantries, Daisy got right to the point: "Mr. Thompson, I think your sister was murdered," she said.

"Well, no shit."

"Sorry?" she asked.

"Ms. Scott, was it?" he asked.

"You can call me Daisy. But, yeah."

"And who did you say you were with?" he asked.

"I didn't."

"Well, say now."

Daisy knew there was no time for games. She had to be honest with the guy.

"*The Brooklyn Believer.*"

"I haven't even heard of it," he said.

Thank God! Daisy thought.

"Look, Daisy…" Mr. Thompson said, "my sister chose to make her living by airing the dirty laundry of the most powerful people in the country. Did someone want her dead? Yeah, fucking everybody! It was just a matter of time. We all warned her for years, but she kept pushing. And pushing. She reported on the federal government, arms manufacturers, Wall Street, insider trading, 3M, Boeing, OpenAI, Meta, McKinsey & Company. She exposed corruption by both Republicans and Democrats. They passed a bipartisan bill in two days to stop reporters from accessing a database because she'd used it to demonstrate a senator had misappropriated funds. EVERYBODY wanted her gone! She got death threats, bomb threats, and was followed constantly. Do you know that guys showed up at *our* house? Here, in Bakersfield?"

"No..." Daisy said.

"Yeah, they go after the families too. When you screw with people like that, they pull out all the stops. It becomes their mission to ruin you, and they have all the money and power in the world to do it. But she kept going. She wanted to be some kind of muckraking hero. Of course she was murdered. Probably by whoever she was investigating in New York City."

"What do you mean?" Daisy asked. "Her file said she was here on vacation when she died."

"No, that's probably the bullshit Monica was telling people. She was working on a story and said she had to follow it to New York. She said she was onto something HUGE, but couldn't discuss it. Monica was alway like that. Anyway, Daisy. Here's some free advice: find another line of work. This isn't the 1950s. Journalism is dead in America. It's either propaganda or fluff because the real thing can get you killed. You've seen it with your own eyes now. And there's no glory in that when it can't change anything. Be careful out there."

He hung up.

Eagle came downstairs dressed for the night's activities in a charcoal gray three-piece suit, with a navy wool coat, Chelsea boots, and a short cashmere scarf. Coney explained that, before they'd arrived, she had removed the spooled edges from her stack of hospital computer printouts and scanned all the pages so she could search for names. The results had confirmed their suspicions: Cortelyou Health Systems had been an unwitting accomplice to most of Catalina's murders.

Eagle recapped what he'd learned about Catalina's volunteer work and then explained the plan for that night. Thanks to Daisy's experience with the storage room on Catalina's roof, they had exactly one advantage—Catalina didn't yet know that they'd found her den. They had the element of surprise.

The plan was for Eagle and Daisy to leave before the sun set and then stakeout on separate high-rises near Catalina's building. They would watch the storage room from their respective safe distances with binoculars until they saw activity. Once they knew Catalina had left on a raid with her lower half behind in the den, Eagle would enter the storage room and destroy her legs. Checkmate. With that completed, it wouldn't even matter if they killed Catalina. She'd be stuck, unable to ever reverse the metamorphosis and would die with the morning sunrise. The evil bitch's reign of terror would be over.

Daisy watched as Eagle inspected his elaborate weapon displays to find tools for the night's job. He selected a different whip than the night before. This one was so dark it was almost black, but had a similar stingray tail affixed to the end.

"The whip can inflict injury but the best way to kill a manananggal is always a stake through the back," Eagle said.

"In all fairness," Daisy pointed out, "that's also a good way to kill anybody. How will you sabotage her lower half?"

"Easy," he said. They walked over to a different display shelf which had a row of hot sauce bottles and he selected one. "With this."

Daisy looked at the bottle. It was standard-issue hot sauce, ingredients: water, vinegar, chiles, garlic, and spices.

"You're joking?" she asked.

"I never joke about hot sauce."

Daisy noticed an odd-looking item on the top shelf of the display. It looked like a red headband with a fake bat attached to the front. She tried it on her head and looked at her reflection in the glass door of Eagle's knives and daggers display. It looked ridiculous.

"What's this for?" she asked.

"Stop touching my things!" he complained, pulling the bat headband off her head.

Daisy's phone chimed in her back pocket. Even before she had unlocked her phone, a wave of relief washed over her as she saw it was a text from Jordan.

Then, she saw the message. And screamed, dropping her phone to the ground.

"JORDAN!!!!" she moaned.

Eagle picked up her phone and saw what she had—the horrible image.

Someone had texted a photo from Jordan's cell phone. It showed Jordan, tied up and bleeding somewhere. His eyes were closed and he was covered in wounds and bruises. Honestly, it wasn't clear if he was alive or dead.

"Daisy, sit down," Eagle said, taking her hand.

The next thing Daisy knew she was on the couch, Coney's arm wrapped around her. She noticed her hands were shaking wildly so she tried to steady herself. Intense emotion was burning inside her. But it wasn't fear or loss or guilt.

It was anger.

Catalina had taken too much. She had crossed a line. No matter Jordan's prognosis, Catalina had done the unforgivable and things would never be the same again. Daisy felt a rage inside her that inflated like a balloon until it put pressure on her eyeballs.

"You said a stake through the back?" she remembered, through tears. "That's how I kill it? Tell me exactly! Because I'm done with the "need to know basis." Tell me *exactly* how I kill this fucking thing."

"Daisy, our plan has changed now, obviously…" Eagle said. He was trying to choose his words carefully.

Daisy retrieved her phone to look at the image again. Eagle tried to stop her, but she insisted. This time, she dismissed her emotions and studied the photo carefully. There was something familiar there… THE RED RAILING. She knew where Jordan was! She'd been there. It was the small, upper-level roof of Catalina's building.

"I know where this is!" Daisy said. "It's right above the storage room. Let's go now. Let's fucking get her."

"Daisy, we've lost our advantage here," Eagle pointed out. "She's set a trap for us, if we spring it now then she wins."

"I don't care. You can stay here. I'm going to help my friend. He needs me."

"Daisy…" Eagle sat down next to her. "I need to be very blunt with you. I don't know that your friend Jordan is okay. I just don't. I can't promise you that. I also don't know what I'm gonna find on that rooftop. But I can promise you this. One way or another, I will stop Catalina tonight. No matter the cost. This has gone too far. I swear to you I will put an end to this. And if I can save your friend Jordan–IF that's still possible–I swear that I will do that too. But you have to stay here."

"NO!!"

"Daisy, you're in no shape for this. What you went through last night alone! It'll take the rest of your life to come to terms with that. Believe me, I know. This is too dangerous. Someone is going to die tonight. It's just a fact now. I can't risk you being there, and that person being you instead of Catalina."

"What about the legs?" she asked. "You can't fight Catalina, rescue Jordan, and also destroy the legs."

"I'll do it," Coney said, with determination.

"No! Absolutely not," Eagle said.

"Daisy went last night, and you just met her! When are you going to trust me?!" Coney demanded.

"Coney, now isn't the time," Eagle said.

"Then when will it be the time?!" she roared. "Why don't you trust me?!"

"It's not about TRUST, Coney!" Eagle said. "I've seen things… things in this world, so dark. I don't even mean monsters–I mean PEOPLE–made of such evil, that it makes me sometimes question if all this is even worth it. Maybe humans are just like aswang, simply takers, only pretending to care about anyone but themselves, just worthless. But you're different, Coney. You show me what else is possible. Without you, people wouldn't be worth fighting for. That's why I can't risk it."

Coney blushed at the praise, but it seemed to do the trick, and she stopped pushing to go along. That meant Daisy was back on deck.

"The way you feel about her, Eagle," she told him, "is the way I feel about my best friend up there. And I know what we're up against now. No matter what we find, I can do it. I was terrified last night but I still saved your ass, remember?"

Eagle thought for a moment, rubbing his chin.

"I wouldn't phrase it like that…" he said, "but you do have a point."

Eagle finally consented to her coming along, so they made their final preparations. This time, Daisy wouldn't be stuck using her phone's camera flash for illumination. She'd brought along her overpowered tactical flashlight, stuffed with new batteries. Eagle gave her the bottle of hot sauce to store in her jacket pocket until she needed it.

"Be careful with this," he said. "It's top shelf hot sauce."

"I'll be waiting back here at *The Eagle's Nest*," Coney said.

"NO!" Eagle yelled. "Coney, do not let her influence you. We are NOT calling it that."

"Too late!" Coney laughed, "I already changed the Wi-Fi name."

Daisy and Eagle paused outside the revolving door entrance of The Impluvium. Daisy watched some young parents escorting their kids, dressed for trick-or-treating, through the lobby doors and outside to begin their adventure. This night might be one they'd remember for their entire lives. Halloween was always memorable for Daisy at that age.

This Halloween will be one for the books as well, she realized.

A themed Halloween display had been set up on a long table outside the building. There were some fake spiders and cobwebs and a scarecrow that looked more goofy than frightening. But what caught Daisy's eye were the three impressive Jack-o-Lanterns on display, probably the winners of a carving contest in the building. One pumpkin in particular disturbed her. Someone very skilled had etched a detailed, demonic face into the hull of the pumpkin, carving out only thin slivers for the candlelight to shine though as highlights. Inside each of the sinister eyes, a hole revealed dancing flames hidden behind, creating the illusion of the lantern having burning red eyes, like the manananggal. It gave Daisy a shudder.

Was she really doing this again? Did she have it in her? Last time she'd gone into the situation with a misplaced confidence born of ignorance and arrogance. In fact, Eagle had made the same mistake. But now they knew the score. Daisy knew that the manananggal was real and that she could have gotten herself killed confronting it. She'd stalled outside Catalina's apartment last time due to fear of the unknown. But that wasn't her problem now. It was fear of the *known*.

Not to mention, people who saw Catalina's transformation never lived to speak of it. Catalina could never let a *reporter* live to write about it. If Eagle didn't kill Catalina tonight, well...

The new plan was for Daisy to destroy the lower half while Eagle sprung Catalina's trap and engaged her if necessary. Eagle addressed Daisy for a final pep talk before entering the building.

"If you're sensing danger, you're correct," he said. "Daisy, listen to me, because this is important."

"Okay," she said.

"I need you to protect yourself both spiritually and mentally for what's about to happen."

"What?" she asked. "What the fuck does that mean?"

"Look…" he demurred. "Coney usually just rolls with it when I say stuff like that."

"Sure, but what does it mean?"

"Look!" he said. "I'm just giving you some useful feedback! When that happens, you're supposed to just internalize it and then move on."

The pair reached the roof and repeated Daisy's journey from the week before to reach the upper level where their paths would split. Knowing Jordan was right there above her, Daisy had to fight the instinct to run to him, up the final stretch of stairs. But she knew Eagle was better prepared for that assignment. She would stick to the plan, enter the storage room, and sauce Catalina's legs into a fucking pile of goo.

"Remember what I said about being brave?" Eagle asked, eying the top level. Was he talking to her? Or himself?

"That it's doing things even though you're scared," Daisy remembered.

"That's right. We do it anyway because we have to. Daisy, many more people will die if we fail tonight. There's no one else but us."

He stared at her with an intensity, and an *earnestness*, she hadn't often seen in people, outside of film performances. He was a man of true conviction in a world of pretenders. She had to admit, no matter what happened next, she was thankful to have crossed paths with Eagle Valdez. A person's life is only as interesting as the people they surround themselves with, and just knowing Eagle felt like opening doors to exciting other worlds.

Daisy thought about all the victims—migrants, the homeless, pregnant women, young children, *babies*… It was a collection of the most vulnerable. It was all the people we were supposed to protect in a supposed "free land."

"I'll see you on the other side, Eagle," she said, walking towards the storage room.

"Don't be so dramatic, Daisy."

"Yeah, *I'm* the one that's dramatic."

Daisy turned on her flashlight as she walked along the narrow platform, dodging piles of equipment, and then pulled open the door to the storage room at the end. She aimed her flashlight inside before entering so she could see the full layout of the space. Again, the terrible smell burned in her nostrils, and she saw the racks of equipment and large motors, this time fully illuminated all the way to the back wall, where the path turned to the right. She entered the room and looked for a light switch on the wall, but didn't see anything. The room's lights could be on a breaker somewhere instead. She'd have to make do with the flashlight.

She walked further into the room, proceeding past where she'd stopped last time, and followed the turn to the right. Daisy pointed her beam of light into the new space and immediately encountered a PERSON standing there. She screamed with fright and turned to run back for the door. Only after she'd taken a few steps did the information from her eyes fully reach her brain. She hadn't seen a person; she'd seen HALF a person.

GOTCHA, BITCH.

Daisy quickly returned to the side corridor and checked her surroundings to make sure she was safe. The tactical flashlight was easily powerful enough to light up the back area around the legs and there was nowhere in the alcove for Catalina to hide. It was safe.

The legs looked absurd. They weren't lying on the ground; they were vertical. It really looked like Catalina had been standing in place and someone just removed the top half of her body. How were the legs freestanding? She touched one, pushing it with her finger. The skin was taut–the muscles felt engaged, but they were locked, stationary. There was a blue skirt wrapped around the legs and then a human anatomy lesson protruding out of the top. It was disgusting; Daisy saw blood and guts, intestines, and what looked like the ridge of a pelvic bone emerging from the layer of gore atop the skirt.

It was no wonder Catalina went to such lengths to protect herself. Daisy considered how vulnerable the manananggal actually was if you found its den. She put the handle of the flashlight in her mouth to free her hands and removed the hot sauce bottle from her jacket. She opened the lid and took a whiff.

YIKES! It's spicy! Her eyes and sinuses burned just from smelling it. At least they weren't wasting the good stuff.

Here goes nothing, Daisy thought, as she began shaking the bottle to release dollops of fiery vinegar onto the exposed waist. Daisy had worried beforehand that the results of the hot sauce might be subtle, and she might not know if it was even working. But as each drop of hot sauce landed, it made an audible sizzling sound and released a little puff of smoke. As Daisy shook the bottle more vigorously and the sauce began to flow out in larger spurts, she saw the manananggal's tissue begin to shrivel and distort, like a chemical reaction. The guts began to boil and steam, sending up a noxious cloud that burned in Daisy's eyes, but she kept going...

* * *

Eagle climbed the metal stairs to the small upper roof level and looked around before stepping out onto the concrete. Daisy's friend Jordan was there, against the back railing in a lump on the ground. He couldn't tell if he was breathing.

Eagle studied the skies in all directions, knowing Catalina could be anywhere. She was likely nearby and watching him. All she had to do was wait. She'd set the perfect trap. A manananggal was most effective in open spaces. New York City was actually a terrible place for Catalina to make her home—an island of steel and concrete, nothing but safe hiding places that she couldn't penetrate. It's why he'd never considered the notion of a manananggal in NYC.

The one and only environment in the city where a manananggal had the same advantages as back home, was the place Eagle was about to enter—an exposed, unprotected rooftop.

Well, that's the gig.

Eagle quickly crossed the roof level, keeping his eyes on the sky, and crouched down next to Jordan. He found a weak pulse—he was still alive—but he was unconscious and there was a pool of dried blood underneath him. Eagle pulled up Jordan's shirt to look at his stomach.

DAMN. Poor guy.

It was bad. Catalina had fed on him and it didn't look fresh. It had probably happened the night before. It was a miracle Jordan was still hanging on at all. Catalina had purposely left him lingering at the cusp of death, just to serve as bait. It was such cruelty, and so devoid of honor, that it turned his stomach.

Where is she? Eagle wondered.

It was a trap. And he had sprung it. Now what?

* * *

The sizzling pile of organs writhing from the hot sauce began to remind Daisy of a stew boiling in a pot, except the awful smell—something like burning cheese and rotten eggs with an astringent finish that burned her lungs like chlorine—could never be mistaken as belonging to anything edible.

Daisy noticed movement in her peripheral vision, outside the beam of her flashlight.

The attack came from the left.

Daisy was knocked to the ground by an immense weight and found herself pinned to the floor. The flashlight went tumbling and fell to the ground, pointing in the wrong direction.

A kaleidoscope of pain shot across Daisy's left thigh. It was a dish with too many flavors—pains that were sharp, dull, hot, cold, searing, and some so profound they seemed connected to strings of fire that ran through every inch of her body, like her entire nervous system was boiling inside her. In the dark, Daisy didn't know if she had been scratched or bitten. It didn't matter! It hurt like hell!

She got me again! Daisy thought in panic. Catalina had been hiding behind the giant motors for the fucking elevator. She'd pulled the SAME trick as last time… and it had worked!

I'm a fucking idiot!

And this time, Eagle wasn't there!

"Eagle!!!" she screamed. "She's in here! EAGLE!!!!"

It was no use. He'd never hear her. The door to the room had closed and Eagle was on the other side of a thick layer of concrete above her.

The manananggal was on top of her. She could feel it breathing. Daisy couldn't see, but she knew the tongue was probably coming out. Thank God she couldn't see!

Is this how I die? she wondered. Would Eagle find her body later, knowing he'd been less than twenty feet away, clueless, while it had happened?

As Daisy's eyes adjusted to the darkness, she noticed her bag was on the ground next to her. She could almost reach it! But was there anything of use in there? Perhaps her mace, but she was pinned to the ground and couldn't stretch her arm far enough. She would never get to it. The only thing her fingertips could even reach were her drumsticks, sticking out the top.

My drumsticks!

With nothing left to lose but her life, Daisy poked at a drumstick with her finger, inching and sliding it closer until she could grab it in her fist. Then, she smacked the tip down on the concrete, breaking it, and thrust her improvised wooden stake as hard as she could into the manananggal's chest.

It HOWLED in pain, releasing her.

Daisy didn't waste time. She shoved the creature off her and scrambled to her feet, as her thigh screamed in pain. She left her belongings on the floor and bolted out the door, running along the ridge until she reached the ladder to the top level. Daisy knew she hadn't finished with the legs. Eagle had said to use the entire bottle, but she'd only emptied a fraction of it before Catalina jumped her. But that would have to wait.

"She's here!!" Daisy screamed as she limped up the steps to reach Eagle and Jordan. "She got us again, Eagle! She was in that room! She attacked me! I poured some hot sauce on her guts but I don't know if it was enough."

"Are you okay?" he asked.

This time, she noticed, Eagle already had his whip out and ready to go. *Good.* At least he'd learned something from last time, even if she hadn't. Then, she saw the bloody lump in the back corner of the railing.

"Jordan!!" Daisy ran over to her friend, sobbing as she held him in her arms.

"He's alive," Eagle said. "But we need to get him out of here ASAP."

"I'll call an ambulance," Daisy said, getting out her phone.

"Do it quick, while I keep watch. Then, we'll go together to finish with the legs."

One second, Eagle was standing there talking to her. The next, he was just GONE. It happened so fast, it was just a blur. The manananggal had swooped down like a falcon, picking Eagle up off the ground and carrying him away—just gone.

"Eagle!!" she screamed, rising to her feet.

What if Catalina dropped him on the street? They were too high up! He'd be killed! Where had she taken him?!

Then, Eagle crashed to the ground in front of her, HARD. He'd fallen from a significant height onto the concrete.

"*AGUY!!!*" he cried.

Eagle stumbled to his feet, clutching his right leg, and limped over to retrieve his whip off the ground. It looked like he was having trouble putting weight on his leg. Daisy wondered if he'd broken something.

"Get down!" he yelled.

HE WAS TALKING TO HER! Daisy crouched quickly, only just avoiding the manananggal's dive-bomb. Catalina was still going! They were sitting ducks up there!

Eagle curled his whip in his hands and sucked his teeth as he watched the creature circling in the sky. He looked like a pitcher at the mound in a baseball game. As Catalina came in for a third attempt, this time targeting Eagle again, the monster hunter stood firm until the last moment. Then, he parried to the side, avoiding a collision, and pivoted his body to follow her as he reared back his arm and then ripped his whip through the air, where it coiled around the beast, lassoing around its chest.

"Got you!" he yelled.

The creature dropped to the roof. Its wings were caught in the coil, and it tumbled around, unable to fly. The manananggal instead dug its claws into the concrete and began dragging itself, pulling Eagle like a shark on a fishing line.

Eagle tugged at the whip, trying to reel it in while struggling to stand his ground, but the manananggal's wings managed to break free of their bondage and started flapping. The creature looked like a dying insect, flopping around on the ground, trying to take flight. It almost looked comical… Until the wings started beating more furiously, creating a surge of wind on the roof like it was a helipad.

The manananggal became airborne, now dragging Eagle on the other end of the whip–pulling him like a giant, evil kite. The wings flapped harder and harder, moving him toward the side railing. Eagle bent his knees and dug in his heels, fighting against the creature, but it was futile against the power of the manananggal's giant wingspan. She was trying to fly away, and Eagle wasn't heavy enough to hold his ground.

Catalina dragged him to the edge, where Eagle leveraged himself against the red railing, leaning back with all his strength. But Catalina was stronger. Daisy watched as Eagle Valdez was yanked from his protection behind the railing and carried away into the sky, dangling from his whip and holding on for dear life.

"*Hoy matandang hukluban!*" he yelled at Catalina, as they disappeared from view.

* * *

Eagle didn't panic. Not now. Not ever.

Eagle Valdez fully expected to meet his end on the job one day. He had assumed that burden by choice and did not fear death. More importantly, Eagle understood that panic was useless in life-or-death situations. It can only lead to bad outcomes. It's a self-fulfilling prophecy, so he didn't do it. When the end came, he would go down fighting and planning. He would recalculate at every new development until he had no more moves and reached his final breath. A clear mind maintains its potential, and in no moment was that as essential as when one was being dragged through the skies of New York City at the end of a whip, a couple hundred feet above the asphalt.

The first move he made was always the most important. It would determine what he had to work with later. First thing, he was too vulnerable at the end of the line; he needed to climb up. Eagle held firmly onto the leather, reaching upwards to pull himself higher, until there was enough slack for the handle of the whip to reach his knees. The manananggal was flying erratically from his added weight. She flew higher, heading for the roof of a large apartment building near the East River. She was trying to hit the edge of the roof and knock him off the end of the whip!

Eagle gripped the whip hard with both hands as he collided with the top edge of the building's roof deck. His hands held firm, as he bashed against the side and was pulled upwards. Once he reached the top, Catalina dragged him over the edge and along the roof as he staggered to his feet. Again, he tried to reel her in. But the manananggal ripped him away from the protection of solid ground and he was flying once more.

This time, Eagle quickly climbed up the whip again until he could grab hold of Catalina's shirt and heaved himself up onto her back. For a moment, he felt like Atreyu on Falkor's back in *The Neverending Story*. His shifting weight threw off the manananggal's balance as he clutched with all his strength and positioned himself right in between her wings. They beat him from both sides as she flew.

Eagle noticed something sticking out of the creature's chest. What did the writing say?

VIC FIRTH?

It was one of Daisy's drumsticks! CLASSIC! She had stuck Catalina; it just hadn't gone in far enough. Eagle reached his arms around the beast and grabbed Daisy's drumstick, pulling it toward him–deeper. Catalina screamed, tumbling in circles though the air. Eagle lost his balance. Which way was up?!

He noticed they were heading for another high-rise. It was close! But they were too low this time! They weren't heading for the roof!

Eagle and the manananggal collided into the side of the building, falling into the balcony of an upper floor apartment. Eagle went tumbling into an outdoor table and chairs and lost his grip on the whip. He rose to his feet as Catalina also recovered. She began flying and paused in front of the balcony as she uncoiled the whip from her body and dropped it to the street, far below, giving him a big jeering smile, which said, "I won."

And then, she just stayed there for a moment, grinning. She hovered in front of him. The whip was gone. He was stranded on a high balcony. And she was right there, JUST out of reach. There was nothing he could do and they both knew it. And she was savoring it.

Eagle looked into her awful red eyes. That face, it was unchanged from the first time he'd seen it. Old, buried memories suddenly resurfaced and became so fresh they made his heart pang. In a moment of weakness, Eagle flashed back to his childhood. He could remember it so clearly now. He had been terrified, and he'd looked to his father to help. He'd needed his father to be brave for him....

Then, Catalina turned and began to fly away.

What? Why doesn't she finish me off?

She was saving him for later! The bitch wanted the satisfaction of leaving him stranded up there with his defeat.

No! That wasn't going to work for him! Eagle reburied the memories and focused. He didn't think. He felt. And without hesitation, without a single thought to the danger, he ran, and JUMPED...

Eagle didn't consider the altitude, only Catalina. He soared through the air, untethered, over two hundred feet above the ground. If the arc of his leap didn't connect with Catalina, there would be no second chances. He had just jumped to his foolish death.

But that was the thing about Eagle, he never made a jump if he didn't intend to survive it. His gut had told him he had a chance. And so far it hadn't been wrong.

Eagle crashed into Catalina, who was completely caught off guard this time and they began tumbling down–FAST!–towards the streets below. The sky, the approaching ground, and windows of buildings flew past him in a revolving parade of colors, but he only focused on the creature clutched in his grasp. *It's all that matters!* He pulled himself closer and grabbed for Daisy's drumstick again, gripping it with both hands from around Catalina, and he HEAVED.

The manananggal bellowed in pain and the wings became erratic. The pair began falling faster–TOO FAST–spinning in the air until they both crashed to a hard stop that put his window washing fall to shame. Eagle was dazed from the landing and his entire body screamed with pain. What had they hit? He was alive! But what about Catalina?!

He saw they'd crashed into a dumpster! And he'd landed on top of the manananggal, sparing him from the worst of the impact. Catalina wasn't moving.

Groaning in pain, Eagle rolled off the creature and lifted Catalina's head to look at her.

OH MY GOD.

It was no longer the beautiful young woman from his childhood. The creature in front of him had turned into a shriveled old hag. She'd become wrinkles on bones, with the sharp end of Daisy's drumstick protruding out the back of her ribs.

I'll never make a drummer joke ever again! Eagle promised himself.

He tried rising to his feet. Nothing felt broken except potentially his right leg from his first fall. He'd really gotten lucky with the way they had landed. His survival had somewhat fallen to chance. But luck had been with him again that night, it seemed.

Then, he saw Catalina's head move. Was it a "last gasp?" A death rattle? It had been known to happen with aswang. She might still try a final attack. He saw movement in the mouth. Was it the tongue coming out again?

NO!!!

Eagle lunged for Catalina's open mouth with his hands, but was too late. He watched, utterly helpless, as a tiny black chick emerged from her lips and then fluttered away into the Queens sky.

CHAPTER 24

Daisy Scott: Investigative Reporter

* * *

Publishing the full, unbridled truth had never been an option. No one would believe Daisy, even if she had Catalina's head in a bag as proof, and Eagle had disposed of her body. Plus, to share every detail of her adventure would put Eagle and Coney at risk. It could hurt the work they were trying to do, which was more important than her career, and she couldn't allow that.

Instead, she had woven her new evidence into a think-piece about the city's reaction to the murders and about our relationship with the underprivileged. Her findings strongly suggested Dr. Rhinelander had been innocent, and her article was the first reporting in NYC to mention the other murders. Twice, police officers questioned her about her knowledge of the cases. She stuck to the script Eagle had given her, which omitted the events of Halloween and focused on her investigation of the other deaths. Since she wasn't able to reveal Catalina's identity, the article implied that a serial killer was still on the loose in the city, but Daisy knew the NYPD would never connect the trail of bodies to Catalina, and the wave of fear her story incited would blow over eventually since there would be no additional victims.

Like any *Believer* article, she at least towed the line of indulging the most far-out interpretation–the truth–that a real manananggal had been on a killing spree in NYC. But Daisy's article mostly concealed reality under a safe sheen of allegory.

Daisy called attention to the fact that it took a rich white woman's death for the city to even take notice that a couple dozen poor people had been murdered. What Daisy couldn't write, was that Catalina's fatal error had been messing with a rich person. That had been the mistake that got her. Otherwise, Daisy herself might never have made the connections.

Manananggal in New York, by Daisy Scott, didn't change the world. It didn't make Daisy a superstar or significantly alter her career trajectory. But it *was* a sensation, the most-viewed story of her career, and it generated higher traffic than anything Jerry's paper had run in years.

Tiffani had responded by pointing out that Daisy had spent over a week on the story and, financially speaking, the article's extra traffic didn't fully justify her man hours.

Jerry had responded by bringing Daisy up to *The Believer*'s roof after work to celebrate with beers and reminisce. He was in such a good mood, he'd even agreed to pull Tanner off the "invisibility" story and give it to her after all. It felt like she was the top of the pecking order again. Maybe to Jerry, Daisy's successful article meant she was back on track as his protégé, ready to assume command of the paper when he retired. But that wasn't what she wanted anymore.

"What's next, kid?" Jerry asked, as they looked out over Queensboro Plaza from the roof deck.

Daisy thought about the L.A. reporter Monica Thompson and how her brother had described her work–poking powerful people in the eye and shining a light on injustice. She liked the sound of that. There were a lot of CEOs and politicians she'd like to tear up so badly they developed a third asshole. And now, she realized, she had some powerful friends too.

"Maybe it's time to think bigger," she said.

After all Daisy had seen and overcome, she still questioned if she'd witnessed anything paranormal. The manananggal was certainly *unexplainable*. At least, for the time being. But deep down, Daisy didn't believe it was "supernatural."

SUPERNATURAL. What does that word even mean?

It means that something is beyond explanation, that fundamentally, on some foundational level, it is permanently beyond the realm of explanation. But how could that be true of anything? Take any example: a ghost, an alien, BigFoot; if these entities agreed to sit down to answer your questions and be studied, you would find your answers, whatever they may be. Your suspicions might be confirmed, or your mind might be blown, but the paranormal would become normal.

Supernaturalism isn't a description of phenomena, it's a *mindset*.

And Daisy did not have that mindset. She was still a skeptic deep down. She was a scientist at heart, believing the world operated according to a set of principles which could be fully explained if she had the time and resources. But her years at *The Believer* had also shown her that a person's heart can grow cold from being overly focused on dissecting and refuting every inspiring notion. Somewhere along the way, she had forgotten that it was the thrill of *discovery*, not the work of unraveling mysteries that had inspired her in the first place.

As Daisy looked out over Queens, the World's Borough, she was no longer afraid of the future. Hell, she even felt a little bit like a reporter.

EPILOGUE

* * *

Eagle cursed in two languages as Daisy helped him drag an oversized Christmas tree through the back door of his hideout. His louder slurs were in Tagalog, so the finer context was lost on her and she relied on his furious tone for context clues. He'd picked too large a tree and it didn't want to squeeze through the door. Daisy tugged from the inside as Eagle pushed from outside. She began sweating even though it was early December and freezing outside. She considered taking off her jacket. Soon, it would be too cold for her leather jacket—all patched up save for a few battle scars.

"HEAVE!" Eagle commanded, and Daisy tugged again with all her weight. This time, they got the bulging bottom of the tree through the door frame and into the large room.

"Okay! You're on your own from here," Daisy reminded Eagle. "And it's time for that beer you promised me. I'm sweating like a pig. Why not get a fake tree? You can just store it."

"Blasphemy, Daisy! Blasphemy!" he screeched.

Coney had been spared from physical labor since any sort of athletics was not her strong suit. She approached Eagle with some papers.

"Another autopsy report got posted," she said, handing the printouts to Eagle.

Daisy had learned that Eagle stored important documents related to his work in a huge file cabinet. The outside looked like a safe and it had two layers of biometric security before it could be opened. The inside, however, looked just like a basic file system–just drawers of file folders, filled with documents. In the weeks since Daisy had met Eagle and Coney, she'd been dying to get a look inside the files, but she knew even Coney had only partial access.

Eagle scanned his thumbprint and then stared into an optical sensor and the giant case unlocked. He then took the files Coney had given him and started filing through the contents looking for the correct folder to place them in.

Daisy snuck closer to get a peak. She might have assumed such a wealthy, hi-tech guy would have relied on a digital file system, but she'd learned Eagle employed a "best of both worlds" approach to balancing the old ways with the new. He only cared about what worked.

Eagle's phone rang. He checked the caller ID and then answered. He began walking away, leaving the drawer open!

"Priya, darling. What can I do for you, dear? Are you still on Governors Island…"

As Eagle walked away, Daisy stared at the open safe with desire. She'd had a taste of forbidden knowledge now. And the answers to her biggest questions were stuffed in the folders in that cabinet. How could she resist?

With Eagle distracted, Daisy risked a quick look through the files. They seemed to be organized by species name in alphabetical order. There was a hanging file for each letter of the alphabet but most of the letter folders were empty. The "M" folder, which Eagle had just added to, was thick with contents. With no time to spare, she went immediately to the back of the files to search the 'V' folder for "vampire" and settle the debate about their existence once and for all. She was heartbroken to find the 'V' folder completely empty. They really hadn't been kidding. It was the final nail in the coffin for vampires.

Oh well, she thought, *I still have my Christopher Lee.*

The following folder, however, was stuffed to the gills. Daisy pulled the file from its place in a frenzy, like a child opening Christmas presents ahead of time knowing her parents might catch her at any moment and every second mattered.

A military-style stamp on the front indicated the materials were classified but Daisy wasn't sure what agency was responsible for the designation or if it was even from the government. She gathered only one cryptic clue from the folder's label—it was branded with the phrase *"SIREN POINT."*

What's Siren Point?

She opened the folder and a photograph on the very first page sent her heart racing. It was a low-resolution night vision image from a trail camera in a swamp in Louisiana. The outline of the creature captured in the pixels was unmistakable.

My God. IS THIS REAL?

Vampires might only be fiction, but this monster would be one hell of a consolation prize. Eagle wouldn't have a photo like that if it wasn't genuine, she knew that. But how could it be possible?

"Hey! Put that back!" Eagle yelled, running back toward her.

Damn. BUSTED!

"Eagle, is this for real?" she asked. She was too desperate for the answer to care how much trouble she was in for reading his private files. "Are they real?!"

"This stuff isn't for you, Daisy," he scolded, pulling the folder from her grip. "You're like the intern here, understand? Stay out of the safe."

Oh no.

She realized he was right. Was she like Eagle's Liam? The dumb, eager new intern? There was a funny irony to the idea. But she couldn't let her question go. She had to know the answer.

"Eagle?" she asked again. "Was that real? Have you seen one?"

He didn't respond, only gave her a stoic stare. But Daisy got her answer. Because Daisy Scott knew faces. Not even Eagle Valdez could hide his micro-expressions from her fucking attention to detail.

HOT DAMN.

Eagle returned the folder to its home and relocked the file cabinet, but Daisy's pulse continued to beat with a quick, steady rhythm as she imagined what else Eagle might know and what might lie ahead.

She could be patient. Because she knew it would be worth the wait. That "W" folder had been so thick with secrets.

The trio put on coats and stepped out onto the back water access desk to drink beers.

"How is your friend Jordan," Coney asked. "When are we finally going to meet him?"

"Soon," Daisy said. "I hope. I don't know. He's weird with new people. I'm working on it. He hasn't been answering his phone."

Jordan hadn't exactly made a full recovery; he was missing a chunk of his liver and would have impaired function for the rest of his life. But, otherwise, his doctors had been stunned at his recovery. Jordan was a little neurotic, but he was a fighter, like her, and he had pulled through. Still, she hadn't seen him in person since he'd been released from the hospital. It was starting to get annoying.

"I'm gonna go try him again, actually," Daisy said. "I'll be right back."

* * *

"She looked at my files," Eagle said to Coney, after Daisy had walked away.

"I can't believe you're so comfortable having a reporter around this place," Coney said. "Don't get me wrong, I love Daisy, but she wants answers, and to publish them. Isn't that gonna be a problem for you?"

"*Reporter*," Eagle laughed. "Please. Have you seen her work? She interviewed a man who claimed his air fryer was self-aware and had passed the mirror test."

"I liked that one," Coney said. "Besides, you should know better than to underestimate her."

"I'm not at all! She's smart and has good survival instincts. She could be useful. Besides, Coney. Whoever controls the media, controls the mind."

Coney stared at the Manhattan skyline through the trees of the little creek and picked at the label on her beer bottle. She wasn't much of a drinker and preferred Diet Dr. Pepper.

"You never told me, Kuya," she said, "and I need to know. What did you do with Catalina's body?"

Eagle sipped his beer, silently.

"You destroyed it, right?" she asked.

"It's someplace safe."

"You didn't, Eagle?" Coney asked. "Tell me you didn't. Did you sell it?"

"Shhhh!" he said. "It's in the safest place it could possibly be. Let's just leave it at that."

"We're gonna need to have a talk one of these days," Coney advised. "All of this big money is going to your head. Remember what you said a few weeks ago to Daisy? No one's ever put a manananggal in a cage and studied it before? That's a GOOD thing, Eagle."

"Relax, Coney," Eagle said. "The manananggal's body is useless without the black chick. But not everyone knows that. Get it? And I saw the bird fly out of her. I sold a useless, shriveled corpse."

"So why aren't you smiling?" she asked Eagle.

"Because we don't know where the bird went," he said.

"Don't worry, Kuya. It probably got run over by a car. And if not? You killed this one, you'll kill the next. No aswang allowed in our city, right?"

She held out her closed fist.

"Yeah," Eagle said. "That's right." He bumped her fist. "Not in our city."

* * *

"I'm just worried about you, Jordan. I haven't seen you since Halloween and you didn't look very great at the time."

Jordan had answered his phone after a couple rings. It sounded like Daisy had woken him up, so she didn't plan to keep him on the phone long.

"I just want to see you," she said. "I know you're getting over a lot. But I can help."

"I know," Jordan said.

His voice sounded frail. Did he have a cold on top of everything else?

"Soon," he said. "I promise."

"Okay. I'm holding you to that. Get some sleep, Jordan. You sound awful. Bye."

* * *

Jordan's grip on the phone slipped and it fell to the ground, landing in a puddle of his vomit. It didn't fall very far; he was lying in a fetal position on the floor. In the dark, he couldn't see the devastation inside his apartment. He couldn't see the damage he had done.

He could only see the foamy pool of bile and blood in front of him, an island of yesterday's undigested Spaghetti-O's sitting proudly in the center.

The thought of eating made him wretch again. His insides howled with pain, and he clenched into a ball.

And as he whimpered and cradled his aching stomach, his tired eyes burned red in the darkness.

THANK YOU FOR READING!

IF YOU ENJOYED THIS BOOK, PLEASE TAKE A MOMENT TO LEAVE US A REVIEW.

Reviews and recommendations
help us expand our reach and ensure
we are able to continue writing.

www.woodsidepublishing.com

COMING 2026

𝕮𝖆𝖏𝖚𝖓 𝕸𝖔𝖔𝖓
The Siren Point Series: Book 2

*A shared secret in the swamps of
Terrebonne Parish...*

Sabina Barbot and her husband Henri, a French
immigrant living with schizophrenia, struggle to run their
failing plant store on Chartres Street, in the French Quarter
of New Orleans. As outside forces threaten to upend their
lives, the couple will be forced to recon with Henri's most
persistent psychotic delusion, the belief that he is a werewolf.

Inspired by French werewolf myths from the 16th and 17th
centuries, Cajun Moon is a fresh spin on the subgenre.
Lycanthropy, Voodoo, and magick collide, in a new
gothic horror romance thriller from Sanders & Zabat.